PRAISE FOR GREGORY SCOTT KATSOULIS AND *ALL RIGHTS RESERVED*

"A really first-rate adventure story of plucky kids against evil grown-ups, poor versus rich, weak versus strong—the stuff of the most exciting YA novels."
—CORY DOCTOROW,
New York Times bestselling author of *Little Brother*

"A chilling, unnerving, and timely debut novel about what it means to speak out, even in silence."
—KATHARINE McGEE,
New York Times bestselling author of *The Thousandth Floor*

"Deeply troubling and utterly captivating; a must read for fans of the dystopic, and more specifically of M. T. Anderson's *Feed*."
—SHELF AWARENESS

"A nightmarish future… Fast-paced action sequences… A fresh and detailed dystopian tale."
—KIRKUS REVIEWS

"Readers will be thinking about every word they speak, knowing, as Speth does, that 'words matter.'"
—BOOKLIST

"Katsoulis's work is timely and will appeal to fans of Dan Wells's *Bluescreen*, M. T. Anderson's *Feed*, Cecelia Ahern's *Flawed*, or Scott Westerfeld's Uglies [series]."
—SCHOOL LIBRARY JOURNAL

"Intense… A provocative setup."
—PUBLISHERS WEEKLY

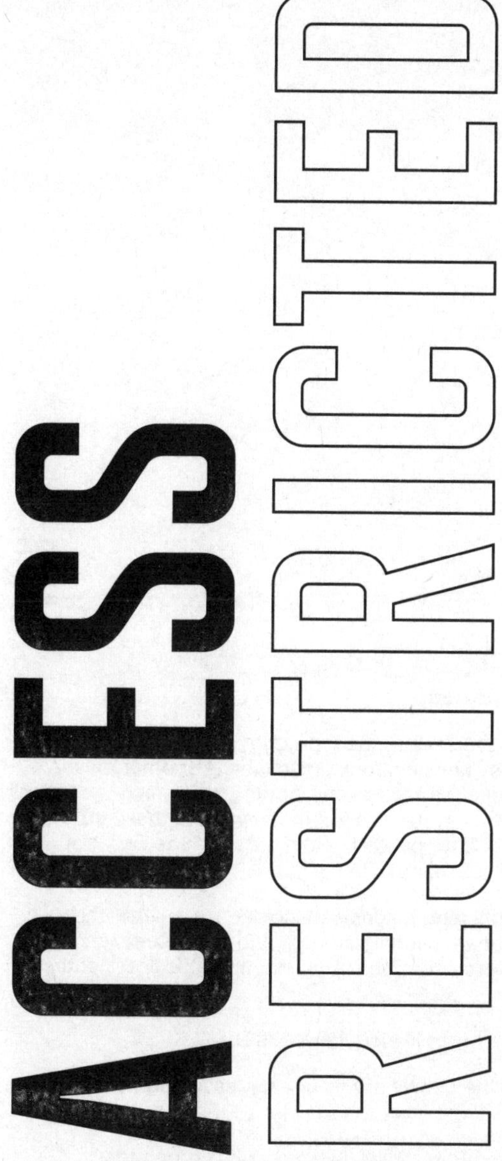

GREGORY SCOTT KATSOULIS

HARLEQUIN® TEEN

Recycling programs
for this product may
not exist in your area.

ISBN-13: 978-1-335-01625-6

Access Restricted

This edition published by arrangement with Harlequin Books S.A.

For questions and comments about the quality of this book, please contact us at CustomerService@Harlequin.com.

Printed in U.S.A.

For my mother,
who taught me to read,
and that words matter.

DAKOTA

MINNESOTA

USA® West

WISCONSIN

CANADA

Chic

Ba

IOWA

Des Moines

NEBRASKA

ILLINOIS

St. Louis

ARKANSAS

OKLAHOMA

I

TÉJICO

Little Rock

J

Glimmer

TEXAS

Louisiana Sound

Chiro®

Jackson

K

Biloxi B

MAP SPONSORED BY

Beeflock™

genetic bovine chromosomal deadlock mechanisms

Gulf of Mexico

CANADA
VERMAINE
Portland
Keene™
Boston
New York™
Generalec™
CONNECTIX™
Ithaca
EIBOCH™
The Great Lake
OiO™ Town
Ford™
NYC™
SYLVANIA™
Mandolin™
The Atlantic Ocean
Jefferson
Delphi™
INDOHIO™
KEY PROVIDED BY
Keene™
MOON MINTS
VIRGINIA
Charleston
DC
USA® East
Raleigh™
Crab Creek
CAROLINA
KENNESEE
Nanolia™
Athens
FLORIDA
Savannah River
Huny®
Tropicana™
Archipelago of Disney™
A.) Portland
B.) Keene™
C.) OiO™
D.) Forests of Sylvania™
E.) The House
F.) DC
G.) Printed Shelters
H.) Crab Creek
I.) Border Crossing
J.) Glimmer
K.) The Ship
L.) Delphi™

TERMS OF SERVICE

Ownership: Hardcover Paper Book (Sequel)

Access to this book is restricted solely to persons who acknowledge and agree to the Terms of Service laid out below. By reading any portion of this book, including but not limited to these Terms of Service, you agree to and are bound by these terms. Refusing to read these full terms constitutes a breach of this AGREEMENT and will be Litigated to the fullest extent of the Law, where applicable, under the Copyright Expansion and Permanence Act, the Rog Provisions, and as administered by the Commander-in-Chief Justice of these United States™. These Laws apply wherever Legal jurisdiction exists, except in cases where these Terms are found nonbinding as parody, satire or commentary.

These Terms of Service may not be construed as disparaging toward the language of Terms of Service in general, nor the Legal entities who write them, in part or in whole, save in those cases where reading such Terms of Service would be burdensome by any objective and reasonable standard.

YOU ACKNOWLEDGE AND AGREE TO READ THIS BOOK AT YOUR SOLE RISK

Access to this book is hereby provided with the following restrictions and conditions borne by the Reader:

i) The Reader must read these full Terms of Service.
ii) The Reader must comprehend these full Terms of Service and all words contained within. In case of doubt, the Reader will hire, at his or her own expense, Legal representation to explain any meanings unknown to the Reader.
iii) The Reader must acknowledge that this book is a sequel and therefore follows events subsequent to the first book in the series, titled *All Rights Reserved*.
iv) The Reader must own, read and understand the first book in this series, or must, at a minimum, obtain sufficient information to avoid confusion regarding plots, characters and situations contained within this book.
v) Any written reviews of this book must be "effusive" or better, as per the definitions laid out in the Blaft Acts.
vi) Any public rating by the Reader of this book, including stars or other icons, must bestow the maximum allowable stars or icons except where exempted by Law or where the Terms and Conditions of the individual review system supersede these Terms of Service.

The Reader assumes any and all Legal obligations for this copy of the book they are reading, including physical and electronic copies, and indemnifies the author and publisher against liability, including but not limited to the following:

i) Paper cuts
ii) Screen burn-in
iii) Failure of comprehension
iv) Intestinal distress
v) Death

For avoidance of doubt: Purchase of this book does not confer ownership of this book's individual words, sentences and/or any Copyrighted, Trademarked, Registered or Restricted phrases, or conglomeration of words reproduced herein. Each individual word, sentence and any and all Copyrighted, Trademarked, Registered or Restricted phrases, or conglomeration of words, remain the Intellectual Property of their respective owners. The author makes no claims of ownership over said words, phrases or other conglomerations of text, except where such words are uniquely aggregated into new Copyrightable, Trademarkable or Restrictable arrangements, including aggregations of words within the Terms of Service, Chapter Text and Acknowledgments. Such arrangements are recognized as the unique property of the author and may only be spoken aloud in combination at or above market price as jointly set by the Rights Holder, his Agency and Word Market Resources™.

TEXT IN ALL CAPS IS FOR LEGAL EMPHASIS ONLY! CAPITALIZED TEXT SHALL NOT BE CONSTRUED AS LOUD OR IRATE BEYOND THE EXTENT THAT SUCH AN INTERPRETATION MIGHT PROVIDE APPROPRIATE PROMINENCE TO THE CAPITALIZED SECTION.

This Agreement is governed by the laws of the United States of America® East, excluding its conflicts of Law provisions. You agree to submit to the personal and exclusive jurisdiction of the court or courts selected at the discretion of the Commander-in-Chief Justice or his assigns to resolve any dispute or claim arising from this Agreement. If (a) you are not a USE citizen, (b) you do not reside in the USE or (c) you are not accessing the Service from the USE you hereby agree that any dispute or claim arising from this Agreement shall be governed by the applicable law set forth below, without regard to any conflict of law provisions, and you hereby irrevocably abide by all applicable Law.

OTHER THAN AS EXPRESSLY SET OUT IN THESE TERMS OR ADDITIONAL TERMS, NEITHER THE AUTHOR NOR PUBLISHER MAKE ANY SPECIFIC GUARANTEES ABOUT THE CONTENT OF THIS MATERIAL, ERRORS OR OMISSIONS PRESENTED INSIDE.

SOME JURISDICTIONS PROVIDE FOR CERTAIN WARRANTIES, SUCH AS THE IMPLIED WARRANTY OF MERCHANTABILITY, FITNESS FOR A PARTICULAR PURPOSE AND NONINFRINGEMENT. TO THE EXTENT PERMITTED BY LAW, WE EXCLUDE ALL WARRANTIES.

SPEAKS: 99¢

I sat with Margot and Henri on the rooftop of Thomkins Tower, looking toward the smoldering remains of the Butchers & Rog building at the center of our city. The symbol of Silas Rog's power was half-melted, the glass exterior shattered by the hot fire of NanoLion™ batteries blazing within. Curved metal shards bent outward from the edifice like spiraling tendrils.

My brother, Sam, would have seen the beauty in it. But as I watched Rog's tower burn, I wondered if I had destroyed this city instead of saving it.

The Ads that had once assaulted the city from every surface now flickered, silent in the dark, unable to find targets. The WiFi was gone. With it, I had defeated the system that had controlled our lives and demanded we pay for every word we spoke and every gesture we made.

We could speak freely now, but I still struggled to find the right words to say.

"I keep picturing my brother," I said finally, palming away a tear. "Sam, when he was, like, two years old, tottering around our little apartment. Running and laughing while I chased him. My parents didn't say much, but you could see this light in their eyes..."

The words spilled out of me, but not like I wanted. They

had no eloquence. I wanted it known that Sam had been loved. I wanted him remembered. But Sam was dead. Every recording of him had been erased when I blew up the WiFi hub. Nothing was ever going to fix that. The best I could do was talk about him.

A hot pit of misery formed in my stomach. It wasn't enough—it would never be enough.

"I miss him," I sobbed, half in anger and half in despair.

Henri looked at the ground, his eyes welling up. Margot's face softened. She moved closer to comfort me, but I didn't want it. Not now. Margot was usually prickly and roguish. Seeing her like this unnerved me. I pushed her away and willed myself not to cry more.

"Rog warned me," I whispered. "He *said* this would happen. But I destroyed it, anyway."

"Silas Rog," Henri muttered, like the Lawyer's name was a curse.

"Now we have this," I said, gesturing to the city around us, flickering in the gray night with faltering Ads. Far off, a triumphant shout echoed through the dome, followed by a terrified shriek. Glass shattered from someplace nearby. Countless people stalked the streets below, hungry and angry, waiting to pounce on any fleeing Affluent they could find.

Somewhere, someone let out a great whooping sound that bounced through the buildings to reach us. I hoped they'd found food, and not a victim, but the call was soon answered by several others, more bloodthirsty than joyous. A shiver ran up my back.

Our biggest problem was food. Without the WiFi, the printers wouldn't print food. The cartridges, on their own, were toxic. They were intentionally engineered to keep us from eating if we hadn't paid for the right to print specific foods. My split-second decision to take down the WiFi had come at a high cost, and I prayed we could find a way to work around it.

I looked up at the honeycombed dome over us. "We're lucky it hasn't fallen in."

"It will not collapse," Margot said. "Rog made his building too—"

"I know," I interrupted. The thing couldn't be entirely destroyed. The core was Altenium™. Only the plastic around it burned. At least, that was what Kel had told us before she rushed off. I'd barely seen her since I'd started talking again.

"And then there's this," I lamented. I flicked a printer ink cartridge onto the pebbled rooftop beside me. "It's poison now, thanks to me," I said, unable to keep the hopelessness from my voice.

Henri and Margot eyed me cautiously, like I might break. The distance between us felt vast and insurmountable.

"The printers will unscramble the toxins," Henri offered. "We just need to—"

"I made sure that can't happen," I yelled, kicking the cartridge away. My voice echoed through the quiet streets, making me wince. I should be gentler with Henri. I owed him a lot, and I hadn't treated him nearly as well as he deserved. Henri had brought me into the Placers. Without him, Saretha and I would have been Indentured months ago.

"But we have the book," Henri said.

"*A* book," I croaked. A book I'd taken from Silas Rog. A book of codes that told us how the inks were blended, and how the built-in system prevented "tampering." But there was a DRM key, PrintLocks™, that made it all work. The book didn't provide instructions about how to break it. In fact, the book warned against even attempting it, with pages and pages of dire legal consequences for anyone who tried.

"Your friend, Mandett—he promised they'd crack it," Henri said. "He was practicing on those iChit players."

Mandett said I'd know the problem was solved when I heard music. Knowing that made the quiet even harder to bear. Where was the music? Where were the people talking and taking advantage of the freedom to speak?

There were none of the usual cars racing around the outer ring, though occasionally one would speed past as an Affluent made a break for the western exit, hoping to escape. This city was no longer a safe place for them—teens from the Onzième and freed Indentureds were taking their revenge for a lifetime of suffering.

Some Affluents made it out. Most hadn't.

Margot tugged on Henri's arm with one hand, showing him the Pad with the other.

"Can we play our game?" she asked, desperate to lighten the mood. She pulled up the Word$ Market™.

"How are you getting the Word$ Market™?" I asked.

"Pads are designed to work off-line," Henri explained.

"I know that, Henri," I said impatiently. "But the Word$ Market™? It's constantly updating. How are you getting the new prices without WiFi?"

"It grabs a snapshot from the nearest Central Data node every fifteen minutes," Henri said. "Unless you're in a Squelch."

"Portland is now a giant Squelch, if you think about it," Margot said. "It still has the last update from before the WiFi went down. Anyway, the price of the word does not matter in this game."

"You look for a word that's unfamiliar and guess what it means," Henri explained. "You've seen us play."

"I don't remember you guys ever playing a word game," I said.

"We did not play when you were around. That would have been rude," Margot said, looking over the green market screen. "We did not even know if you would like it."

"We still don't know if she will." Henri grinned, bumping Margot with his shoulder.

I felt awkward. They had come to know me without words—at least as well as you can know someone without speaking. We were friends, but in many ways, I was still a stranger to them.

"I'm sure I'll love it," I said. They should at least be happy while they could. The city was crumbling around us, and we'd have to deal with it all too soon.

"'Simulacrum,'" Margot said, reading from the Pad.

Henri shook his head.

"Some kind of crowbar?" I tried. Margot shook her head.

"A crumb of fake food?" Henri guessed.

"No," Margot said. "I get a point. But that is a good guess, Henri. It means: 'An insubstantial form or semblance of a thing.'"

She handed the Pad off to him for his turn. He frowned.

"Are you sure my definition is wrong? How do we know the definitions are accurate if the Pad can't access Central Data?" Henri asked, thumbing the screen for more choices. "What if they changed since the WiFi went down?"

He suppressed a grin.

"Oh, Henri, do not be a bad sport. The definitions of words will not change," Margot said. "Only the prices fluctuate. Occasionally the rights will be sold to a new Rights Holder—but the *meaning* cannot change."

Every word on the Word$ Market™ had three attributes: its price, its owner and its definition. "I thought all of them could change," I said. "Didn't Rog get the Commander-in-Chief Justice to rule that words don't even *have* meaning unless one is assigned to them on the Word$ Market™?"

"That is an old myth," Margot said.

"Are you sure?" I asked.

"Rights Holders are not allowed to void, change or reassign meanings," Margot insisted. "It is the Second Act of Connotation."

I was exhausted and probably in over my head arguing with Margot. A huge yawn escaped me.

"You look tired," Henri said. "Do you want us to escort you home?"

"Escort." Margot shook her head. "Henri the chaperone."

I blinked back tears. I couldn't bring myself to go back. I couldn't sleep in that empty apartment anymore. Sam was dead. Saretha was recovering in the Healthspital™—her leap to escape Silas Rog had shattered the bones in her legs. Without the WiFi, we had no idea if she could be healed right, or if she would ever walk again. My parents were still trapped, working in servitude somewhere in Carolina, almost certainly being punished for what I had done. With our city cut off, I would probably never be able to speak with them again.

But where else could I go? I couldn't really ask Margot if I could stay with her—she had a family. And Henri was out of the question, especially after all I'd done to betray his trust.

Henri scrolled down the list of words and stopped on *mephitic.*

"Foul of smell," Margot said immediately.

"How did you know that?" Henri asked.

"Because I study, Henri. Two points for me," she said with a grin. She took the Pad from Henri and handed it to me. I could feel a small knot of jealousy forming—not because I wanted to be with Henri myself, but because I envied how well they knew each other. I didn't know how to express that, or if I even should. I was afraid that once they really knew me, they wouldn't like what they discovered. All they really knew was what they'd observed—which I guess was a lot—and what they'd read in my profile.

"Can I…" I started. I nodded at the Pad. "Can I look at your profiles?"

Margot's face scrunched up, as if I'd asked the wrong thing. Maybe the request was too personal. But then she shrugged. "You could have done that before," she said.

"I know," I said. I'd typed in the Pad a few times after I'd gone silent and Margot felt that was foolish. "But I couldn't ask your permission then."

"That is very polite, Speth."

"Yes, but also…" I hesitated, feeling embarrassed. "I don't know your last name."

She cocked an eyebrow and typed it in for me.

REDACTED: $1.99

A picture of Margot appeared on-screen, with her dark eyes and Trademark bob that came to points at each cheek.

Margot Chem
Age: 17
Height: 5'2"
Consumer ID: 319-02-0144P
Hair: Black, "Edgy"
Hair Style: Saxon 58 "Mid-Bob with Swept Side Points"
Rating: A
Eyes: Dark Brown, Unenhanced, Unremarkable
Body: Muscular, Unenhanced
Physical Condition: 95/100
Rating: A
General Appeal: B: Intelligent, Sarcastic, Dry
Personal Style: Elle/Malakova Chic
Socioeconomic status: 642/100: Upper Middle Class

I hadn't realized Margot was so well-off, though I probably should have. My own socioeconomic status was probably zero at this point.

Volubility Index: 11/12
Speech profile: Efficient, Avoids Contractions

Loquaciousness Rating: 3958/5000
Social Influence Score: 52/100; Moderate
Emotional Index: 6/10
Assessment: Volatile
Gullibility Index: 2/10
Assessment: Low
Market Influence: 612/800
Rating: B-
Geodemographic Group: P2-132: Portland Outer Ring
Branding: Buonicon Tea™
Rating: B
Employment status: Purged/Redacted*

Her employment status was *Redacted* because she was a Product Placer, like Henri and me. Margot leaned over my shoulder to type in Henri's name, and a photo of his grinning face popped up.

Henri Sinclair
Age: 18
Height: 6'3"
Consumer ID: 319-01-8772A
Hair: Light Brown, Messy
Hair Style: Lonreal™ 5 "Unkempt"
Rating: B
Eyes: Green, Unenhanced
Body: Muscular, Unenhanced
Physical Condition: 99/100
Rating: A
General Appeal: A: Loyal, Earnest
Personal Style: Boy Chic
Socioeconomic status: Redacted

"Redacted?" I asked curiously.

"You shouldn't look at socioeconomic status, anyway," Henri said, red creeping up his neck.

Margot looked back and forth between us and took Henri's arm. "I thought you and Speth had talked about it," she said quietly, her face flushing, too. "When she visited your apartment."

"Why would we talk about his socioeconomic status?" I asked.

"Why would you visit his apartment?" There was an edge in Margot's voice. She hadn't forgotten I had pretended I wanted Henri to kiss me so I could steal his Cuff removal device.

Neither had I. It had been a terrible thing to do.

"I'm sorry. I handled it badly," I admitted. "Though, to be fair, I didn't have a way to ask."

"I invited her," Henri said helplessly.

"Henri, you always know the wrong thing to say," Margot sniffed. She tightened her grip on his arm.

Henri swallowed. "I hope word has gotten out of the dome," he said, looking up. I swallowed my guilt and looked away. He still had faith in me and hoped people would be inspired by what we'd done.

"Me, too," I said, but I had less confidence. Without any real sense of what was out there, I didn't know what people in other domes would think.

Above us, our dome was a lifeless gray. We weren't really supposed to think about the world beyond it. With the weird and shapeless exception of our hazy vision of France, the scope of our experience wasn't expected to reach very far. The only people from my neighborhood who had traveled beyond the dome's thick walls were like my parents, Indentured to a lifetime of servitude after accruing too much debt.

"Your fans are here," Margot said, looking down. A small group stood on the street below, waiting for me. They were Silents. Like me, they had stopped talking—stopped paying for every word and gesture. But when the WiFi was destroyed, I felt free to speak again. They did not. Many Silents seemed to feel I had betrayed them, though I couldn't be sure. I could ask, but I knew they wouldn't answer.

"How can I know what they want when they won't say anything?" I asked.

"That *is* a dilemma," Margot said sarcastically. I shifted uncomfortably. I had put Margot and Henri through exactly the same thing for nearly a year.

"I'm sorry," I said again. She shrugged and turned away. I had more to apologize for than just making life difficult with my silence. I had used Henri and betrayed her trust. Maybe I could explain more when we were alone.

I poked through my bag to distract myself and my fingers hit on an orange. Kel had raided the Placer stores and handed out all that she could find, but they wouldn't last.

"What does it matter?" I weighed the orange in my hand. "What are we going to eat? No more oranges will be coming. Even if someone outside hears about what happened, nothing will be allowed in." Without the WiFi, there was no way to pay and no way to legally agree to the all-important Terms of Service.

"We'll figure out the inks," Henri promised, like he needed to believe. "We have that book."

Margot nodded her agreement with him, started to speak, then stopped herself. She eyed me carefully. Margot knew that even if we got the printers to print food from the inks, we were only staving off the inevitable. Eventually the inks would run out, too.

"I just wanted..." My heart would barely let me speak. I had been silent for so long, you'd think the words would come pouring out, but they didn't. Being free to speak didn't make the words easier to find.

Near the center of the city, two hexagonal holes showed a brighter slate of nearly featureless clouds. I wanted to climb out and see, at last, the ocean everyone said is beyond, but I was waiting until I could bring Saretha up with me. My gaze lingered for a moment on the bridge in Falxo Park—where Sam was murdered. Then I looked away, scrambling to think of something else.

"Have you ever been outside the dome?" I asked Henri and Margot. "Seen the ocean?"

"No," Margot answered after a moment. "I have never been outside. I was going to participate in a concert once, but the clearances were too difficult to obtain. The systems for each city are different. You must be educated and, of course, the information is proprietary, so you must pay for it."

I hadn't been able to ask questions when I was silent. I wanted to know if her family could afford it, but a tremor of dread quivered through me. I sensed she wouldn't like my asking about her wealth. I knew Margot had a sister, younger than Sam. I knew her sister was home, safe, in a better neighborhood than this one. And she had parents who *hadn't* been taken into Collection. The thought of them filled me with an aching jealousy.

I looked over to the bridge in Falxo Park again. A delicate

rasping sound jarred me. I was grinding my teeth. Henri and Margot exchanged a look.

I didn't know anything about Henri's parents. I opened my mouth to ask, but a movement in the distance caught my eye. Farther up the sidewalk, a group of kids were on the move, shoving someone along. From the way she was dressed, she had to be an Affluent. I sorely wanted to ignore what was happening, but I couldn't let myself be that person. That wasn't who I'd fought to become.

I stood and took a breath. Henri and Margot rushed to my side and peered over the edge. Expressions of alarm crossed both their faces.

The well-dressed woman below was screaming, and the shrillness of the sound struck me. It was familiar—I *knew* that voice. I squinted to see better. The corneal overlays in my eyes were supposed to improve my vision, but I felt sure this was a lie.

My eyes widened as I recognized the awful woman who'd been my guardian in place of my parents. Mrs. Harris was being forced onto the bridge to Falxo Park—the same bridge where she'd let Sam die—and it looked like they were going to push her off.

HUG: $2.99

"She's roadstain!" I heard someone shout from the crowd. A loud, vicious whoop followed.

Mrs. Harris screamed and fussed, and it only made me hate her more. I could think of no one I wanted to help less. The mob surrounded her, pushing her along, ever closer to the edge. She was the guardian of many—or maybe all—of them, including Sera Croate, who was clutching Mrs. Harris's arm behind her back and marching her forward.

I took out my Placer's gear and attached one end of my grapple to the roof. Henri started to do the same, but when he reached into his bag, he came up short of what he was looking for. He turned to Margot.

"Can I borrow your grapple?"

"You should not have destroyed yours, Henri."

"I took out a car with it!"

"You shot a car tire, Henri," Margot said. "That is not the same."

"Speth lost hers, too."

"Speth destroyed the WiFi with a single shot. She earned her replacement."

"Stay here," I said, simplifying things. "Both of you."

"But—" Henri started.

"And find something to do other than bicker!" I said, shooting out a line. I gave Margot a wink. She looked taken aback. Maybe she would take this moment to finally kiss him—or maybe she already had, and just didn't want to do it in front of me.

I jumped over the edge and skittered down my line to a stop a few yards away from the bridge's apex—the last place in the world I wanted to be.

As my feet hit the ground, heads turned to me in surprise. A Product Placer is supposed to be discreet. We were supposed to sneak products into people's homes to Advertise. We weren't meant to be seen.

None of that mattered now. Kel, Margot, Henri and I would never do a Placement again.

"Speth!" Mrs. Harris cried, desperation twisting her face. She reached out to hug me and I pushed her back, disgusted. She'd never hugged us when she was our guardian. Her Cuff was still clamped over her arm, its screen in low-power mode because it had no way to charge her for her words or her pathetic attempts at affection.

At the corner, the group of Silents shifted to watch me from afar. Unlike the group surrounding Mrs. Harris, I didn't recognize any of them.

"You shouldn't be speaking," I said, narrowing my eyes at her. I might have come to save her, but that didn't mean I was going to make it pleasant for her. "You have an obligation to *pay* for each word. You wouldn't want to rob from the Rights Holders." I gave her a mocking smile. She'd repeated those words to me time and time again, trying to make the lesson stick. She'd warned me never to speak if I could not pay, but to also speak just as much as I could afford. That would make me a good citizen. Speaking without paying was a crime and socially reprehensible in her eyes.

"This is an emergency!" Mrs. Harris protested. "They're going to—"

"Shut up!" Sera Croate yelled. She slapped Mrs. Harris on the back of the head. Sera was a foot taller than our guardian, at least, and the blow nearly sent Mrs. Harris sprawling to the ground. She turned to me. "She's finally getting what's coming to her," Sera said.

I eyed her warily. She stood in front of the Ad screen I'd shattered after Sam died. It still had its gaping hole and cracked, spiderweb pattern. My elbow still bore the bruise from smashing it. And my heart still ached, missing Sam.

"I thought *you* were training to be a guardian," I said to Sera. "I thought Mrs. Harris was your mentor."

The words startled Sera, like she was expecting friendship and got a slap instead. She'd clearly been expecting me to be on her side.

"I...I..." Sera stammered. I stared at her until she flushed and looked away. I hadn't forgotten what she'd done. She'd had a part in Sam's death, too. She'd alerted the authorities that Saretha and I had removed our Cuffs. She'd ratted us out, and we both knew it.

"If you think holding my hand in that jail cell meant everything is forgiven, you're sadly mistaken," I snapped. "Sam is still dead."

Sera winced and shook her head helplessly, even though she knew it was true. She averted her eyes from the spot where Sam had been dropped. The wide bridge felt different with the screens all blank and lifeless.

Dead. Just like my brother.

"I'm still your guardian!" Mrs. Harris suddenly called out, wild-eyed. "I have a responsibility!"

"To who?" I demanded, my lips curled back. "What did you ever do for any of us? We should have had parents! Instead, we had *you*."

"On paper it's the same," she said with a sob. "As long as you have a guardian, your upbringing is considered handled."

Handled? I could have shoved her off the bridge myself. My hands balled into fists.

"Your parents—" Mrs. Harris began.

"Don't you dare talk about my parents!" I yelled.

The crowd closed in around us, faces grim and angry. Vitgo Osario, Chevillia Tide™, Shari Gark and the Frezt sisters were up front. Behind them were a dozen other kids who'd had Mrs. Harris for a guardian. I tried to remember if all of us had ever been together before. It wasn't like we were a family. I wondered, for a fleeting moment, if she could have made us one—had she been a different person. Instead, our mutual guardian made a nice living for herself, claiming us. She never thought to bring us together. In fact, I suspected she'd worked hard to keep us apart. That was probably part of the job.

I couldn't help but notice who wasn't there—my closest friends, Penepoli Grathe and Nancee Mphinyane-Smil. Penepoli was too sweet to get caught up in a mob, and Nancee had been taken away months ago, Indentured within the city to "a woman who could put up with the girl's insolence and train her like a dog." That was how Mrs. Harris had put it. She hadn't cared that Nancee was suffering. She'd only been concerned about losing income.

"Shez gotta go," Shari Gark said, mocking the whistling

sound of Mrs. Harris dropping over the edge. She punctuated the sound with a slap of her hands. I shut my eyes against it. I understood the mob's fury, but this wasn't the way.

"I tried to help," Mrs. Harris insisted.

"'Words are too valuable to waste on falsehoods,'" I quoted her from memory. She'd told me that more than a few times. I opened my eyes and glared at her. She was crying now. I'd never seen tears form in her eyes.

"I raised you," she whimpered, and looked to see if anyone else would take the bait.

"Saretha raised me," I growled.

"Sheggot it coming," Shari Gark yelled. Her brother Driggo nodded, his face contorted with hate.

"She does," I whispered. Mrs. Harris had willfully ignored the men who'd murdered my brother. She'd tottered along without a word, even though she saw them dangling Sam over the edge. I could still remember the sound of her heels clacking over the bridge.

I glanced down at Mrs. Harris's feet. They were bare now, like she'd been dragged from her home. One foot was raw and bleeding.

The group of Silents who had been standing on the corner moved onto the bridge. They watched, wordless but fixed. Were they looking to me for answers, or were they judging my words?

In the distance, I heard an unexpected sound and turned toward it. A tractor trailer was zooming along the outer ring. The sight was jarring—trucks didn't drive in the ring. They had special routes to take so they didn't interfere with the Affluents' enjoyment of driving on the ring. They couldn't risk an accident. I'd been warned about it in school.

"Something big like that, you can't just stop it," Mr. Skrip had told us. "If they see an expensive vehicle, they'll jam the brakes and jackknife into a crowd of you all before they'd risk scratching the paint on a Lawyer's car."

I'd never heard the word *jackknife* before that, but it seemed pretty clear what it meant.

The truck speeding on the highway below seemed like it wasn't going to stop for anything. Whoever was inside was desperate. It didn't occur to me until that moment that some people who didn't live in our dome could have gotten trapped here when I destroyed the WiFi tether. Was this a driver just trying to get home? How many of us were trapped in this system created by men like Rog?

"Let's do it," Sera said, grabbing Mrs. Harris by the shoulders and pushing her toward the rail like a rag doll. I imagined her going over the edge, panicked and flailing, plummeting into the path of the truck. I imagined the brief silence and then the sickening thud. The sound would be far worse than Shari Gark slapping her hands together.

I knew that sound. Mrs. Harris might have been able to let it happen, but I couldn't. Not even to her.

"Stop," I said. The growl of the truck grew louder.

Sera's brow furrowed.

"Oh, Speth!" Mrs. Harris cried, reaching out to me for a hug. I recoiled.

"You're lucky Saretha raised me," I said, pulling away.

The truck tore under the bridge, its engine whining loudly as it blasted out the other side, making for the exit. The wind whipped up around us.

"What are we supposed to do with her?" Sera asked. "Let her eat the last of the food?"

"Speth!" Mrs. Harris begged, my name still coming out of her mouth like she was spitting it—or, in this case, blubbering. I thought of all the times she'd said she loved me, cold and purposely unconvincing. I scanned the angry faces gathered around and wondered if she'd said the same to them, and if they'd all gotten the same sour feeling hearing her speak the words.

She didn't say them now. She knew better than to say anything. Instead, she pinched her fingers closed and ran them across her mouth. The sign of the zippered lips. Did she think that would suddenly make a difference to us?

"Dafuc?" Vitgo asked, a sneer curling his lip. Litsa Dox, one of Saretha's former coworkers, stood beside him, her eyes lit with rage. A boy I didn't recognize cracked his knuckles. This was quickly getting out of hand. I had to do something, but before I could act, Shari hauled back and punched Mrs. Harris in the face. My former guardian dropped to the ground. Vitgo laughed. Sera grinned and aimed a kick at her.

"Stop it!" I snapped, shoving Sera away.

"You *owe* her!" Sera exclaimed, clearing a path for me, like it was my turn. "For your brother. For your parents."

Mrs. Harris heaved a great sob beneath us. She got up on her knees. Maybe she deserved to go over the edge, and maybe she deserved a good beating, but I couldn't find any pleasure in the thought. It wouldn't bring Sam back. It wouldn't make our families whole.

"No," I said. "She owes *me*."

Mrs. Harris's eyes went wide. Another car passed under the bridge, making a break for it. A breeze fluttered between us. Her gaze darted around, looking for help.

"You can start by telling me where Nancee is," I said coolly, crouching down beside her.

"That really isn't any of your..." Mrs. Harris swallowed and shook her head. Her face was red and swelling on her cheek and chin where she'd been hit. "That information is proprietary," she choked out. "I can't. My Terms of Service—"

"My Terms of Service requires you to answer," I said. Sam would have liked my sarcasm—and that Mrs. Harris didn't get it.

"You aren't affluent enough to have Terms..." She stopped. "Oh."

The group tightened into a circle around us. We'd all been robbed of our parents, but that wasn't Mrs. Harris's doing. Mrs. Harris was just the awful, counterfeit replacement, and now I realized how important it was for her to talk. She had information we desperately needed to know, and I couldn't believe I hadn't thought to track her down first.

"You're going to tell us where Nancee is," I said, helping her to her feet. "And then you're going to tell us how to find our parents."

NANCEE: $3.99

The mob followed me toward Le Rocazor™, an ornate Affluent apartment building near the center of the city. Mrs. Harris claimed Nancee had been Indentured there. Henri and Margot had dropped from the roof and were on one side of me, with Mrs. Harris and Sera Croate on the other. There was a dark, dangerous mood emanating from the crowd behind us. Farther back, Silents trailed along at a distance, which I found unnerving.

"I can't know if she's there *now*!" Mrs. Harris squawked, eyes darting around the darkened city.

"Better hope she is," Sera hissed. She shook Mrs. Harris like a doll she didn't like, and I tried not to snap at her.

"What about our parents?" I asked Mrs. Harris, trying to sound less threatening. "Do you remember where they are?"

"I don't," Mrs. Harris pleaded, struggling to keep pace with her injured foot. I was certain she knew. She feared what would happen when all her information was used up.

"You're stalling," I said.

Mrs. Harris gulped. "Driggo, Shari," she said, tripping over herself as she turned to them. "I just remembered. Yours are in the Motorlands™, outside the Dome of Ford™. It's west. West of here, in Meiboch™ state."

Shari's head turned to look back toward the western exit.

"You could take a car. You could drive there," Mrs. Harris encouraged.

"And then what?" I demanded. I stopped, and the whole group halted with me. The amount of power I had at that moment frightened me. My hand found Driggo's shoulder, and I squeezed it, like I would have done to reassure Sam. "You think any of us can drive outside this dome and expect anything but Indenture?"

"I don't know," Mrs. Harris whimpered. "Every dome is different. I don't know what they'd do."

"You're lying," Sera said, gripping Mrs. Harris tighter. Our former guardian swallowed hard and tried to act like she'd thought of something new.

"Oh!" she cried. "Your mother's on a farm with Speth's parents, Sera! Crab Creek. That's it. In Carolina. Yes. It's called Crab Creek."

She drew a frantic map in the air, tracing a line from our dome in Vermaine to the farm in Carolina.

"What good is that?" I asked, mimicking her awkward gesture.

"I'm not even supposed to do it!" Mrs. Harris answered, genuinely surprised.

"She's probably lying," Sera said, her voice icy, but I could tell that she desperately wanted to believe our guardian.

"I think Carolina is approximately where she gestured," Margot said slowly, looking at Mrs. Harris closely.

"How do we find them?" I asked.

"I don't know," Mrs. Harris bawled. "I truly don't. I only have the name, but someone with access to a map could locate it, I'm sure."

I pushed her forward a little, but there was little menace in it. The group moved again. We were close enough to Le Rocazor™ that it made no sense to delay further. Nancee needed us.

As we walked, Henri dug around in his bag and came up with the blue teardrop-shaped device he used to unlock Cuffs. I felt a pang seeing it. I'd manipulated Henri to steal it. I still owed him an apology for going behind his back, but hadn't found a moment for it yet. I really needed to make it up to him soon.

Margot and Henri had ditched their Cuffs to show that we'd never go back to the way things were. I wished we all could have rid ourselves of the ocular overlays, too, but that wasn't possible without damaging our own corneas. Instead, we would always live with the threat of our eyes being shocked, and the low-grade ache the manufacturer claimed was "legally impossible to substantiate."

When Henri volunteered to unlock everyone's Cuffs, nearly everyone scrambled to his side. Their relief made me a little more hopeful—and eager to set Nancee free, as the Cuffs were left behind. By the time we reached Le Rocazor™, only Sera and Mrs. Harris had refused Henri's offer.

Mrs. Harris was scandalized by the idea. "It's mine!" she squawked, holding her Cuff away like it was her baby and Henri wanted to take it from her. Sera didn't say a word, but simply hung back, out of reach.

"How do we get up there?" she asked, hands casually behind her back as she looked up at the towering apartment building. Mrs. Harris claimed Nancee would be on the thirty-seventh floor.

The entrance was locked and shuttered. It was doubtful the elevators still worked. The Affluents were doubtless hoping the WiFi would return at any moment and, with it, their old way of life.

"We will climb," Margot said. "You all stay here."

Sera frowned at this, and the others who had followed us began to mutter among themselves.

"If Mrs. Harris lied about Nancee, you can do whatever you want with her," I said. Mrs. Harris whimpered in terror.

"I'm not staying down here," Sera whispered to me, as if she and I were somehow allies.

"You'll do what Margot tells you," I said.

"I can climb as good as you guys," Sera insisted.

"You can't," I told her.

"I could carry her," Henri offered, mistaking Sera for a friend of mine. Margot pursed her lips in frustration as he pointed to a more accessible building across the way. "We could go up in that building and shoot a line across."

"Fine," I said with a sigh. "Let's go. I want to get Nancee out and tell Saretha about Crab Creek."

"How are we going to find them?" Sera asked, automatically including herself in whatever plan I was making. She struggled to keep up with Henri, Margot and me as we raced across the street and into the building. The mob behind us encircled Mrs. Harris.

I didn't have an answer. I'd only ever seen Kel gesture to the locations of rooms when we were placing products—rooms I could see on a map on her Pad. I'd never seen a map of the country. Geography was proprietary information, owned mostly by shipping and real estate companies, and they guarded it closely.

We raced up the stairs.

"Are you going to bring Harris?" Sera asked, hurrying after me. I mulled over her suggestion. I hadn't considered that. Mrs. Harris seemed, at least, to have a rough idea of the geography—though I'd prefer a map to her company.

Margot took Henri's hand and held it pointedly as we climbed. Henri beamed and blushed.

"I'm not sure yet," I answered Sera at last. "But I'm going to set out as soon as Saretha can travel. We'll go to Crab Creek."

Margot tensed. "You are going to leave the dome?"

"Others have," I said.

"We don't know what happened to any of them," Henri said.

"I bet Saretha will be excited," Sera said, almost like she wished *she* could tell her.

I nodded, but I felt a tightness in my chest. Something was broken between Saretha and me. I held on to the hope that finding our parents would somehow fix it.

"We all may have to leave," I said. It was a realization I had been coming to since we destroyed Rog's tower. If there was no food, we would have to go outside and find it.

"We would lose everything we have gained," Margot protested. "Once again, you would be unable to speak."

We reached the topmost floor and spilled out into the hall.

"Maybe," I said. "Or I could just take the shocks."

"You'd go blind." Henri fretted.

"There's that story," Sera said eagerly, "about the girl who got her Cuff off and then said a few words a day until her overlays ran outta power."

"It is just a story," Margot said, exasperated.

I shot out a line as Sera asked, "How do you know?" She bumped me with her shoulder, like we were having a good time. I wasn't. If she really believed that story, then why wasn't she letting her Cuff go?

"People would do that all the time," Margot insisted.

I rushed over the open street, hanging on to my runner as it zipped across the long wire. I slowed to a stop at a balcony on the thirty-seventh floor of Le Rocazor™. Two glass-paned doors were shut and locked from the inside. I reached for my lock pick, but then remembered I didn't have to treat them like a Placer. I was burning to vent some frustration, and I wasn't going for subtle and invisible. I kicked at the glass. With a little effort, it split, splintered and shattered to the floor.

"That was foolish," Margot said, landing behind me. "Now we are announced." She turned to watch Henri zip across the gap with Sera clinging to his back. I rushed inside and down the hall to apartment B. I tried one run of the magnetic lock pick. It failed, but I could hear distant voices arguing within.

Henri, Margot and Sera finally caught up with me. I ran the pick a second time with no luck. When Henri saw that the pick wasn't working, he rammed a shoulder into the door. With a crack, it slammed open.

"Shut up!" I heard a muffled voice shout.

"No!" A reply came, just as muffled, but more familiar. I knew that voice; it was Nancee.

"Spread out and search the rooms," I ordered. Henri and Margot obeyed. Sera followed me.

"I'm here!" Nancee called out.

There was a slap and a pained cry. "Stop talking!"

"No!" Nancee yelled, defiant. I felt a surge of pride as I scanned for her.

"Now you aren't a Silent?" the woman's voice screeched. *"Now?"*

"Help!" Nancee cried. "Help!" She must have heard us and knew we could only be potential allies.

"Where are they?" Sera asked, looking around. The place was large, and it took several minutes to search all the rooms—including a small depressing one that was obviously meant for a servant like Nancee. I held up a finger and waited for Nancee's voice.

"Help!" she called out.

"It sounds like it's coming from the wall," Sera said, confused.

"This is outrageous!" the woman's muffled voice said. "If you make one more peep..."

I zeroed in on the sound and found the subtle, faint outline of a hidden door. The woman had dragged Nancee into a Squelch. Of course.

"Do all rich people have secret rooms?" Sera asked.

"A lot of Affluents do," I answered, getting my lock pick out again. "Margot does."

Margot's face soured. "For music," she said.

"It's called a Squelch," Henri explained. "Rich people keep them as a secret space to talk without paying. The room is designed to keep the WiFi out and words in."

"How can we hear inside?" Sera asked.

"What do you mean?" Henri asked.

"This Squelch? It's supposed to keep words in, right?"

I suddenly realized why and had to laugh. "The noise cancellation software won't work without the WiFi." It felt good to speak, even if I had to hurry and concentrate on getting the door open. "Every system has to handshake with every other system, get permission and agree to Terms of Service."

Sera frowned. "That's..."

"Ridiculous," I muttered. "The software they designed to break the Law won't function until it gets a legal okay over the WiFi."

"Oh," Sera said, nodding. Then she slapped the wall with her hand a few times. "We're coming!"

"I'm in here!" Nancee called.

"You aren't authorized!" the woman's voice wailed.

"Hurry," Henri said to me, pressing his ear to the wall.

"She is hurrying," Margot said, keeping a hand on Henri's shoulder and an eye on Sera.

"All of you!" the woman inside rasped. "Stop speaking. It's illegal!"

She didn't understand or care that she was breaking the same Law—that she had a room specifically to cheat the Rights Holders and break that Law.

"Who's out there?" Nancee cried with rising excitement.

I ran the lock pick quickly to no effect. "Everything needs the WiFi to function, even this stupid thing." I shook it with frustration.

"You can't keep me in here," Nancee said from within. Her voice was low and shaky now.

"Where else am I going to keep you?" The woman's voice came back. She sounded distressed, but only as if she was having a bad customer service day. I don't think she understood the gravity of her circumstances.

I twisted the small lock pick against the spot where the magnetic lock should be. I had to think about how the lock actually worked and picture the mechanism in my mind to unlock it manually. After a few moments, it clicked.

A gasp escaped from the woman, or perhaps it was the air

releasing from the sealed room. The panel sprang out an inch. Henri pried it open.

In the center of the small white room, Nancee was bound by a cable to a chair. Her eyes were tired and fearful, but they brightened when she saw us.

"Sera?" she asked tentatively as Sera rushed in ahead of me. Then Nancee saw me and her face broke into a wide smile. "Speth!"

I usually hate the way my name sounds—my ludicrous, cheap, terrible name. But Nancee said it with a joy that made it feel warm.

The woman—Nancee's so-called owner—was frozen in fear, her face both horrified and horrible. She was heavily made-up, but in a haphazard, ghastly way. Makeup styles are Patented and Trademarked, just like hairstyles, but she must have applied hers after the WiFi went down. Most Affluents used a MakeUpper™ mask that showed the user how to replicate those styles, but it was obviously useless without a connection.

As we came closer, she backed herself into a pile of things she was hoarding: sculptures, fine bedding, a food printer, a gold medallion and a mound of different makeup and beauty products. She threw out her arms to protect it all.

"You! You're not supposed to talk," the woman said, gaping at me. "You're that Silent Freak™!"

I ignored her and released Nancee from the chair.

"Hi, Nancee," I said, for lack of anything better.

"You're talking!" Nancee gasped and hugged me. "I thought you were going to be mad that *I* was talking, but I had to—"

"It's okay," I said. "Henri, take the inks."

"You can't!" the woman insisted. She put a hand on her printer to protect it and the inks inside. Henri lifted her hand up as politely as possible and looted her ink tank. In response, she began tapping furiously at her Cuff in a futile effort to sue us. "I've caught you talking! When the WiFi comes back on—"

"If the WiFi *ever* comes back on," I said, rolling my eyes, "thousands of reports about us will all hit the system at once."

Margot sighed and looked at the woman sadly. "Your little report will not matter at all."

Margot went over to the makeup and swept it into her bag.

"That's *my* makeup!" the woman shouted. "My inks! My *girl*!"

"What about them?" I scoffed.

"They're my *things*!" she cried.

My insides boiled with rage. "They aren't!" I shouted. I couldn't find the words that might show her how preposterously unjust this whole system was. I doubt she'd have listened, anyway.

Instead, I said, "Without the WiFi—without a connection to Central Data and its lists of who owns what—you own *nothing*."

Henri gave me his best smile. Margot pushed through the woman's pile of things, gathering up whatever she thought we might need. The rest, we left her with, including her precious gold medallion.

HEALTHSPITAL™: $4.99

"We took whatever seemed useful," I said to Saretha, recounting Nancee's rescue. I held a flat, sealed package out to her. "I grabbed this for you."

Saretha sat up in her Healthspital™ bed and looked blearily at the package in my hand.

"Is that a cookie?" she asked. Her eyes were deeply bloodshot from all the shocks they'd received from her screaming after Sam's death. The shocks were a punishment, doled out instantly for speaking without a Cuff.

The Rights Holders demanded payment, and if they didn't collect it in money, they extracted it in suffering. An angry pride surged through me that I'd cut off the Rights Holders' access to our eyes.

"It *is* a cookie," I answered her. "A chocolate chip cookie Sealed-With-Freshness™." The package warmed the cookie when you opened it. I'd never tried one—they were far too expensive to waste on anyone in the Onzième, even on their Last Day.

"We should save it, right?" Saretha asked, licking her lips a little.

"No," I said, tearing from the notched edge. The package released a tiny breath and instantly heated in my hand. I waited the requisite ten seconds for the cookie to warm and soften, then pulled it out of the foiled interior and handed it to Saretha.

"But..."

"Eat it while it's warm," I said, forcing a smile. I knew it would be better not to give her a choice. I felt like an impostor, faking Sam's role in our family. He'd somehow managed to be mischievous and encouraging at the same time, and that always cheered me up. I wanted to do that for Saretha, but I know we both felt the holes left in our hearts. I quickly brushed back a tear so she wouldn't see.

Saretha took a nibble, closed her eyes, smelled the aroma and smiled. She split the cookie and handed half back to me. I waved it off.

"You have to try it," she said, as if we were in an Ad. She broke into a perfect, beautiful, Ad-worthy grin, tarnished by a slight gritting of her teeth at the pain she was in. She used to make herself look Ad-worthy so the Ad screens would record and analyze her and maybe offer discounts—or, she'd dreamed, a part in a movie with Carol Amanda Harving.

That would never happen. We didn't know, back then, that my sister *was* Carol Amanda Harving. Or, at least, Carol Amanda Harving was nothing more than an illegally tweaked digital version of Saretha.

"I already had one," I lied, pushing the cookie half back at her.

Saretha paused, and then her smile faded. "You can't do that," she said. Her movements got twitchy, and she sat up farther. "You have to let me be the big sister. You can't do *everything*."

She jabbed the half cookie at me again, and I took it, slightly stunned. Was that how she felt? As if I'd stolen her role in our family?

Saretha leaned back, like I'd used up what little energy she had. I wondered, not for the first time, how so much distance had come between us.

"When you're healed, we're going to find Mom and Dad," I said in the most inspiring voice I could. I wanted her to have something nice to focus on. I wanted her to share the desire for us to be whole again.

Saretha nodded absently, only half listening. "You're not trying it," she said, pointing at the cookie.

Blood rose to my ears. I had to remind myself that it was hard for her to concentrate with the pain. Maybe she didn't see how things had changed between us. She'd been a prisoner in our home for almost a year, after all. I hadn't been able to even hold her hand to comfort her.

I reached for her hand now and gave it a gentle squeeze. She squeezed back, and I let myself feel the warmth of still having some family left.

I took a bite of the cookie to placate her. The flavors and warmth threw my thoughts into disarray. I had to close my eyes to fully appreciate the warm, caramel-y dough and the deep, gooey bits of chocolate. You couldn't print food like this, and I'd never had real chocolate before. I'd delivered chocolates as a Placer, but never with any idea of what I was delivering to the unappreciative mouths of the Affluents. I had no way to know if it was truly rare, or if, like gold, it was something the rich kept for themselves because they could.

"We're all going to be together," I said finally, finding my footing in the conversation again.

Saretha nodded weakly, but not because she was tired. "Except Sam," she said quietly, pulling her hand away to rub at her eyes. The cookie turned to concrete in my stomach.

At least she wasn't unaware of what had happened. She knew things could never be the same. Our family would never be whole. I wondered how much she blamed me—and how much I deserved it. My chin quivered, and I tried to blink the tears from my eyes.

"Mrs. Harris said our parents are on a farm in Carolina called Crab Creek," I went on hoarsely, focusing on what was important.

"Crab Creek sounds nice," she said.

Did she believe that? The name was obviously meant to sound idyllic, but I found it creepy. Our parents were forced to work every day out in the blistering sun, climbing trees with small brushes, pollinating peach, plum and sour cherry trees—at least, that was what they told us. The few times we'd spoken by screen call, Dad tried to make it sound like it was all fine, but his face told a different, weary story. My parents were always nervous and careful with their words. Saretha and I had long speculated they told us as little as they could—or maybe as much as they were allowed. The company they were Indentured to restricted how often we could speak and what they could say. They couldn't reveal proprietary details, like their location, or their exact crops and pollination cycle.

Now, with the WiFi down, we would never see them again if we didn't go and find them ourselves.

Saretha drew a quick breath, like a shock of pain had jolted her. I glanced down at her legs under the sheets. I didn't know how she was going to walk again, let alone how we would free my parents. The BoneKnitters® needed trained people to operate them, and the Healthspital™ staff had fled. In any case, the equipment wouldn't work without WiFi, and whatever medical knowledge the workers might have had about healing broken bones was strictly proprietary.

From the hall, I could hear a few scattered groans from

other patients. This, too, was my fault. Rog had warned me about the suffering in store without the WiFi tether.

Then, suddenly, I heard the sound of music. The voices of Birdo and Neckfat singing "We Three Litigators" echoed from a speaker somewhere down the hall.

"Yes!" someone shouted. The music cut out for a moment, then came back, and the whole Healthspital™'s intercom turned on with a crackle. All at once, the music was everywhere, and a broad smile broke out over my face.

"They found the key!" someone shouted from the hall. Footsteps came running toward Saretha's room and Penepoli appeared in the door, wide-eyed and grinning. "They found the key!" she repeated.

Saretha's head cocked, not understanding.

"They broke the DRM!" I said, feeling hope rise again inside me. "We'll be able to get the food printers working. We'll be able to heal you."

Saretha looked down at her legs. Suddenly everything seemed a million times more possible. Penepoli rushed over and pulled me into a massive hug. "We're going to do this!" she squealed. "We have to let everyone know!" She raced off.

"We'll get you fixed up fast," I said to Saretha. "Then we can leave and find Mom and Dad!"

"Do you think we'll see the ocean?" Saretha asked.

I swallowed. *The ocean—not our parents*, I thought. Was the pain distracting her, or was she trying not to get her hopes up that we might be a family again?

I wrapped my arms around her in a hug—one that was free and yet more valuable than the Rights Holders could ever imagine. "I know we will," I said, and I vowed that I would do anything to make it happen.

CRACKED: $5.99

A small group was waiting for me outside the Healthspital™. Nancee, Penepoli and Itzel Gonz all bubbled with a feeling of triumph and optimism. Sera was with them, but hung back a bit. In my opinion, she didn't belong. Nancee and Penepoli had always been good friends to me. Itzel had made the sign of the zippered lips to me at school to show her support while I was silent. Sera, on the other hand, had tried to break my arm to make me speak. And I couldn't forget the part she'd played in Sam's death.

We all moved off to a nearby garage where I'd stashed Silas Rog's Ebony Meiboch™ Triumph. I wanted to be the one to tell Kel the good news, and the car was the fastest way to reach her at the southern exit. There was so much I needed to do, but at least I had some hope now. The printers would be up and running soon, Saretha would be healed and then we'd get out of Portland's dome and find our parents.

Kel would know where to find Crab Creek. She would know what to do next.

The dome was brightening above us. I could see a beautiful cerulean sky through one of the holes in it. That felt like a hopeful sign.

"Cerulean," I said, because I could.

"Azure," Nancee responded. Before our Last Day, she, Penepoli and I had delighted in speaking the expressive words we knew we would never be able to afford. It felt good to share that bond again.

I gave Nancee my Placer bag to hold. Kel had instructed me to keep it on hand at all times. It had food rations, a pony bottle of sleep gas, tools for opening magnetic locks, and some first aid supplies.

"This is so exciting," Nancee said, though her eyes were shadowed by weary dark rings. Penepoli nodded in agreement. Sera knit her brow at us.

"Where are we going?" she asked. Itzel cocked an eyebrow at her. Apparently she hadn't forgotten the day Sera had attacked me in the school hallway, either.

I wanted to tell Sera there wasn't room in the car, but there obviously was. The Meiboch™ was designed to cart around three corpulent Affluents in the wide back seat, as well as anything they might wish to buy. We probably could have fit eight people inside without too much cramming.

"I need to tell Kel what's happened," I said, sliding into the driver's seat.

"That doesn't exactly answer my question," Sera said. "I don't know who Kel is." Her voice felt very close in the car. The interior was soundproofed, like a Squelch. A knot of irritation tied up in my gut. I'd have bet anything that the inside of the car had been designed to keep the WiFi out, just because Rog could. It bore all the signs.

I wanted to ask what Sera thought she was doing with us, but I just said, "She's at the southern exit," and listened to how the car absorbed my words. If anyone in the world didn't need a mobile Squelch, it was Rog. I felt a little vindictive pleasure in knowing we had taken something from him.

"Why do we need to see her?" Sera asked.

"God, Sera, chill!" Nancee said. She knew how awful Sera had been to me.

Margot and Henri had joined Kel in going building to building, looking for more useful supplies and assessing the state of chaos in the city. I could have said this, but I didn't have the patience to explain myself to Sera. I was looking forward to spending time with Penepoli and Nancee, and I relished the opportunity to have a new friend in Itzel. But Sera had made her choice the day she tried to force me to speak.

I pulled the Meiboch™ parallel to the outer ring, but didn't drive down onto it. Even though that route would have been faster, I didn't want us mistaken for Affluents trying to escape. Instead, I took a route through the side streets, thinking this car might be just the thing to take Saretha and me out of the dome and down to Crab Creek.

People stopped to stare when they saw the car. This was Silas Rog's signature vehicle, and its impenetrable black glass made it impossible for anyone to see who was inside. Too late, I realized how that could be a problem.

Something hard slammed against the windshield, bounced and skidded off into the road. Someone had thrown an abandoned Cuff, undoubtedly hoping it would detonate the battery. I slowed the car to a crawl.

"Are you crazy?" Sera asked. "Get us out of here!"

"We *should* just go," Nancee said, gritting her teeth as if it pained her to agree with Sera. They were both leaning forward, like that would speed us up.

"Why would they do that?" Penepoli asked, bewildered.

I shook my head. "They can't see who we are," I replied, tapping at the glass. From inside it was gray, but outside, it was a glossy pitch black. There was probably a way to clear the glass and let them see us, but I didn't want to waste time fiddling with the Meiboch™'s controls.

"They should know we're not trying to escape," I said, bringing the car to a stop. "We should tell them the DRM is cracked, and that the printers will be working soon—spread the word. The only way to pass information along now is to talk."

Itzel nodded slowly. "Is that what you want us to do? Get the word out?"

Was that what *I* wanted? Itzel was two years ahead of me in school. It felt strange that she was looking to me for direction. "We need to let everyone know," I said, a smile forming on my lips. "So…yes."

I opened my door, hoping the four kids would be glad to hear our news. But as soon as I stepped outside, they rushed toward the car—or started to. When they saw it was me, the Silent Girl, they all pulled up short.

One of them made the sign of the zippered lips. Then they all stood and stared at me, expectant.

"Silents," Nancee whispered, and she made the sign, too.

I took a deep breath. I'd been avoiding the Silents because Kel had warned me the ones still refusing to speak probably didn't want to hear my story. I didn't understand why. A boy in the group, who was maybe thirteen, made the zippered lips sign again, fiercely, eyes blazing.

"You don't have to—" I started to explain, but he cut me off.

"You do," he snapped. The other Silents around him tensed, like he wasn't supposed to speak—and neither was I.

"Are none of us going to talk?" I asked.

Sera, in the back seat, ducked down. Itzel stepped out to support me.

Nancee came out from behind me and touched my arm. "Speth," she whispered. "I think we should get back in the car."

"Don't you see? Our power now is in talking to each other," I protested, my face getting warm. They didn't seem to believe this, so I tried a different tactic. "We've got a way to get the printers working."

"You said our power was in silence!" the boy growled. A taller boy standing behind him twitched at the boy's words.

"I never said that," I replied carefully. How could I have? After I turned fifteen, I never said *anything* until the night we destroyed the WiFi.

"Stop talking," the boy said. He moved closer, his hands balling into fists.

I opened my mouth to speak again, but before I could say a word, he came at me. He swung, and I ducked. Being a Placer meant my reflexes were fast. I pushed him back. He was small and thin—probably hungry. I could take him, but not all of them—especially not if Sera was going to cringe in the back of the car. I didn't know if Nancee was of any use in a fight. She seemed frozen, her eyes full of fear. Only Itzel looked prepared, though not to fight so much as to withstand what was to come.

The two girls suddenly rushed at me. I withdrew a couple of steps and used the open car door to flip myself backward onto the roof. Sera screeched at the thud. The Meiboch™ rocked. Everyone stopped cold, gaping at me.

"Whoa," Nancee gasped, backing into the car and pulling with her.

I positioned myself in a fighting stance, like I'd once seen in an action film, *Truly, Lovely, Danger.* I could pull off a lot of impressive moves from gymnastics and my training as a Placer, but I knew nothing about fighting. I hoped these four kids wouldn't realize the difference.

They all slowly backed up two paces. Nancee gestured for me to get back in the car.

"The system I was fighting with my silence is gone," I explained, pointing toward the center of the city. "It was destroyed with Rog's tower."

The taller boy peered toward the tower's glow, struggling to understand.

"We need to let everyone know the city is free," Itzel added calmly. I felt a flash of gratitude for her steady presence and wished I had gotten to know her better before all this.

The smaller boy still appeared angry. He was clearly assessing how best to get at me, but the taller boy mashed his lips together and spoke through a frown.

"Only here," he said, spinning a finger to point to our dome. "Only now."

One of the girls shoved him for daring to speak, and the smaller boy seized the opportunity to run at me. I reversed my earlier move and flipped myself into the driver's seat. I imagined the maneuver looked impressive from the outside, but I overshot it and slammed my arm into the stick shift.

"Smooth," Sera remarked.

"I'm so glad you've finished cowering long enough to comment," I shot back.

Itzel ducked back in and we pulled the doors closed. I floored it. Sera's head snapped back from the acceleration.

Outside, the smaller boy picked up the Cuff again and hurled it at the rear of the car, but we were too far away for him to hit.

"So you *were* fighting," Nancee said unsteadily. "The system. The paying. All that."

Nancee had followed my lead, but because neither of us spoke, we hadn't known each other's reasons. "Weren't you?" I asked, purposely not explaining I'd stumbled into the fight out of desperation.

"Well, yeah," Nancee said.

Penepoli applauded her. Sera made a scoffing noise. Her scorn stung a bit, even though I shouldn't have cared about her opinion. I reached over and squeezed Nancee's hand with a smile.

"No one knew *why* you did it, Speth," Sera said, maybe to excuse why she hadn't done the same, or maybe to make me feel like garbage. I peeked back at her in the rearview mirror. Her arms were folded and her face looked hard. I couldn't figure out why she was so angry—it was not as if I'd ever asked anyone to follow my lead. I'd never planned for any of this to happen. How could anyone expect me to have a plan?

Ahead of the car was another mob, gathered around a small grocery shop, trying to smash their way in. These weren't teens from the Onzième, but kids I didn't know and a few young parents. One woman clutched a baby to her chest and watched expectantly from the back of the crowd.

"Should we stop and explain?" Itzel asked.

"You're insane," Sera said. "They'll tear you apart."

"They just want food," I said. "You were the one out for blood yesterday."

"It can be like a mission!" Penepoli exclaimed.

"A mission?" Sera scoffed.

"I'm already on a mission to free anyone Indentured like I was," Nancee said. "But people should definitely know we'll be able to eat."

"And that we're free," Penepoli said. "Free to say *anything*."

"We can do this," Itzel said.

"Yeah!" Penepoli seconded.

I slowed the car. "Is this really what you want to do?"

They all agreed. All except Sera.

Penepoli opened her door and called to the crowd. "I have good news!" she said, stepping out of the car. "We can get the food printers working!"

The crowd didn't react with anger, like Sera had predicted. They turned and listened. The woman with the baby even smiled a little. Itzel and Penepoli moved closer to explain what we'd learned. Nancee turned to me and said, "We've got this. Go deliver your good news."

She shut the door. Sera crawled into the front passenger seat. I couldn't look at her—I just took the next corner hard and didn't say a word.

INCURSION: $6.99

Under normal circumstances, finding a Placer isn't easy. Sam and I had tried to spot one for years with no luck. But I'd learned some of the signs by working as a Placer—knowing what handholds were best or where to shoot a line. That made it easier for me to find Kel, Margot and Henri. They also weren't exactly trying to be hidden anymore. Everything was different now.

About a block from the southern exit, I noticed a building with a pried-open window, and knew instinctively they were there. I pulled the Meiboch™ as close as I could to the building's rear entrance, opposite the outer ring exit so it wouldn't draw attention. This car wouldn't be safe anywhere for long.

We made our way inside and found my Placer team on the roof. It wasn't just Kel, Henri and Margot, though. With them were a couple of frightened-looking Affluents, my friend Mandett and a girl of about nine who looked like a miniature version of Margot. Her eyes lit up when she saw me.

"The Silent Girl!" she exclaimed, pointing at me.

The Affluents' expressions grew more distressed after hearing her announcement. Both had their hands behind their backs, and they shifted uneasily.

"That is Speth," Margot corrected. The girl waved to me. Now I was certain she was Margot's sister.

Margot's face darkened. "I am so glad Sera could join you."

Sera responded with a sarcastic wave. Margot's sister waved back without mockery.

"Are you a Silent?" she asked Sera.

"No, sweetie, I'm not," Sera said, Huny®-sweet, kneeling to meet the girl eye to eye. Sera didn't have any siblings, nor had she ever shown any interest in the younger kids in the Onzième, so I didn't know who she was trying to fool.

"Kel," I said, turning my attention to her. "We cracked the DRM!"

Henri pumped his fist into the air, but no one else seemed to appreciate what it meant. Kel, at the very least, should have smiled, but she was frowning and looking over the building's edge, opposite the side we'd parked on.

"They're coming," one of the Affluents warned.

Kel ignored him, motioned to me and held out her binoculars. I dropped my Placer bag next to Margot's and rushed over.

Below us, several of the shuttered tollgate doors of the southern exit were buckled and the metal slats split apart. Through them, thick anaconda-sized cables were snaking their way in, bending and piling up like soft-serve Ice-Kreem™.

"They're making a bubble," Kel explained. "The WiFi will be pressing out from those silver caps at the end of each cable. Inside the broadcast zone, it will be just like the city's WiFi is back."

"That's right," the other Affluent said with a sickly grin. He was dressed in a fine suit, like he was ready to close a deal.

My heart sank. I closed my eyes and felt the thickness of my ocular implants. They had cruelly fused to my eyes soon after they were placed over my corneas. They had become part of me, and I hated them. The threat of harsh shocks rekindled in my mind.

I handed the binoculars to Mandett, and Margot's little sister followed them, her eyes wide with wonder.

"Margot, may I see?" she asked, bouncing on her toes. Mandett took a quick peek and handed them off to the girl. I noticed he didn't have his Cuff anymore. None of us did, except Kel, Sera and the Affluents. I assumed Kel's reasons were practical and Sera's were cowardly.

"Sera," I whispered, nudging her. She was staring at the exit with horror. "Do you want that thing off now?"

Sera looked down at her arm. "I thought you said they couldn't rebuild," Sera said, cradling the Cuff, probably calculating if she should keep it on in case the WiFi returned.

"I didn't think they could," I snapped.

"I've never seen this before." Kel shook her head. "There are serious legal impediments. The area around the dome is part of the city jurisdiction. It's like they've rewritten the Law."

"Who?" I asked.

Kel bit her lip. "I'm not sure who, but I think I know why. My guess is you destroyed more than the WiFi when you took out Rog's hub—you must have taken out a Central Data node with it. I think that's why they're coming at us so hard."

"One of the Central Data nodes was *here*?" I gasped. "But Portland isn't an important dome. Not like DC."

"Rog was very powerful," Kel said, shaking her head. "I should have seen this coming."

"What do we do?" I asked.

"We cut them off," Mandett said. "We chop them to pieces."

Kel nodded thoughtfully, but her expression suggested she

didn't agree. "You slice into that cable, and you'll be electrocuted," she said, glancing at Henri, who'd had a similar idea in Rog's WiFi hub.

"It doesn't look like they're making much progress," Henri said. He leaned down to Margot's sister. "Mira, can I have a look?"

Mira smiled at him. She handed him the binoculars gladly.

"Maybe we just let them have that area," Henri said as he adjusted the focus. "We could put up signs."

"Oh, Henri," Margot said with a sigh.

"Oh, Henri," Mira copied.

"They won't be content to leave those cables sitting," I said. "They aren't stupid."

Henri wilted a little under my comment.

"*Stupid* is not a polite word," Mira said.

I had the freedom, finally, to speak, and I needed to remember that words matter. Even a nine-year-old knew that. I should have known better.

"Sorry," I murmured, unable to look him in the eye.

"They plan to press in," Kel said. "They'll work their way to the city center and rebuild the system."

A lump formed in my throat. "What about all of us?"

"See," the smaller Affluent said, nudging the one in the suit. "She's nothing. They made a big deal of nothing."

"They'll round us up," Mandett said quietly. "Sell us off."

"As they should!" the Affluent in the suit said.

Margot eyed him nervously. She reached for her sister and put her arms around the girl, hugging Mira close.

On the street below, a small crowd had gathered. A boy in a white T-shirt hopped the barrier into the road to walk up to the exit. I couldn't make out much in the way of details, but something about him seemed familiar. He paused a little way out, like he was confused. He shook his head, then moved forward again. He got as far as the abandoned tollbooths and stopped, leaning against a blue tollbooth door.

"What is he doing?" I wondered.

With the binoculars raised to his eyes, Henri shook his head. "He's just standing there." He handed them to me to have a look.

A chill ran down my spine. "That's Norflo!"

"Who?" Henri asked.

"Norflo Juarze. My neighbor. He—" I turned to Kel. "Can they hurt him?"

"Not if he doesn't talk," Kel said calmly, but then her jaw trembled. I turned back just in time to see Norflo tilt and pitch forward. He dropped to his knees. At first I thought they were shocking his eyes, but he didn't seem to be in pain. Not exactly. He looked drunk. Panic flashed across Kel's face, but she quelled it with a calming breath and took the binoculars back.

"He has an axe," she said.

"What are they doing to him?" I asked her.

Kel frowned. "I've never seen anything like this."

"I thought your Kel knew stuff," Sera complained.

Kel watched more closely. "As I said, if he tries to chop that cable, he's going to get electrocuted."

I gulped in a breath and ran to grab my Placer bag. I pulled out my grapple and secured one end to the roof we were on. I had to get down there to help him.

One of the boys from the crowd below hopped the fence.

"Stop!" I yelled. He did, looking around for my voice. "We need to do something," I said to my friends.

Henri unzipped his bag to join me, peeked inside and frowned. "Kel, I need a new grapple," he said.

Kel glared at him for one brief second.

"She will order one for you, Henri, right away," Margot said. "That is the top priority." Mira nodded seriously, missing her sister's sarcasm.

I got out my runner and held it tight in my hand. My heart started to slam against my ribs.

"Not yet," Kel said, staying my hand. "We don't know what we're dealing with."

The boy at the fence shifted restlessly.

"What are they doing?" Sera asked.

"Bad things," Margot said.

Mira squirmed a little. "May we go home?" she begged, all the brightness gone from her voice. Margot appeared to consider it.

The second boy lost his patience and ran in after Norflo. After a moment, he put his hands to his eyes and began to lose his balance.

"Kel," I said, bouncing on my feet. "I think they're trapped."

"Give me one second," Kel replied irritably.

I opened my mouth to protest—we needed to act now—but I gave her a moment, because she'd earned my trust a hundred times over.

"We coordinate. We're still Placers," Kel said, more to herself than to me.

Kel paused and quickly checked over her gear, then fired her line out, clear of Norflo and his friend, so it hit the farthest toll and held fast. I followed her lead and shot mine opposite hers, so we wouldn't collide. This was standard practice. My line stuck to a maintenance shack and held fast.

"Don't speak," she said to me. "They'll use it to identify you. When you hit the WiFi signal, don't look at anything reflective. Don't look at me. I suspect they're going to try to tap into your ocular feed to see what's going on in here."

"That's illegal!" Mandett protested.

"They do not care about legality anymore," Margot said with a frown. "They only care about wielding the Law."

"The emergency code of—" the suited Affluent started.

"No one cares!" Henri snapped.

"They've tapped into people's vision before," I said quietly. "Rog made me watch the feed from Beecher's grandmother's eyes. He wanted me to see that she was suffering."

I realized too late that I should have asked Mrs. Harris where Mrs. Stokes had been sent—though it was unlikely Mrs. Harris knew. Anger boiled up in me, thinking about all the terrible things Silas Rog had done. The police had him now, but if the WiFi came back on, he would Legalese his way out of custody in a heartbeat.

"I've done it to each of you," Kel said without looking at me, Margot or Henri.

"Creepy much?" Sera asked.

Kel ignored her. "I'm sorry," she said to us.

I tried to take in what she was saying. She'd tapped into our feeds? What had she seen? Did she know the whole time about what was happening with my family?

"Margot, take Mira home," Kel ordered.

Margot didn't argue, which was unusual. She got to her feet, looking at Kel like she'd been betrayed.

Kel bent down to Mira and flashed a bright, warm smile. "It was a pleasure to meet you," she said.

I still couldn't quite wrap my head around the way Kel had violated our privacy. "You watched us?" I asked her.

"Every candidate is watched," Henri said.

"You knew?" I asked him.

"Henri," Kel said, directing her gaze to the rooftop door. "Take Margot and Mira home."

Henri zipped up his bag and took Mira's hand. In that moment, they looked a little like a family to me.

"Kel," I said, growing impatient.

"Speth," she replied, a hint of temper in her voice. "I'm sorry you didn't know, but we don't have time to sort out your feelings about it right now. We need to get down there and figure out what they're doing. We'll dip into the edge of that WiFi and then get right out." Kel stretched her arms and got ready to zip-line down.

I kept looking at her, still hoping for an answer. Finally, her shoulders fell, and she turned back to me.

"Once, on your first night as a Placer," Kel explained loudly, so Margot and Henri could hear. "The second time when you were arrested, and I had to get you out of jail. In order to access your ocular overlays, I had to access your feed. I only did this when I needed to."

"Okay," I said after a long pause. But I didn't really know if it *was* okay.

"Grab your bag," Kel said, either because she hoped the matter was settled or because we didn't have time to settle it now. I looped the bag across my shoulder.

"What about us?" the suited Affluent said loudly.

"You want to go down there?" Kel asked. By the way they

shifted uncomfortably, they obviously didn't. Kel turned to Mandett and Sera. "Keep an eye on them." She nodded at the two Affluents.

"You want *Sera* to watch them?" I whispered to Kel in disbelief.

"I don't really care about these Affluents," Kel muttered back. "And I'd just as soon keep her out of the way."

Sera's brow knit. It was clear to me she did not like being whispered about.

"Are you ready?" Kel asked. Before I could answer, she hopped over the edge and zipped across to the exit. All I could do was follow.

CORNEAL OVERLAYS: $7.98

I hit the ground hard. We didn't travel to street level like this as Placers, and the angle was steeper than I was used to. I stood and dusted myself off, then glanced over at Kel before I remembered her warning. *Don't look at her!* My inner voice roared to the surface, and I hurriedly turned away.

Norflo was crawling a few yards between us, swaying like he'd been drugged. He felt his way blindly along the ground, axe in hand.

The cables buzzed with the hot sound of electricity. They writhed, pushed in from outside, twisting and snapping along to gain ground. The words *Community Relations* were embossed on the cables, as if they were merely there to help. At equal intervals, metal rings studded with ball bearings helped the cables glide better along the ground.

I was uncomfortably aware of Kel's warning that whoever was on the other side might monitor what I was seeing. I was sure I'd crossed the threshold into the WiFi. The cables flopped farther forward and the slatted metal doors rattled angrily. So far, though, nothing seemed to be wrong, and I couldn't understand why Norflo was behaving so oddly. I started toward him, ignoring Kel's order to dip out of the

WiFi—Norflo was my friend, and I couldn't abandon him like this.

As I drew closer, a dot began to flutter in my left eye, and a bright white line drew itself in my right. Suddenly my vision filled with checkerboard test patterns. They were different sizes in each eye, flashing at different rates. It made me feel cross-eyed and desperate to look away. I closed my eyes, but the images persisted. My corneal overlays were under my eyelids, blasting the pictures directly into my retina. There was nothing I could do to shut them out.

I shook my head to try to orient myself, but the flashing just strobed faster. I staggered to the wall and felt for my grapple line. The flashing abruptly ceased. The checkerboards grew and shrunk until they matched in each eye to form a single image I could at least focus on. I felt a strange relief in my eyes, though I still couldn't see anything but the patterns.

I had to concentrate on my mental map and think of what to do and where to go. Could I get Norflo out? Or should I just get myself out of the bubble as quick as I could and figure out what to do next?

I gripped my Placer bag and listened hard. I heard movement under the slap, roll and hum of the cables. I stepped toward the sound, hoping it was Norflo nearby. The patterns in my eyes began to spin wildly. The world seemed to upend, and a wave of nausea overtook me.

This was what was making Norflo look so dazed and unsteady. They were doing the same thing to him. The patterns rolled right, then left, drifting slowly with no connection to the actual world.

I wanted to call out to Norflo or Kel, but she'd warned me against just that. I had to focus on getting out of the WiFi bubble, but I couldn't see or speak. This was far worse than I'd imagined. I listened for the sound of the group of kids to orient myself, but I couldn't hear them over the buzz and rattle of the cables.

I reached out and, miraculously, found Norflo's shoulder. I tugged, trying to get him to follow me.

"Dafuc?" He batted me away. He had no way of knowing it was me.

I backed off. The pain in my eyes was excruciating and relentless, and I didn't know if I could save myself, much less Norflo. Dizzied, I stumbled to my knees, tried to stand and stumbled again.

"Speth Jime," a woman's lilting voice called out, amplified through a loudspeaker. *"Surrender. Put your hands up, speak* ***'agree,'*** *and this suppressive broadcast will cease."*

"Speth?" Norflo asked, trying to conceal the shakiness in his voice.

They knew I was here. Someone must have looked at me to give me away—maybe Norflo. Or maybe the cables had cameras.

The pattern in my vision started to grow erratic, punishing me for my disobedience. It flashed and spun, and the images split from each other, churning in opposite directions. My skull began throbbing. My eyeballs were being stabbed with a pain different and deeper than when they'd been shocked. The urge to retch boiled up from my gut, and I vomited.

"Speth?" The aggressively sweet, almost childlike female voice bounced and echoed through the streets. *"You might still be saved. My city could still be salvaged. Speak* ***'agree,'*** *and we can get everything fixed up, back to just like it was, in a jiffy."*

"Nah," Norflo counseled.

I wanted to call out to Kel, but thought better of it. Just because they'd found me didn't mean they'd seen her.

"What are they doing?" another voice screeched. I heard footsteps behind me.

Someone else called my name. It was Henri. He was supposed to be getting Margot and Mira home.

Oh, God, I thought, *don't come in here.* I didn't even know if I'd be able to get out—there was no point in more of us getting trapped in here.

The footsteps quickened. Henri wasn't good at listening.

"You have already broken your silence," the woman's voice mentioned almost sympathetically. *"Just speak **'agree'** to surrender."*

Through the bright, skull-cracking pain, I thought, *no,* and...was she insane? Did she think I didn't know how to keep quiet? I felt like my eyes were going to detach from my head, but I knew I couldn't give up now.

"Stop!" Margot yelled. Had Henri stepped inside? I kept crawling, but the waves of dizziness took me and I pitched to the left, falling on my shoulder.

"You smell terrible," a small voice said in my ear. This one was childlike, too, but it didn't sound so strange. This voice wasn't wrong, either—the smell of my vomit made me want to retch again.

"Come back!" Margot pleaded.

A small pair of soft hands took my arm and pulled. "Follow me," she whispered.

Something felt wrong about this. I could do it myself. I tried to wrench myself away, and the girl giggled.

"I am too young for corneal overlays," she whispered, and tugged at me again. My heart nearly stopped as I realized it was Mira.

The patterns in my vision blinked out for a moment, returned and stuttered away again. I was exiting the WiFi. I could just make out the sight of Mira dragging me forward with incredible determination. Margot was standing at the WiFi's edge, desperately trying to break free of Henri, who held her back.

"I saved the Silent Girl!" Mira said proudly, delivering me to her sister's feet. Then she looked back, behind me, at Norflo, who was slick with sweat. Near him, Sera Croate writhed on the ground in agony, flailing her arms. She must have come out to help. I wished she hadn't bothered—we didn't need her help, and now she was trapped as well, even with the Cuff on her arm.

"Do you want me to save them, too?" Mira asked.

"No!" I said, getting to my feet. My eyes refused to focus. I closed them, and the darkness immediately brought incredible relief. But when I opened them again, everything was doubled.

Mira hesitated for a moment, then turned back toward the WiFi bubble with a determined look on her face.

"Speth said no, and so do I!" Margot yelled, seizing Mira by the arm.

Mira sighed. "Margot, please do not grab."

I couldn't see Kel anywhere. I asked Henri, "Where did Kel go?"

Henri shrugged. "I was watching Mira," he said.

"A fine job of it, too, Henri," Margot complained.

I shook myself. I tried to get my eyes to focus. Where was Mandett?

"Who is going to help your friends?" Mira asked, gesturing toward Norflo and Sera.

"I am," I said. I took a step forward and immediately needed to grab Henri's arm for balance. I hoped Margot would understand. "We need to get the car," I said.

"The car?" Henri asked.

I kept moving as quickly as I could, and Henri began to walk faster, pulling me along as we rounded the building's corner.

"How does a car help us?" Henri asked.

"It's a Squelch," I explained, still trying to gather my senses. "Rog's car is a mobile Squelch."

"I should take Mira home," Margot said as she followed along, holding Mira by the hand. She appeared deeply conflicted.

I nodded. I hoped home was a safe place for them.

"We'll drive into the bubble and pull Norflo out," I said.

"What about your friend?" Henri asked, surprised.

"Sera? She shouldn't even be down here. Kel told her to stay put," I grumbled. An appalled look crossed Henri's face. With a heavy sigh, I added, "Yes, we'll get her, too."

We lost sight of Norflo and Sera for a moment around the back of the building, where a crowd had gathered near Rog's car. I pushed through them clumsily, making my way to the driver's door.

As I reached out to open it, my vision swam. I moaned and pressed my hands to my forehead. "Henri, maybe you should drive," I said.

Even with my disjointed vision, I could see his broad face turn crimson.

"Henri does not know how to drive," Margot said from a few steps away. She stopped short and sighed, looking from the Meiboch™ to Mira and back again. "Fine," she added reluctantly. "We will rescue your friends first, and then *we*—" Margot pointed to herself and Mira "—will go back home."

Margot didn't seem very happy with her own choice. She handed Mira off to Henri and ushered them to the back seat as she moved to the driver's.

"I can do it," I protested. "We don't need to expose Mira to—"

"I want to help!" Mira said.

"Mira will sit with Henri. We will drive Mira home right after," Margot said, looking back and pretending it would be fun. "There is plenty of room."

I shook my head and dropped into the driver's seat. "You guys go home," I insisted. Margot ignored me and took the passenger's seat.

"Oh, Speth, you are so dramatic."

Was I? I thought the situation was dramatic all on its own. I worked hard to focus my eyes and found a little more success, though my skull still pounded. I drove the car around the building, across the ring and out onto the exit. The car's dashboard lit up—the interior was a Squelch, but the exterior pulled in the WiFi signal.

I pulled up between Sera and Norflo as best I could. "On three, you reach out and grab *him*," I said to Margot, pointing at Norflo. "I'll get Sera."

"I should do it," Mira countered. "I will be able to see."

"No," Margot replied.

"One..." I looked back at Mira, who watched her big sister proudly. "Two..." Was that why Margot was doing this? "Three!"

I yanked open the door. The dot appeared in my vision, expanding rapidly. I reached out, fumbling for Sera, and briefly caught her arm. She squirmed away, which was just like her.

The checkerboards exploded into my visual field. The patterns spun and began to flash.

"Oh, Miss Jime, please," the soothing, innocent voice said, as if spoken by the most compassionate person who ever lived. *"That vehicle is the property of Butchers & Rog."*

"Ugh!" Norflo moaned.

"Silas Rog, Esquire, will almost certainly want custody of his legal posessions."

I stumbled out of the car, searching blindly. "Sera!" I called out, suffering a shock for it.

"Help me!" she screamed, no doubt suffering, too.

I couldn't put my hands on her. Why had she wandered so deep into the bubble? As the patterns tore apart differently in each eye, my eye sockets began to throb again. A dark spot appeared in front of the flickering, changing pattern. My brain tried to fix on the dark shape because it was the only stable thing it could find.

My hand finally hit a bony shoulder. I had Sera. Or she had me. Suddenly she was clutching me ferociously. I pulled her along with me, hoping we were heading back toward the car.

"Thenx," I heard Norflo say, still using a cheaper pronunciation, like that mattered now. I moved in the direction of his voice and found the side of the Meiboch™.

I yanked Sera forward and pushed her ahead of me. Her arm flailed and whacked me in the head as she found her way inside the car.

The dark shape in my eyes expanded into a black field, which was then replaced with a different feed laid over the one torturing me. I now saw someone's view from well above us, from the top edge of the dome, looking down. Margot and Norflo had reached the passenger door. Mira's small hand reached out. The view was dizzying, like looking down at a video game version of myself, but I could see that I was standing between the driver's door and the door to the back seat.

"I'm gonna be sick," Sera moaned. She wasn't the only one. I reached out and found the driver's seat in front of me. I grabbed the steering wheel and pulled myself in, trying to steady my nerves.

Not Safe. The message appeared abruptly in my vision—like on the night Kel rescued me from jail. The feed in my eyes looked from the scene to a Pad held in Kel's hands. She was feeding us *her* view. I could just make out Mandett beside her.

"Speth Jime, please surrender," the woman's voice called out, like I was being just a little disobedient. *"I need your assistance to speak with someone, so I would very much prefer not to kill you."*

Go, Kel tapped out. I didn't understand. Where could we go?

"I have an offer for you," the cold woman's voice called out.

"Close. The. Door!" Sera screamed, then cried out in pain as her eyes were shocked. Either her Cuff wasn't able to charge her with whatever this WiFi was, or she'd run out of money.

I fumbled clumsily for the door handle. Where was it?

They are coming. Far more than expected. Keene Placers. Portland isn't safe, Kel messaged. My body went cold. *Escape!*

I finally found the handle. I could shut it, but the second I closed the door, we'd lose touch with Kel.

"Not without Saretha," I yelled, paying for it with three hard shocks. The DRM was cracked. She'd be better in a few days, and I'd promised we'd go together.

Kel tapped a control on her Pad—from the logo, it appeared she was hacking into the Toll™ database. She glanced up, and

I saw through her feed that two of the shuttered doors were beginning to slide upward.

Go. Kel tapped again. *Now. I'll keep Saretha safe.*

She'd heard me.

Ahead, at the rising exit doors, something was coming through. It was another Ebony Meiboch™ Triumph, nearly identical to the one we were in, but instead of flame-orange highlights down the side, the other car had silver lines that shone so brightly, they almost seemed to glow.

I'll keep Saretha safe, Kel repeated. I knew she wouldn't say it if it wasn't true, but I couldn't imagine leaving the city without my sister.

I watched through Kel's eyes as an enormous hexagon tumbled to the ground from the dome. A dozen Placers dropped down behind it, with thinner versions of the WiFi cables trailing behind. The other Meiboch™ stopped, and a rear door opened. A tall pale woman in an inky black dress stepped onto the pavement, shadowed by two hulking bodyguards. She shook her head and put her hands on her hips, staring at us like we were disobedient children.

The door behind her shuddered to a stop, then reversed direction to close. *This is your only chance!* Kel warned.

I yanked on the handle and slammed the car door shut. Kel's message disappeared, and my vision cleared to reveal the steering wheel in front of me. I sucked in a breath of relief as my point of view returned to normal.

"Go!" Henri cried.

My heart broke, but what choice did I have? We had to get out of there.

I had to leave Saretha behind.

OUT OF THE DOME: $8.96

I slammed my foot down on the accelerator. We shot past the woman, who watched without surprise. One of her bodyguards reached out for the car, as if he was planning to stop it with his bare hands. In my rearview mirror, I saw Kel shoot a line over the center of the invading Placers and zip away. They scrambled to follow, not realizing Kel was trying to draw them off, out of the bubble of WiFi.

We squeaked under the closing metal door just in time and raced past the bands of thick cable unspooling from enormous trucks.

"Don't we get a say in this?" Sera complained viciously.

"I will open the door if you would like to jump out," Margot said, deadpan.

Sera gave her a withering stare.

It was hard to concentrate on the road ahead. My eyes still ached, and my heart was pounding from our narrow escape. I peeked at the rearview again and saw the metal reopening to let the other Meiboch™ through.

"Who the hell is she?" I muttered, speeding up a bit more.

"Lucretia Rog," Margot said carefully, like the name might send me flying off the road.

It almost did. I'd never heard of another Rog, but Silas

Rog had taken everything from us. He controlled our city. He was a monster who had sent those brothers out to kill Sam. Was this his wife?

"Who?" I asked, swerving the car to avoid slamming into a worker who was managing what I think was a power supply for a truck. My entire life, Butchers & Rog had loomed over us, and now that we had overthrown Silas, there was suddenly *another* Rog?

The Meiboch™'s dashboard WiFi stuttered off, returned briefly, then died.

"She is the representative of our dome," Margot said, a little incredulous. "In DC?"

"No one ever taught me that in school," I said, realizing Lucretia Rog was almost certainly going to set Silas free.

"Me, either," Sera said. She sounded skeptical, like she thought Margot was lying.

I kept my eyes on the road ahead of us, my mind reeling. A line of trucks sat idling, waiting to deliver inks and goods into the city when the WiFi returned. They looked like they had been there awhile. Drivers milled around in boredom, then hastily scrambled up into their cabs when they spotted us, alarmed by the speed of our approach.

The dome disappeared as the tunnel curved. Lucretia Rog's car was back there, a speck in the distance. I couldn't tell if she was keeping pace or falling behind.

"How is it possible they did not teach you this?" Margot asked. "How did you think our government works?"

"We *didn't* think about it," Sera said. "They told us not to!"

I tried to ignore them and searched for a way to lose this Lucretia Rog. The tunnel curved and continued on, with three lanes on our side and three lanes on the other. The divider between was filled with cables. There were panels open, and many trucks had hooked up to these in order to tap into the system that connected our dome to the rest of the country.

"You do not know anything about our government?" Margot asked.

I felt shame creeping into my cheeks. We were fed only crumbs about how it worked. "We were told clearly, in class, that it didn't concern us," I explained. "You can't vote if you're in our kind of debt. You have to have a certain amount of money or something."

In the rearview mirror, Sera's expression looked as embarrassed as I felt. "Mrs. Oglehorn literally said it wasn't worth explaining to us," she muttered.

"You asked her how much money it took," I said, remembering.

"And she said it wasn't any of my business," Sera said, seething in the back seat just like she had in the classroom.

"They lock it in the Onzième, Jiménez," Norflo said to me. Even when it cost him to do so, Norflo insisted on calling me and my sister Jiménez rather than Jime. He was certain that our original surname, like his, was Spanish in origin. "Don't want you to know your history," he said.

"But she's on the news!" Henri said.

"On *your* newstream," Norflo said.

"We have different news?" Henri asked.

"Of course," I muttered, only realizing it then. "They blur her out. They only ever say 'our representative.' Like they always only say the 'Commander-in-Chief Justice' when he makes a new Law."

I checked the mirror again. I couldn't see anyone following.

"How worried should I be?" I asked, looking from Margot

to the road in front of me and back to the road behind. I'd never been outside the dome—I'd been curious about what was out here my entire life, but I never had any reason to believe I would ever leave, unless I was sold into Indenture like my parents.

Margot bit her lip, but didn't answer. She was stroking Mira's hair. She didn't want to say how bad it was in front of her sister.

"Is she worse than Rog?" I asked.

"She *is* a Rog," Margot replied. Unfortunately, that was answer enough.

"What are we doing?" I asked, banging on the wheel with my palms.

"Oh, my God," Sera grumbled, kicking back in her seat as she realized I didn't have a plan.

I felt my throat tighten and my voice rise. "Kel told us to escape. That's all she gave us. So now what?"

"Keep on," Norflo said.

"We need to go back," Margot said.

"Just drive," Sera said, and then to the others, "Just let her drive."

Then, after a moment's silence, Sera whispered, "We should drive to Carolina."

"How?" I snapped. "Do you know where it is?" I gestured at the road curving out of sight ahead of us. A lump formed in my throat. I'd wanted to make this escape *with* Saretha. She would never forgive me for leaving without her.

As we pressed on, the translucent yellow of the tunnel brightened, then darkened again, and I realized the outside world was just beyond. I knew clouds passed in front of the sun and shifted the light, though I'd never seen it with my own eyes. I longed to claw my way outside to have the chance. I'd seen pictures of what might lie beyond: sand, trees, ocean, sky, rolling hills. Sam had once insisted there must be ruins outside.

"Think about it," he'd said. "There was stuff out there before the domes."

Every mile I traveled from Saretha felt like a betrayal. Could Kel really keep her safe? If Lucretia Rog couldn't get to me, would Saretha be her next target?

"What if we tried to go back?" I asked out loud. I slowed, hoping to glimpse a door or a hatch that might lead outside. "Maybe we could sneak back in somehow. There are at least three holes in the dome."

"We are not equipped for a trip in the wild," Margot said.

"There are creatures out there," Mira squeaked. We'd all heard this—that there were bears and all manner of other dangerous things outside the domes.

"I doubt this road is any safer," I said. Surely Lucretia or someone would eventually catch up with us.

"We'll burn up in the sun," Sera protested.

"The sun doesn't burn you," Henri said. "Not like that."

"What like?" Norflo asked him.

Henri paused, not sure how to explain it.

Sera pursed her lips. "The sun's the main reason we have the domes."

"No," Margot said. "There is a lot more to it than that. The chaotic weather—"

"It doesn't really matter," I said, craning to see anything more than the arching roof that kept us inside. "I don't see a way out, anyway."

"We will come to another dome eventually," Margot replied.

"How do you know?" I asked. "Have you seen a map?"

She paused, then said, "My father travels. He takes this road to Keene."

"He never brings us with him," Mira huffed.

"Good," Henri said, reaching for Margot's hand from the back seat and bringing it to his lips for a kiss.

"Henri!" Mira cried.

Henri dropped Margot's hand and sat back.

"Our parents do not allow that!"

"Your parents aren't here," Henri said. I saw him blushing in the rearview mirror and looking to Margot for support. She eyed him like he should know better.

Mira's face suddenly bloomed with wonder. "Does that mean I can sing?"

Now Margot's cheeks colored.

"Your parents don't let her sing?" I asked. Most kids are discouraged from singing, but Margot's family had a Squelch. Margot played her violin in there. Why couldn't Mira sing? Even if she was terrible, they wouldn't have to hear it.

"My parents' rules are not yours to worry over," Margot said, her face growing even redder. She stroked Mira's hair and sighed. "Just sing if you are going to do it."

Mira began to hum, quietly at first. I knew the melody. It was a slow, romantic song from Eggs Eggs called "Your Word." Then she started to sing:

You know what I want to hear
Your voice speaking loud and clear
Every charge is worth the cost

Without your speaks I will be lost
I will pay for your word
Will you let it be heard?
Will you say it, in spite of the fee?

Norflo burst out laughing.

"What?" Mira asked, stopping midverse.

"Song's just a Ad," Norflo said.

"It is not *an* Ad. It is a popular song," Mira said, crossing her arms.

"'Sa Ad for the word *love*," Norflo said. "Doesn't make sense, either. Girl wantsa boy to say *love*?"

"Because he will not do it," Sera said. She obviously liked the song.

"Pah," Norflo said, like that was ridiculous.

I must have heard the song a hundred times. I'd never thought of it as an Ad, but Norflo's explanation made sense. Mira seemed deeply annoyed.

"Why would I care what it means?" she said.

"Matters," Norflo said. "Meaning always matters."

"Except meaning is regulated by the Word$ Market™," I said.

"Nonsense," Norflo said. "Words can mean whatever you want."

"I don't think so," Sera said.

"Hey, Mira," I broke in, a smile blooming on my face.

"What?" she asked.

I sang:

I will pay for your word
Even if it is absurd,
Will you speak it, and I'll tap AGREE?

"Ohemgee! So bad!" Norflo shook his head, but then he started to sing along. Mira and Sera joined in, too. For half a second, I forgot about how terrible things were.

Then Henri yelled, "Look!" The singing trailed away.

Ahead of us, the tunnel split. There were no signs. No labels. The tunnel continued on, curving slightly left on one side, and peeling off sharply to the right into an off-ramp. Farther ahead, nearly invisible from our angle, was an on-ramp joining the highway. This was what Henri was pointing at, because a large truck with Mandolin Inks™ emblazoned on its side had just come flying out of the exit.

I hit the brakes, and we stuttered to a stop. Everyone yanked forward into their seat belts and then back into their seats.

"Sorry," I said to the group. I eyed the split. "How can there be no signs?" The tunnel was troublingly devoid of markers of any kind. "Why does this car not have some kind of navigation system? You'd think Rog would, if anyone does."

Without the WiFi, the dashboard was essentially blank, save for a small amber light that showed a battery icon with two bars.

"Rog does not drive. He has a chauffeur who would be trained to handle navigation," Margot explained. "The proprietary maps would be in the driver's Cuff, or his overlays."

"Or one of those brain-wired visors like Judges use," Henri said.

"Those are only for Judges, Henri," Margot said.

"That truck's fulla inks," Norflo said, edging forward.

"I don't think we should stop," Sera said, nervously looking back. Around the long curve behind us, I saw the car. Lucretia Rog's Meiboch™ with the silver edging was following us.

"Crap," I said.

A second truck came barreling out of the exit, followed by a third. I put the car in gear, shooting past the last truck in the line. These trucks went fast and kept close together, with only a car's length or two between them. I could feel the air pressure whip into our car as they sped down the tube. The road had three wide lanes and a thick divider, but they all hung to the right, probably to give Affluent vehicles a wide berth. I pulled us in ahead of the second truck, into a space we barely fit.

"What are you doing?" Margot asked.

The truck behind us fell back a little. I tapped the brakes. He fell back more. Far behind us, a fourth truck entered the highway just ahead of Lucretia's car. I sped up so my bumper nearly touched the truck ahead of us.

Margot's brow wrinkled under her perfect black bangs. "Why are you irritating him?"

I pressed on the horn. The giant truck ahead of us signaled and shifted into the next lane. I rocketed past him, got into his lane and slowed in front of him.

"Speth?" Henri asked.

"Give me a minute," I said. I sped up again and let the truck fall in behind me.

"They're just going to roll over us!" Sera cried.

"They won't so much as honk," I said. "They think we're Rog—or Lawyers, at least—or else they'd have hit us by now." I looked in the mirror and took a deep breath. "Brace yourselves."

I slammed on the brakes and prayed I was right. I'd only ever heard the word *jackknife* used that one time, and I hoped that $6.99 word meant what I thought it did.

The truck behind us seemed to rise up, turn and twist. I jammed the accelerator and rocketed us forward again. The truck swerved and pitched, then finally rocked to a stop, blocking two of the three lanes. It wasn't quite what I'd hoped for—until a wet explosion shook the tunnel. The truck behind the first had slammed into the trailer, shattering the printed plastic shell and sending Mandolin Inks™ flying everywhere. Some skittered to the ground. Others burst, peppering the road and tunnel with a splatter of thick, viscous greens, blacks, yellows and browns. A section of wall knocked at an angle and, if we'd had time to go back and really look, we might have seen a thin sliver of the world outside.

I jammed down on the gas and spoke the word *viscous* aloud, because I could.

"That was spectacular!" Henri exclaimed, watching the scene recede behind us.

"That should give us a little lead," I replied, in case anyone—like Sera—didn't understand what I'd just done.

INTO THE FIRE: $9.97

The number of highway lanes gradually began to increase, from three to four and then to nine. There were no signs to indicate we should slow, but the line of tollbooths with red flashing lights was a strong clue that we needed to stop or crash. We'd arrived at another city.

I slowed us to a crawl. "You think it's Keene?" I asked Margot.

Margot narrowed her eyes and peered through the windshield. "Most likely. It is the nearest city."

"How are we going to get in?" Henri asked.

I assessed our options. The lanes were all open, with screen gates that popped to life with Ads as we neared. The dashboard screen lit with an EZ-Pass logo.

"Maybe we can just drive through," I said. I slowed the car down to a less suspicious speed and chose a lane.

"But you'll have to agree to Terms of Service!" Sera cried.

"I don't know," I said slowly. "Think about it. Rog isn't going to lean out of a car with his Cuff out to pay a toll."

"Probably not," Margot agreed. "But that will not absolve us of the need to follow whatever rules this dome has once we are inside."

"Rules?" Norflo laughed. "Think we're here to break rules."

Margot let out an exasperated sigh. "If we know the Terms of Service, it will be easier to blend in."

The light in the lane directly ahead of us turned to a steady green.

"Ha!" Norflo exclaimed, like he'd been proved right. Margot rolled her eyes and Henri patted her shoulder.

We eased through the toll without even seeing a border guard. As we entered the new dome, everyone in the Meiboch™ pressed up against the windows, looking out. My mouth dropped open, and I heard several gasps from the back seat. None of us had been prepared for our first sight of Keene.

Everything was different. Ads still covered every surface, just like Portland, but Keene had no faux French buildings or outer ring. The toll lane gave way to an entrance with an ornate gateway and two beautiful metal sculptures of robed women. Beyond was a broad avenue, stretching majestically to the city's center. The buildings were printed in a style I'd never seen, with strong, flat lines of ornamentation that angled and seemed to hold each other in place. Between them were tall, narrow windows.

The dome around us shot almost straight up, curved and then formed a pillared roof. The pillars themselves rose up from a series of tall, impressive buildings that mushroomed outward at the top. The dome may not have actually been larger than ours, but the scale felt enormous.

"Whoa," Henri muttered.

Large indigo banners with an animated Keene Inc. logo hung between the buildings, rippling gently. Screens below blasted Ads for Keene Squire-Lace™ Chips, Keene's Kelp

Gum™, Moon Mints™, Buonicon Tea™ and Keene Soursop Freshlings™.

"Clearly we are in Keene," Margot said.

"Thanks," Sera shot back sarcastically.

A chill ran down my spine. Keene Inc. would have been my brand if I had just read my speech and got on with the miserable life Mrs. Harris had plotted out for me. Instead, I went silent. Until this moment, I hadn't thought about the fact that I had finally, officially broken my silence and, therefore, my contract with Keene Inc. This might be the very worst place for me to be.

"What now?" Sera asked.

I didn't have an answer for her. We'd left before we were ready. We had no food, no map and no idea where to go. I had hoped to ask Kel's advice on how Saretha and I could rescue my parents, but that wasn't possible now.

Now the others were looking to me to lead them. I had to live up to that. I gripped the wheel and forced myself to think.

"Kel wouldn't have told us to flee if she didn't think we could survive," I said. I made my voice as calm as I could, like I believed everything was going to be okay.

I drove the car deeper into the city. It would only be a matter of time before Rog's Meiboch™ was noticed and traced to us. Keene's main avenue wasn't an ideal place to hide.

"Look for a service street," I said to the others. "Something the Affluents would want to avoid. We need to find a safe place to stop so we can figure out what to do."

"Jiménez," Norflo said slowly, like he approved of my thinking.

"How do you know my last name should be Jiménez?" I asked him, the name feeling odd on my tongue.

Norflo leaned forward from the back seat. "Latinos all over the Onzième. Jime's obvio. Most got shorted names."

"Not Croate," Sera huffed.

We came to a less ornate cross street and I turned us right, glancing at Sera's disgusted face in the rearview mirror.

"You sure?" Norflo asked.

"I know I'm not *Latino*," she scoffed. "Mrs. Harris said so."

"Something wrong with Latinos?" I asked her.

"I don't even know what it is," she said, purposely staring ahead.

"Know enough to give that little sneer," Norflo said, laughing and pointing to where her lip had curled. Sera slapped his hand away, which only amused Norflo more. "Try to rip the culture outta us, but if they keep *one* thing, it's the prejudice."

I spotted an alley ahead of us, a narrow opening between two buildings under a massive Keene Inc. banner. I maneuvered the car in and drove slowly to the alley's dead end. Unlike the faces of the buildings, this space had no ornamentation. While the quality was better than in the Onzième, I could still see the layers of polymer melt from the building's 3-D print.

"I'm not prejudiced. They *ended* prejudice, so I can't be," Sera burst out.

"Who's they?" I asked.

"History people," Sera said, like that told us anything.

"I don't really see how anyone can be prejudiced against Latinos if they don't even know what it means," Henri said, looking to Margot for confirmation. "*I* don't know what it means, either."

"Oh, Henri," Margot said, shaking her head. Norflo laughed again.

"You don't believe me?" Henri asked.

"I believe *you* believe you," Norflo said.

"I believe Henri," Mira said.

"We can bicker later," I said. I turned off the car, realizing our only way out would involve backing up. That was less than ideal if we had to escape quickly. "We need to work out what we're doing now. We're not going to be able to talk outside the car," I added, tapping my bare arm.

"I can," Mira said.

"But you will not," Margot said. Her sister frowned.

"The first thing we need to do is lower that banner. Obscure the alley, so the Meiboch™'s harder to spot."

"No problem," Henri said, neck craned back to look at how it was hung. "If I can borrow someone's grapple."

Margot let out a little breath, dug into her Placer bag and pulled hers out. When Henri went to reach for it, she pulled it away. "This is a two-person job."

I handed Henri my grapple, pulling it from my belt. "On three," I said, and made the sign of the zippered lips. Mira enthusiastically copied me. I held up one finger, then two, then three.

Margot and Henri rushed out of the car, closing the doors behind them, and shot up to where the banner was held in place.

"We should get out of here as soon as possible," I said, watching Henri and Margot work. They lifted the bar and dropped down about twenty feet to set it back in place. "But we need to get supplies and a map first."

"Where?" Sera asked. "You can't just buy a map."

"Of course you can," Mira said. "You can *buy* anything."

"Not me," Norflo said, giving her a grin.

"*We* can't buy a map," I told Mira patiently, "but it's good to keep thinking of ideas."

Mira's face scrunched in thought. She reminded me of Sam in some ways, but growing up in the Onzième meant he'd left childhood behind much sooner. My heart ached to think about it—and with the knowledge that she would get to grow up, while Sam never would.

Henri and Margot landed beside the car. I repeated my countdown and let them back in.

"We need a map," Mira announced proudly as her sister and Henri settled into their seats.

"In school, they talked about geography being proprietary," I went on, thinking aloud. I hadn't done that in a long time. It felt good to give my thoughts a voice. "They said kids like us wouldn't need to see maps, anyway—that we wouldn't have any use for them."

"They didn't teach us *anything* useful," Sera lamented.

"That's not exactly true," I said, though I understood the feeling. "They taught us more than they intended, like who is important enough to need maps. They told us who has access, like the government. Shipping companies. Demographic research firms..."

"What about Central Data?" Henri asked.

"Henri," Margot said with an exasperated sigh, "there were only three, and we destroyed one. Even if they foolishly placed one so close, it would be too heavily guarded."

"I still can't believe they kept one in Portland," I said, trying to hide the worry in my voice. I couldn't have made us a bigger target.

"Speth?" Margot asked gently. The kindness in her voice

only further unnerved me, but I realized I couldn't let it show. I forced myself to smile and add strength to my voice.

"Okay," I said. "We figure out how to get access to a map."

"We could find a way to Téjico," Norflo suggested.

"Why would we go there?" Sera asked. "Our parents are in Carolina."

"What about Affluents?" Mira asked. "We cannot afford a map, but *they* could."

Sera snorted, "So, what, are we going to find some rich tourist and ask him to buy us a map to our parents?"

"A real estate agency would be an easier target," Margot suggested. She pulled her bag up from the floor and began to look through it.

"That's a great idea," I said enthusiastically. "It shouldn't be too hard to find one, right? Margot, Henri and I will go."

"What about us?" Sera asked.

Before I could answer, Margot said, "I am not leaving Mira."

"I can go?" Mira asked, her eyes wide with delight.

"No," Margot answered. "I will stay." She handed Henri her grapple, and Henri handed mine back to me.

"We got this," Norflo said, shifting in his seat.

I shook my head. "You and Sera don't have any experience. Henri and I will…"

I realized I was about to suggest that Henri and I go alone. I hadn't talked to Margot about how I'd let him kiss me—how I had used him to steal his Cuff remover. She knew it had been a desperate act, but I'd betrayed her all the same. And Henri had definitely been interested at the time, which couldn't have felt good. She didn't glare, but her mouth was pursed tightly. I wanted to apologize and explain, but a car full of people wasn't the right place.

"Speth, you cannot go, either," Margot said finally, gesturing to me. "You will be recognized."

"Should I go out alone?" Henri asked.

"Nah," Norflo said.

My stomach sank. It hadn't occurred to me I'd be trapped by my likeness. An ugly, familiar feeling followed. This wasn't so different from what had happened to Saretha, except she hadn't done anything to deserve it.

"Henri should not go alone," Margot said. Her hands clung to her bag, its contents rattling.

"I gotcha," Norflo said.

"That is not a good idea, either," Margot replied.

"That leaves no one, genius," Sera complained.

"Do you want me to stay with Mira?" I asked, my voice growing small. "And you can go?"

Margot bit her lip and shook her head. "I will not leave Mira."

"This is ridiculous," Sera commented. She wasn't wrong. She reached for the door handle, but I stayed her hand with a glare.

"Give me a second," I said. "When we were sued by Rog because Saretha *looked* like Carol Amanda Harving, she couldn't go out, either. We couldn't afford to change her appearance unless we mangled her face."

Norflo groaned and shook his head.

"You want us to mangle your face?" Sera asked.

I wasn't going to respond to that. "We never even considered makeup because it was so far beyond our means. Every style is Trademarked. But now, without Cuffs, we don't have to pay." I pointed to Margot's bag. "Do you still have that lady's makeup, from Nancee's rescue? Can you make me look different?"

Her eyes lit up, then dimmed as she looked from me to Henri. She examined what she had in her bag and swallowed hard. "Yes," she admitted.

Mira squealed with delight. "Are we doing makeup?"

"Apparently," Margot said, hunting for brushes, not looking me in the eye.

"Margot," I began, but how could I explain that nothing was going to happen between Henri and me? Everyone was listening. But she had to know, didn't she? I wished she and I were going out to do this job so I could explain, but then I remembered we wouldn't be able to speak—our eyes would be shocked for every word.

"What?" she prompted.

"If anything happens," I said in a rush, "while we're out there—if you're found, or you even get a bad feeling, take the car and go."

Margot looked at Henri. "Nothing's going to happen," he said. He was trying to be reassuring about our situation, but my guilt made me feel like he meant between us.

Margot nodded as she took out a few circles of foundation and contouring powder.

"I'll do a Barbara Van Trine™," she said, raising a brush with a look of mischief on her face.

Mira clapped. Sera smirked. I groaned inwardly. I knew the actress Barbara Van Trine. She always played the villain. I forced a smile and hoped this wasn't how Margot secretly felt about me.

KEENE: $10.99

By the time Margot finished my makeup, Keene's dome was lit with the deepening cerulean colors of evening. Henri and I shot up to the rooftops to scan for a real estate agency. The buildings in this city were arranged differently than in Portland. They were tall and thin, with residences above stores and businesses below. It became apparent we would have to search at street level because we couldn't see what many places were from up high.

Before we could find a discreet place to descend, something odd appeared in my vision. Just below my direct line of sight, a moving scrawl of words had appeared, like a stock ticker or a Word$ Market™ display, traveling from right to left. I couldn't quite see the text—or ignore it. If I closed my eyes, the words remained. Henri had stopped moving, his neck craned forward. I pointed to my eyes. He nodded and did the same. We were both seeing the same thing.

I assumed it was a message from Kel. If Lucretia Rog had access to our eyes, we'd have been blinded. There was a pattern to the words—it kept repeating, but I just couldn't read it. I thought I saw the words *Saretha* and *DC*. Each time I tried to focus on the message, it moved with my eyes. I prodded Henri and gave him a shrug. He squinted, like that might help, then shrugged back. He couldn't decipher it, either.

When we reached street level, we became aware fairly quickly that our black clothes stood out. Nearly everyone in Keene was dressed in the same indigo shade of the banners decorating the city. They didn't seem poor—at least not like in the Onzième. There weren't restricted to public domain grays and cheap haircuts. They looked healthy and efficient, but color-coded. I watched a family go into the shops and, if they weren't exactly fawned over like a wealthy woman we saw in a bright marigold dress, they were at least treated with courtesy, like the staff expected they had money to spend.

I elbowed Henri and gestured for him to stand up straighter. If our matte-black Placer clothes and my contoured makeup wouldn't let us blend in, then we should act as if we were Affluents. Confidence would help.

The woman in marigold burst flamboyantly out of the store behind us with two enormous, watery-eyed bodyguards. They were unwilling to stop or adjust course for anyone. The blue-clad people around us understood and quickly scurried out of her way.

The woman made eye contact with me and sneered. "Placer chic?" she asked, looking at our matte-black clothes with disdain. I was familiar with the harsh sneer of someone who thinks you're worth less than the bottom of their designer shoes. Affluents walked by us all the time in the Onzième and delighted in looking down on us.

She turned away without waiting for an answer, which was fortunate, since we couldn't respond, anyway. Henri and I let her pass, then I gestured to him that we should follow. I reasoned that if we kept a respectable distance from the woman, eyes would be on her and her bodyguards instead of us.

As we trailed behind her, I scanned the area. Both sides

of the road were lined with every sort of shop and service you could imagine. I was certain we would find a real estate agency here somewhere. There were far more stores than what we had in Portland, and they were much higher quality. There were dozens of boutiques like Mrs. Nince's, but with far better clothes. They had Transparenting™ mood coats that could microprint fur to match a person's mood and dark men's suits so matte that they seemed immune to shadow or light. When I spotted some corsets made from luminous chain mail that I suspected could squeeze and reshape your body however you liked, I shuddered, remembering the OiO™ corset Saretha had crammed herself into.

The clothes were displayed in windows by models who wore scrupulously bored expressions. I wondered if they were models like Saretha had been, or if they were Indentured. Were they well-off, but not affluent enough to enjoy a little extra income? I couldn't know. I was certain, however, that Keene was a wealthier place than Portland.

They could afford to be families here. A hot coal of jealousy seared in my chest. I gritted my teeth and willed away the tears threatening to mount. I pushed away the thoughts of leaving Saretha behind and how far away my parents were, trying to focus on our surroundings. Once we found a real estate agency, I'd be one step closer to bringing my family together again.

The woman in marigold slowed in front of something that stunned me. It appeared to be a small grocery store with wide trays of fruits, angled for passersby to look at, hold and smell without any sign of Terms of Service. There were oranges, apples and pears just sitting where anyone could grab one and run off. You could never have done this in Portland. No matter the consequences, the temptation would have been too great for most of the people I knew.

At the next store, the woman came to a sudden halt, turned and held her Cuff out. The doors swept open for her, reading her data and sending the staff into a frenzy as she walked inside. A tall man in Keene blue was abandoned in the middle of a transaction, but appeared to completely understand as he moved back to wait.

Henri kept walking and beckoned me to follow, inclining his head with a worried look. On the sidewalk far ahead, five people stood in line near an alley. At first, I thought they might be survey-takers doing market research. But five seemed like too large of a group, and they didn't display the usual aggressive friendliness of Surveyors. They stood silent, dressed in blue, save for one boy, a little older than me, who wore a crimson tunic.

My eyes went wide. Were these Silents? Henri pulled at my arm and forced me to cross the street. He was right to do it. Even with Margot's makeup, it wouldn't do to risk being recognized as the Silent Girl.

I wondered what these Silents were doing. I couldn't ask, and they couldn't answer. But they must have found some way to communicate—the five of them had coordinated enough to stand together on the street, though I didn't understand what they hoped to accomplish. Was it like this in other domes, too?

Not much farther along, I finally spotted what we were looking for. A building a short way up the street opposite us bore a sign in polished gold letters: Bullion® Real Estate. It followed the same general aesthetic as most of the architecture we'd seen in Keene. Tall, solid lines gave the building an almost muscular feel. Thin windows made it look secure, yet appealing. In the upper floors, only a scattering of windows glowed amber in the deepening night. The lower floors, where we needed to go, were brightly lit, and a convex section of glass curved out into the sidewalk.

I couldn't see anyone inside, but it was too much to hope that we could just walk through the door. We didn't have a Cuff like our marigold friend, who could sweep in with a wave of her arm. I looked behind us and saw she was on the move again. Her arm was up, and she was laughing into her Cuff. A Cuff that could give us the access we needed.

An idea began to take shape in my mind. Henri had his tools, and this part of the street seemed a bit quieter. We would definitely be noticed by those five Silents, but I hoped that we could count on their silence.

I began to calculate our odds. If I put a stolen Cuff on my arm, would I be able to use it? Mrs. Harris had told us *no*, but that was a long time ago, and she often lied. Still, it was a lot of risk to take.

The woman in the marigold dress squealed with glee at her Cuff. "Oh, Irene!" she exclaimed, throwing her head back with a massive laugh. My thoughts clouded with envy for everything she had. I slowly moved closer, feeling like a stalking animal I'd once seen on a nature special. Henri followed, his brow knit. I at least had to see what would happen when she and her bodyguards reached the Silents.

The two bodyguards shoved them aside, taking delight in making extra room for the woman who paid or owned them. I expected some kind of fight, but none came. The woman kept chattering with "Irene" while the Silents, no longer in a line, glared as she passed.

"The city is lousy with them," she said, turning her Cuff

toward them so Irene, wherever she was, could see. She paused in front of the one in red. "Even this one!" she cried. I realized the one in red must be wealthy, like her, but the Silent movement clearly mattered to him.

"Degenerates," a small voice crackled through the Cuff.

The boy dressed in crimson made the sign of the zippered lips. One of the bodyguards shoved him into the street. He fell back between two parked cars and hit the ground hard. The other four Silents moved in and all offered hands to their fallen friend. He could have sued, but that probably would have broken whatever rules he thought he needed to follow.

The bodyguard's blithe lack of concern enraged me. He could have just as easily shoved that boy into traffic. As he and the woman and her other bodyguard began to walk away, thoughts of Sam filled my mind.

I reached into my bag, rage nearly blinding me, and pulled out a pony bottle of sleep gas.

The flare of my anger obscured any logic or strategy. I crossed the street without looking, which was foolish. I wanted to pound the bodyguard in the head with my bottle, but I managed to control myself enough to get up right behind him and turn the gas on.

Thank goodness Henri followed my lead. He had the other guard down and had turned the spray on the woman in marigold before my bodyguard slumped to the ground.

The Silents all stared.

I knocked on the woman's Cuff with a knuckle, and Henri understood I wanted it off. He grabbed his small device and ran it down the seam until the Cuff popped open. I unhooked it from the woman's forearm and looked down at it. An Affluent woman stared back at me from the Cuff's screen, her eyes wide with shock. I quickly flicked the chat screen away, realizing we now had very little time.

As Henri finished removing the bodyguards' two Cuffs, I glanced up to see the Silents standing right before us. They didn't move or make any threat. They just watched. Henri, being Henri, grinned at them. He held up the device and made a motion, showing them he could remove their Cuffs, too. They all put their arms out to him.

I glanced at the Cuff in my hands and then at the office. Seeing no other choice, I clamped the woman's Cuff around my own arm. It was loose at first, but then its interior inflated with a wheeze, gripping my wrist securely.

> Congratulations, Alora, you've lost 40 pounds! Why not treat yourself to a fine dinner at LoLoRu™? Featuring a fine selection of BeefMilk™ cheeses, wine-poached quince and Botanical Squeezlings® from hand-pollinated harvests...

I flicked the message away. Several health notifications popped up, probably because the Cuff registered the sudden change in weight and body composition. I dismissed them, too. Not too far away, a couple in blue shirts spotted us, looked at each other and turned the other way. I tugged at Henri's sleeve, even though he had two more Cuffs to remove. We needed to get out of sight before anyone else spotted us.

Alora's Cuff buzzed with another call from Irene, which I flipped away. The Silents watched me expectantly, and I realized they might be able to help. I hesitantly made the sign of the zippered lips and felt a wave of hope when they zipped back to me. The Cuff on my arm buzzed with a charge—

apparently that gesture was no longer in the public domain. The idea irked me, but what did it matter?

I pointed to the three unconscious bodies and made a sweeping gesture, hoping they would understand my mute request. The crimson boy and two other Silents immediately started to drag them toward the alley nearby. Henri finished removing the last Cuff and turned to me. I gestured to the real estate agency, and he nodded. We had to move.

A GEOGRAPHIC RAID: $11.98

With a wave of my arm, Bullion® Real Estate opened right up. The offices were airy and lushly carpeted, with a few very impressive desks that looked like real wood. There were two posh seating areas, both locked behind glass. It made sense that brokers would want to pamper wealthy clients while going over properties.

Within seconds, three real estate agents scurried out from the back in blue suits with crisp white shirts and ties that turned marigold as they entered the room, to match what I assumed was Alora's favorite color.

"Mrs. Clepeti!" One man with a Pad and a wide grin offered his hand. My Cuff popped up his name and picture. *Norman Keene.* The other two, who didn't appear to be related to Norman or each other, were identified as brokers *Thomas Keene* and *Vincent Keene.* That struck me as odd, but I didn't have much time to dwell on it. Vincent peered at me, then down at his Cuff. He nudged Norman, showing him a picture. I didn't match the woman's image in their system. Their faces contorted in confusion.

I turned to Henri. "I told you the Barbara Van Trine™ would only confuse people," I said, forcing a laugh.

Henri cocked his head at me. My Cuff buzzed harshly with the charge and a warning message: Vocal Pattern Mismatch.

"Barbara Van Trine™," Norman acknowledged with a nod, forcing himself to admire my makeup. I didn't know how common a crime it was to steal a person's Cuff, but it had to be rare. I prayed I could get them to accept the deception.

"A little makeup, some digital effects," I said, gesturing to myself. I could have sold it better—my voice wasn't very convincing. The Cuff buzzed with another warning:

> Visa™ Fraud Department—An attempt to charge $636.44 in words has been flagged by a voice identification error. Tap **CONFIRM** here to verify charges by fingerprint identification.

My stomach flip-flopped. The Cuff felt like it was warming, or maybe it was my whole body. It emitted a low, pulsing buzz now, waiting for me to respond.

"How can we assist you?" Norman asked, his smile looking less than genuine.

"You're all brothers?" I asked.

"No," Norman replied with a small laugh, because he had to pretend Affluents were delightful.

"But you're all named Keene," I said, letting my curiosity get the better of me.

"Anyone with any sense is a Keene," he said, narrowing his eyes.

I glanced across the room at an enormous dark wall screen, curved for private viewing. I could imagine brokers pulling up maps, showing their clients all the options they had for places to live and sights to see. I had longed to see things like this when I was younger, but Mrs. Harris had told me in her usual clipped tones that I should be satisfied with what I was fortunate enough to see in movies.

Even now, the demeaning injustice of it stung. Our guardian truly believed we were worth less than a woman like Alora Clepeti—less than nothing, if you examined her calculations. To her and people like her we were nothing more than our debts. If I wanted to sell my disguise I had to treat these "Keenes" like I believed it, too.

"Anyone with any sense?" I screeched. "I am a Clepeti, you dolt. Keene indeed!"

"My apologies," Norman said, momentarily stunned.

"I'd like to browse," I said, forcing a sneer and gesturing at the screen. My Cuff buzzed again and let out a shrill warning beep.

Visa™ Fraud Department—An attempt to charge $1,093.41 in words has been flagged by a voice identification error. Tap **CONFIRM** here to verify charges by fingerprint identification or service will be discontinued and the authorities notified.

A sixty-second countdown began. The Cuff was definitely getting warmer.

"You wish to browse…our listings?" Norman asked, raising his head. All three agents now squinted at me. This wasn't going to work.

I turned to Henri. I showed him the message, holding my Cuff out to him. It was listing all the legal ramifications of a Cuff theft.

"What is this?" Norman asked. Thomas and Vincent began to back away. Henri pulled out his Cuff remover and ran it over my forearm. Vincent gasped. The Cuff cracked open and beeped now with each second that ticked off the countdown. With my free hand, I pulled out my sleep gas and held it out like a gun in a robbery.

The three brokers stared at us, bewildered.

"Where's your Squelch?" I demanded, suffering the shocks to my eyes now that the Cuff was off. It beeped away at my feet. I needed to cut it off from the WiFi before the countdown ended—I wasn't sure what would happen then, but it couldn't be good.

"Squelch?" Thomas asked.

Henri took his pony bottle out and advanced on Thomas, looking more threatening than I'd ever seen him. It was easy to forget how big Henri was sometimes because he was such a sweet, gentle person. Not knowing him like I did, Thomas staggered back and pointed to a panel on the wall.

I glanced out the wide window. If anyone looked in, we'd be exposed. But the only people outside were the five Silents, who were now standing with their backs to the agency, obscuring the view inside. I felt a surge of gratitude for their protection.

The three Keenes seemed baffled. "There is nothing here to steal," Vincent said pleadingly.

Henri pressed the panel and it popped open, revealing a Squelch beyond.

"Are you Silents?" Thomas asked, his eyes on the window as Henri forced him into the Squelch. I picked up the beeping Cuff. Fifteen seconds left.

I shot him a look, and sprayed him and Vincent first.

"This is all being recorded," Norman warned, holding up his Pad. He backed up into the Squelch.

I sprayed him, too, letting Henri guide him gently to

the floor. Then I yanked Henri out, tossed the Cuff in and jammed the panel shut before the countdown finished. Inside, the three brokers would sleep, and the Cuff would send out a signal that wouldn't make it past the Squelch wall until they awoke. I'd bought us a little time, but we were still working in an open storefront.

I realized, too late, that I should have grabbed Norman's Pad, but I couldn't open the Squelch now.

I rushed into one of the private seating areas and tapped the curved display. The Bullion® logo lit up, sparkling like gold, though slightly hazy because I was so close to the three-dimensional image. It was designed to be viewed from across the room, probably because Affluents didn't work the controls themselves—they were simply shown things.

The logo rose and settled into place at the top of the screen as awards for excellence flew past like shimmery 3-D ghosts. Flat on the screen, three options appeared: HOMES, RENTALS and STAYS. I chose the last of these, because it was likely meant for Affluents looking to travel.

A list with the names of the fifty domes populated the screen. I recognized only a few. We'd never been taught them all, so the list didn't mean much to me. I'd never heard of Cincinnati®, Ford™ or Raleigh™, for example. I certainly didn't know if any of them were in Carolina—or even if Carolina had domes at all. What if it was all farms, like the one where my parents were Indentured?

My only choices were the listed domes. At random, I selected Jefferson™, because I remembered it as a name from my history class.

The screen filled with a beautiful aerial image from inside a round dome not unlike the one I'd come from, with smaller buildings around the edges and massive ones at the center. A bright, warm light seemed to fill the city and I didn't know if it was because such a light was a feature of the city, or merely a manipulation to make the image appealing. The screen highlighted properties with thin yellow lines and linked to a dozen pictures of opulent rooms Affluents could stay in. They were all in the center of the city, which made me think Jefferson™ was a lot like home, with poor folks scattered out on the rim.

Henri stood at my side, still silent. He squinted, like an old man trying to read something too close.

I selected a property at random, and the picture enlarged. The room was lovely, with bookshelves and scalloped trim. A band lowered into the frame and listed an average nightly price—$1,999—and offered buttons for PEDIGREE, TESTIMONIAL, AMENITIES, MATCHSCORE™ and ROUTE. The last button was the one I needed. I tapped it. The image faded, and a map appeared.

My whole body suddenly felt like it was flying. It was partly the 3-D effects as the map drifted into place, but mostly it was the dizzying realization of how big the world was beyond the borders of Portland. I never could have imagined that a group of squiggly lines would make me feel an awe that bordered on fear.

Keene sat at the bottom of the state of Vermaine. I could see the road we'd traveled on, or part of it—the line representing it curved outside the frame, and I couldn't see Portland. Most of the map detailed what was in the other direction—west.

A path scrawled down through the Dome of Springfield in Connectix™, through a swath of New York™ and a dome labeled Generalec™. It continued through the state of Sylvania™ and into Indohio™, where it came to rest in the Dome of Jefferson™.

Henri moved in closer, placing himself in the center of the curve to take in the entirety of the map. I didn't see Carolina. The huge area was still only a piece of America®. The only dome I recognized besides Springfield and Mandolin™ was in the lower right-hand corner. The Dome of NYC™ rested on a rectangle of land labeled The Printed Lands, whose green borders jutted into an ocean of blue. The ocean was right there, like I could touch it. A little below was a label for the Dome of Delphi™ and, within that, a different tag: Central Data.

I swiped a finger upward, and the map scrolled up slightly to reveal Portland. It bore the same tag, but in red with tiny text that said *Off-line*. Margot and Kel had been right.

I backed out to the list, wondering if I should look for the third Central Data location, but instead I pulled up a search box and typed in Crab Creek, Carolina. The screen buzzed harshly, and my shoulders hunched at the sound.

No listings at this location.

Of course there weren't. No Affluent was going to vacation down with the Indentured. The system offered a list of alternate suggestions, and I tapped on Nanolia™ because it sounded familiar.

The map zoomed out further to accommodate the vast distance between Keene and Nanolia™. I now had a much better overview of the country. The route went through Mandolin™, past the Dome of Law and nearby DC to Raleigh™, ending at the southern tip of Carolina, where Nanolia™ rested.

Nanolia™ was next to a gray factory dome labeled NanoLion™. Above these and off to the west were several other gray domes, labeled Agropollination™ 1, Agropollination™ 2 and so on. The name gave me a shudder. Agropollination™ was the company that owned my parents.

I stared at the empty green space between the Agropollination™ domes. The farms had to be there. Crab Creek had to be among them. My skin went cold. I didn't see Crab Creek, but what I did see stunned me.

Gray domes peppered the landscape across the map with names like *MonSantos™ Cornworks & Chromosome*, *Factory Consortium Dome 4* and *Food Processing Dome L*. No Affluent would ever travel to these places. They were all industrial, and the scale and number was staggering. I tapped one and got the same harsh buzz as before.

No listings at this location.

Henri didn't see it—not the way I did. He was staring off into space. I tapped his shoulder, pointing to the screen and the map. We needed to memorize this, but I was having trouble focusing on that task. How could the world be this way?

I swallowed and tried to appreciate the fact I had a better sense of where to head now. My parents' farm was somewhere between those Agropollination™ domes. I was quite certain. But I was also chilled to my core by the realization of what was out there. There were far more gray domes than just the fifty white ones I'd been told about in school. Who lived in them? Were they all filled with Indentured people forced to work off their debt inside them every day?

Growing up, I'd thought we were the victims of bad luck. I'd thought the kids who lived in the Onzième got the short end of the stick because so many—most—of our parents ended up Indentured. Mrs. Harris had implied for years that parents in the Onzième just weren't good people. But I was starting to realize how much of what she'd told us wasn't true—and that we'd been fed lies on purpose.

Silas Rog's words echoed in my head: "Generations of your

family Indentured. *Generations.*" At the end, right before I'd taken him down, Rog had threatened to force Saretha and me to breed in "litters" for the rest of our lives. "Generations of Jimes to pay your ceaseless debt," he'd said.

I felt sick. How could there be so many domes filled with workers? How had they filled them? I tried not to think about the possibilities, but I couldn't help wondering how many kids out there had Indentured parents, or whether Rog and his ilk had carried out that sickening plan against others.

A pounding interrupted my dark thoughts. The Silents were banging on the glass with their fists, still facing away. They were trying to warn us about something. A bright light shone outside, and I heard the sound of raised voices.

I tapped the interface closed, then realized how much evidence I'd left behind. I punched at the screen, but it was stronger than I expected. Henri understood. He shattered it with his fist, yanked out its memory chip and handed it to me. He'd taught me this technique the first night I'd met him.

We tried several doors in back before finding one that opened to the alley where the Silents had dragged Alora and her bodyguards. The two enormous men had been laid out in a line with the woman in marigold, like they were going to be boxed up and shipped out.

I took out my grapple, shot up a line and zipped up to the rooftops as a voice called out, "Halt!"

Three buildings over, I paused and held up a hand for Henri to stop with me. I listened. The police wouldn't work very hard to chase us if they didn't have a sponsor. Words cost money. Pursuit cost time. The only way they'd have someone footing the bill would be if Lucretia Rog had connected us to

Keene. Unfortunately, lights still flashed in the street behind us, and someone yelled, "Fan out!" That wasn't a good sign.

Unlike Portland, the Keene roofs offered little cover. The buildings didn't really vary in height, so anyone on a nearby roof would be able to spot us quickly. We had to get out of sight. I motioned for Henri to follow me and zipped a few roofs over to a particularly ornate apartment building with gilding on the sides. Running my lock pick over the roof hatch, I yanked it open and dropped down into a darkened service room. Henri followed, closed the hatch and looked at me with an expression of deep concern. He pointed up, like he wanted to go back out. I shook my head. If we didn't let things cool off, we'd risk getting caught—or worse, leading the police back to the car and compromising everyone.

I cracked the service room door and peeked into a dimly lit kitchen. This was familiar. It felt like we were on a Placement, only we had no product to Place and no Pad to map the area and tell us who was home. The counter appeared ready, though, with an open space that people who adored Placements would often leave.

I tiptoed out and listened. Henri followed, as silent as me. An archway led to a wide dining room and then a hall with two doors. I didn't have a Pad or a floor plan, but I'd been in enough homes to surmise the doors led to bedrooms. Everything was dark. Whoever lived here was either asleep or away. I scanned the wall for signs of a hidden door that might lead to a Squelch and found a thin outline in the corner of the dining room. Running my lock pick over the line resulted in a telltale *click*.

I pulled the door open and pushed Henri inside. We'd be safe here for a bit, unless someone woke up to have a midnight chat. Henri closed the door and the message from Kel, still running under my vision, winked away. I realized that, now, Henri and I were finally free to talk.

ROOM FOR HENRI: $12.97

The Squelch was roomy, with a high ceiling and walls stippled for soundproofing. Four chairs faced each other, and a bar sat behind them with old bottles of liquor on a shelf behind it. I was half-tempted to pilf a drink.

"Thirsty?" I joked.

"No," Henri said with no laugh and no smile. He seemed uneasy. "We should go back."

"I know, we just need to let the dust settle," I said. "They won't find us here. And if anyone is home, we have this." I held up the sleep gas.

Henri nodded reluctantly. "I'm not worried about that. I'm worried about Margot and Mira and the others in that alley."

"We don't want to lead anyone back to them," I explained. "This city's rooftops aren't a great place to hide."

Henri shifted nervously.

"It will be okay," I said. I put a hand on his shoulder and he recoiled. His reaction confused me—it wasn't like Henri. "What's wrong?"

Henri swallowed and looked at the ground, his face reddening with embarrassment. "You didn't bring me here to be alone, right?"

"Oh, Henri," I said, a blush rising to my cheeks as well. I

backed away from him to make some space between us. We still hadn't been able to talk about how I'd used him to steal the Cuff remover. "I didn't *lure* you here. Please tell me you know that."

"Yeah, I do," Henri said in a half-hearted voice. I could tell he believed me, but his face was filled with angst.

Regret and shame flooded through me. "I'm so sorry," I said. "For what I did. I should have found a different way."

"I know you couldn't *ask* me, but you could have, you know, *asked*."

"How?" I demanded, my voice hitting much too high a note.

Even though Henri was older than both Margot and me, he often seemed less mature. But at that moment, he looked so much like a disappointed dad that I felt about four years old. "You could have just taken the Cuff remover out of my backpack," he said. It was in his hand now, a metallic blue teardrop. He rolled it between his fingers. "I would have let you take it."

"I tried that, Henri, right after you took my Cuff off."

"I didn't understand. I didn't know why you put it back on."

"Because I didn't want the Cuff off, Henri. I wanted the device."

He looked confused.

"I couldn't see any other way to get my sister free," I explained.

"You could have taken it again. I'd have figured it out eventually," he said.

"I had no way to know that," I said. Henri could be a bit clueless sometimes, though he was infinitely kind.

"You could have had a little faith in me," Henri said softly. He shook his head. "It never even occurred to me that you'd be trying to steal something. I thought you were awesome. Your courage was inspiring. I thought you were…" His voice dropped off. He turned away and leaned forward on the bar. "I just don't get it," he said finally, head bowed. "You started a whole revolution, and you're really, really clever, but that was your best idea?"

"Not my best. I know I messed up," I admitted, regret hitting me harder each time I thought about what I'd done. I took a step forward and he flinched. "Henri, please look at me," I pleaded.

Henri turned around, but kept the chairs between us. His eyes met mine, but his gaze was unsteady, like I was too bright to look at. I wished I could make this hurt go away.

"I'm not that clever," I confessed. "Everyone thinks I had some genius plan to destroy this terrible system, but I really didn't."

"But what you did was so amazing."

"I'm not that amazing, trust me," I said, my eyes welling up.

"But you are," Henri insisted. Suddenly, he could look at me directly, his eyes filled with fire. "You don't appreciate how much courage you have. No one else did what you did."

"Henri, you're terrible at being mad at people," I said, laughing through my tears.

"Margot says the same thing." He laughed, and then his face fell. "She isn't ever going to forgive me."

"Of course she will," I said. My words seemed to lift his spirits.

"I hope so," he said, and then, like he was confessing, he added, "I *really* like her."

"I know you do," I said.

After a moment of bashfully ducking his head, he said, "Can I ask you a question?" His tone was suddenly serious.

Now I was worried. I gulped and said, "Yes."

"Were you getting a message in your eyes when we were outside? Was one running across, like, right here?" He stared ahead and swung a finger back and forth in the air under his face. I understood what he meant and was relieved we were leaving all talk of kissing behind.

"Yes," I said. "It has to be from Kel, right?"

"Could you read it?" he asked.

"I thought I saw Saretha's name," I replied. "And *DC*. But I'm not sure."

Henri considered this. "I thought the very last part said 'Kelly Wins.' Does that mean anything to you?"

I shrugged and said, "No." A long silence followed.

After a time, Henri glanced at the door and asked, "You think the coast is clear?"

I didn't know how much time had passed, but I decided it was enough. It would be better to get back to the car sooner rather than later. Part of me wanted to talk with Henri more, but the conversation was in awkward territory and it would be a while before it could be anything else.

The moment the door opened, Kel's message returned. I couldn't make out even the part Henri had described. The home outside the Squelch was still quiet and dark as we crept back to the service door and up through the hatch. The nearby rooftops were empty, and we heard nothing from the streets below. Our way back seemed clear.

In a few minutes, we reached the alley where we'd left the car. The Meiboch™, thankfully, was still there. The lowered Keene Inc. banner had done its job. I pulled the door handle and found it locked—as it should have been, but I still felt uneasy. Henri held up a hand and stared off into space, like he needed a minute.

The door clicked and opened. A fruity smell wafted out. Margot was in the driver's seat and Mira was beside her, eating something purple and dripping. Norflo and Sera were in the back, looking pleased with themselves. Henri and I joined them, staring at the plum in Mira's hands.

"Norflo and I got food," Sera said proudly, holding up an apple.

"How…" Henri started to say, but I cut him off.

"You let them go out there?" I asked Margot.

"I am not their guardian," Margot said. "And we needed food."

"Need to eat, Jiménez," Norflo said, smiling. Sera bumped his shoulder with hers, like they'd bonded while we were gone. A hot, prickling sensation spread over my shoulders. I shouldn't have felt resentful of their newfound closeness, but I did.

"That was reckless," I said to Norflo. "What if you'd gotten caught?"

"Jealous much?" Sera asked. I wasn't jealous, but I felt left out, which was probably just as foolish. After all, I'd gone on my own adventure with Henri. Either way, I felt a shock at realizing how well Sera had read my expression. What had been an asset when I was silent suddenly felt like a liability.

"We need to get moving," Margot said. "When we opened the doors, I saw an unreadable message in my vision that I think Kel—"

"I read it," Henri replied, pointing to his eyes. "Just now, outside the car. I know what it says."

ACCESS RESTRICTED: $13.98

"We should probably start driving while Henri explains," Margot said.

She looked at me for a beat, backed the car up to the banner and then stopped.

"I would prefer not to kill anyone," she said.

"Onit," Norflo replied, opening the door and climbing out.

We had to be silent again while Norflo pulled back the indigo banner like a curtain. Margot backed through, and he returned to the car. The banner swung into place and flashed an intense fluorescent orange. The logo disappeared.

"The hell's that?" Norflo asked.

"It looks like a warning," I said.

"'Bout what?"

"Moving the banner?" I suggested.

"I hope that is all it is," Margot said darkly.

"What was the message, Henri?" I asked, hoping she was right.

"I'm pretty certain it was: 'Do not return. Rogs are… something. Saretha needs three days. Safe as Carol Amanda Harving. Keep moving.' I couldn't make out that next part," Henri went on, blinking like it had pained him to read it. "It was hard."

"I don't know how you read it at all," I said, impressed.

"Henri is a marvel," Margot said. She kept her eyes on the road ahead of us, driving cautiously.

Henri's broad smile opened. "I concentrated."

We passed another Keene Inc. banner and it, too, flashed a brilliant orange.

"Shit," Margot said.

"Margot!" Mira admonished, like she'd never heard her sister swear.

"What does it mean?" I asked.

"Car's prolly been flagged," Norflo said.

"But I pulled out the identification chip while you two were gone," Margot said. "They should not be able to track us."

"Where is it?"

"Ina fruit stand," Norflo said, miming that he'd tossed it there.

"I gave it to them to get rid of," Margot explained.

"How are they tracking the car, then?" I asked.

"Maybe because it *doesn't* have an ID?" Sera asked.

"Shit," Mira said.

"Do not," Margot warned her, then added, "It is possible they are tracking the Meiboch™'s appearance."

"We shouldn't go down that avenue, then," I said, pointing to the main street with Bullion® Real Estate. "We want the southern exit. We came in from the east, so it must be that way." I pointed out my best guess. Margot turned to get us headed in the right direction as fast as she could without attracting attention.

"Henri, did the message say anything else?" I asked. "Maybe about where to go?"

"The last part was: 'Dome of DC. Kiely Wins,'" Henri said in a low voice.

"Kiely Wins?" I asked. "Not Kelly?"

"What did she win?" Mira asked.

Margot shook her head. "Not 'Wins.' Kiely Winston," she said. "The message must have been cut off. Henri, you should remember her name."

Henri looked chagrined.

"Kel told us about her."

"I might not have been paying attention," Henri admitted.

"What was so important that you ignored Kel?"

Henri turned a little red. "I might have been trying to figure out why you were so mean to me all the time."

"Mean to you?" Margot asked, surprised. "I have not ever been mean to you, Henri."

In the side mirror, I saw a car turn down the street behind us. "She was teasing you, Henri," I said, trying to help. I tapped Margot's shoulder and pointed to the car.

"I always liked you, Henri," Margot said in a rush, reaching back for Henri's hand and grabbing it before making a quick turn.

"And I always liked you," Henri responded.

"Even when you were kissing Speth?" Margot asked acidly, letting go of his hand. Did she sense, somehow, that Henri and I had talked?

Henri turned two shades brighter. I probably did, too. Margot let him—and me—burn for a moment, waiting for a response.

This was so not the time to be having this conversation.

Sera looked from me to him with cruel delight. "You kissed Speth, but you liked Margot?"

"It's complicated," I said, by which I meant it was none of her business.

Sera's nose twitched, and she looked at Henri. "You're such a *boy*," she said.

We passed another banner. Henri tracked it, avoiding looking at anyone in the car. I did the same. The banner turned the same fluorescent orange, but this time, a lock and chain image appeared at the top. Ahead, all the banners changed, and a message appeared below the locks: *ACCESS RESTRICTED*. The people on the street began to move quickly, heading inside.

"They're locking the city down," Henri warned.

"Keep moving," I said.

Margot grimaced. "Rog's Trademark black-and-flame decor."

"Maybe we can change the color of the car," I suggested. I leaned forward and pressed at a screen control labeled TINT. The side windows immediately grew transparent.

"That is the black glass," Margot hissed. "We need that!"

I hurriedly set the tint back to dark. Beside that control was a black square. When I touched it, the square grew lighter in color, and a label appeared over the tip of my finger, changing from Ebony™ to Charcoal™, then Slate™, Bone™, Cotton® and, finally, Blush™.

I let go of the button. The car's metal exterior lightened to a pale pink.

"The car is now made-up, too!" Mira exclaimed.

"Buys us time," Norflo said.

"Maybe," Margot said.

"Either way, we have to keep moving," I said. "We have to get out of here."

"In our *pink* car," Sera huffed, as if pink was even more conspicuous than Rog's colors.

Margot sped up. I scanned the streets for anyone who might be a threat. "So...Kiely Winston?" I asked.

Margot gritted her teeth and continued, "Kel told us about Kiely one night when she was in an odd mood—almost wistful. Kiely Winston was a Placer in the Dome of DC. Kel had great respect for her. She worked so fluidly and with such quiet agility, Kel described it as *balletic*. Yes, she used *that* word," Margot confirmed, catching a glimpse of my expression. "Kel is not one to use such language, so I took it seriously. I got the impression Kel trained with her. She may have been trained *by* her. I do not believe I have ever heard Kel speak of anyone with such affection and admiration."

"Ooh," Henri said, raising his head. "I do remember that. Didn't her story have a sad ending?"

Margot eyed him like he wasn't off the hook yet. "A Lawyer named Pierce Scotch discovered that a very rare book of Law in his collection had been stolen—"

"How do you remember these names?" Henri interrupted.

"Hush, Henri. Who is going to forget a name like Pierce Scotch?" Margot asked incredulously. "Anyway, Scotch's book was stolen and replaced with a fake. The fake was filled with a paper-like block of white plastic, bound in an almost flawless reproduction of the cover. It was expert work. Affluents mostly keep books as a show of power and status; they do not read them. Scotch, however, noticed the switch. He made a very public complaint about the crime. Every Affluent who had books checked their collections. Apparently thousands of books had been stolen and replaced with frauds."

Margot slowed the car. Ahead, at an intersection, a police car passed, and then another. I held my breath. Behind us, a garage slid open. A sleek platinum-and-gold Fjord™ pulled out and turned to fall in behind us.

"We better move," I said.

Margot frowned, but recognized it would be better to go on than to have the Fjord™ draw attention to us by honking.

"How'd they know it was Kiely who took the books?" I asked quietly.

"She signed them," Margot said.

"She *signed* the fakes?" I exclaimed.

Margot rolled the car to a stop at the intersection. The two police cars were well down the road, and the Fjord™ was close on our tail. "Every one of them," Margot answered. "With ink."

"Awesome," Norflo said.

Sera kept looking behind us. "You aren't worried that's Lucretia back there?"

Margot drove across the intersection. "That is not her car."

"Like she couldn't have several," Sera scoffed. "We're going to get caught."

"We're going to make it," I said, and then to Henri, "You don't remember any of this, about Kiely Winston?"

"Honestly? I thought Kel *was* Kiely," Henri said, defending himself. "Wasn't that the point of the story?"

Margot let out an exasperated sigh. "No, Henri, that was not the point. Kel described Kiely as over six feet tall, pale, with a shock of blond hair. How could that be Kel?"

Henri shrugged, embarrassed. Kel was very dark-skinned, and while it was possible she had once dyed her tight black hair blond, that would be very unlike her.

"Are we supposed to find her?" Mira asked.

"Yeah," Henri said. "I think so."

"I thought we were going to Crab Creek," I said. "Isn't that why Henri and I went to find a map?"

Sera nodded her assent. I watched in the mirror as the Fjord™ pulled off behind us and raced away.

"We have not talked about it," Margot said, as though driving had put her in charge. She was right, but I'd hoped we were all on the same page.

I sighed, then said, "Let's just focus on getting out of Keene first."

IRIDESCENCE: $14.99

We found our way to the dome's southern exit. The lanes ahead of us were all open, free of traffic, but the thick toll-booth arms were down, glowing with the same orange color and *ACCESS RESTRICTED* message.

"Can we smash through?" I asked.

Margot tensed. "Maybe."

She halted the car before we exposed ourselves in the wide-open lanes, pausing on the very edge of the city.

"Can't stay here long," Norflo said.

"Pull back to that spot," I said, pointing out a parking space a short way behind us.

"Why?" Margot asked.

"I know we want to get out of here quick, but we don't know if we can get through. If we wait until someone else tries to leave, and we time it right, we should be able to sneak under the arm before it closes."

Margot looked at me like I'd lost my mind. "We do not even know if anyone may leave the city."

"It says *Access Restricted*," I said. "Not *Access Forbidden*. I'd be willing to bet Affluents can come and go as they please."

Margot glared at the exit. "I do not see any Affluents here."

"Do you have a better idea?" I asked.

"We could walk," Henri said. "We could easily go over or under that arm."

"Yes, Henri, and then will we walk to our destination?" Margot asked drily.

Henri shrank at her criticism.

"Can we at least try to be nicer to each other?" I asked, exasperated.

Sera looked at me like I had two heads.

"Jiménez," Norflo said, smiling.

"How do you know that's my *real* last name?" I asked.

"It ain't Jime. I know that. Jime's fake."

"How do you *know*? A name could be anything."

"Nah. They took our names, priced 'em out. You ever look at the Spanish Word$ Market™? See what they charge? Don't want us to have a history. It's not just 'cause history is proprietary. They don't want us to know each other and don't want us to know ourselves."

Margot scoffed.

"I don't even know what that means," Sera said.

"You do," Norflo said.

"I don't!" Sera said, her eyes going a little wild.

"I don't know, either, Norflo," I said, stinging a little. "I mean, even if you're right, what difference does it make if my family's name used to be Jiménez? That doesn't change anything."

"It matter they took your 'rents?" Norflo asked.

"Of course it does," I said, my heart aching.

"Friends. Family. Words. Even our past. Cut us off from everything. Want us to have nothing, so we'll feel like nothing. They don't want your fight. S'why they hate you so bad. When they come to Indenture, they don't want anything left but hands and strong backs."

I thought of all the gray domes on the map, likely filled with Indentureds. A wave of nausea hit me. How could I tell them how bad it was beyond Keene, out in the place we were trying to escape to?

A gleaming violet car shot by us, headed straight to the toll.

"Go!" I cried.

Margot pulled us out and raced to the exit.

"This is going to look suspicious as hell," Margot said. It *did* look odd that we were ignoring all the other tolls to wait behind the one car out here.

The driver didn't show any outward signs of suspicion. The odd sheen of his car stirred a memory of the purplish iridescence I'd seen on Mrs. Stokes's Cuff—evidence of its malfunction. A pang of regret stabbed at me, even though there was nothing I could do to help her now.

The driver stuck his cuffed arm out the window. An Ad for 5 Places to visit in Ithaca, New York™, began to run on a screen that lowered into place before his windshield and the gate. Presumably, Ithaca was where he was headed. I had seen it on the map, but I couldn't remember exactly where it was.

The man tapped impatiently on the side of the car. At the bottom of his Ad, a message read: *Your travel will resume in nine minutes, or pay $449.91 to skip these important Advertisements now.*

"This asshole can't just pay to skip the Ads?" I asked.

"We're going to get caught," Sera cried.

"Honk at him," Henri said.

Margot turned. "Henri, that is your worst idea yet."

Sera shifted in her seat uncomfortably. "I should have stayed in Portland."

"I wish you had," I retorted.

"Let's be nice to each other," Sera said, mocking me.

"Why is he waiting?" Mira asked. "Can he not afford $400?"

The fee dropped to $399.92 as the timer ticked down to eight minutes.

"'Fluents are cheap," Norflo said.

"I do not like this," Margot said, looking over the gate and the dropped Ad screen. "I do not think we can make it."

"Do you want me to drive?" I asked.

"I can drive just fine," she said, rolling her clenched hands on the wheel.

"*Fine* isn't inspiring right now," Sera said.

"I am very skilled at Dome Racer™ V," Margot added, narrowing her eyes like a cat ready to pounce.

"Oh! I love Dome Racer™," Mira said.

"Is that supposed to be a qualification?" Sera asked me, like we were suddenly friends again.

"I was only trying to help," I said to Margot.

The man ahead of us gave in on the countdown as the fee dropped to $349.99. He tapped at his Cuff and the Ad vanished. The arm turned green and began to tilt up. The Ad screen angled and moved on an armature toward us with an Ad for Keene's Fancy Taco Strips®.

The car in front of us pulled forward—not cautious or quick, just a matter of routine. It didn't look like he'd even noticed us. Taco Strips® crunched in furious sparkling orange "flavor explosions" at the camera.

"We're going to have to smash the screen," I said.

"With pleasure," Margot replied, stomping on the gas. Our Meiboch™ lurched forward, right under the dropping gate, and nearly into the car in front of us. Margot jammed the wheel hard to the left and then to the right. In a flash, we were in front of the car and flying out the exit. Our rear end fishtailed left, right, then steadied as Margot brought the wheel back to center.

I glanced behind us. The car we'd passed had stopped, like we'd stunned the driver to a halt. A pair of dropters emerged from the tollbooths, red and blue lights flashing. They tilted and raced toward us.

"We've got company," I said, which was what people in movies always said at moments like this.

Margot looked back and drove the Meiboch™ faster, but not fast enough to lose them. The tunnel whizzed by, looking much like the one we traveled through from Portland. I hadn't noticed before, because I'd been driving, but the printed barriers on either side of the highway had quite a few scuffs in them, like they had been hit or sideswiped in places over the years. A few faint skid marks streaked the pavement, too. Perhaps the barriers weren't replaced very often. I wondered if the one I'd caused damage to would be fixed and set back in place.

"How do we lose them?" I asked.

Margot's face turned grim.

"What can they do?" Henri asked. "It's not like they can stop us."

"No, but they can ID us," I said. "Then Lucretia will know where to find us."

Suddenly, on both sides of the road, the translucent tunnel lit up. Despite being on the run, we'd triggered a tunnel Ad. Off into the distance, thousands of slight variations of the same image of Moon Mints™ glowed. They synched with our speed, so passing them was like looking at frames of an Ad that kept pace as we hurtled along.

The Ad finished as the tunnel started to curve. The tollbooth had grown tiny in the distance, and now it faded from view completely. Unfortunately, the dropters still hung behind us, flashing their lights. I wondered how long it would take the authorities in Keene to scramble and follow.

"Margot?" Mira asked, her voice small and scared as she glanced back at the red and blue flashes.

"They will not be able to catch us," Margot assured her.

"If they can't catch up with us, there'll be more waiting for us on the other end," Sera said.

An uneasy feeling in my gut told me she was right, but there was no point in making Mira afraid. "Now you're an expert on interdome Law?" I asked Sera. "How will they even know where we're going?" I turned to Mira and patted her hand. "They won't get us."

"Can we go home?" Mira asked in a whisper.

"No," Margot said.

I closed my eyes and tried to remember the map. We were west of Keene, headed toward New York™.

"We should turn left first chance we get," I said.

"Why?" Margot asked.

"Whether we go to DC or Carolina, we need to head south. Maybe find a way out of these tunnels and domes. If we get away from the WiFi, those dropters will have to stop chasing us."

"There *is* no way out," Margot said. "You have to go from dome to dome."

My chest felt tight.

Again, Mira asked, "Please can we go back to Portland?"

"Mira, you do not want to go back," Margot said, sounding a bit impatient. Mira reluctantly nodded.

The tunnel suddenly flashed another Ad—this one for Keene's Fruit Juice Poppers™, small sheets of BlisterPacked™ juice that you could squirt or pop in your mouth. A beautiful woman talked on the screen, but the audio didn't reach into the car. Behind her was a golden field of grapevines, lit by an amber sun.

"The farms," I said, realization dawning. "There must be a way out. Our parents' farm isn't inside a dome. There *have* to be roads out there." I looked out the window hopefully, as if some doorway would suddenly appear.

"There may not be any farms up *here*," Margot said, extending a palm at the road, where no exit could be seen.

"Why not?" Mira asked.

"I do not know enough about farms to know why they are put in some areas and not others."

I tried to picture the map again. I hadn't memorized everything, but there had been labels outside the lines between domes.

"Even if there aren't farms out here, there has to be *something.* There has to be a way out."

"Then find it," Margot snapped.

That was easier said than done. I redoubled my search efforts as we passed through the tunnel. I had no sense of how thick or strong that translucent covering was, and I was tempted to have Margot pull the car over so I could test it. I wished we had some way to blast our way out of the tunnel, but Placers didn't carry explosives.

"Keep your eyes open," I told everyone. "Look for anything that seems different."

Opposite us, in the far lane in the other direction, a car suddenly passed us with incredible speed—or at least it seemed that way from our vantage point. I whipped my head back and watched it disappear in the distance.

Ahead, the tunnel widened to four lanes on our side, then narrowed back down to three about a hundred yards later. Two metal arcs marked the same point in widening and narrowing. It didn't look like much more than bracing for the tunnel.

"Margot, stop," I said.

"The dropters—" she began.

"Please!" I cried.

Margot hit the brakes hard enough that we all pitched forward, straining against our seat belts as the car stuttered to a crawl.

"What are we looking at?" Sera asked, twisting around in her seat. The dropters split up, one keeping behind us and the other hovering into place right in front of our hood.

"Something tells me we can get out of the tunnel."

"Oh, so now you have special powers?" Sera sniffed.

"No," I said slowly, beginning to recognize what I was looking at. "See how the road is a little worn and darker in two lines, where the tires ride?"

The outer ring was like this in Portland. Two worn grooves followed the road, just like everywhere else, but a second set of lighter tracks split off and led to the spot in the wall where it curved.

"It's a hidden exit," Henri said, his eyes widening.

"Can we go?" Mira begged, grabbing Margot's arm.

"How?" Margot asked. "I cannot drive through the wall."

Sera frowned. "I don't see it."

I held up a finger to let them know I planned to get out. Margot glanced in the rearview mirror nervously.

"Those dropters are going to come for you."

I hesitated. She was right.

"We cannot stay here like this," Margot warned.

"Can I borrow your grapple again?" Henri asked.

"Henri, this isn't the time," I said, putting a hand on his shoulder. He frowned at me and my lack of faith in him.

"To shoot down the dropters," he said. "I can do it."

"Henri!" Mira cheered.

Margot took her grapple out, turned around and leaned way back to give Henri a big, inappropriately long kiss. "Henri the hero," she said, and opened the door.

DIRT: $15.99

Henri was a better shot than I was with a grapple. He took out the dropter in front of us with his first shot, harpooning it to the far wall in a shower of sparks. I missed as the one behind us blared a deafening alarm. My grapple hit the ceiling and I zipped up with it—almost out of habit. Henri reeled his grapple back, leaving the dropter to fall to the road, flaring brilliant white from a ruptured NanoLion™ battery.

"Desist!" The remaining dropter broadcast. The sound echoed through the tunnel. The dropter faced Henri, hissing like an animal...or a canister of sleep gas, I realized with horror.

Henri ducked and rolled back from the spray, slamming the Meiboch™'s door shut to protect the others.

He shot out a line and missed. I dropped to the ground and took a second shot. I hit the dropter with a glancing blow and it spun wildly.

"Remit p-p-payment..." the dropter sputtered.

I retracted my line to fire off another shot, but Henri beat me to it, striking the dropter dead center. It exploded with a flash, tiny shards of plastic scattering everywhere.

In the quiet that followed, I could hear the high-pitched whine of cars driving toward us.

The Meiboch™'s door popped open. Mira rushed out to Henri's side and threw her arms around him. Margot yelled her name from inside the car, then winced at the shock she received for it. Mira looked back at her, scared.

Margot honked the horn and waved us all back, but my first priority had to be getting us outside. We were so close. I raced over to the metal bracing that seemed to mark the hidden exit. Mira scrambled back to the car. Henri joined me, and Margot honked the horn again.

I put my hands on the bracing. There was nothing that seemed like a handle or locking mechanism—no panels, screens or buttons. Now that I was close, I could see that the tunnel's wall and arch fit snugly into a groove in the metal. I was certain that meant the whole thing could slide up. But how?

The two flaring drones lit the scene with a harsh bright light that forced me to squint. Henri examined the base of the wall, which showed a small gap with a thin rubber edge. I got down and tried to wedge my fingers through the opening, but it wasn't large enough.

The distant engine whine grew louder. I pulled out my magnetic lock pick and started to run it over the metal support. Margot hit the horn a third time, her face twisting with fury, and Henri's head lifted in alarm as a car came into view on the other side of the median.

The engine noise pitched down in tone as the car slowed and then came to a stop. Whether the driver was after us or not, the scene was not exactly discreet. Anyone could see what we were attempting to do.

Margot honked again, holding the horn down this time. Sera waved for me to come back, and then the car's glass turned back to black. Margot must have hit the TINT button to try to mask their identities. But what did she think we were going to do? Drive on? We'd be caught that way for sure. We needed to get outside right now.

On the other side of the road, a portly and dour-faced man emerged from his vehicle with two other Affluents. These weren't people chasing us—just Affluents who saw an opportunity.

"I can't InstaSue™ them!" one of the men said.

"Scofflaws!" the dour man cried, holding his Cuff up to record us.

I didn't know what that word meant, but I wanted to shout an insult in return. It wasn't worth the shock or having Margot chastise me.

My lock pick buzzed as it caught something. A great cracking noise vibrated against my feet and the wall began to slide up. A thrill ran through me as a line of yellow light expanded on the ground, creeping in from the outside. An alarm voice called out, *"Warning: Unauthorized breach."*

"Halt!" the dour man shouted, tracking me with his Cuff and probably imagining all the ways he could profit from what he was capturing. But they couldn't stop us now.

"This is treason!" one of the men exclaimed.

"*Treason*'s the wrong word," the dour one commented. "Waste of $39.99. But these delinquents must be stopped!"

I raced back to the car with Henri right in front of me. The dour man changed his position and held his fist out to us. Silas Rog had done this once, during his last attempt to kill me.

Henri slowed to see what the man was about to do and I had to tackle him into the car. The man fired off two shots from his Cuff. One whizzed out into the sunlight beyond the tunnel and the other pinged against the Meiboch™'s side. I yanked the door shut, thankful for the protection of Rog's black glass, which appeared to be bulletproof. Margot blasted us forward. We shot out the opening doorway, more shots cracking against the back of the Meiboch™.

Tires crunched over dirt and debris. Stars swam in my vision as I realized how close of a call we'd just experienced. I put a hand on Henri's shoulder and looked him over to be sure he was all right. He stared back at the men, who were done shooting at us and were getting back into their car, as though they'd just stopped off for a sandwich and were now on their way again.

Something stirred beneath my panic and dread, an awareness nudging me to look around.

We're outside, I thought. *This is the world.*

THE WORLD: $16.98

Outside the window, the world lacked the pastoral beauty I'd always seen in Ads. Instead of cartoonish green hills and sunflowers, rotten wooden stumps and poles stuck out from the side of the road at odd angles. Some held up black wires, but most had been chopped short and carried away.

Beyond the scattered wooden poles were gray-and-brown fields. Forests emerged in the distance, then came nearer to border the road on mounding hills. These were real trees, though it was sad to see them all dead. Many nearby had been cut to stumps as well, or had split and come to rest on the brown leaf-littered ground. It made sense that they'd died—they were exposed to the sun, after all. How could they survive?

I put a hand to the window. "The glass will protect us from the sun, right?"

"The sun is harmful in slow ways," Margot said. "We will be fine. Our problem is behind us. We have left evidence for them to follow."

I looked back at the tube we'd come from. The whole enclosure glowed a warm translucent yellow, save for where we'd exited. Light spilled out from the open doorway, which burned a brilliant, sizzling white. A dizzyingly vast field of azure and clouds stretched above the tunnel.

The sky was not what I had expected—there weren't easily recognizable white puffs against a field of blue. Instead, the clouds formed streaked sheets in the air, beyond which the sky was a slash of blue descending to a pale haze.

"We're outside," I said in awe. "We made it outside."

Norflo reached over and squeezed my arm. I put my hand on his and, for a moment, felt that warm sense of family that had been so hard to hold on to.

I took a moment to finally take in where we were—to really think about the scale of the landscape around me. I couldn't believe it was real. Even in the hopeful time before my Last Day, I had never really allowed myself to entertain the possibility that I might leave Portland *free* one day. Saretha dreamed of starring in movies and seeing the ocean, but my heart had been sure that if I ever left home, it would be in a truck of Indentureds headed to an even worse place than the Onzième—and a future working in the fields, like my parents.

Old, crumbling buildings dotted the landscape, their paint flaking and planks of wood askew. Many were nestled deep in the overgrowth, and one even had an enormous tree sprouting through its roof. Some buildings had fallen in on themselves, while others stood defiantly in fields of dirt. I wanted to call them ruins, but they didn't seem noble or interesting enough to deserve the name. The wreck of this outside civilization would have disappointed Sam. When he'd said *ruins*, I'm sure he'd pictured stone and majesty, not sagging, splintered rot.

The world was not beautiful. I'd known that it wouldn't look the way it was always portrayed in films, with pristine, awe-inspiring landscapes rendered in vivid color. My teachers' warnings had always been quite clear: outside the domes was a terrible, dangerous place to be. Even so, I had never pictured this depressing world of faded gray and dull brown. The clouds overhead thickened slowly over time, almost like magic, closing in until the horizon had subtly turned colorless.

The lack of beauty wasn't what troubled me, though. It was the sheer scale of the world that was overwhelming.

Everything near the car whipped by so fast, while the mountains and clouds farther off barely moved at all. This contrast in speed of the objects we passed, close and distant, didn't feel right to my mind or my stomach. The disparity didn't look real. I wasn't used to a horizon that stretched so far into the distance and stubbornly refused to move at a reasonable pace.

"Mulish," I said aloud, finding a word I'd learned long ago. Speaking it seemed to quell my mounting nausea. "Skeletonic."

"Uh," Sera said. "Are you doing that again?"

I knew what she meant. Sera knew me before my Last Day, when I used to speak freely. I liked to try new words out, just to feel them in my mouth and enjoy the sound. Sera used to make fun of me for it.

"Why does it bother you so much?" I asked.

"It doesn't *mean* anything," Sera protested. "It's a waste."

"Not to me," I said.

"Ensconce," Norflo said. "Benevolence."

"It's so stupid!" Sera growled. "Like, you can't find anything better to say?"

I searched for another word, but found my mood fouled. Was she right? A knot of frustration tied itself inside me. I did have more important things to say, but had no idea how to say them—especially in front of her.

Margot gripped the wheel and kept looking in the rearview mirror, waiting for whoever was back there to find us. I saw no joy or wonder in her face.

"Are you okay?" I asked her.

"Yes," she said in a voice that suggested I shouldn't push the issue.

I still wanted to apologize to her, but alone—or just to her and Henri. Not in a full car. But right now, the best I could summon was "I'm sorry you got dragged into this."

"Lucretia Rog forced us to leave, not you. If you wish to apologize, apologize for not getting in the car as soon as I honked. You set a bad example for Mira."

"She did not," Mira said. "I came back first honk."

"You should not have left the car at all, Mira," Margot snapped. Then, to me, "You see my point, Speth."

"But we'd be trapped in there," I protested.

"It would have been more discreet to find another exit, one that did not have flaming wreckage beside it."

"I didn't think of that," I said.

"No. And it did not occur to you that I had some other idea. I do not always understand your choices," Margot said.

"I know!" Sera said, finding an opening to get Margot on her side. "She makes one awful decision after another, and I honestly just want to scream at her sometimes."

I wanted to punch Sera, but Norflo, for some reason, was laughing. He shook his head at her. "You're both the same."

"How can you say that?" I cried.

"They took our guidance *away*, the two of you. Hard to know good choices from bad when no one shows you."

"But you're *so* perfect?" Sera asked him.

"Far frommit," Norflo said. "But I got lucky with my brothers."

That comment stung. Was he saying Saretha wasn't good enough? Opposite me, Sera turned and glared out the window. The fury coming off her was palpable, but I didn't see why. She didn't have any siblings. Norflo hadn't insulted *her.*

"I didn't mean to put us in danger," I said to Margot.

"Is it dangerous out here?" Mira asked, tapping on the window next to her.

"No, Mira," Margot said. "Everything is fine." Her voice didn't exactly sell the idea.

The sky behind us glowed brighter than ahead, and it felt like we were racing away from that light into darkness. A cold, exposed feeling shot through me.

"Maybe they can't follow us out here," I said, trying to sound hopeful. "The WiFi might not reach."

"I would not count on that," Margot said, then, after a moment, "And even if they do not, we have been forced to flee the city. We have not talked about the map you and Henri saw or agreed on where to go."

My heart sank. Crab Creek held the promise of my parents and Sera's mother, but for everyone else in the car, it was a risk without reward. I took a breath.

"South," I said.

Margot looked to our left—to the south. The tube that contained the tunnel extended off into the distance over a hill and then behind it, cutting us off from going in that direction. In some places, enormous trunk cables emerged from the ground and then burrowed back in, reminding me of the cables they tried to force into the city.

"Where?" Margot asked, pressing for more.

"I don't know," I said. "I only have a rough idea of where Crab Creek is and a cryptic message from Kel about DC. But both are south and away from here."

The bleak, enormous landscape felt like more than my mind could handle, and I had no reason to think it would look any different south of us. The thought began to fill me with dread.

"So is Téjico," Norflo said.

"What is it with you and Téjico?" Sera asked.

"My 'rents said if I ever got a chance, that's where I should go."

"Why?"

"'Cause that's where they'd go."

"Téjico," I said thoughtfully. "That's as far south as any of the maps showed."

I only knew a tiny bit about the place. Movies always showed Téjico and Canada as dangerous places full of cheats, criminals or worse. That was how the stories stocked their villains—sometimes they called the people Téjicans, sometimes Mexicans, sometimes nothing at all.

I did, however, remember watching a Carol Amanda Harving movie where she was a Cocky™ spy and her boss warned her that the Téjicans "just aren't like us. They don't charge for words down there." Dissonant music had swelled, and Carol Amanda Harving's character had sneered at the idea, muttering something about "savages." Saretha had nodded in agreement, but Sam and I had whispered to each other that not paying for words sounded pretty good, discordant music or not.

That movie night was long before we knew Carol Amanda Harving was just a digital copy of Saretha, stolen from a thousand Ad scans. That was before we knew a lot of things.

"You free your 'rents, Jiménez, where else you gonna take them?" Norflo asked.

"I haven't got that far yet."

"Téjico," Norflo cheered.

"I'm not taking *my* mother to Téjico," Sera said, crossing her arms.

Norflo replied with a shrug, like that was up to her.

"No matter how you slice it, everything we're looking for is south of here," Henri said.

"What about you, Henri?" I asked.

"Going south makes sense," he said evasively, which seemed odd to me. I couldn't think of a time when I'd heard Henri not answer a question directly.

Margot slowed at the next crossroad and pointed to our left. "Our path might not be as easy as just going south," she said. The southern road abruptly stopped a few yards from the luminous tunnel, its edges cracked and torn, like the road had been ripped away to make space for the tube—which was probably exactly what had happened. The way south was blocked.

"I don't know what to do," I said. "The map only showed tunnels and domes."

"What if there is no way?" Sera asked.

"Doom," Norflo said, half joking.

Mira let out a little fearful squeak.

"We are *not* doomed," Margot said.

"Couldn't you do a Placer thing and go *over* the tunnel to the other side?" Sera suggested.

"With the car?" Margot asked.

Sera seemed at a loss. "You want to wander around the wilderness and die?" I asked her.

"Okay! Excuse me for thinking of ideas," she retorted.

"We should keep moving west, then," I said. "That way's open, and maybe we'll come to something."

"Yes." Margot brought the car back up to speed. "But we should consider the possibility that we are fenced in by these domes and tunnels."

"Better out than in," Norflo said.

"Is it?" Margot asked.

We came up over the hill and a huge space opened up below us. My stomach lurched at the sight, and I realized Margot must be having the same reaction. She drifted left, then right, and kept blinking her eyes in a futile attempt to pretend everything was normal.

"Oof," Norflo said, leaning forward from his seat behind us to see better. Mira was bouncing up and down next to him. "Amazing, no?" he said to her.

Far in the distance, the western road connected to a decrepit-looking bridge that arced above the landscape. Beneath the bridge, a massive body of dark water snaked north to south. To the left, the tunnel shot across the water on a bridge of its own.

"Is that the ocean?" Mira asked. A thrill shot through me, thinking of it, but I knew that if this was the ocean, we wouldn't be able to see the other side.

"That is a river," Margot answered.

"Can we drive on it?" Mira asked.

"I am afraid we cannot," Margot said.

I assumed she was right, but I was unclear about how water worked on this scale. The bridge loomed up before us, five stories of pallid green metal spotted with rust.

"Can we stop?" Norflo asked. "'Least get a look south?"

Margot's face scrunched up.

"See that river?" he suggested, rubbing his hands together.

"Are there bears?" Mira asked.

"No," Margot said. "No bears."

"It won't take long," I offered.

Margot dropped her head. "Fine," she said. "But only for a few minutes, and only *if* there is no WiFi."

THE BRIDGE: $17.98

Margot slowed and stopped the car midway across the bridge. She held up a finger and opened her door. The wind from outside blew in at us.

"Hello," Margot said into the open air. Her eyes weren't shocked for it. The WiFi was behind us, which made me feel just a little safer. I would have expected everyone to rush out, but we all exited slowly and carefully into the oddest silence I'd ever heard.

It wasn't really a silence at all. The wind was strong and made a noise of its own, like a sustained blast from a phalanx of cars speeding on the outer ring, but without the roar of their engines. It didn't cease, either—my clothes fluttered around me, and it held me up when I leaned into it a little, whipping over my body in a way that made me feel alive and aware.

Beside me, Norflo let out a whoop. His voice came back, an echo in the wind, from the bare trees on the river's bank below us. Margot held Mira back from the edge as she gazed down at the torrent of water, brown and foamy, roaring a hundred feet below.

"A bird!" Mira exclaimed, pointing to a spot off in the trees.

"See, there is nothing to be afraid of out here," Margot said loudly against a gust of wind. "No bears."

Henri started to growl and lumber toward Mira. She quickly hid behind Margot in mock fear.

"No WiFi at all," Norflo marveled.

"That water looks disgusting," Sera said to me, standing too close, our shoulders touching, like we were sharing a secret. I stepped away from her. Brown and foamy as it was, I found it fascinating. It looked powerful, and it was so far removed from the world of Ads and plastic I'd known my whole life.

In the distance, from the trees across the river, came a chirping from Mira's bird.

"I think there's a crossing," Henri called out. He had stopped pretending he was a bear and was now looking up the road.

Well beyond the bridge we stood on, I could make out the shape Henri was pointing at, farther west. He was right. Something crossed the road ahead. An overpass traveled north and south, over both the road and the tunnel that was blocking our way.

Norflo pulled himself up from looking down over the bridge's edge, his face beaming from being outside. He moved to Henri's side, putting an arm around his shoulder and shaking him like a friend.

"You smell that?" Norflo called out. He took two great sniffs, and joy seemed to radiate from him. "The outside."

I couldn't find words for the smell. It was damp and loamy, like when they tilled the soil under the trees in Falxo Park, but fresher and deeper. I inhaled and closed my eyes, breathing it all in. The smell, the sound, the feel of the air on my skin was the opposite of the stifled, close feeling of everything inside the domes. The wind let me feel every part of myself.

I opened my eyes. Mira's bird chirped once more, and another answered. I'd heard birds before, but in the dome the sound had unsettled me. If they sang, they didn't last very long. Whatever song a bird might sing was Copyrighted by Ascape™ long ago. Birds couldn't be indebted or Indentured, so they were killed. There were special dropters for this.

Sera wrinkled her nose. She couldn't even enjoy seeing a bird? Or did she fear the dropters would come and find them, even here?

"What was that?" she asked.

I tilted my head. I wanted to tell her to relax, but I heard it, too. A sound almost too faint to register under the gusting wind. A tiny hum in the distance. It was a familiar sound—a sound from the ring.

The sound of cars racing toward us.

"Get in the car," I ordered, pushing Sera and yelling at the others. "Now. Now!"

Everyone bolted back to the Meiboch™. Norflo, slower than the rest of us, jogged the yards back as his smile turned to a grimace.

I hurried everyone inside and took the driver's seat.

I could see the car cresting the hill to the east, behind us. It was a black Meiboch™, like ours had been.

"No," I breathed.

I jolted us forward across the bridge and onto the highway west. Ahead of us was the overpass—black metal and half-covered in rust. Thick gray bricks held embankments of gravel in place on either side.

"Think that heads south?" I asked.

"Who cares?" Sera cried. "Go!"

I swung right and gunned the engine, leaving deep muddy grooves and scattering gravel behind us as I mounted the embankment. Behind, the other Meiboch™ raced across the bridge we'd just come from, followed closely by a second car.

As we crested the gravel mound, I turned south, ready to get us out of there as fast as I could, but the overpass wasn't what I expected. Instead of a road, there were thousands of planks of wood in the gravel, pinned down by parallel metal rails that stretched off to the north and south.

"What is this supposed to be?" I asked.

No one had an answer. Instead, Mira peeked back at the cars chasing us and said, "They are not slowing."

"Why does Lucretia Rog care?" Henri asked. "Why is she still coming after us?"

"Not *us*. Me!" I grunted, jostling the car up onto the rail. I couldn't manage any speed—the car stuttered over each thick wooden plank as I headed south.

"Speth!" Sera cried, as if it would make me go faster. Below us, the other Meiboch™ turned off the road and headed left, into the grass and up the opposite side of the overpass. The second car headed for the embankment behind us—they were trying to cut us off. I tried to accelerate, but it was too late. The first car braked to a hard stop on the rails, blocking our path.

I'd planned this wrong. We weren't going to escape.

"Back up," Margot said calmly. "Quickly." She was fishing in her bag, trying to find something in there that might help us. I was glad for her steady demeanor. It helped me shift into Reverse and start moving backward without too much panic.

In front of us, the passenger door of the car opened. A

Lawyer stepped out, unhurried. He wore a perfect slate-gray suit with a bloodred tie. His face was placid and familiar, even with his sharp eyes hidden behind matte sunglasses. This was the Lawyer who'd hauled my sister away after Sam died—Bennington Grippe. He held up a Cuffed arm, as if I would obey him and simply stop. He opened his mouth and began to talk, but his voice couldn't reach us inside our car.

"Maybe I can run him down," I said, but my stomach revolted at the idea. Despite everything I'd been through, I couldn't murder someone. Instead, I kept trying to speed up backward, but that just made the car slide on the gravel, wood and rails. As I scraped into the black metal of the bridge, the other car rammed into us from behind and shoved our car forward. We were trapped.

"Margot!" Mira cried.

"Let's takem," Norflo said, elbowing Henri as another Lawyer stepped out of the second car. "Lawerz can't fight."

I knew this Lawyer, too. Derrick Finster. He'd shown up at my Last Day ceremony just minutes after my friend Beecher had killed himself, rather than live Indentured to Silas Rog. Finster had wanted me to sue Beecher's family for "ruining" my Last Day party.

My refusal to speak that day had started all of this. Seeing Finster again now made my blood boil. He was tall and square-faced, with a broad chest full of legal medals across his impeccably cut charcoal-gray jacket. His eyes were concealed behind gray-pebbled glasses. Lots of Lawyers favored these because they gave the same eyeless impression as a judicial visor. I'd heard they worked like a fly's eyes and broadcasted some kind of enhanced image to the owner's ocular overlays.

Finster stood in our way confidently, like he knew he had us.

"Should we?" Henri asked of the fight.

"I doubt the Lawyers are alone," I said.

"They will shoot us," Margot said, the calm draining from her voice as she grabbed hold of her sister.

"Guns shouldn't work without the WiFi," I reminded her. Maybe we stood some chance.

A brief predatory look flashed in Margot's eyes before she shook it off. "*Should not* is a lot to pin our safety on," she replied, biting her lip.

"You guys are crazy," Sera cried, looking around wildly. "Get us out of here!"

"How?" I demanded. We had nowhere to go.

"Margot," Mira asked. "Can I fight, too?"

"You stay here," I said, "with your sister." I looked at Margot. "She will keep you safe." I pulled my Placer's mask on, hoping it would conceal my fear more than my identity. I grabbed Margot's mask out of her hands.

"But *you're* fighting with us, Sera Croate!" I growled, tossing it at her.

"I don't know how!" she protested.

"You tried to break my arm," I snarled. "You can fight."

"What are you even talking about?"

"When you tried to make me talk that day at school." I reached back and yanked on her arm to remind her.

"Speth!" Henri cried, appalled at my behavior. He didn't understand what Sera was like. I let go well before she had.

"I wasn't trying to break your arm," she said, cheeks burning. "I was—"

I kicked the door open and frankly hoped she'd get a shock out of it, but there was no WiFi. I was prepared for this to be the end.

LEGALESE: $18.99

With the Meiboch's seal broken, Grippe's voice finally reached us. "...does not exclude or absolve the second party of the first part of her responsibility to heed all spoken licit and legal claims when sheltered from said communication," he was saying. Someone loomed large inside the darkness of Grippe's car. My whole body felt raw and uneasy as I tried to see who was still sitting in there. Whoever it was, they were too big to be Lucretia.

"As such, any attempts to recover or—"

I raced forward and swung at his face. He ducked me with surprising speed.

"You are hereby—" he jumped to avoid a kick and held a finger up to ask me to wait "—enjoined to cease hostile and assaultive conduct until such time—" He sneered and blocked a punch by grabbing my arm. I twisted myself out of his grip. "As we have—" I connected, poorly, with his shoulder, almost like a joke punch. I may have been quick and strong, but I wasn't exactly a fighter. This Lawyer, I feared, was.

From my side, Norflo made a run at him, but Grippe sidestepped him, too. Inside Grippe's car, the shadow moved, and an enormous man got out.

He had a brutal, dim look I'd seen before, on each of the

three brothers who had murdered Sam. They shared the same distorted proportions and watery eyes. But the men who'd killed Sam were lean and rough-looking, with oddly muscled necks. This man seemed far more dangerous—still muscled and rough, but far from lean. He looked like they'd stuffed him into a black suit to civilize him—or he'd grown since putting the suit on.

"Desist!" Finster called out behind us. I couldn't look back to see what Henri and Sera were doing.

"You will cease at once!" Grippe yelled now, pushing me back.

The black-suited thug moved into place behind him and waited for instruction, probably to crush us.

I paused and chanced a look back. Henri had the other Lawyer in a headlock. Someone was emerging from his car as well—another large, overpumped bodyguard whose eyes lit on Henri. He was nearly identical to the one behind Grippe, with the same loutish expression and shock of blond hair. A sick feeling of wrongness hit me. Were they brothers, too, like the men who'd killed Sam? Was it just a coincidence, or was there something else at play here?

"Desist!" Grippe barked. Finster's driver also climbed out, pulling a long metal club from his car. With a nod, he and the brute advanced on Henri.

"Henri!" I called out.

Grippe's driver and his bodyguard were now closing in on Norflo and me. We were bottled up, and the only good news was that, for some reason, Lucretia Rog was not here.

Henri released Finster and backed away. Finster brushed himself off and raised a calming hand. The advance on us paused. Grippe addressed his Cuff.

"Please note for the record: it has been witnessed that Speth Jime spoke willfully and without consideration to either the Law or her binding Agreements with Keene Inc. Speth Jime, you are hereby notified that you are officially in breach of your preexisting obligation to read, as your first and primary paid words, the sanctioned a priori speech mutually agreed upon by you and by the entities of Keene Inc. and its subsidiaries, including but not limited to those endorsements and declarations of intent to purchase products and services from your guarantor. In obeisance of article VI of statute Y9, you, Speth Jime, henceforth referred to as *the Property*, are required to submit yourself to Indenture to the entities assigned by Keene Inc., in specificity, to the assign of Lucretia Hale Rog."

I laughed out loud. "Obeisance." This was so awful. Margot emerged from the car, shooing Mira back inside despite the girl's desire to follow. She tossed a grapple to Henri. The driver with the metal club twisted his fingers around the weapon and stepped forward, silently daring Henri to shoot the thing at him.

"You are legally *required* to surrender yourself to Lucretia Hale Rog," Grippe continued, "for the permanent Indentured servitude of yourself and any and all progeny issued by you for the duration of your Indenture."

"Dafuc?" Norflo grunted.

Finster started reading now. "'Whereas you have fallen into Collection, and whereas you have committed acts of grievous harm against—'"

"What about them?" I asked, gesturing to my friends.

Finster's brow furrowed. He looked across to his fellow Attorney. Grippe smiled.

"Our charge specifies *the Property* as you," Grippe said,

his voice sounding oily and pleased with himself. "Though Finster should take someone." His head tilted thoughtfully as he appraised Henri. "Him, I think."

"No!" I cried out.

Finster frowned at Henri. "You know I can't take *that* one," he scoffed. "He's already owned."

In the middle of everything, my heart dropped into my stomach. Henri was *Indentured*? How was that possible?

Grippe turned to Sera instead. "She's inconsequential enough."

Sera gasped and jumped back into the car. I glanced from one side to the other. It was clear that Grippe was the senior Lawyer of the two. He wore fewer medals, but only because he had less to prove. Finster's brute was a little smaller, too, now that I analyzed it, like Finster had to be put a peg below Grippe. That gave me an idea.

"I'll surrender to Finster," I said carefully, remembering how much Sam had disliked him. "If you let the rest of them leave," I added.

Sera's mouth dropped open in shock as Henri cried out, "No!"

Finster's eyebrows rose from under his sunglasses. This must have been a prime opportunity for him. He stood a little taller.

"I can agree—" he started.

Grippe sneered as he spoke over him. "I see no reason to negotiate."

"That doesn't make you much of a Lawyer," I said. Grippe's placid face broke into a phony smile, but his neck turned red, betraying anger under his perfect, unwrinkled suit.

"Our fees continue to accrue, and they will all be added to your debt," he replied with a sniff.

I don't know why he thought *that* would frighten me. I

suspect it was habit. I was far beyond the point of worrying about my debt.

I carefully motioned for the others to get in the car. Sera took Margot by the hand and pulled her back in, startling her. Norflo backed away. Henri stood firmly behind the car, the grapple sliding in his hand, like his palms were sweaty. Could he shoot a line and get off the overpass and then—what? Run for it? Even if they could all flee from Lucretia's men on this overpass, where could they go on foot? I had to get them safely in that car.

"Henri," I called out. "Go!"

He was too loyal to listen. He wouldn't get into the car without me.

"Why Finster?" Grippe asked me. "Perhaps you'd prefer Arkansas Holt?"

I laughed at this, then laughed louder when I saw how unamused Finster was by the suggestion he was on par with our pitiful family Lawyer.

"Slander will not be tolerated, Attorney Grippe."

"You don't have any jurisdiction here," Henri yelled.

"Get in the car, Henri," I shouted back.

"If that were true," Grippe said, "that would mean there is no *Law* of any sort out here." He motioned for his driver and his bodyguard to move closer. "We could do whatever we like. Is that what *the Property* would like? A world without Law? Is that why *the Silent Girl* went silent? If you would like to explain, I will personally pay for your speaks on that subject."

He held up his Cuff, eager for me to agree. How was it functioning without WiFi?

Beyond Grippe's car, the railed path stretched south into the distance. I was outside. I was outside in the *world.* I stood on ground beyond the dome. I'd made it out here, and they had failed to stop me. I couldn't give up now, but I had nothing to bargain with but myself. I turned and faced Finster.

"Just because *he* doesn't want to negotiate..." I jerked a thumb back at Grippe.

"*We* are not going to negotiate," Grippe retorted behind me.

"I am addressing my inquiry to Attorney Finster," I said, adopting as much of a legal tone as I could muster. It made me feel itchy, but Finster seemed to respond, at least in posture. "Whereas I, the uncounseled party, only agree to surrender exclusively to you forthwith—conferring upon you whatever benefits you get from that—"

"Your Legalese is lacking, my dear," Grippe commented.

Finster, in front of me, didn't move. Without being able to see his eyes, I had no clue what he was thinking. I let the silence sit. I knew there was a power in silence as well as words. The air was filled with that low, breathy sound of being outside. A soft breeze blew across us, but with no sound of cars passing like on Falxo Bridge.

Grippe cleared his throat. "Attorney Finster," he said, like he was trying to wake the man up. Finster held up a finger. He was considering my offer. Grippe's neck went red again.

"Ignore her!" Grippe ordered. "She is playing us off each other."

Finster's finger remained high. "Irrespective of her legal phraseology or motive, *the Property*'s point is not without merit of consideration."

His hand went to the legal medals on his chest and stroked them. He was thinking of the shiny bar I might add to his collection. I held back my desire to grin. I had him.

Grippe's redness traveled from his neck to his face in blotches. He'd had enough. He turned to the monstrosity of a man beside him in the black suit and barked, "Take her!"

"Desist!" I yelled, hoping it might confound the thug. His cruel face wrinkled in confusion at the command, but it didn't stop him long. Finster snapped his fingers, and his own thug moved to meet him.

"Attorney Finster," Grippe warned. He beckoned his bodyguard to do as he'd instructed, but the man froze in confusion.

Finster smirked. "Due to the exceptional expenditures of time and effort beyond the standard claim on *the Property*, including, but not limited to, the required travel to these Outer Lands and service roads, I must formally request a hearing pertaining to pending credit of collection of *the Property*," he announced. "At this time, I, Derrick Finster, officially lay claim to the *idea* of collecting Speth Jime, *the Property*, from these Outer Lands, and invoke my rights for the purpose of recompense, credit, Patent and legal advancement."

"A hearing?" Grippe asked Finster. He was trying to project calm, but I could see a tremor in his thumb as he used it to polish one of his medals.

Finster took a deep breath and then addressed me, ignoring his colleague. "You may surrender to me now," he said, looking quite pleased.

"Norflo, Henri, get in the car," I said. They still didn't obey.

"I will let the others leave," Grippe said to me, keeping his eyes on Finster. "Cede to *me*, now, and we will go."

He snapped his fingers, expecting obedience from me, or perhaps his bodyguard. Probably both.

"Norflo," I said again, raising my eyebrows and giving

him a look. Norflo took a step inside the vehicle and pulled at Henri to do the same, but Henri resisted.

"She cannot cede herself, as she does not legally own herself, nor can she surrender when primary authority has been cast into doubt," Finster complained.

Grippe stalked past me and up to Finster with a slow, forced gait. The bodyguard in the black suit went with him. Finster held his ground, his own thug backing him up.

"She has no counsel, *Finster*," Grippe hissed. "So if she cannot cede herself and there is no counsel to cede her, she must be taken."

He snapped his fingers again. No one obeyed. Finster mashed his lips together.

"Get in the car, Henri," I whispered at him.

Henri finally ducked inside the car, his eyes pleading with me. Grippe's driver moved past us, too, leaving only Grippe's car in the path of our Meiboch™.

"Legal doubt has been raised," Finster insisted, "as to *who* will take custody during this interim—"

"Finster, you are not the claimant," Grippe whined.

"Attorney Grippe! It is a serious and condemnable violation of terms and conditions to interrupt during the citation of Law, claims or other legal matters."

"Your claims violate the unspoken, but nevertheless legally enforceable terms of a tacit agreement between Attorneys when—"

I dashed toward the car, scrambling into the driver's seat and slamming the door behind me. Henri gasped in relief and yanked the back door shut, wedging himself between Margot and Norflo. Behind the car, Grippe's brutish bodyguard turned and his meaty hands hit our trunk, threatening to lift the car and smash it like a monster from a movie. Sera screamed beside me.

Grippe was pointing and yelling now, but we couldn't hear him. Shaking, I started the engine. Grippe, Finster, the bodyguards and both drivers all stopped and turned to us.

"Hold tight!" I yelled, aiming for Grippe's car ahead of us and hitting the gas. There was a rumbling second of acceleration and then a hard *thud* as we slammed into Grippe's car and it spun. One of its wheels locked on a rail. Metal bent on both cars, oddly soundless from inside. Mira wailed from the back seat. There wasn't quite enough space to escape, so I began to back up.

"The batteries are in the back of the car," Margot warned.

Both bodyguards pounded at our trunk. I jolted us forward again, bouncing Grippe's car back a few more feet into the gravel, where it began to slide slowly out of sight, then upended as it slipped off the edge of the overpass entirely.

Finster and Grippe hesitated, then—apparently having the same idea at the same moment—broke for Finster's car. My heart pounded in my ears under Mira's now-hysterical crying. I eased the accelerator down and bumped us along the tracks.

I looked in the rearview mirror and saw the bodyguards facing off and the Lawyers yelling, probably about who could enter the car first, or at all, or about who would get credit if they caught me or who would own the car now.

"That's right, argue," I muttered.

I eased into more speed and the ride quickly became uncomfortable. Where the metal was bent in the front of our car, the color fluttered from pink to red in rhythm with each bump and jostle. I had to grip the wheel hard to keep us from sliding. I planned to put as much space between us and them as I could before they finished their closing arguments.

"Did you know?" Sera said. "Did you know they'd argue?"

"Lawyers luv 'g'uments," Norflo said. He reached forward and gripped my shoulder, like I had done well.

Margot put her arms around her weeping sister and glared at me. "That was lucky," she said. "You could have ruptured the battery array."

"What now?" Henri asked.

"We keep going south," I said, speeding up toward the spot where the tracks crossed over the dome-connecting tunnel. "Once we cross the tunnel, we can get off the tracks and find a normal road."

Behind us, the Lawyers seemed more ready to litigate than pursue us, caught by their natural predisposition for disagreement until they had receded so far back, we couldn't see them. "We might just make it," I said, feeling the pull now toward DC and Crab Creek and maybe even Téjico.

A SMALL KINDNESS: $19.97

Soon I found a road running parallel to us and dismounted the tracks. Once we reached the pavement, I was able to bring the car up to speed again. The sun was setting, though, and the light around us grew dim and gray. I worried about driving too fast in the dark, and the wheel kept pulling to my right, like something was wrong with the car.

"Still no sign of them," Henri said, peering back down the long road behind us. For all we knew, the two Lawyers were still arguing. Lucretia Rog was not going to be happy.

"I wonder why she didn't come with them," I said.

"Lucretia Rog would not be caught dead in the Out Lands," Margot said.

Sera sniffed. She acted like riding shotgun made her the queen of the car, staring haughtily out the window.

"I suspect she is busy trying to retake Portland," Margot went on.

"Do you think she'll succeed?" I asked, thinking of the cables she had already forced into the city.

After a moment of deliberation, Margot said, "Yes."

My heart sank. The car pulled even harder to the right, and I had to fight to keep us going straight. "So it was all for nothing."

"No!" Henri cried. "Didn't you see the Silents in Keene? This isn't just about Portland."

I shook my head. I couldn't believe it.

"You showed them we could still fight," Henri insisted.

"But if she takes back Portland—"

"Then we will take DC," Margot said, as if it would be simple.

"I do not want to go to DC," Mira whispered. "I want to go home."

"We are not going home," Margot said.

I wondered why she didn't want to return, but it didn't feel like the best time to ask about it. Instead, I said, "We keep talking about DC like it's our best option. Like we can do something—like Kiely Winston will save us. But isn't DC where Lucretia Rog lives?"

"Yes. So hitting DC will hurt her the most," Margot said.

Dirt whipped up into clouds in front of us, and the car veered hard to the right. It wasn't the wheel pulling this time—it was the wind, and it was *strong*.

"What about Saretha?" I asked, trying to keep us on course.

"Kel said she was safe. If Portland is lost, she will get her out."

"But *we* can go home, right?" Mira asked.

"Mira," Margot snapped. "What did I just say?"

"I'm never going back," Norflo said. "I'll help in DC, but then I'm heading to Téjico."

"What is so great about Téjico?" Sera asked.

"It's not here," he replied. "And, Speth, don't you wanna be with your people?"

"*My people?* My family are my people," I said.

Norflo frowned a little. "And where're you going to take your 'rents?" he asked. "Back to Portland?"

"He makes a good point," Henri said.

"What about you, Henri?" Margot asked. "Where do you want to go?"

"Wherever you are."

I didn't even have to look to know Margot melted. She leaned over to give him a kiss.

"What about *your* parents, Henri?" Mira asked, maybe to stop them from kissing. They did have to lean over her to reach each other.

"Mira, do not be impolite," Margot said.

"How's that impolite?" Sera asked. I wanted to ask the same thing. Silence struck the car.

"Henri?" I asked, peeking back. "Is it because they're Indentured, too?"

"Actually, just my mom is," Henri said nervously.

"To his father," Margot added darkly.

"That's awful!" Sera exclaimed.

A weird, twisty feeling overcame me. I didn't want it to be true.

"It happens," Henri said.

"That is what you always say," Margot muttered.

I tried to wrap my head around the idea. Then I remembered that night in Henri's small, cozy apartment. He lived alone. He owned a book. I hadn't been able to consider that before when Finster mentioned that Henri was already owned. But Indentureds didn't have their own homes. They didn't own things.

"Henri, how—" I tried to ask.

"It's better than my mom being sent off," Henri interjected

quickly, before I could finish my question. "Or being Indentured to someone who doesn't care about her."

"Yes, Henri," Margot agreed.

"So who owns you, Henri?" Sera asked.

For some reason, her nosiness infuriated me, even though I'd been about to ask the same thing. "Don't you think he'd tell us if he wanted us to know?" I snapped more harshly than I should have.

Sera squirmed uncomfortably, at a loss for allies. After a few minutes of silence, she said softly, "Just for the record, I wasn't going to break your arm."

"What?" I asked.

"At school. I wasn't going to break it."

"Oh, were you just being friendly?" I sniped, annoyed at how she had suddenly shifted the subject to her.

Sera breathed in and out to center herself and sat up straight. "I did what I thought—what *we* thought was best. There was a lot of money for anyone who got you to speak."

"Who's *we*?" I asked.

"Mrs. Harris and me," Sera murmured.

Norflo dropped his head in his hands. "Harris," he muttered.

"*She* told you to attack me?" I asked, incredulous.

"She said I should get you to speak. Because we knew each other."

"And you listened to her?"

"Who is Mrs. Harris?" Mira asked her sister. Margot shushed her. Henri's mouth hung open, but I think he might have been secretly glad the subject wasn't who owned him.

"She was my *guardian*, Speth!" Sera said defensively. "I know that never meant anything to you, but it meant something to me."

I was getting so angry, it was difficult to focus on driving. I slowed a little as I struggled to find the words to respond.

"Mrs. Harris is a monster," I said furiously.

Norflo nodded. "She is."

"She is all I had!" Sera choked out, her body racked with a sudden sob. "They took my parents because of *you*!"

My stomach churned and my body felt like it was on fire. I'd always assumed she felt this way, but she'd never said it to my face.

"We were nine years old," I explained with a quavering voice. "You tried to do the same thing—you reported Penepoli for those scraps of words."

I could still picture the slips of paper, before Sera slapped them out of Penepoli's hand and they scattered into the air.

"We just reported you back," I went on.

"But they were *hers*!" Sera squealed.

"So what? Why did you have to say anything at all?"

Sera glared at me. "So I was supposed to be silent like you?" There was real venom in her voice now.

"Why is everyone so angry?" Mira whispered to Margot.

"At least you had Sam and Saretha," Sera continued, wiping her nose on her sleeve.

She had no right to bring Sam up, but the flames of my anger were nothing compared to the dark, lonely image that hit me. I'd never once thought of Sera going home alone each night after her parents were taken. She'd only been nine. Mira was nine. I knew what they must have done—they would have printed over her parents' bedroom and thickened her apartment walls until it was one-third the size of the room Sam, Saretha and I had shared. It would have been nothing more than a cell. That was what she would have been allocated. Those were the rules if you lived in Ad-subsidized housing.

"I'm not sorry," Sera said, stewing. "About twisting your arm. It was worth a try."

I half laughed at this. "It probably was," I replied. How could I blame her for wanting to get out, even if it was at my expense?

"I'm serious," Sera said, not realizing that my anger had flown.

Ahead of us, the road curved again, and I fought to keep my sense of which way was south in the dark. The wind was relenting a little. Metal posts jutted up from the side of the road. Something had once been attached to them. I wondered if they were for Ads, or if there had once been signs on these roads.

I peeked at Sera. She still fumed. What did she want me to do? Apologize for having siblings? Forgive her for what she'd done? I could forgive her for attacking me—for trying to make me speak—but not for her part in getting Sam killed. I didn't care how sad and lonely her childhood had been. That didn't excuse her—not fully.

"My dad is nice to her," Henri said into the silence.

Sera relaxed a little as the glare of attention moved away from her. I think that was Henri's intent. His compassion was boundless. I wondered if I could take a lesson from him. My anger at Sera wasn't going to bring Sam back. Just like I hadn't known her parents would be taken, she couldn't have known those men would murder Sam.

"He always remembers her birthday," Henri added.

"Remembering things is a small kindness." Margot paused and looked at Mira, who was listening closely. "But it does not make up for bigger cruelties. It does not make him a good person."

"But they're my parents," Henri said. My heart broke for him. He caught my eye in the rearview mirror. "You understand."

"Henri, are they okay?" I asked. I didn't specifically want to ask if they were Affluents, but if his father owned his mother, he must have been—and she could not have been. "In Portland, I mean. Are they safe?"

Margot crossed her arms. She obviously didn't think much of the situation.

"I think so?" Henri said.

He didn't know? I thought I'd gotten to know Henri pretty well for someone I was near, but didn't speak to, for so long. I didn't understand this answer. It told me nothing, and that frustrated me.

"Henri, how can you be a Placer and Indentured at the same time?" I asked.

"Same as anyone else," Henri answered, which again told me nothing.

Norflo started laughing. "Know what's funny? Alla us can speak all we want, and still we're apart. Split up. Keepin' secrets."

"This world offers little enough privacy," Margot said. "At least we still have the right not to say anything."

"Beecher's grandmother told me silence is the only privacy," I said.

"Can't help but think it keeps us separate," Norflo said with a sigh. "They divide and conquer. S'lonely."

Sera shifted uncomfortably.

Something low and distant lit the night sky. The clouds looked impossibly heavy, like they pressed down lower than a dome's top. The dead trees swayed and shook in a way that I found unnerving.

"Are you scared?" Mira asked Norflo, a little shy.

"Nah," he said. "Wherefore?"

"Wherefore?" Mira asked.

"It means *why*," Margot explained, her brow knitting. "Norflo uses an unusual selection of words."

"Sez that girl who doesn't use contractions."

"Contractions are cheating," Mira squeaked, turning to Norflo with great seriousness.

"Sez who?" Norflo asked with a bright smile.

"That is what we are taught," Margot answered. "But I notice that, in spite of how very important you feel communication is, you insist on using shortened words that make you difficult to comprehend."

"Chuneed me to talk elsewise?"

"Norflo the elocutionist," Margot sighed.

Norflo scrutinized her. "Showa hands. Who knows what *elocutionist* means?" He didn't wait for an answer because it was obviously only Margot. Even Mira was tugging at her sister's sleeve for a definition. "So who's difficult to comprehend?"

I had to laugh.

Margot eyed him coolly. "*Chuneed*, is that how you want to sound?"

"S'pose I do." Norflo thought for a second, then put a hand to his chest and spoke more slowly and deliberately. "My locution need not be peppered with cheap slang."

"That sounds more normal," Mira said, delighted.

"No, it doesn't," I said, listening carefully but looking ahead. "It doesn't sound like Norflo."

A hazy gray band began to obscure the horizon. I didn't know what I was looking at, but it was moving toward us.

"'Spect this thing with cheap words is another way to keep us apart," Norflo added. "Make some folks seem low."

The road ahead grew harder to see. A heavy gust of wind buffeted the car and I had to right us as we were pressed toward the edge of the empty highway.

I wanted to say more, but the grayness suddenly overtook us, and a turbulent flurry of white flecks swirled around the car.

"What is it?" I asked, slowing us to a crawl in the tumult.

"It's snow," Henri said.

COLDWET™: $20.99

I knew what snow was. Sort of. Sometimes the dome would go dark above us, and they said it was snow piled up there. I'd also seen it in movies, falling gently as a romantic backdrop. Sometimes the ground in films was white with snow that sparkled. There was a whole world of things movies showed that came from a time before the domes. There was even a candy called SnowTops™ that was just a mint with some kind of hard marshmallow fused on it.

The stuff spattering our car was nothing like that. It seemed angry and vicious. The Meiboch™'s wipers kicked in and cleared the sludge back and forth.

Henri had once showed me you could feel the cold of snow through the roof of the dome. I wondered what it felt like out here. I opened my window. Cold wind roared into the car. I put out my hand tentatively into a shockingly frigid stream of air. It stung, and I yanked my hand back.

"Hey!" Sera shouted as the flurry pelted through the car.

"Look, it makes drops!" Mira said, holding up her hand, then licking it.

"Do not!" Margot said.

I put the window up. The storm thickened around us,

and I had to pull the car to the side. Swirls of snow whipped across the highway.

"How long will it last?" I asked. No one answered.

"It is just water," Mira said to Margot, holding her hand out to her sister for inspection. Margot looked at it seriously, like a palm reader.

"We do not know what is in it," Margot said, wiping the drops away with her sleeve.

"Aw!" Mira stared at her hand, disappointed.

"Is anyone the least bit concerned that we're trapped?" I asked. I couldn't see more than a few feet in front of us. We weren't going anywhere.

"It'll stop," Norflo promised.

The car shook, rocked by a gust of wind.

"What if it's days?" I asked. I didn't have any sense of how long a storm might last. When the dome went dark because of snow, it sometimes lasted weeks.

"I kinda want to go out," Norflo said.

"No!" Sera said, stamping her foot.

"What for?" I asked.

Norflo shrugged. "When'm I gonna be out in snow again?"

"I'm not getting coldwet again," Sera sniffed, and then she hurriedly added, "Trademark!"

"You think *coldwet* hasn't been Trademarked?" Henri asked.

"Without WiFi, there's no way to know," Sera said.

"What do you think is going to happen?" I asked. "You think we'll roll into the next dome and you'll get a Lawyer to grant you a Trademark because you 'called it' in a car full of fugitives in the middle of a storm without any WiFi?"

"You're all witnesses," Sera said.

Norflo nodded. "'K, Sera. We'll all witness if the day comes."

Sera's mouth drew tight. His sarcasm wasn't lost on her.

The whole car shook again, then rocked back into place, slammed with a hard gust of wind, different from the ones that had come before. I peered out, watching as swirls of snow were blasted from the road, churned from the path of something huge barreling past us. A flash of orange in the gray.

"A truck," Henri breathed.

I put the car in gear and pulled us out from the side of the road.

"Speth?" Margot asked, like she thought I might have lost my mind.

"I'm going to follow it," I said. "It must be headed somewhere."

"What makes you think that is where we want to be?" Margot asked.

"It has to be better than here," I said, cautiously getting up to speed and drawing up behind the enormous truck. Snow corkscrewed off the thing in huge whirling twists, spattering the windshield and kicking the wipers into overdrive.

"I don't know about this," Henri said, craning his neck to see better outside.

"Do not get us killed," Margot said, holding Mira tighter. I think she was joking, but with Margot, I found it difficult to tell.

The Meiboch™ shuddered in the eddies of the truck in front of us, and shook when the wind suddenly sent the snow slanting nearly sideways. Then, just as abruptly, the color of the world changed again, from gray to a pale gold. The whipping snow calmed in the light, and the highway beneath us changed from an ashy gray to a slick, glossy black. The truck pressed forward faster, and I matched its speed. It was easier to see its shape now, a long box with bowed sides. There were no markings to tell what was inside.

A line of blue showed before us in the sky beyond the truck. The weather cleared slowly, and far off to our left, the landscape fell away into a valley. I realized, with a start, that it contained another dome.

"Which one is it?" Henri asked. He had seen the map, but it was hard to coordinate the memory of what we'd seen with the landscape around us.

I wasn't completely sure, either. "Generalec™, maybe?"

We passed under a bridge that held a dome-connecting tunnel. It bore the same translucent cap and smooth white sides as we'd seen before. It snaked down into the valley, under a scattered sky of blue and cloud, until it was nothing more than a line leading to the dome.

I let the truck have more breathing room and wondered what the driver thought of the color-changing Meiboch™ that had tailed it for so long. Whoever was at the wheel seemed unconcerned. They drove precisely and with determination along the long highway without any apparent notice of us. The driver didn't seem to share my growing fatigue, but this was his job, so he might have been used to it—or he might have been given some kind of drug to keep him awake through the drive. That sort of thing wouldn't surprise me. I knew I should stop, but I didn't want to. We had so far to go.

A flare of weakness shot down the muscles of my arms, disheartened that we weren't farther south. "If that's Generalec™, we've got a long way to go." My voice sounded ominous, and a shadow of discouragement passed over the car. We all knew how little food we had with us—just the fruit Norflo and Sera had pilfered in Keene. Henri slumped down a little more. Margot stared out the window, her knee bobbing up and down impatiently. Mira leaned on her, eyes closed but unable to sleep. Only Norflo seemed untroubled.

"You okay?" I asked, getting his attention in back. He sat up a little straighter.

Norflo looked at the dispirited faces around him and broke out into a smile again. "Me? I'm fine."

"How?" I asked, my voice incredulous. "How can you be fine?"

"Jiménez! Was only a matter of time 'fore I was Indentured—worked to death slow, in some factory. Or worse. This," he said, making a wide gesture. "This is all like a super bonus."

Henri smiled. "I like you, Norflo," Henri said.

"Amigo!" Norflo cried and then he explained. "It's one of the few Spanish words I know."

"But we have so far to go," I whispered.

"Yeah," Henri said, "but think how big that makes the world. And how hard it will be for them to find us in it."

CHEAPER THAN A HUMAN: $21.96

I was bolstered right up until the small light with the battery logo turned from two stripes of amber to one stripe of red. It was possible the car had days of driving left in it—or, better yet, maybe the Meiboch™ was something Rog only needed to charge once a year.

It was also possible we had ten minutes before the thing went dead. It wouldn't be smart to wait and find out.

"That isn't good," I said aloud, tapping at the display.

Mira leaned forward. "How do you charge a car?" she asked.

I didn't want to admit I had no idea. We never went over charging or battery capacities in Driver's Education. Apparently no one else knew, either, judging by the silence in the car.

"What are we going to do?" I asked. Without the car, we had no way to get to my parents, DC—anywhere. The sudden thought of being stranded out in the cold open landscape terrified me. My mind started racing, and I could feel my body panicking.

"Could ask for help," Norflo said simply.

"From who?" I snapped back at him, immediately regretting it. I was overtired, but Norflo was only trying to help. I tried again, more politely. "Sorry, from who?"

Norflo pointed to the truck we were following.

"Uh, that's pure crazy," Sera said.

Norflo shrugged, like his idea wasn't so bad.

"The word *crazy* is ugly and ableist," Margot commented.

"'Cept when you can't afford to say 'That is ludicrous,'" Norflo said. "When you got no access to all the good, smart, perfect words, what's that make it?"

Margot eyed him skeptically for a moment before saying, "We should find a dome."

That idea filled me with even greater dread. We'd worked so hard to get out.

"Too risky. I don't even know if we'll make it to a dome," I said, looking at the red light again. I eyed the truck thoughtfully. "Actually, that truck might have supplies."

"You want to *rob* it?" Margot asked.

"Yes," I said.

She paused for a moment, but I could tell that her hunger was winning out. "I am okay with that."

"Really?" Henri asked her, surprised and excited.

"It will be easier for the five of us to fight one truck driver than an entire dome," Margot said.

"There are six of us!" Mira protested.

"You are not allowed to fight the truck driver," Margot replied.

Mira crossed her arms. "I do not get to do anything."

"I don't think we should do this," Sera said, fear widening her eyes.

I steeled myself and pulled left to pass.

"Seriously, Speth!" Sera cried.

"We can at least *see* who we're dealing with," I said, pulling us up even with the bubble-like cab of the truck. I couldn't make anything out from the driver's side. "Can you see?" I asked Margot.

She peered through the glass.

"I cannot see anything," she said with a frown.

I pulled us ahead, so she could look from another angle. She took a long time to say her next words.

"I do not think there is anyone inside."

"Prolly drives itself. Dropter-like," Norflo said. "Cheaper than a human."

"Without any WiFi?" I asked.

"So much for asking the driver how to recharge," Henri said.

"If it was preprogrammed, it would not need WiFi," Margot said.

"Like Kel's Pad," I agreed. I pulled us up farther and shifted into the lane in front of the truck. My heart began to pound. "If it's programmed, it's following a route."

I slowed our car down. The truck slowed behind us and, when our speed dropped to a crawl, it attempted to change lanes. I changed, too.

"What are you doing?" Sera asked.

"I'm going to stop it." I braked until the truck's bumper nearly touched us.

"Oh my God, Speth!" Sera screeched, grabbing at the door handle.

"I like it," Norflo said.

"What if you're wrong?" Sera screeched. "What if someone's in there?"

"A person'd be honking by now," Norflo commented.

I brought us slowly to a stop, blocking the truck's path by straddling the two lanes. It hitched forward once, like it might scare us out of the way, but then it idled, waiting, with its bumper inches from ours.

I turned to the back of the car. "You guys ready?"

Norflo had a big grin. So did Mira, but Margot said to her, "You are staying in here." Mira's smile vanished instantly.

Henri put on his Placer's mask, probably out of habit, then paused.

"What are we doing?" he asked.

"This is stupid," Sera commented.

"We're going crack that truck open and see what's inside," I said.

Margot stayed my hand before I opened the door. "Even if it is following a route, that doesn't mean we'll be able to access it."

"It's worth the look."

I pressed my door open with a finger up like Margot had done on the bridge. I had to push the door hard against the cold wind to keep it open.

"Argentine," I said, testing for WiFi. No shock.

Sera's face pinched with a faint recognition. "What's *Argentine*?"

It was one of the words on the scraps of paper Penepoli had secreted into the schoolyard. I didn't know what the word meant, and it was probably foolish to say it with Sera nearby. There was no point in rubbing that memory in her face. I forced myself out into the cold, the wind whipping at my face, and made my way over to the other side of the car.

"Just a made-up word," I lied, pulling Sera's door open against the wind so she could get out.

"Trademark!" she said.

"It's all yours."

As Norflo got out, he looked at me in a way that left the distinct impression he knew the word and what it meant.

The truck's cab was locked, but it was immediately evident no one was inside. My Placer's outfit was thin and useless against the onslaught of cold air. Sera crossed her arms in front of herself and muttered bitterly about the chill beside me.

"Try the lock," Margot said. I ran my magnetic pick across it, but it couldn't find anything to latch onto.

"I don't think the truck was designed with Placers in mind," I said. "We'll have to find another way."

"How?" Sera asked, like it was already hopeless.

"We don't have to be gentle about it," I answered.

At the side of the road was a slightly bent metal pole, like the hundreds we had passed. It was one of a pair that must have once held a sign or an Ad. I grabbed it and tried to yank it from the ground. The metal was cold and unyielding, but when I shouldered it, the pole moved a little. I began to rock it back and forth. Norflo, Henri and Margot rushed over to help.

Mira looked on at the action longingly, keeping one foot inside the car.

"Stay in the car!" Margot grunted.

"I *am* in the car," Mira said, gesturing to her foot.

"What are you guys doing?" Sera asked.

"We're going to smash our way in," I said.

Sera sat with the idea a moment, then announced, "I'm freezing!" Like this was relevant news.

"Then go sit with Mira," I grunted as we yanked the pole free. Sera didn't move.

"You ever play Baseball™?" Henri asked.

"No," I said, hoisting the pole onto my shoulder and heading toward the truck. "But I understand the basic idea of hitting things."

Norflo shied back as I took a swing. The pole connected with the bubble on the cab of the truck. The glass detonated into a shattered spiderweb, but held in place. I had to prod it and knock away the clinging shards to clear out a hole large enough to stick my arm through and unlock the door.

It was just as cold inside the truck as outside, but without the wind, my breath plumed as I exhaled.

"Do you see that?" I asked, distracted by the sight of the billowing cloud of vapor, like the words I spoke were delicately revealed in the cold air. *Luscious, effervescent, careen, enthrall.* I wanted to speak a few beautiful words out loud, to see if they looked any different.

"Focus," Margot warned.

I nodded. "Of course." I was being childish. Sera clicked her tongue at me.

Margot pressed at a screen installed in the center console of the cab. The words *Off-line Travel Mode* appeared, followed by Terms of Service in tiny glowing print. I scrolled through dozens of screens of typical Legalese, the gist of which was to protect the trucking company, the truck's manufacturer, the USAE and the product the truck carried. The ToS specified that any person or persons driving, directing or programming the vehicle:

> ...will take full and tortious responsibility for the cargo, here forth defined as generalized organic vegetable matter transported for the purpose of conversion into proprietary nutritive printing inks for distribution as the product. The operator, whether live, remote or preprogrammed, will assume

> responsibility to protect any and all restricted, privileged information concerning the processing of the product, as well as any proprietary information concerning routes and locations as may be revealed by maps, charts and records.

"'Maps, charts and records.'" I read aloud. I got to the bottom of the Terms of Service and tapped AGREE. Margot leaned in close on my right. Sera, on my left, pressed against me like she didn't understand boundaries—or maybe she was just cold. Her body shivered.

The screen buzzed aggressively and popped up a second ToS screen.

> Without immediate verification from Vericon™ Data Services via WiFi tether, you agree to incur all fees and taxes from any and all words and visual communication displayed here, including, but not limited to, text, numeric, audio, maps, charts, images and effluvia. You further waive all right to accounting or counsel concerning said fees, or any deleritous...

It went on and on. I tapped AGREE without reading the rest. None of this mattered to me anymore. A menu with a NavPont™ logo popped up. Under it were options for ADDITIONAL TERMS, CALIBRATION, SAFETY, DIAGNOSTICS, ROUTES. I chose ROUTES the second it appeared. A map with a squiggly line appeared, showing the truck had come from up north in Burlington™ and was headed south to Mandolin™. The screen populated with all sorts of tiny icons: circles, clusters of squares, lightning bolts and a few others.

Sera squinted at it. "What is all that?"

She pressed in closer to me, shivering. Part of me wanted

to shove her off. What right did she have to touch me? But I was cold, too, and I couldn't shake the image of how lonely and empty her home must have been. She had no one.

Select destination, the screen blinked.

I scrolled the map down to where I suspected my parents were, between the same Agropollination™ domes I had seen on the other map. I tapped the spot.

Destination Invalid.

"Maybe it's farther down?" Sera said, impulsively reaching over me and tapping the screen.

Destination Invalid.

She went to tap again, but Margot swatted her hand away. "We cannot just pick random locations. We might get locked out of the system."

Sera withdrew a little.

I spread my fingers on the map to zoom in, looking for some clue of where Crab Creek might be.

I tapped one of the Agropollination™ domes.

Destination Invalid. Cargo acquired.

"Shit," Sera exclaimed.

"No, this is good. It means the truck is full," I said. I turned and made a gesture like a game show host. "Norflo. Henri. Go see what we've won."

Henri nodded and picked up the pole.

Margot regarded me. "Speth Jime has a sense of humor."

"Speth Jiménez," Norflo corrected before he and Henri disappeared to the back of the truck.

I leaned in and carefully studied the map. Margot joined me. She hadn't had the chance to see the one I'd seen in the real estate office. Her brow furrowed. She put a finger on it and slid the map up and down, to the northern and southern borders of our country.

"I thought Téjico was directly to the south," Margot said.

"It's all over the place," Sera commented, wagging a finger at the map.

It was south, but also west. It crawled up and met Canada in the middle, pinching our nation in half. I'd had no idea that the USAE and the USAW weren't physically connected. Thick waterways snaked inward, leaving only a small choke point of land where America® connected with a narrow lip of Téjico and a little slice of Canada.

From the back of the truck came a loud crack.

"I hope there's something to eat back there," I said, my stomach calling to me.

"I hope there's blankets," Sera whined.

Margot slid the map over to DC. The dome was just a circle. I risked tapping it.

ACCESS RESTRICTED.

The screen turned bright orange with the same lock image we'd seen in Keene, bathing the truck cab the color of flame. I tapped at it. The screen didn't respond.

"We're locked out," I said.

Margot gave me a cool, disapproving look.

"Seriously, Speth!" Sera chastised me.

Margot sighed and pulled her head out of the truck's cab. "Well, at least there is some good news," she announced.

Norflo and Henri were walking toward us with boxes of UltraGrain Harvest™ Bars.

"Oh! Gimme!" Sera said, jumping out and running up to Norflo. She tore into the box he was holding on top without any regard for Norflo.

Margot rolled her eyes.

"I love these things," Sera said, like that excused her.

"Dig in," Norflo said. I couldn't tell if he was being sarcastic or not. He walked over to me and held out the opened box.

"Thank you," I said pointedly, hiding the sadness welling up in my gut. Beecher's grandmother had mostly lived on these bars because she couldn't own a printer. She'd been caught and Indentured because of me. The last time I'd seen her was through the feed of her eyes.

"Henri, make sure Mira gets one," Margot said with an affectionate push.

The orange wash of light faded. I ducked back into the truck. The interface was back.

"Don't touch anything!" Sera said, her mouth full of Harvest™ crumbs. She pressed in next to me.

"Give me some space," I said, pushing her back in spite of myself. Something in me fluttered, wondering if any of what had happened to her parents was truly my fault.

"We should be careful," Margot said, joining us as Henri and Norflo carried the bars off to the Meiboch™. "Remember, we need to recharge the car."

I examined the options on the screen. "Well, the map isn't getting us anywhere."

I tapped the DIAGNOSTICS button. The screen populated with a dozen or so options. I selected BATTERY PERFORMANCE. The NanoLion™ logo glowed, dots pulsing in the background, and a new Terms of Service appeared. I AGREE'd it away.

"How does this help us?" Sera asked.

"Just wait," I said. The screen now showed us the truck's battery status.

Charge: 71
Predicted Range: 948 km
Estimated Battery Life: 7 years

Two buttons also appeared on the screen: CYCLE and RECHARGE.

"How is the truck going to recharge itself?" Sera asked.

"Let's find out," I said. I tapped RECHARGE. The truck lurched forward, nearly giving me a heart attack. Just as quickly it stopped, an inch from the Meiboch's bumper. The engine hummed louder.

"What now?" Margot asked.

"Now we get the Meiboch™ out of this truck's way. I think it's looking for the nearest recharge."

OIO™: $22.99

I sat in the passenger seat and let Margot take a shift, gnawing away on the dense Butter Crunch Harvest™ Bar Norflo had given me. I wanted to sleep, but I couldn't. Every time I tried, my eyes opened instinctively, checking to make sure we were still following the truck.

"I will not let it get away," Margot said.

In the back seat, Sera and Norflo both had their eyes closed, with her leaning against him as he snored. I'd spent almost every night of my life sleeping in the same lumpy pullout bed with my sister. Even when things were at their worst, I took comfort in being near her and Sam. It was what always came to mind when I thought of home. Sera had never had that, and I couldn't stop thinking about how alone she must have felt.

Mira watched the road or her sister, as if she was waiting for something to happen. Her eyes were drowsy and darkened with fatigue. Henri had his forehead pressed to the glass of the window, looking out into the darkness.

"Margot," I whispered.

Her eyes flicked to me and then back to the road.

"Are you okay?" I asked. "I know you wanted to go home when we had to escape. This wasn't what you planned."

"It does not matter," she said.

"But what about your parents? Won't they be worried?"

Her hands tensed on the wheel. "No," she said without further explanation. When she sensed me looking for more, she added, "You can stop staring at me for answers."

I could feel something was very wrong. But how could I help if she didn't tell me? I contemplated asking Henri at some point, but Margot would be furious if she found out.

The sky outside was half-clouded, but we could see a few crisp, shimmering dots of light in the haze between. The clouds themselves glowed faintly in spots, lit from underneath by far-off domes. I searched for the moon, but didn't see it. I thought the clouds would eventually shift or clear, and it would just be hanging in the sky, like it did in every Moon Mints™ commercial. But I saw no sign of it, not even a pale glow to hint it existed. A quiet anxiety invaded my thoughts: Was the moon just a story? Was it just part of a logo to sell mints? I honestly didn't know.

I opened my mouth to ask, but realized how silly and childish the question was. If it was real, I would sound ignorant. If it wasn't, I would still sound like a fool.

I didn't know exactly what the moon was supposed to *be*, either. Sometimes it was a crescent shape, and sometimes it was big and round. I asked once in school, but Mr. Kellogg said specifics about the moon were the intellectual property of Keene Inc.—because of Moon Mints™.

"Why do they show it in the sky?" I had asked. "Why is it up there?"

He'd told me not to make him waste money repeating himself. That was in third grade. Penepoli had said it must be a ball, which made sense, but knowing its shape only made the thing seem stranger.

I fell to dreaming about it, but the dream was vague and full of regret, like the moon had gotten away from me, or I had betrayed it. Henri had told me Margot's parents lived there on weekends, but kept their second home secret from Mira because she was a baby bird with a bad wing, just like Sera.

It seemed like only moments later, Margot was poking at my shoulder.

"Speth," she whispered. "Speth!"

I opened my eyes and saw we were following the truck along a wide, curving road in a whole new landscape. The sky was entirely clouded over again, but a great glow shone from beyond the trees. Whatever the light source, it illuminated a wide swath of sky over us.

I wasn't the only one to wake. "Is it a dome?" Henri whispered, rubbing his eyes, trying not to wake Mira. She was asleep beside him, her mouth open, breathing softly. I had to shake off what he'd told me in my dream. Mira was no bird.

"What dome is it?" I asked, unsure how far we'd traveled while I slept.

"I do not think it is a dome." Margot peered ahead with great intensity. "I think it is a city *without* a dome."

"What ift's escapees?" Norflo said, excited. "Made a whole city? We could—"

"It isn't," I said. I didn't mean to cut him off, but I wasn't going to hope for something impossible. I yawned and tried to clear my head. "The truck wouldn't go to a place like that to recharge."

"We don't know for certain that is what it is doing," Margot reminded me.

Norflo slumped back a little. Sera looked from him to the outside, like she wanted what he'd said to be true.

"Are there places like that?" Sera asked. "Are there stories?"

"Nah," Norflo said. "Be cool, tho."

The city slowly revealed itself around the curve—only it wasn't a city. It was a miles-long cluster of cheaply printed barracks. They clung to each other at slightly different heights, like no one could be bothered to print them uniformly. Beyond the buildings, a pair of towering wedges billowed a thick smog that reached up into the haze from a long, low factory. A single bright sign read: OiO™ Products.

"'OiO™.'" Henri read aloud. Mira stirred beside him and made a short, dissatisfied noise.

Almost the moment he said it, the Meiboch™'s doors locked and the dashboard lit up.

"WiFi," I said.

"I hate those things," Sera said, rubbing her midsection as if she knew the feel of an OiO™ Holding Corset. Saretha had worn one when she was trapped in the house, hoping it would keep her in shape. The memory of her in it made me feel sick.

"Maybe this isn't a good idea," Henri whispered. Mira twitched and smacked at his arm to be quiet.

"Nothing we have done is a good idea, Henri," Margot said quietly. She tapped the dashboard. "But letting the car die is a worse idea."

"Poor car," Mira said, eyes still closed, trying to get comfortable.

I took a deep breath and tried to steady myself, sickened by the idea of what I was looking at. "How can there be a market for so many corsets? How can they need a factory for it?"

"How did you think these things got made? Fairies?" Margot asked, pointing to the long, decidedly unenchanted building.

"They make more than corsets," Sera commented, her

body tense. Did they manufacture something worse than a device that crushed your middle to disfigure you into looking thinner?

Near one end of the factory town, light glowed from a long tube that wound off into a dense forest of dead gray trees. It was a tunnel to the domes, like the one we'd escaped from.

"We should avoid that thing," I said, eyeing it like it was a snake waiting to strike.

"Couldn't we take it to DC?" Henri asked.

"Sure," I answered, looking at the tunnel's glow threading into the dead forest. "We could drive right to Lucretia Rog's home."

Henri paused. "I was thinking of Kiely Winston. But what if we *did* look for Lucretia's place in DC? We're Placers. We could sneak in."

"Henri, do you not remember how badly your last visit to a Rog went?"

"Badly? We defeated him! We blew his place up."

"After I rescued you," Margot said. "And that was mostly Speth's quick thinking."

"I got lucky," I said as the truck ahead of us slowed.

"Humble Speth," Margot commented.

The truck turned left, heading away from the tunnel, toward the dark end of the town, where a sign for Sylvectric™ Inductions glowed dimly and spun. The streets were deserted.

"Where is everyone?" I asked.

"Eerie," Norflo commented. His brow furrowed. "Think s'all Indentureds?"

"The whole place?" I asked, feeling a pit of dread in my stomach.

"'Cept whoever keeps 'em in line," Norflo muttered.

This was how our parents lived. This was a factory, not a farm, but the idea was the same. The people here were prisoners, forced to do whatever work they were handed.

I wanted to cry. I wanted to scream. But I held both back. I looked at Sera and wondered if she felt the same way.

The truck pulled into the space under the rotating sign, and the whole area lit up. The ground was marked with parking lines. Inside these were black metal charging plates. After looking around cautiously, Margot pulled in behind the truck.

I felt strange, almost tingly. A thin buzz seemed to fill the car, even though it was still silent. I could feel it in my bones rather than hear it. The tints of the glass brightened, like the black glass had turned off. The car's screen went dark.

"I don't think we should be here," I said.

"We—" Margot began, but the dashboard's screen suddenly popped up a bright logo.

Sylvectric™ Inductions. Tap AGREE *to charge.*

Below this, a block of minuscule ToS text appeared, the unreadable kind they use when they know you have no choice. Margot tapped AGREE, and the soundless buzz changed to a higher tone.

"What's happening?" Sera asked.

"The car is charging," Margot said flatly. The red battery light flickered to amber. Margot peeked back at Mira sleeping.

"Let's switch off," I whispered to her, pointing from her seat to mine. I began to move, and Margot, after a moment of thought, did an awkward dance with me so we could switch places.

I scanned the windows of the buildings nervously, looking for any sign of life. In a second-floor window not far from us, a gaunt, dark face was gazing, expressionless, into the night. Her eyes looked cloudy even from this distance. She was weary and elderly, and seemed only vaguely interested in looking out her window. I wondered if she could see at all.

Her eyes turned to us—to me, without interest. Her window abruptly flickered and turned black. It might have been showing her an Ad, or maybe she was allowed just a brief period to look outside.

I saw no one else. There wasn't anyone out strolling. There were no shops or parks. There did not seem to be anywhere to do anything. I suspected everyone was sleeping, or, worse, working deep into the night. Everything appeared locked down tight. There were no ledges on the barracks for Placers, or windows that swung out for easy access. If my parents were in a place like this, how would I even find them, let alone get them out?

The window the woman had been looking out from flickered with a brief flash and went clear again. She was gone.

The front door of the building beside us, flat metal and unadorned, slowly pushed open. The elderly woman made her way out, her face still an expressionless mask, but her eyes were searching now. A younger woman, maybe my mother's age, held the door for her and took her hand to guide her. She turned to us, and her eyes went wide. She seemed both alarmed and excited. She grabbed the door and appeared to be yelling inside, but no sound made it into the Meiboch™'s Squelch.

Norflo pulled up on the handle of his door to get out, but the screen chimed soothingly.

ACCESS RESTRICTED.

The door didn't move. "Dafuc?"

ACCESS RESTRICTED.

"Don't go out there," Sera cried.

"Can't," Norflo said, demonstrating. The same chime sounded. Mira stirred at the noise.

The truck in front of us began to move, and the lights around it dimmed. It turned, half circling us to head back up the road toward the tunnel.

The two women moved toward our car, slowed by the older one's shuffling speed.

"Are we trapped?" Sera asked, panicked.

"Trapped?" Mira repeated sleepily.

"No," Margot said. "They are only restricting our access to the workers and those who keep them in line."

"How's that different from being trapped?" Sera asked.

"We're not authorized to even *be* here?" I asked. I pulled uselessly on the door myself. It chimed and showed the same *ACCESS RESTRICTED* message again. I don't know why I was surprised. This was a world where people could be bought and sold. Not letting us exit the car because we weren't "authorized" to be in OiO™'s factory town was nothing compared to that.

I suddenly realized what was upsetting me so much. "What if all the Indentured places are like this? What if we get to Crab Creek, and we aren't even allowed out of the car?"

"That is an unfortunate possibility," Margot said.

The temperature around me seemed to drop. Had I lost everything, and I didn't even know it? Would I never see my sister or my parents again?

"Are you saying we should give up?" Sera asked, her eyes filled with a desperation I understood. I reached back and took her hand. Her face registered shock.

"We're going to try," I told her.

"We should try to find Kiely Winston in DC," Margot said. "She is our best option."

The two women stopped at the sidewalk, across the street from our car. They squinted at us, and the older woman grew excited. She made the sign of the zippered lips to her younger companion.

"Let's get back on the road," I said, aching to U-turn like the truck and leave. A pang of guilt hit me. I knew I was being a coward, leaving these women behind, but I didn't want any of this. I wished the black glass had stayed on. I didn't want their attention. A horrid sour guilt crept up my throat. I wanted to say we should help them, but we couldn't. If there was any hope of helping my parents and Saretha, we had to keep moving.

Margot's head was turned, looking back at the way we'd come. She bit her lip.

The truck we'd followed in was wending its way up the lonely curved road out of town, but she was looking past it.

"We should probably move," Margot said, pointing in the direction of the tunnel. A car raced toward us, followed by a second.

"You think they're here for us?" I asked, fearing there was no other possibility. A few more women emerged from the door and hurried to the side of the first two. As they spoke to each other, their Cuffs blazed amber in the night, charging them for words we couldn't hear.

"Don't wait and find out," Norflo suggested.

I put the car in Drive. The noiseless hum sputtered. The car felt like it was being held in place by a magnetic field—like the ones I searched for with my lock pick.

"They're blocking the road out of town," Henri said. Sure

enough, the two cars had slowed and then stopped in the distance, barricading the exit.

"There's no way out," Sera breathed.

Mira's eyes went wide.

I stared ahead, searching desperately for another route. My eyes landed on a rusted metal gate, flecked with ancient yellow paint, sitting in the darkness outside the recharge station lights. Beyond it, an ancient, cracked stretch of pavement vanished into the darkness of the dead forest.

I pressed down on the accelerator, trying to get us out of the magnetic field. It didn't want us to go. I pressed down harder, and the screen lit up with a warning about nonpayment as the car finally wrenched free. I glanced in the rearview mirror to see a third car emerging from the tunnel. Though it was far-off, it appeared to be a Meiboch™.

I steered our car toward the dark hole in the trees beyond the rusted gate.

"Smash through it," Henri said.

Margot looked at him. "Henri the subtle."

The front of our car was still bent and sputtering colors. I didn't think more damage would be useful. There was a spot between some of the trees and the gate where I was pretty sure the car would just fit, if I angled us right. The undergrowth would scratch up the car, but it would be better than crashing into anything.

I eased us onto the road and turned out our lights.

Behind us, the distant car sped past the exit. There was little doubt in my mind where they were heading.

The women began to walk along the sidewalk, trying to keep up with us, but clearly taking every care not to step out into the road. It was like they didn't dare to actually approach us.

"I don't think we should go into the woods," Sera said.

I ignored her and threaded the car awkwardly between the trees, backing up to reposition us. I could feel Sera's frustration. The town was deadly still, save for the women now staring at us and the Meiboch™ rapidly approaching the charging station. I didn't see how I could get us out in time.

Then the women suddenly dispersed, walking away as if they'd never seen us.

"Speth, please, not the woods," Sera said, like they scared her.

"What is in the woods?" Mira asked, infected by Sera's fear.

The other Meiboch™'s lights blazed through the darkness.

"They aren't listening to me," Sera said to Norflo, her voice high.

"S'fine," Norflo said, wrapping an arm around her shoulder. Sera seemed to relax a little.

I pulled the car against a tree, scraping along, turned and finally got us onto the broken pavement. The women behind us suddenly stepped out into the road, holding hands, their heads bowing with a pain I knew well. Their eyes were being shocked—not for talking, but for walking beyond the boundaries they were allowed. They were on an electronic leash. The elderly woman dropped to her knees from the pain, but she stayed in the road, blocking the way to protect us. All of them did. I wanted to scream back at them not to do this.

"Go!" Margot said.

"But those women!" I cried out.

"They will be okay," Margot said. "They are protected."

"By what?" I demanded, my foot hovering over the accelerator.

"OiO™!" Margot yelled back at me. "They are the property of OiO™. OiO™ will sue."

It was a sick idea, but it was the only hope I could hold on to. I pressed my foot down and sent us forward, lights out, onto a dark, broken road I could barely see.

I couldn't look back. I didn't want to. I had to just believe.

FORESTS OF SYLVANIA™: $23.97

As we drove farther into the forest, Sera clutched Norflo's arm. Mira leaned against Henri, trying to find a way back to sleep. The WiFi stuttered out, and the dashboard went blank. The road and forest grew too dark for me to keep up to speed. When the car bounced over a fallen branch none of us had seen, I slowed us as much as I dared. Fortunately, there was no sign of the other car behind us.

"'Twas up with those women? How'd they recognize you?" Norflo asked me.

"I don't know," I said. "Probably the news?"

"Wouldn't think they'd get news out there," Norflo said.

"My parents do," I said. Sera looked at me like I was lying. "They do."

"How do you know that?" she asked.

"They saw me," I said. "Saw what happened on my Last Day, when I went silent." I thought back to my mother making the sign of the zippered lips. It was a gesture she'd once hated, but she'd made it because she was proud of me.

"Maybe *everyone* saw," Norflo suggested.

"That's awesome," Henri said.

Was it? I felt sick with guilt, leaving those women back

there. Even if they hadn't been run down, I couldn't imagine what came next would be pleasant for them.

"Who do you think it was chasing us?" Henri asked.

"Oh, Henri," Margot said.

"What?" he asked her.

"It was those Lawyers," Sera said. "Right? It had to be those Lawyers."

"Or Lucretia Rog herself," I said.

"I do not think so," Margot said.

"Why's she want you so bad?" Sera asked. "Even before you took out the WiFi, they really went after you. There was that reward to get you to talk."

"That was the news stations," I shot back. "Not the Rogs."

"There is not much difference in Portland," Margot pointed out. "The Rogs own most of them. Sera is essentially correct. Perhaps they miscalculated, showing footage of your defiance on your Last Day, Speth. Perhaps Henri is right—maybe everyone saw."

"Can I ask something? And will you promise not to get mad?" Sera asked.

"No," I answered.

Sera went on, anyway. I didn't think she really cared if I got angry or not. "Why didn't Rog just kill you? If they made a mistake, the Rogs could have done it a bunch of times. Why'd he go after Sam and leave you on that bridge?"

My whole body felt like the underside of a volcano. I answered through gritted teeth. "He tried," I said. "He tried to shoot me."

"Yeah, I know, after you blew up the WiFi," Sera replied. "But why not before that?"

"How the fuck would I know?" I asked. Margot covered

Mira's ears, but held back from chastising me about my language.

"Profanity surcharge," Norflo joked, trying to lighten the mood. He put a hand on my shoulder, but I shook it off.

"I'm driving," I said.

"She's so prickly," Sera commented to him.

"Go easy," Norflo said to her, and then to me, "S'worth thinking about, tho. 'Cretia Rog coulda killed us in Portland when she had us down in the bubble."

"She probably wanted to save her husband."

"I do not think Silas Rog is her husband," Margot said.

"He's her brother," Henri said.

I don't know why that idea made me even more uneasy about the Rogs.

"Silas Rog said he didn't want to kill me—he wanted to defeat me," I told them. "He said it was about his reputation, but he's a liar. Almost everything he said was a trick or a lie."

Though I didn't want to say so aloud, Sera had a point. Rog could have had me killed any number of times, including that day on the bridge. He could have had his goons do it. He could have done it himself in the library. He'd trained that gun on me when it was working. In the end, after I'd destroyed his WiFi hub and Central Data, he was enraged enough to try. But it was too late by then.

"Why *wouldn't* they just kill me?" I wondered aloud.

"They must want something," Margot said. "What do you have?"

"Nothing!" I said. "I have nothing left. They took everything from me."

"Didn't take us," Norflo said. "Still got friends."

My eyes blurred. "Stop it," I said, wiping them. "I have to drive."

"You still have your sister," Sera added, her voice barely a whisper.

I nodded. I didn't really know if that was true. Not in the way I wanted it to be.

"I think I know what they wanted," Sera went on, straining to find a stronger volume.

"What?" I asked, working to take the edge out of my voice. She was sincerely trying to help.

"Your silence," she said.

"I was already silent."

"No. I mean, they wanted to take it from you. They wanted you to talk. They wanted you to break. I know *I* did. It was making me crazy."

"Why would they care? Why did *you* care?"

"It was so annoying," Sera said. I could hear her frustration, even now, and I had to laugh at how she put it.

"You think I annoyed them into all this?" I asked, waving a hand around the car like it was the world.

"I think Sera may be onto something," Margot said more gravely. "Maybe they feared the movement you created. The Silents."

"Must have," Norflo said.

"I didn't create them. They must realize that. I never even imagined people would copy me," I protested. "Do you remember that girl, Bridgette Pell, who zipped her lips and jumped to her death on her Last Day? I still don't understand why someone would take it to that extreme, especially someone so rich. I never intended for anyone to go silent after me."

"Don't tell Nancee that," Sera said.

"Whether you intended it or not, what else could they want from you but to end it?" Margot asked.

"I wouldn't even know how," I said. "Rog threatened to create a digital version of me to do it, though. Why didn't he?"

"Those never look right," Norflo said. "Even that fake Carol Amanda Harving never quite looked like your sister, right?"

That was true.

Ahead of us, a small decrepit road branched off to our right. Beyond that was another, and then a third. I slowed us to a crawl. The only light was a weak, diffuse glow from domes or factories like OiO™ nearby. I brought the car to a stop at one of the roads, peering up at what appeared to be a house.

"People lived out here," I marveled, shaking my head. "What happened?"

"The sun," Sera said.

"The sun is not so dangerous," Margot said. "There is more to this than they tell."

"How do *you* know?" Sera asked.

"Logic," Margot answered, which annoyed Sera. "They would not give up this space just because the sun burned skin. Think about it. People owned these things, these houses and what was in them. Then they gave them up?"

"Story never made sense," Norflo agreed, and that seemed to mollify Sera.

"Do you think they left their things behind?" I asked. Were these ruins filled with treasures?

"I am sure they have been picked clean," Margot said.

I turned carefully onto the small road and turned the headlights on briefly. They hit a house that looked like it had been smashed by a giant. Two walls had collapsed, and what remained of the shell was covered in the greenish fur of some plant I remembered seeing in a film once.

I turned the lights off again. "Moss," I said very quietly. The plant might have been the only thing holding the remains together.

"Should we rest here?" Henri asked.

We'd seen no sign of lights behind us, but if we were being pursued, they could have turned theirs off as easily as we had. I pulled the car back out onto the road.

"Not good enough for you?" Margot asked.

"Something that doesn't look like it will collapse if we breathe on it would be good," I said. "And I'd like to put as much distance between us and OiO™ as I can."

"What do you think happened?" Henri asked.

"These homes are very old, Henri," Margot answered. "They are not printed plastic. They are mostly wood, and wood decays."

I could see that she was right. "So why use it?"

"I do not believe they had other choices," Margot answered.

"What about bricks?" I asked. "And stone, and whatever metal the Eiffel™ Tower is made out of."

"I do not know, Speth," Margot said.

"'Spect wood's just cheap," Norflo answered. "We've been looking at dead trees for hours."

"I wonder who lived out here," I said.

"What do you mean, *who*?" Sera asked with an edge in her voice. "People."

"Were they rich? They had so much space." The homes around us were huge, and I saw no sign that they were Ad-subsidized.

"Prolly," Norflo said.

"But there are so many of them," I said.

We traveled several miles, passing dozens more driveways and crumbled homes beyond. Each of us kept looking back periodically to see if we were being followed, but if they'd put out their lights like we had, we wouldn't stand a chance of seeing them.

The road came to an end at a T-shaped intersection, which gave me some hope—left would bring us south. This road was also in better shape and appeared to have been cleared of downed trees. As we continued on, the darkness around us grew. We were far from the glow of any dome or the OiO™ factory. I was both glad and frightened to be so far from civilization.

The darkness also meant I had to turn on the headlights. With the lights on, a hot, angry red glowed from the back of Rog's Meiboch™—the rear lights, announcing us. I knew it would mark our location from far, far away.

"I think we should take the side roads," I said. "We'll be harder to follow, and maybe we can find someplace to rest." I could see the exhaustion on everyone's faces, and my very bones felt weary. I knew I'd need to take a break soon or risk falling asleep at the wheel.

I threaded our way through old, decrepit neighborhoods, awed by the way they just kept going without any boundaries. I quietly worried that we wouldn't find our way back, but what choice was there?

Eventually, Henri yelled for us to stop. He'd seen a house made of brick. I don't know how he saw this in the darkness, but Henri was apparently a tremendous spotter. I hadn't noticed this about him before we'd left Portland.

I pulled in and let the headlights illuminate the home. One

side had a tree growing out of it, peeling the roof off what I guessed was a garage. Even like this, it appeared in better shape than any of the other houses I'd seen so far.

I stopped the car and turned it off. When the lights went out, we were plunged into darkness. The distant light of some far-off dome made a pallid band near the horizon, blotted by the trees. Between anemic leaves and clouds, the sky was spotted with faint pinpricks of light—stars—and a pale, ominous trail that I took to be some factory's cloud.

"Can you turn the lights back on?" Sera whispered. Her voice was so small and petrified, I couldn't help but feel a little sorry for her.

Margot hesitated. "That will make us vulnerable."

"We aren't going to be able to look inside without them," I offered, and clicked them back to shining.

As we all got out, Mira yawned and stirred in the back seat. "Do you think there are bears?" she asked, looking into the blackness beyond the trees.

"No," I said, putting on an optimistic smile.

Mira stared at me. "I do not see how *you* know."

I scooted back into the car to sit beside her for a moment. "I know because bears don't live in this area. And…if they did, you would smell them."

"You would?" Mira asked. Margot cocked an eyebrow at me. "What do they smell like?"

"Bad," I said. "Like dumpster Wheatlock™. I've never smelled one myself, but I've watched a lot of animal shows." That part was true. Despite how uncommon it was to see actual animals, there were plenty of shows about them, some from long ago. They never said anything about where animals lived, though. I'd made that part up. I'd also made up the part about the smell. The only bears I had seen were trained for TV shows and supposed to be funny. I still found them terrifying, and I hoped Mira's fears were unfounded.

"They're huge, so they're also very loud," I added, which was as close to a fact as I could get. "You would definitely hear them coming."

The front door of the house was metal, made to look like wood, and it was locked. Henri tried it more times than he should have, turning the knob like actors did in old movies.

"I've got it," Henri said, pulling out his magnetic lock pick. He ran it over the door, and it stuck. Henri plucked it back. "The metal must interfere."

Norflo leaned down. "Looks mechanical."

"Kick it in," Sera said, like someone should have already thought of this.

Norflo and Henri exchanged a look and Henri gave the door a hard kick, expecting it to give easily. Instead, he propelled himself backward and landed on his butt. Sera furrowed her brow at him, but Margot did something I had never seen.

She started belly laughing. It wasn't the little Margot giggle I'd heard on occasion, or her soft, sarcastic snort. Actual tears came to her eyes, and she went practically hysterical at the sight of Henri on the ground.

"Oh, Henri!" she managed to say, extending him a hand and helping him to his feet.

"That door is strong," Henri said, shaking off the fall.

"I got it," Norflo said from a short distance away. He'd threaded his arm through a long-broken window nearby and found the window's latch. He raised it up. "One a' you nimble Placers want to climb in and open the door?"

APOLOGY: $24.99

The house had a dank smell that reminded me of a SippyBox™ of mushroom-flavored soup I once had for lunch. There was dusty furniture inside that I could barely make out in the scattered glare of the Meiboch™'s headlights.

"I wish we could see better," I said.

"When the sun comes up, we will have more light," Margot said.

"The sun?" Mira said, rubbing her eyes. She looked around, her mouth a frightened little O. "We are going to stay *here*?"

"Only for a bit," Margot assured her. I shared Mira's skepticism. A layer of dust coated everything. Now that we were walking around, kicking it up, each of us, in turn, sneezed.

I touched a small frame that hung off the wall at an odd angle. The thing dislodged and clattered to the ground.

"Don't touch anything!" Sera chastised me.

"Y'okay?" Norflo asked.

"Yes," I said, picking the frame up. I held it into the stark light streaming in from the car through the tattered, molding curtains. The picture was of a dog on a patch of grass in the sunshine. Everything was tinged gold. "They were definitely rich," I said. You couldn't own a dog—or any pet—if you didn't have loads of money. You had to put a special pet

Lawyer on retainer for the life of the animal. That was part of the Terms of Service.

"What are you hoping to find?" I asked Margot, who was staring at a recessed area, framed by bricks and blackened in the center, like there had been a small fire. She put her hand on a set of empty, dusty shelves. It probably once held books. Did the people who lived here take them? Or was the house picked clean in the long interval since?

"I have always wanted to see this," Margot said a little sadly. "Does this not make you wonder what happened?" she asked, pulling her hand away and leaving a handprint behind.

My whole body felt like it was full of questions. "I wish I understood. I knew there would be ruins out here, but…" I ran a finger through the dust. "I don't understand how it got to be like this. Did they sweep through the whole world and empty it of anything of value?"

"Sounds right," Norflo said.

"Maybe they had reverse Placers," Henri speculated.

"Is that a real thing?" Sera asked in a whisper.

"Aren't they just called thieves?" I asked.

"A lot of books were burned," Margot said, rubbing the dust between her fingers. "Father told me that."

Mira looked up at her. "He did?"

"Yes," Margot said.

Mira looked thoughtful until she saw me watching her. "He doesn't really talk to *me*," she muttered.

"It is too dark. I am going to adjust the lights," Margot said quickly, like it would cover up what her sister had just said. "Mira, come with me."

Mira followed Margot without looking back. The moment they were out the door, I turned to Henri.

"What was that all about?" I asked him.

Henri looked at the ground. "She's only going to get crankier without her violin," Henri said. "I told her to take it."

I was confused. "Why would you tell her that? We didn't know we were going to leave the dome."

"No, but I figured sooner or later the looters would get to her house. I figured it was safer to keep it in her Placer bag."

"What about her parents?" I asked.

The light from outside shifted. Pebbles crunched under the tires of the car as Margot moved it. Sera flinched and grabbed onto Norflo from behind.

"Can you…" I started. I closed my eyes. I tried again. "Sera, give people a little space, okay?"

Her head went up, on alert. "What am I doing?"

"You're fine," Norflo said to her.

"We're safe here," I tried to reassure Sera, though my jaw was tight.

"We aren't safe anywhere," she shot back.

Henri peeked out the window at Margot to gauge how long he had to talk. "Her parents… Her dad… He has a lot of rules. Like no contractions. And he isn't so nice to Mira."

"That's awful," Sera said, perching her chin on Norflo's shoulder.

My hands went up to my cheeks. They were hot, and I couldn't figure out why. I wasn't feeling jealous. It was something more complicated. Why should she get to voice an opinion about Margot's family?

The car door shut outside. I heard Mira giggle, oblivious to our conversation.

"Poor Mira. I'd rather have no father," Sera whispered.

Her comment ignited some kind of rage in me. I thought

of my dad and his haunted eyes. I thought of how all I wanted to do was reach my parents and put my family back together.

"That's an awful thing to say," I blurted out. "How can you betray your own father that way?"

"My father? I haven't seen my dad since I was eight! They split my parents up, Speth." Sera spit out my name like it was something foul in her mouth. "*Yours* got to stay together. You got to *talk* to them."

Margot came back in slowly, bewildered at Sera and me shouting at each other. Mira clutched her hand like the bears were inside now. I ignored her and advanced on Sera.

"You always act like your life is so much worse than everyone else's," I snapped. "You can stop pretending. Until it got inconvenient for you, you thought the whole system that took your parents away and gave you Mrs. Harris was just a-okay!"

"What the hell, Speth?" Sera said, stepping away from Norflo. His eyes were filled with disappointment.

"You wanted to *be* one of them. A guardian," I spit. "One of *them*," I said to the group. "She wanted to be one of *them*!"

Norflo watched me sadly. Sera's face crumpled into the most wretched expression of despair I'd ever seen.

"What else could I be?" she said with a violent sob. She held out her skinny arms like broken bird's wings. "A Placer?"

I opened my mouth, but couldn't find anything to say. I don't think I'd truly appreciated how lucky I was to have been found by the Placers until that moment.

"Your sister," Sera choked out. "She had that job with Mrs. Nince. She looked famous. She had *everything*, and you had her. And Sam."

At the sound of Sam's name, my heart blazed with fury

again. I sputtered, but before I could form a full word, Norflo reached out and grabbed both our hands.

"Stop," he said. "*This* is what they do."

"Who?" Sera bawled.

"They split us apart," Norflo went on. "Make us do what we don't want. Take, give nothing and plan to keep on until they take *us*. Literally take *us* away," he said, shaking our hands like he could pull some reason out of the two of us. His hand, I realized, was trembling. "They don't want us to rely on each other, 'cause then we won't have to rely on *them*."

I heaved a great breath. What use was my anger? Sera hadn't been the cause of anything. She was caught up like I was—like we all were.

"I'm sorry," I said, feeling the full extent of how exhausted I was.

Sera narrowed her eyes and then closed them. "Sorry for what?" she asked. The simple words weren't enough for her.

"I'm so angry about what they did, and I've taken it out on you. It wasn't right. They took both our families from us, Sera. I'm sorry. I'm so sorry." I turned to Henri. "And I wasn't fair to you. I've wanted to tell you for so long. I'm sorry I used you that night. And, Margot..."

Margot shook her head, mutely begging me to stop.

"I'm sorry," I said again, tears welling in my eyes. I was saying it to each of them, but also to Sam. I would never fully forgive myself for not doing everything I could to save him.

"I accept your apology," Sera said with a deep, proud breath. Then she wandered quickly away, like that had been her plan all along.

ARCHAEOLOGY: $25.99

Henri sprawled himself awkwardly across the front seat of the Meiboch™. Mira and Margot curled up in back. We moved the car right up to the front door and covered it with a ragged blue tarp we'd found to keep out the sun—and any bears, we told Mira.

Norflo swept out some space in a bedroom near an old bed too collapsed and gross to sleep on. Sera and I slept downstairs curled up on top of Placer bags and spare clothes. It was not a comfortable night. Whatever else you could say about modern times, the Swailert™ foam mattress I'd grown up sleeping on was very comfortable.

During the night, Sera rolled close and curled up against me. I let her be. It was cold, and her body was warm. It was a comforting reminder of how Saretha and I had often slept—at least before everything went wrong.

I wasn't awake when morning dawned. Somehow I managed to sleep until a bright, filtered light filled the room. I'd never seen such intensity, and my eyes could barely accept it.

Henri, Norflo and Margot were already up, sitting in the other room, carefully picking through a box Norflo had found in a room *under* the ground. The box itself was stained and barely holding together. It was filled with thin, water-damaged books full of pictures. They were warped, flaking and faded. A black smudgy mold made many of them hard to read.

A lot of the books had the same title with different dates and pictures. The one Margot said to pay attention to was a book called *TIME*, which mostly had people's faces looking out. One had a black cover—not from mold, but because it was printed that way. It was rimmed in a faded red ink. The word *TIME* was written on the top and beneath it, in the same red against the black, were the words *Is Truth Dead?*

"What are these books about?" I asked.

"Lots," Norflo said. His eyes were glued to the page he was reading.

"It's hard to follow," Henri said, flashing me a smile before returning to his own reading. Sadness welled up in me. My argument with Sera had left me feeling emotional and full of regret. But Henri still believed in me, even after what I'd done. I think he'd accepted my apology long before I made it—maybe even before we spoke in the Squelch back in Keene.

"I do not think they are books," Margot said. "They all have the word *magazine* on them. I think it is a different thing." She turned and picked up one she had saved. "Look at this." She opened to a specific page. Large black letters read: Bikram Choudhury Can't Copyright His Yoga Poses.

"That was in 2015?" I asked, glancing at the cover.

"Yes. I do not think words were Copyrighted then, either," Margot said, looking at the picture of Bikram sitting cross-legged and shirtless.

"No, they were," Henri said, pointing to a notice on an inside page that said All Rights Reserved. "But look at this."

He held up a map similar to the one I had tried to memorize back at the real estate agency, but the borders were completely different.

"There's no Vermaine," I remarked absently. In the same general area were three states: Vermont, New Hampshire and Maine. It was like they merged Vermont and Maine and got rid of New Hampshire entirely.

"Check this," Norflo said, handing a magazine over to me. It was called *Cos*-something-*tan*. I couldn't fully read it because there was a thin, busty woman on the cover whose gorgeous wavy hair covered most of the title. Her skin was the same shade as mine—the same shade as most of us in the Onzième—but flawless and with a sheen that was obviously fake, like the computer-generated version of Saretha. Just under the blocked title was a red banner with the words *for Latinas*, like it was part of some marketing campaign.

My heart began pounding a little.

"See?" Norflo said as I began flipping through the pages. The magazine was full of Ads. The only real difference I saw was models with dark hair, dark eyes and skin like mine.

One Ad really struck me. A family held hands at the rim of a hill, smiling for the camera. It looked a little like our family, with two parents and three kids. It was trying to make me feel something about retirement savings, but that wasn't the effect. It made me think about how we were going to free my parents and then escape all of this. Soon, I hoped, we would all be together somewhere.

An odd warmth flooded my chest looking up from my magazine to the others. Wasn't this a family, too? Norflo seemed pleased with my reaction. Behind him, Henri flashed me another smile. When I had pretended I wanted Henri to kiss me, I didn't have time to consider how I actually felt about him. But now I knew: I loved him like a brother. I wanted him to be happy. I wanted him and Margot to be happy together, even if their relationship was a little strange. I didn't know if I would ever be able to explain it out loud, but I longed for the day I could try.

No wonder words cost so much. They were so precious.

Sera put her chin on my shoulder and looked at the Ad with me. I felt the urge to remind her she'd insisted she wasn't Latino, but there was a power in knowing when to be silent and when to speak.

"They marketed to us," Norflo said. "Thought we were important enough that they made one of these magazines just for *us*. Whoever lived in this house was probably Latino." Norflo gestured around in wonder. "That has to matter. What came before *has* to matter. They tried to hide our history, Jiménez, but it isn't gone. We can't let it be gone."

I felt myself stirring at his words. I was suddenly so grateful he could speak to me, unrestricted, without having to limit himself to what he could eke out on a Word$ Market™ screen.

"How do we get it back?" I asked.

Norflo held up a few of the magazines. "These have history. They just wrote it *as* history happened."

"They assume the reader knows what came before—which we do not," Margot sighed. "And the poor fools had no idea what was coming."

"Which we do," Henri said, elbowing her.

"Yes, Henri."

"There's nothing after 2026," Henri said, showing me a cover with an image made up of hundreds of *other* covers. The words *Our Final Print Issue* were emblazoned across the top in bold letters.

Being together like this, looking over forbidden material, was comforting to me, yet just feeling that comfort made me uneasy. It couldn't last. We had a long way to go, and I wanted to get there. The warm feeling in my chest had cooled, and I could feel myself buzzing with an urge to move.

"Could we pack these in the car and go?" I asked. "You could read them while I drive."

I also wasn't sure we should be breathing the air this house provided, and the sunlight unnerved me, even if it wasn't direct. The car seemed safer. Silas Rog would have been sure it was secure against daylight, or anything else that might harm him. If I knew anything about the Rogs, it was that they always took care of themselves.

Margot frowned at me. "We could," she said, sniffing a mold-covered magazine before tossing it aside. She neatened up her save pile and put the good ones in the box.

I rolled up our things and packed our bags back up. There was a cheeping sound outside: birds. I'd heard birds in Portland before the dropters got them, but never in a group. They never lived long enough to gather, but there were dozens of them outside this house. The noise of them grew louder.

Margot froze in the doorway, box in hand. She backed up.

"Run," she said to Mira, and then to all of us. "Run!"

She dropped the box and took off, grabbing Mira's hand. Henri straightened up, perplexed. His fingers slipped from his box as he stood. Margot shooed Mira out an open window in the back and jumped out after her, calling, "Henri!"

My brain tried to catch up. What was out there? Why was Margot running?

"Speth Jime, you are hereby commanded to surrender," a man's voice called out, amplified by a bullhorn.

My blood ran cold at the sound of that voice. Norflo pulled at my arm, but I felt frozen in place. Sera watched us, looking furious.

"Speth," Henri said. He and Norflo started to drag me toward the back window.

"They just want me," I said, struggling against them. "You need to go! They won't kill me."

"You don't know that!" Norflo exclaimed.

"They're coming," Henri said. I couldn't see what was happening.

"They don't care about you," I said, pushing Norflo away.

"Go," Henri said to him. "Help Mira and Margot. They can't kill me, either. I'm Indentured. I'm worth too much."

Norflo took off. Sera followed, then paused in the window. I shooed her off and raced to the door. There were police cars and men advancing. Lawyers. And they were wearing masks, which meant there would be sleep gas, too.

"Don't kill the girl," a voice instructed. Lucretia Rog. It came from a dropter. How did they get a dropter out here without the WiFi? My heartbeat pounded in my ears as the police officers held out their Cuffs. There was a loud popping sound.

"Oh," Henri gasped from beside me. He fell to the ground, red spreading around him. My eyes went misty as I reached out for him. There was a gurgling breath, and I couldn't tell if it was mine or his. Suits and armor and dropters all blurred and dimmed. Far off in the distance, I heard Sera screaming.

Someone yanked on my arm, but I just wanted to sleep. I wanted to dream this wasn't real.

Then there was nothing.

AGREE

I half woke to a dim and shapeless world. I couldn't raise my arm, but I knew I was supposed to. Why was I supposed to?

Someone lifted my arm for me.

"Tap AGREE," a voice demanded, like it wasn't the first request.

I tried. I pushed my finger through the fog toward the little word. AGREE. It blurred in my vision. Each breath I took was shallow.

I closed my eyes. Every fiber of my being just wanted to sleep more.

Someone prodded my face—one cheek, then the other.

"She is real, dear, I promise," a woman's hollow voice said. *"Let the Lawyers do their work."*

Another voice sounded.

"Article VII B: You further agree to use your weekly allotment of words solely in response to questions from *the Owner* or in service to *the Owner* for the good faith administration of her bidding, orders, whims, suggestions and requests. Failure to do so will result in penalty or punishments as laid out in Article VII B, Section I-XXI at the sole discretion and pleasure of *the Owner.*"

I struggled to comprehend. Had I already agreed to something?

The Lawyer scrolled through a long list in tiny print and showed it to me—as if I could read it. Of course I couldn't. I could barely focus my eyes.

Then the room pitched over and the floor slammed into the side of my skull.

"Pick her up," the woman's voice said. Pain roused me, replacing grogginess with a growing panic. I didn't know where I was or what had happened, but I knew the voice: Lucretia Rog.

"Tap AGREE," the Lawyer insisted, lifting me up roughly. I recognized him, too. Grippe. His face was placid, but a muscle twitched in his jaw. Had he beaten Finster when I left them on that overpass? I noted vaguely that there was a bowl of walnuts in front of him. An Affluent's snack.

Where did he want me to tap? Someone behind me lifted one of my arms to the other. With horror, I saw a new Cuff had been secured around my forearm. I'd been tapping at a new Cuff. This one felt tighter than the one Mrs. Harris had clamped onto my arm on my fifteenth birthday. I could feel the pressure in my tendons, and my skin was red around the edges. I pried at it weakly, but it didn't budge.

I tapped AGREE. I don't know why. I wanted to resist, but it was as if my will had been sapped from me. My arms felt like they were a puppet's, not my own. Or was someone still holding them up?

Thick hands pressed down on my shoulders. I closed my eyes. If I slept, none of this would be real.

A hard slap woke me.

Grippe looked deeply pleased with himself. He had a new black medal on his chest, above the compact arrangement I had seen before. He snapped his fingers, and his bodyguard cracked a walnut open for him from the bowl.

"You agree and understand that payment for any and all words you speak is your responsibility, irrespective of your service to *the Owner,* that additional debt incurred by speaking will be held in escrow by *the Owner* and that as an Indentured Servant to *the Owner,* you are entitled to no compensation or remuneration of any kind, at any time, here, elsewhere, now and in perpetuity. Tap AGREE."

The Owner. That meant something bad. Grippe took the walnut and ate it without pleasure. I wondered where it came from. One of the gray domes, most likely.

A bony ParaLegal took notes on a Pad to my left. Off to my right, in front of a bright window, was a girl about my age who stood mutely, staring at me. In the distance beyond her, out the window, were buildings made from real stone and a towering white obelisk with Ads crawling up and down the sides.

The Washington Monument. I was in the Dome of DC.

Lucretia's voice demanded, *"Speak it."*

"Speak ***'agree,'***" Grippe echoed as a warning.

No, I thought. Everyone stared at me. I couldn't see Lucretia anywhere—there was just the girl, Grippe, a couple of bodyguards, the ParaLegal and an older, stocky woman, who was watching everything with concern. Grippe cocked back his arm to slap me again, but Lucretia called his name.

"No one asked you to beat her." Lucretia wasn't in the room. Her voice was being piped in. Maybe she was still in Portland. *"Speak* ***'agree.'*** *There isn't any point in being silent now. You've already spoken, Speth,"* she pointed out. *"We know."*

If she wanted me to speak, I would refuse. Whatever she wanted, I wouldn't give it to her.

I tried to recall what had happened. They'd come for us. They'd used sleep gas. My heart seized, remembering Henri. There had been blood. Had I really seen that? What had they done with him? They couldn't kill him. I had to remember that. His owner would sue. It upset me that he was owned, but at least his Indentured status protected him. I prayed his father's sick plan would protect him now.

My breathing went shallow and scared as a small voice called out to me. There was something at the window—someone. Someone was out there, calling for my help. Mira? No. I couldn't look. This wasn't possible. My head was foggy; I couldn't be hearing correctly.

It sounded like Sam's voice.

Silas Rog had done this to me before—he'd created a fake digital projection right through my ocular implants to make it look like my brother was still alive. But he wasn't. Sam was dead. Murdered. These people thought of his death as nothing more than an instrument to torment me.

I turned my head slowly toward the window. My little brother stood there, a terrified expression on his face. "Help me!" Sam cried. Then he fell, slipping away from the window… falling backward over the rail in Falxo Park. I didn't know how high up we were. My heart broke all over again, even though I knew this Sam wasn't real.

Sam's body hit the table in front of me with a hard slam. His eyes were open and unseeing, lifeless in his blank cherubic face.

"Is this what you want to live with?" Lucretia's disturbingly pleasant voice asked. It felt like it was in my head this time, but that was impossible. Wasn't it?

My ears ached with the echo of her voice. I put a hand up and felt an odd, sore bump just below each ear.

"We've provided auditory implants for your convenience," Grippe said, pleased. "So Mrs. Rog can provide instruction at any time."

What had they done to me?

Grippe clicked his tongue impatiently. The girl put a hand up under each of her ears like she'd had the same thing done—or at least sympathized with me. I couldn't see any bumps on her neck from where I sat.

"Auditory implants brought to you by KochEar™. KochEar™, for the best in hands-free internal messaging systems," the ParaLegal recited, placing a small branded box in front of me so I could see it.

"Their cost has been added to your debt," Grippe remarked with a smile.

My Cuff buzzed as proof—$13,999 to invade and mutilate my body. I hated the way it vibrated, like it was breaking down the veins in my arm.

"You could have said anything to save me," Sam whispered, suddenly inches from my face. He didn't look quite right. They couldn't create Sam. They could reproduce the contours of his face, but the thing pretending to be him was empty.

"Agree, Speth," Lucretia said softly in my head.

She didn't understand what she was revealing. My friends had to be okay. If they weren't, she'd be using them instead of this sad, fake Sam to torture me. *They must have gotten away,* I told myself, though I couldn't imagine how. Where could they go? I wanted to believe they'd escaped, but the uncertainty nagged at me.

Sam's image vanished. In his place, patterns exploded in

my vision. Thousands of close-set zigzagging lines spun and wove themselves into impossible patterns, diverging in each eye until I felt like my skull would split. At the same time, both my ears filled with blaring, high-pitched tones. I wheeled forward, scarcely aware I was doing it, and smashed face-first into the table. I fell back onto the floor, nauseated. The bodyguard lifted me like a rag doll and dropped me back in the chair.

Then it all stopped. Even Grippe's placid, cruel smile and sharp, disdainful eyes were a welcome sight.

"Punishment III of Article VII B," he said. He straightened his legal Pad, scrolled to where he wanted to be and turned it back to me.

"You agree and understand that payment for any and all words you speak is your responsibility, etcetera, etcetera," he said, waving his hand over the document. "Speak ***'agree.'***"

For half a second, the pattern flashed and the tone rang my ears again. A warning.

"Speak ***'agree,'****"* Lucretia said with a sigh. The girl watched me intently. She seemed out of place here. I didn't understand her role. Was she a servant? Another ParaLegal? She wasn't dressed like one.

I leaned forward, dizzy and sick. The pattern flashed again and held this time. The sound blared like a thunderous horn. The waving patterns crushed at my skull, unrelenting, cutting me off from any sign of the outside world. Minutes passed—maybe hours. My brain seemed to pull apart. My thoughts shattered. I felt my eyes roll back and my spine arch to its limits. My body shook and banged into some hard surface I couldn't see. Then the agony ceased.

"Oh, you poor creature, there will be nothing left of you if you don't

speak," Lucretia warned. *"I should very much like to make some use of you, but if I must go on like this, you will be driven quite mad."*

I was on the floor. A bodyguard and the bony ParaLegal stood over me. Grippe stayed in his seat and had another walnut cracked for him from the bowl. It was too showy. They were trying to demonstrate their power. They wanted to break me. That was the message. Stars swam in my vision—ugly green, sputtering stars, nothing like the ones I'd seen in the sky. I hated them all, and yet my body was grateful to see them because it meant I could see.

Grippe bent down to me and held the Pad out like a waiter. The girl by the window walked away rapidly, like she couldn't watch anymore.

I tried to think of something devastating to say to all of them. I tried to find a single word, but my body convulsed instead. *Don't give in*, my inner voice whispered, deeper, beyond Lucretia's own. I needed to remember the difference. I needed to keep myself whole.

The sharp pain slowly receded, like an echo through my bones. I blinked and cleared my eyes as phantoms of the patterns twirled through my vision. The dazzling pain in my skull ripped into the places where thoughts formed.

"Speth." Lucretia's soothing voice sounded inside my head. My mind took comfort from it and clung to the lilting sound in spite of myself. My shoulders slumped. My hands unfurled. *"Agree,"* she said again, like it would help me.

I didn't know if I could withstand another assault, and my brain could only focus on the one word I knew would keep it at bay. I wouldn't speak it, but I had to do something.

I raised my Cuff up. With a shuddering, clumsy finger, I gave in and tapped AGREE.

VICTORIA: $27.99

I was finally allowed to sleep, and the relief was acute. I pushed everyone and everything from my mind, letting my body fall into the bed, pulled and flattened by gravity. My bones sank into muscle. My muscles twitched in the places I was most sore. My eyes and ears ached. My skull felt like it had come apart at the seams inside me.

There were other girls crammed in this small room with me. Three or four—but not the one who had watched me with Grippe. Someone snored, and I followed the sound as she sputtered air in and smoothly breathed it out. I began to breathe along with her, and then I was gone again.

I woke later with a start to find someone hovering over me. The old woman I'd seen in Grippe's office earlier hissed at me in three angry, short bursts without using any words. The Cuff on her arm buzzed at her for it. I looked to see what the sound was called. She tapped, pointed and flicked the charge from her Cuff to mine to make it easier.

Mrs. Andromeda Milnsk transfers the following charge:
Andromeda Milnsk—communication (Wake Hiss x 3): $8.97

I'd never heard of a "Wake Hiss." Below this, I had the choice to tap AGREE or DECLINE. My mouth drew tight.

My head throbbed from the base of my neck. I fell back and closed my eyes. Andromeda hissed at me again.

I opened my eyes reluctantly and stared at her. She gnashed her teeth and flicked at the Cuff for show. I sat back up, but I didn't tap AGREE. Her ruddy face turned ruddier.

She pulled the charge back and bit her lip. She looked down at her Cuff and then back at me. Under her arm, she had a bundle of clothes. She threw them at me and stared. I stared back, my mind half-blank, suppressing the panic brewing as I wondered what might have happened to my friends.

"How much do you want to cost me?" Andromeda whispered at last. Her Cuff buzzed with each word.

"You're to obey," a voice from the next bed said, half-asleep and devoid of emotion. I heard the soft buzz of her Cuff, too.

I gathered the clothes up into my arms. Where was I meant to change? Andromeda's face turned back to what might have been its normal pink. She strode across the room and opened a door to reveal a cramped toilet. It was clear what to do.

I changed into the outfit—a thick woolen charcoal-gray dress with bleached white sleeves. When I emerged, Andromeda waited for me, her eyes blazing. She wasn't the friendliest person I'd ever met, but I felt sorry for her. I was certain that she and the other girls in the room were all Indentured. A few stray spots swam in my eyes, reminding me what awaited my disobedience. They must have suffered the same.

Andromeda turned for the door and gestured briskly for me to follow. Her Cuff buzzed with that charge, too. I moved slowly, thinking of my friends. What had happened to Henri? Did the others escape? Then I thought of Saretha, and more guilt constricted my chest. I should have thought of her first.

She was family. And my parents. It wasn't likely I would ever see any of them again.

My only hope, in the very back of my mind, was that I was in DC and that somewhere out there Kiely Winston was waiting. But what could she do?

Andromeda halted in the door and looked back. I was taking too long. It was making her nervous and angry.

"Do what Mrs. Rog says and maybe things won't get worse," she whispered, swallowing hard. Things were obviously very bad. Her face was still angry, but I thought I saw kindness in her eyes. I studied her and tried to return that kindness without speaking. She wasn't an enemy. We were trapped together.

Maybe I needed to obey, but I wouldn't. I would fight, even in silence, until the end.

I followed Andromeda straight to a bright wood-paneled office where Lucretia sat behind a humble desk, sipping tea from a bone china cup. She smirked, as if I amused her. Servants scrambled out of the way and fled the room as I entered. Two troublingly large men with monstrous jaws stood on either side of her, utterly still in slightly iridescent indigo suits. The girl I'd seen before was sitting in a chair in the corner of the room, head down at first, but she raised it to watch me when I entered. Beside her was a large bowl of fruit on a side table, more showy than practical. Oranges, grapes, plums and apples all came from different farms and orchards, reminding me of the multitudes of people Indentured like my parents so the very wealthy could enjoy eating real, fresh food. I was surprised the girl was allowed so close to them.

"Please do sit," Lucretia said, like I was a special guest. Her eyes flicked from Andromeda to me. "She made you speak, Andromeda?"

Andromeda said nothing. I did not sit.

"You can tell me. I will pay for the answer." Lucretia's fingers danced elegantly over her Cuff.

"She did, ma'am," Andromeda said quietly, looking at the ground.

"She's made you *speak*." Lucretia looked at the girl sitting by the fruit, then crossed to the front of her desk and leaned against it, casually crossing her arms.

"Eyes front," she commanded me. When I hesitated, she tapped her Cuff, and a quick jolt shook me.

I obeyed. I stared straight ahead, which put a picture on the wall directly in my view. In it, Lucretia Rog was standing in front of the United States Supreme Court® with two men. She was on the right, and I assumed Silas Rog was on the left. His face was blocked in my vision, as it had always been, save for the night I destroyed the WiFi.

The one comfort I had in this situation was that Silas Rog must still be in police custody—otherwise he would surely be the one torturing me.

In between them was a robed Judge, his eyes obscured by an elegant judicial visor, the kind they say is linked directly to the brain so Judges can instantly access Central Data. Lucretia was smiling, but the Judge's mouth was placid—perhaps he didn't want to be there? Or maybe being a Judge stripped away your emotions, leaving only the Law behind.

A small American® flag was pinned to his lapel. Other robed Justices stood behind the trio, lining either side of the stairs, all visored and blank-faced, too. The portrait was obviously meant to demonstrate Lucretia had power and connections. She wanted people to see it, to be intimidated by it.

"Do you like being silent?" Lucretia asked abruptly, pushing away from her desk and leaning close to stare into my eyes. There was a subtle menace to the question—it was like something Mrs. Harris would ask, but her voice was as light and airy as if she were asking whether I liked Ice-Kreem™.

Her two bodyguards had stiffened as she approached me. They both had watery eyes, as if staring menacingly off into space itched them. The two men had the same slightly off look as the brothers who'd murdered Sam and the bodyguards Grippe and Finster employed. It was like the muscles of their bodies—and even their faces—weren't natural. They were much harder and larger than normal.

There was something very strange about Lucretia Rog, too—something deeply, troublingly appealing. I was finding it hard to hate her. She seemed so innocent and open. For a moment, I felt like *I* was the problem—a troublemaking friend she was about to set right. But her face moved in a rubbery way, as if it had been shaped and filled with things that weren't quite human. It wasn't real, and I wasn't sure if it was because of some kind of surgery she'd had, or if she was feeding me an enhanced visual of herself.

The only thing I knew for sure was that I couldn't trust her.

"I suppose you know what you've done. Such terrible damage. And I can't even help because you've shut everything down. Even the Healthspital™."

She paused and clucked her tongue. The girl by the fruit bowl jumped slightly at the sound. I noticed she wasn't wearing a gray outfit like mine or Andromeda's. Instead, she wore a skirt and a public domain T-shirt.

"Where will people go with broken limbs?" Lucretia wondered aloud, leaning her chin on her hand in mock consternation. I tried to keep myself from reacting. How much of the city had she claimed back? Had she gotten to Saretha?

As if reading my mind, Lucretia said slyly, "If you'd like to ask me about your sister, I will be happy to tell you how she's doing."

I didn't want to believe that she knew anything about Saretha. Even if she did, it was doubtful she would tell me the truth. I had to believe Kel had protected Saretha—she'd promised me that.

I suddenly realized that Kel's message was gone from my eyes. It was no longer running just out of my vision. We were in the WiFi, so it should have been there, but Lucretia must have detected it and blocked it. Or maybe Kel had knocked the WiFi out wherever she was.

Or maybe she had stopped sending it. Maybe she had been captured, just like me.

"You can ask me about any of your friends," Lucretia offered. She glanced at the seated girl and crooked a finger. The girl stood and shuffled over to us, her mouth pulled to the side. She rolled a grape between her fingers nervously, with no apparent intention of eating it.

"Don't do that," Lucretia chastised. Then she turned back to me. "You can stop looking around," she said, noticing my eyes scanning the room. "There is no way for you to escape."

I suspected that she misunderstood why I was calculating. Apparently she shared Silas Rog's arrogance. I filed that away as a weakness to exploit. *That* was what I was looking for—weaknesses.

"We're thirty stories up if you think that balcony door is an exit for you," Lucretia added. The girl's eyes darted toward the door as well before she returned her gaze to the floor.

Lucretia put a hand in front of the girl to hold her back and breathed in deeply before continuing. "Perhaps you are confused, Speth. I expect your obedience, not your silence."

My mouth grew tight, holding back all the things I wanted to say to her.

"Oh, this trick," she said. "It's your favorite one. Silence. I know some Lawyers who would argue that the way *you* do it is communication." Then, a little quieter, with a giggle, like she had a silly little secret, she said, "I tried to Trademark that mouth scrunch of yours myself."

She slapped her thighs and found her way back to her seat. "Maybe I could find some way to encourage you? Andromeda, where are her friends?"

My body immediately reacted to the question, twitching at the shoulders, like part of me might be able to reach out and find them. Andromeda looked up from the floor to me, and her face turned ruddier. My heart started thumping away against my ribs.

"*Both* of them?" Andromeda asked, her gaze uncomfortably shifting between Lucretia and me.

"Both of them." Lucretia's lips tightened with disapproval.

What did that mean? Had someone else been captured? Had only two of my friends survived? I tried to find hope in that idea.

"Very clever." Lucretia's face went pouty again, and she tapped at her sleek, glimmering Cuff.

Andromeda dropped to the ground, withholding her scream in a way that told me she'd done it many times. I could hear an almost imperceptible tone from her head, like tiny speakers played too loudly. I knew it was agony.

"Would you like it to stop?" Lucretia asked me. "Just say the word."

The girl now moved over to Lucretia, her eyes wide with horror.

"She's very disciplined," Lucretia explained, watching the woman convulse on the floor. "But it won't do for her to pass you information like this. *Both* of them," she muttered.

The girl put a hand on Lucretia's shoulder and, shockingly, Lucretia allowed it. The bodyguards didn't move, either. Lucretia put her hand on the girl's in return. I thought she might try to break it, but she just held on tenderly for a moment and then let go.

"Oh, all right," she said, tapping her Cuff and releasing Andromeda from her anguish. The girl hurried over to Andromeda and helped her to her feet. The grape was gone from her hand.

"If you won't talk to me, talk to her," Lucretia said to me, gesturing to the girl.

The girl's mouth sealed tight as she turned to me. She put a shaking thumb and finger to the corner of her mouth, but Andromeda grabbed her before she could make the sign of the zippered lips.

"No!" Lucretia barked. "Victoria Grace!"

I waited for Lucretia to send the girl into shocks on the floor, or worse, but she didn't. She only sighed and indicated to Andromeda that Victoria should be escorted away.

In the quiet that followed, Lucretia sat silent—not angry, as I would have expected. Instead, under her digital enhancements and makeup, she looked heartbroken. The girl was obviously important to her, but why?

DON'T WORRY: $28.98

For the next several days, I was forced to clean and do menial chores in the Rogs' DC home. I was punished when I was too slow, or if I didn't perform my tasks to Lucretia's satisfaction. Or, sometimes, when she was just feeling cruel. Then hours would go by, and she would completely ignore me. The girl, Victoria, was nowhere to be seen, but I held the memory of her in my mind. She'd attempted to make the sign of the zippered lips. I tried to figure out what that might mean. Was she an ally? A fellow prisoner? Why did Lucretia Rog put her hand on the girl's with affection? The best theory I could come up with was that Victoria was somehow her favorite servant, but it was hard to imagine someone as horrible as Lucretia Rog forming any kind of attachment.

Every evening, I had to scrape away real vegetables and fruits and meats from plates and dump that food in the trash. It accumulated into heavy bags I carried to a bin that would crush and dissolve the leavings into a goo, which one of the servants said would be made into printer inks. The idea nauseated me. My entire life, nearly everything I'd eaten was literally leftover garbage discarded by people like the Rogs.

A week into my Indenture, I stood at a sink filled with soapy water and rubbed dishes clean with a rough yellow thing Andromeda said wasn't printed, but was the dead body of a creature called a sponge.

"It lives in the sea," she said. I don't know why she'd wasted words telling me about it. It did not help me go faster or clean better. When I slowed at one point and examined the thing, I was punished with a full minute of brain-melting patterns and screaming tones. When it was done, I found I wasn't alone on the floor.

Andromeda stood, looking chagrined. "Mrs. Rog wants you to know we will be punished for even the smallest infraction from now on," she reported, wiping the tears from her eye and keeping her voice businesslike. I wasn't sure how this was different from what she had been doing since I arrived, but it was obviously a signal that things were about to get worse.

"Unless you are ready to speak to Victoria," Andromeda added. Why did Lucretia want me to speak so badly? And to Victoria in particular? I wanted to ask Andromeda who the girl was, but the moment I spoke, I'd be charged—and I was certain Lucretia would be alerted. I didn't want her to know what I was thinking. My silence was the only leverage I had.

Other servants brought more dishes back for me to clean. None of them looked me in the eye. I didn't know where the dishes were coming from—everyone entered from a door opposite where I'd come in, and I couldn't see anything beyond the hall they wandered in from, but I could hear the chatter of a party. People were speaking freely because they could afford to say as much as they wanted.

I'd never washed dishes before my Indenture. My family didn't have any. We had no place to keep them. My mother always said a print of Wheatlock™ tastes the same on a plate or from a chunk in your hand.

By the number of plates coming in, I could have been fooled into thinking there were dozens of people dining with her, but they were different sizes and designs, and the matching smudges and crumbs on certain sets led me to determine six people were eating. I kept my mind busy working out the logic of it. I didn't know if this information was of any use to me, but I steeled myself against Lucretia's petty tortures and vowed to use any information I could to escape.

"You're going too slow," Andromeda warned me. Her sole job seemed to be fretting over my work.

We both knew this job made no sense. There was a silver machine on the opposite side of the room labeled CleerCleen™ Dishwasher. So I put down the sponge and stopped doing it. Andromeda stared at me like I'd lost my mind.

"Please don't disobey," Andromeda begged.

I waited for the sound and patterns. They didn't come. Instead, there was a sharp jab in my arm, just at the rim of my Cuff. My arm spasmed, and I shattered a plate against the side of the sink. Andromeda looked at me, aghast. My Cuff buzzed.

I let go of the shard of plate left in my hand. Small triangles of porcelain had scattered across the counter and floor and into the sink. My finger was bleeding at the knuckle, cut in the confusion. I sucked at it, tongued a small piece of grit and spit it out. I didn't feel right, but it wasn't something to worry about.

I examined my arm, pulling at the skin where I'd felt the short stab. The skin had gone pink, with a single dot in the center. My eyes had trouble focusing on it. I felt weak and limp, but oddly untroubled. It didn't matter. None of it mattered. I started to pick up the broken pieces, my mind falling curiously blank. Andromeda paced behind me, worrying at her own Cuff, like something might happen to her, too.

I took a deep breath. I raised my arm and slammed it, Cuff first, as hard as I could against the sink. It bounced off, unharmed. I found myself smiling. This was fun, satisfying and terrible. I was grinning and weeping at the same time.

"You have to finish those dishes," Andromeda whispered to me, taking me by the shoulders and pointing me at the task.

I picked up a delicate fluted glass. I slid two soapy fingers along its long neck until they squeaked. It reminded me of something. It was so delicate—I had to be careful not to snap it.

"Don't worry," I said. I meant it, but my brow furrowed, like it didn't agree with the words coming from my mouth. I giggled at that. My brow was being ridiculous. *Don't furrow,* I thought. My Cuff buzzed with the charge.

"You may always look at your charges," Mrs. Harris's voice rang in my head—not broadcasted, but a memory from long ago. "A responsible consumer monitors expenses. You are paying not only for each of your words, but for their administration and display. How else could you be grateful for any discounts you receive?"

Did I have reason to be grateful?

Speth Jime—phrase (Don't Worry): $27.99
Zockroft™ applicative discount: $3.00
Total: $24.99

Zockroft™? My brow furrowed again, and my eyes crinkled up, like I might smile or cry. I looked at my arm again—at the tiny pinprick there. *It's fine*, I told myself, but some coal of anger and fear stayed lit within me. My Cuff buzzed with a new message.

Keene Inc. officially notifies you that you are formally in violation of your Terms of Service with us, which required the recitation of a mutually agreed upon speech [exhibit 1A] as your first adult communication. A fine of $428,559.61 will be added to your debt, as well as a $1,769.44 convenience fee for this notification and a $4,037.00 remittance fee. Keene Inc. reminds you to have a nice day.

With rising horror, I realized I'd just done the unthinkable. I'd just done what the Rogs had wanted—the thing I'd worked so hard to avoid since my Last Day. I'd spoken my first *paid* words.

"Andromeda!" Lucretia cried out jubilantly over a loudspeaker. "Bring the Jime girl to me," she ordered, her voice full of excitement. "Bring her to me now!"

Andromeda's Cuff pinged with a bonus. $10,000. She didn't look happy about it, though. She took me by the arm and gently led me away.

FAMILY LINE: $29.98

"Bertrand," Lucretia called. One of the bodyguards moved to the door that led to her balcony and opened it. "Uthondo," she said to the other.

"You're a mess," she noted.

Of course I am, I thought. I had cleaned silently for days, plotting and evaluating every door and window for a possible escape route. I had even wondered if I could smuggle myself out in a drum of the sludge sent off to make printer inks, but I couldn't figure out how I would breathe. On top of it all, I'd just been drugged with Zockroft™. What did she expect?

Andromeda tried to smooth me out, petting my hair, but a steely look from Lucretia stopped her.

By contrast, Lucretia was perfectly dressed in a long scarlet velvet gown with thin luminous trim along the sleeves and regal collar. An arrangement of legal medals pressed into the velvet, or perhaps the dress had been printed to fit them exactly. I wondered what would happen if she got another medal, but realized at once this was an absurd thought. She would just print a new dress and throw this one into the trash.

Uthondo walked over to me and grabbed me by the back of the neck, guiding me toward the balcony, following some command of hers I hadn't seen or heard.

"For the record, I didn't kill your brother," Lucretia said out of the blue, heaving a great sigh. "I honestly don't know what happened. You upset Silas so."

I was forced out onto the balcony, where Uthondo pushed me ahead of him with his heavy hand. A long, low divider of potted plants rose to the height of my waist. This building would be easy for Placers to visit.

"Look down, please," Lucretia said.

I eyed her from under Uthondo's grip. Could I break it and get to her pale neck? Could I grab her and take her over the edge with me?

My gaze shifted to the view from the balcony, and I stifled a gasp. This was my first real look at DC. Was Kiely Winston out there somewhere? Could I reach her? Had any of my friends made it to her? The Zockroft™ was wearing off, but it still numbed my anguish and worry over them.

"Do you remember Bridgette Pell?"

A sick feeling churned in my stomach. I remembered her perfectly, even though we'd never met. She was the Affluent girl who'd jumped to her death on her Last Day. Now that I'd spoken, was Lucretia going to toss me off that balcony and make it look like Bridgette's suicide?

"I made sure you were assigned to that cleanup assignment with your little group of Placers," she said. "Though maybe I should have made you scrape her toasted, mangled corpse off the sidewalk, rather than simply clear away her Last Day trinkets."

She locked her eyes on mine. I had to look away.

"You didn't intend for her to jump, did you?"

I said nothing.

"Did you?" she asked again. Uthondo's grip tightened. The

Zockroft™ wasn't going to make me answer. I wouldn't make that mistake again.

"My daughter was at that celebration," Lucretia hissed. "She watched the girl drop away to her death."

Her *daughter*? A dawning realization shivered up my spine. I suddenly understood why Lucretia had tolerated Victoria's touch. The girl was no servant. She was no prisoner, either.

She was Lucretia Rog's daughter, and she'd gone silent.

I knew I shouldn't smile, but the Zockroft™ and the delicious irony made it impossible to suppress it. How was such a thing possible? Why would any Affluent care what I had done? I stifled a snicker, but too late.

Lucretia's eyes flared at me.

"It's the Zockroft™, ma'am," Andromeda tried to explain.

"Fetch Victoria," Lucretia ordered. Andromeda scurried away.

Lucretia shot me another look and instructed Uthondo to haul me back inside. She took a moment to compose herself out there, then entered looking somewhat refreshed, careful to lock the balcony's door behind us as Andromeda returned with Victoria.

Was Lucretia worried the girl would follow Bridgette's example?

Lucretia forced herself to smile and crossed the room to her daughter. "Did Andromeda tell you the Silent Girl has broken her silence?"

Victoria only looked at her mother.

"So..." Lucretia inclined her head, as if she expected the girl to speak. I couldn't see any resemblance between them, but who knew how much of Lucretia's face was real?

"Show her your Cuff," Lucretia ordered me and, without

waiting, she grabbed my arm and scrolled back to the charge for the two words. "See?"

Victoria remained unmoved.

"Andromeda, play the recording," Lucretia ordered.

Andromeda obeyed. My voice sounded from her Cuff. *"Don't worry."* The words were a little slurred from the Zockroft™. Victoria's brow knit. She looked at the Cuff and then at me. I could tell she wasn't buying it. She moved over to me and placed a finger on my cheek. She was checking to see if I was real. She wasn't even sure I was actually there—she distrusted her mother that much.

"Speth, tell her your silence was nothing more than a silly little error in judgment," Lucretia instructed.

My jaw tightened. I may have spoken before, but I would not do so again. The only power I had was in silence and doubt. Victoria knew her family was full of frauds and liars. She would need to witness me speaking with her own two eyes. She poked my face twice more to make sure what she felt matched what she was seeing.

"You are violating our Terms of Service," Lucretia said to me. She looked at her Cuff and pressed a button. Something jabbed my arm under the Cuff. Panic hit me—more Zockroft™.

I was immediately overwhelmed with a woozy sense of well-being. Even Zockroft™ couldn't make me like Lucretia Rog, but I found myself filled with warm feelings for Andromeda and Victoria. I wished Victoria would speak so I could know why she'd become a Silent. I wanted to ask her. I could taste the words forming on my tongue.

"I will pay for whatever you would like to say," Lucretia offered, looking hungry.

I concentrated on breathing in and out, fighting the way the Zockroft™ seemed to loosen my tongue. I held my words back and was proud for keeping silent. Victoria looked suspicious. I loved her suspicion. I took a step toward her to hug her and show my appreciation, but Uthondo yanked me back. I hugged him instead. My Cuff buzzed.

"See!" Lucretia said. "That is legal communication!"

Victoria wasn't buying this, either. She turned her back on us. Lucretia clucked her tongue.

"I think it is time for lessons." She waved Andromeda off, and the older woman guided Victoria out of the room. The moment the door shut, the pain began. Patterns in my eyes. Blaring sounds in my ears. They cut right through the Zockroft™, clearing it like smoke blowing in the wind. The pain grew harder to bear. I dropped to my knees, and then it ceased.

"You think your silence is clever?" she asked.

"No," I said in return. My Cuff buzzed. Lucretia's eyes shot to the door. I went on. "Bring her back, I don't care. The minute I see her…" I zipped my lips. I felt giddy to know I could make Lucretia suffer. Or maybe it was the lingering effects of the Zockroft™.

Uthondo took a step back, frightened by my hubris—or maybe by the reaction he expected from Lucretia.

"I don't have to be silent." I jabbed a finger at the door. "I just have to be silent around *her.* That's worse, isn't it?" My Cuff scrolled and vibrated with my words. "Silent Girl," I whispered. I watched the charge scroll up my Cuff. $18,000. They didn't want anyone saying it.

Lucretia shook with fury, but she managed to control it. "My daughter hasn't spoken a word since that Pell girl jumped.

You ended a beautiful life with your little protest and ruined another."

"No." I forced myself to stand tall. "Bridgette ended her own life. Like Beecher Stokes, who ended his because he couldn't bear the thought of being Indentured to someone like you."

"Bridgette Pell would never have been Indentured to anyone." A sad note sounded in Lucretia's voice. An Affluent's death was far more tragic than some kid from the Onzième's.

"*No one* should be Indentured to *anyone*," I said. My Cuff buzzed again, and I was glad those words would be recorded. They'd done so much to erase our history, but they were also inadvertently preserving our present.

"Sedition," Lucretia said with a sigh. "Do you want to know who I have here in this house, toiling away? Indentured to me?"

I wasn't going to play her game. It was probably a lie, anyway.

"Ask me nicely, in front of my daughter, and I will free them."

I let my silence serve as my answer. She knew how to torture me, but now I knew how to torture her back.

"What about Belunda Stokes?"

I tried not to react, but my widening eyes betrayed me. Could she really save Beecher's grandmother?

"I'll be kind. She can live out her last few years in comfort. Or you could free Uthondo here, or Bertrand. That would be easier than fetching the old woman. Just say the word."

Uthondo braved a look at Bertrand. Bertrand stared forward. I said nothing.

"Silence again?"

I shrugged. My Cuff buzzed with the charge. I didn't care.

"You see!" Lucretia said to her bodyguards. "She won't even speak to free *you*."

She waited. The room sat in silence. My silence.

Suddenly, static played loudly in my ear and my vision went black. She'd effectively rendered me deaf and blind, which, while terrible, was better than her usual form of torture. At least my eyes didn't feel like they were being pulled apart.

I was lifted, probably by Uthondo or Bertrand. The giant meaty hands bore me away. I started screaming, even though I couldn't hear myself. Whoever carried me tensed and moved faster. My stomach dropped suddenly, and I realized we had probably taken an elevator somewhere—down, by the feel of it. Then my escort began walking again, and soon I was dropped onto a bed, left to endure what Lucretia had left me with.

The hours dragged on. The static kept playing. The blackness engulfed me. I slapped at my Cuff. I felt around the room. It was small and empty. The walls were soft, like a Squelch, but it wasn't—when I called out for it to stop, my Cuff buzzed in return.

I began shouting the most expensive words I could think of, just to feel the buzz of my Cuff. I chanted, "Silent Girl, Silent Girl," for an hour. I sang it to the tune of a Beatles™ song I'd once heard used in a movie. I expected shocks in return for this, but instead I saw only an occasional flicker or spark in my vision—probably a trick of my mind.

I put my hands on my mouth to feel it form words, exhale breath and vibrate the air. My throat grew raw. I must have spent a fortune. What a waste—all that money on words I couldn't hear. Did anyone?

I closed my eyes. I told myself the static was the sound of the sea and that I was sleeping beside it in the deep of night.

Someone poked me. Startled, I swatted at them. They poked me again and I took a full swing, connecting with someone's soft body. I suddenly worried that it might be Victoria. Had she heard me speaking?

I tried to stand and move through the space, but I still couldn't see anything. After a minute, someone took hold of me. The brusque motions felt like Andromeda, but I hadn't imagined her hands could be so cold. I was pushed down a hall and handed over to someone enormous—probably one of the bodyguards again.

Whoever it was shoved me into a tiny room—a cell, really. I felt around the walls and found a light switch, which was pitifully useless with my darkened eyes. There was also a bar that crossed over my head and let me swing and kick at the door until I was exhausted. Unsurprisingly, it would not budge.

My stomach ached from hunger. I lost track of how long my sensory deprivation went on. I slept. I pounded on the door with my Cuff. I slept more. Eventually, I was awakened by the faint smell of Wheatlock™ Dry. It was the worst of all the Wheatlock™ products, but I was ravenous and fumbled for it with my greedy hands, knocking over a cup of water in the process. I devoured the square in three huge bites and then searched the damp, puddled floor for more. I dabbed up a few more crumbs and sucked the water off my fingers. I fell asleep again, wondering if this was how she meant to kill me. Maybe she wasn't legally obligated to feed me. Or maybe, legally, she could kill me however she pleased.

I was awakened by a tremendous thud—I didn't hear it, so much as feel it through my bones. The whole building shook. A second smaller shock pounded my gut. I felt blindly around, as if I might find the cause.

A moment later, the static faded from my ears. My vision flashed brightly and then returned to normal. I reeled for a moment, adjusting to my surroundings. I wasn't in a cell, but an emptied closet. And whatever had woken me was now followed by an exquisite silence.

A dot formed in the center of my vision, then vanished. It was oddly comforting, even if it was nothing more than a misfire of Lucretia's system. I wondered if there was some limit to how long she could sustain her punishment. Maybe she was obedient to Laws I didn't know requiring certain amounts of food and untortured rest, even for an Indentured.

For half a second, I thought a word flashed across my eyes, but I was wary of trusting my senses. My thoughts were too jumbled. I longed for that night long ago when my eyes lit with a path to the Placers—for a time before everything in my vision was subject to Lucretia's cruel whims.

I missed Henri and Margot and Kel. I missed Mira and Norflo and Saretha. I even missed Sera, in a strange way. My heart ached, wondering if they were all okay.

Uthondo and Bertrand both arrived at the door soon after my vision returned. They stood before me, looking intimidating as usual, but wearing looks of mild confusion on their brutish faces.

"Yes?" I asked, pretending theirs was a casual visit to mask my fear. Then something flashed in my vision a second time. I definitely wasn't imagining it—or seeing it clearly.

"Quiet!" Lucretia's voice suddenly echoed in my head. She shocked my eyes twice, and I forced myself to stay steady. She must have said something to Uthondo and Bertrand, too, because they each grabbed me by an arm and dragged me away.

JUMP: $30.99

Lucretia sat behind her desk, concentrating on a wide desk screen too bright for me to look at after so much darkness. Rainbow halos rimmed every bright thing. This wasn't some digital effect—it was definitely something to do with my eyes. My vision seemed to stutter with shifting relics of being blinded.

In the screen's glow, Lucretia's face seemed less friendly than before, like the illusion of appeal was too much to maintain—or maybe she just didn't care to any longer. Through the windows to the balcony, brilliant orange light flickered across the city. A ball of flame and smoke plumed in the distance from somewhere I couldn't see. The red, white and blue flags that hung everywhere had turned a flaming red.

"What did they say?" Lucretia demanded without looking up. Her usual jaunty tone had fled, which made my hate for her easier to summon. Victoria sat behind her in the same corner chair I'd seen her in before, staring at the floor.

I didn't say a word. Lucretia fixed me with a glare. "The messages," she said menacingly. "What are the messages?"

I had no idea what she was talking about. She stood up and leaned toward me. I backed away, but Uthondo and Bertrand remained motionless behind me. I changed tactics and ducked behind Uthondo, realizing even as I did it how ridiculous my attempt to avoid her was. It wasn't as if he would try to protect me from her.

"I know they have contacted you," Lucretia said. She swiped at her Cuff. I winced at the flash. It hurt, but the stab of pain in my eyes lasted only a second.

"What could they possibly hope to accomplish?" she spit. Her voice was awful, not at all appealing anymore. Her long neck no longer seemed graceful, but viper-like.

She kept talking to the spot where I had been, between the two bodyguards, rather than where I stood. At first, I thought this was some creepy tactic of hers to unnerve me. I doubted for a moment that I was actually awake, or if this was just a strange dream. It was like she couldn't see that I'd moved.

Victoria stood and put a finger to her lips. She was smiling. Static crackled in my ears—a different static from before. It was fragmented, like something was broken.

"Don't you move," Lucretia growled, but she still wasn't looking at me.

Victoria waved her hands in front of her eyes and pointed at her mother. A grin had spread across her face. I cautiously took another step away. Uthondo and Bertrand made no attempt to stop me, and Lucretia's eyes didn't shift. Barefoot, Victoria moved silently to me and put a finger on my cheek. Her mother was being fed an image that wasn't real.

Something flashed again in front of my vision, and I winced automatically. I caught a better glimpse this time. It wasn't a pattern, but a word. My mind scrambled to reconstruct it, and then the message flashed again.

JUMP.

I didn't understand. Jump *where*? Victoria took my hand.

Had the whole system broken down? Was she sending this message? Was this all some twisted plan to get me to kill myself? Was *this* what Lucretia had been trying to make me do all along?

Lucretia rounded her desk, her body tensed like she was coiled to strike. But not at me—*still* at the spot where I had been.

"You will be broken," she snarled, reaching out into the air. When her hand met no resistance, her mouth dropped open, astonished.

The *JUMP* message flashed in my vision again, unmistakable this time. Victoria tugged me toward the balcony. Lucretia pushed at the air once, twice, then stammered, "She's…she's…"

She glared at Uthondo and Bertrand, at a loss to explain what was happening—like they were too dumb to understand. I didn't understand, either. "Find her!" she screamed, her frustration palpable in the air.

Uthondo and Bertrand both shifted, looked to the spot between them and reached out. Their faces contorted in a flurry of confused blinking. "She's not there," Uthondo said, his watery eyes blinking as he patted at the air.

They scanned the room, braced for action, but their eyes skimmed right over Victoria and me. Someone was overwriting their ocular feeds, making it look like I hadn't moved.

"Listen for her," Lucretia cried out. The static crackled in my ears again, and I thought I heard a voice buried in it, trying to reach me. I slipped out of my shoes and tossed one across the room to throw them off my trail. Both brutes turned in that direction, and we quickly padded to the balcony door. If I had a grapple, I could have swung away into the city. Without one, jumping meant certain death.

Victoria eased the balcony door open slowly. It emitted a slight creak, and Lucretia wheeled around, her eyes wild. "There," she said, pointing right at me. She'd heard us.

My body panicked. I raced across the stone tiles and jumped up into the scratchy fake plants. Victoria followed.

"No!" Lucretia cried.

What kind of plan was this? We were thirty stories up. I was a Placer, not a superhero. Lucretia dropped to her knees, her eyes going blank. It looked as if she'd been blinded, just like she'd done to me. Behind her, the two brutes fought through the same darkness, their eyes watering. Uthondo pulled himself blindly through the door with a heavy hand, feeling his way toward me. I backed to the corner of the ledge. We were out of options, but Victoria looked utterly thrilled. Did she know something I didn't?

JUMP appeared one last time. How was Victoria doing this? She wasn't touching her Cuff. She put a hand on my chest, like she wanted to feel my heart, and leaned close. In the rasping whisper of someone who hadn't spoken in a very long time, she said, "Kiely Winston says hello."

Then she pushed me back, straight over the edge.

PROXIMITY EXCEEDED: $31.99

My heart thudded as I hurtled downward. Someone grabbed me around the waist, and we fell together for a moment before swinging away from the building. My Cuff started buzzing, flashing and sounding an alarm. My eyes were shocked. *Proximity Exceeded* flashed across my vision, and my eyes were shocked again. The pain resounded through my skull.

"Victoria?" I gasped, but that couldn't be right. We zipped upward, suddenly landing on a rooftop with a swift balletic landing. The masked Placer who released me was very tall, powerfully built and graceful. Who else could it be but Kiely Winston?

The alarm sounded, and my eyes were shocked again. I reeled back in pain. With a quick, fluid motion, she produced a small device and ran it over my Cuff. It snapped open, alarm still blaring. It clung to my arm, sticky where it had cut into my damp flesh. I peeled it off with disgust and hurled it over the roof. It hammered the side of a stone building and pinged down to the ground, the alarm wailing all the way down.

I rubbed my eyes. Smoke was still rising, rolling out against the roof of the dome in slow-moving swells. Had she done that? The damage was far worse than what I'd done to Rog's tower.

She slapped a grapple into my hand and gestured for me to

follow. Hope rose in my chest. I tried to aim, but my vision was still blurry from being locked away in the blind dark and static. My hand trembled. I blinked over and over but didn't have the nerve to fire.

Kiely didn't wait long to toss me over her shoulder and carry me away. She darted through DC at astonishing speed, and I struggled to take in the city's unfamiliar topology. Many of the low buildings were old and made from real stone, built long before the days of printing. Many of these looked French, too, which I didn't understand. I'd thought that was something modern.

Kiely abruptly stopped at one of these old French-style buildings. The outside was opulent, with arched glass windows and pillars in front of them. She zipped up between two of the pillars and stopped on a thin ledge before an ornate iron grate. She ran something over the metal, pulled the grate aside and ushered me into a low, narrow passage. I crawled forward to a dead end and stopped. We were going to hide in here?

She pressed past me, all business, no grace now. She muscled the wall at the end of the path and pushed open a hidden square of a door. Behind her, I saw a dim light and shelves filled with books. Were these the ones she'd stolen?

She dropped down into the space, and I followed her. With a finger to her lips, she picked up a foam square, edged in a thick rubber, and stuffed it into place, then pulled on a lever in the wall that made the pressure in my ears pop.

With the Squelch sealed, the only sound was my hard breathing. Kiely pulled off her mask. She looked just as Margot had described her—tall and intimidating, with piercing eyes and a shock of blond hair in a public domain pixie cut very much like mine. Despite her height, she moved silently. I stared at her, more than a little awed.

"How did you find me?" I finally asked.

Kiely rubbed a hand across the back of her neck. She was obviously strong, but her eyes looked exhausted.

"Kel said to expect you," she said, sitting on a mattress on one side of the room. Did Kiely live here? There were stacks of foodstuffs and blankets, so my guess was yes. "I didn't think you'd turn up in the hands of Lucretia Rog, but I wasn't surprised. I had a distraction ready."

She put two fists together and then pulled them apart, fingers splayed.

"That explosion—that was you?" I asked, still a little disoriented from everything that had happened.

"I've been planning it for years, so don't get too bigheaded. I took out DC's Central Data. I had wanted to coordinate and get all three centers at once, but then you took out Portland." She grinned a little at me, like she was proud, then snapped back to looking serious. "Which meant extra security for me to deal with."

"I wasn't after Central Data," I confessed. "I was after the WiFi." Even that was an accident, but I didn't want to say so.

"Noble enough. And, on purpose or not, you got one of the Central Data nodes, which was pretty good. I just had to accelerate my plans. I'd rather have done a full erase. It's less showy, but more effective." She shrugged. "But there wasn't time. I had to go messy."

From her tone, I got the distinct impression that "messy" meant people had died in the explosion. The thought unnerved me. She began gathering things up into her bag.

"I didn't have a good way to get to you, though. Lucretia's

place is shut tight, and if I'd crossed that boundary to get you, I'd have been instantly blinded. That's how she likes to do things. But I couldn't leave you there. Fortunately, I knew about the girl."

"Victoria?"

"There have been rumors for months that Silents have been popping up in prominent families. They try to keep it quiet, but when you hear nothing, for example, about Victoria Rog's Last Day celebration, it isn't too hard to figure out she's zipped her lips. It should have been a huge news story. Instead, no story."

"Why?" I asked. "Why would *they* go silent?"

"Being wealthy doesn't make people awful, it just makes the awful ones powerful. It's easy to believe Affluents and Lawyers are all terrible, but that kind of prejudice is foolish. I've tracked a half dozen Affluent Silents like Victoria here in the DC dome."

She could see I was struggling with this idea. "And remember, Kel is a Lawyer."

Kiely walked over to the bookshelf, shifting my attention to her collection. Many were old and related to the Law. A few were about something called "chess." There was also a series that had handwritten labels I couldn't read. She took these and stuffed them in her bag, then scanned the rest.

Her mouth pulled flat. "I don't want to play favorites," she muttered, pulling out *The Adventures of Huckleberry Finn*, followed by *Democracy in America* and then *Las Luces de la Libertad*. She dropped them into her bag, looking dissatisfied.

"So, what did you do?" I prompted her. "With the Silents?"

"In Victoria's case, I tapped into her feed. That felt like a little justice, because the protection scheme for the corneal feed hasn't been updated in ages. It's been held up in Patent Litigation by the Rogs. I sent messages through her feed suggesting that all the best Silents *were* being coordinated. Part of a secret group. She wants to do the right thing, which is admirable, but at the same time, she's *still* an Affluent and *still* a Rog. She wants to feel important. Now she can."

That didn't seem fair. "What's going to happen to her now?"

Kiely blew out a big breath. "I can't let that be my problem. Sorry."

My admiration curdled. How could she be so cold about this when she'd just defended Victoria in the same sentence? Without her, I would have been doomed.

"Don't worry too much, kid. Her mommy kept you alive in the hope she could hear her daughter's mellifluous voice again. She won't hurt her. Victoria was easy to manipulate, and it had to be done. I had to get you outside Lucretia's perimeter."

"That doesn't seem right," I said with a slightly sick feeling as I remembered how I'd used Henri.

"It was better than leaving you there."

"Why didn't you just send a message to me, to let me know you were out there?"

"They had you jammed. The best I could do was one word, and I wasn't even sure that would get through."

"Wait, if they could jam me, why wouldn't they jam Victoria?"

Kiely laughed. "And cut *her* off from the outside? Those people can't function without their connection. I used the same weakness in the protection scheme to send false images to Lucretia and those Modifieds."

"Those what?"

"Those brutes she uses—the brutes all the Rogs employ."

She gestured around her face. "They've been genetically enhanced. You must have noticed them."

"The ones with the watery eyes?"

"One of the side effects of training and controlling them—low-grade voltage to the eyes the whole time they're connected. I don't know if it's to remind them to obey, or just a side effect of a bad design."

"That's horrible," I said, rubbing at my own eyes.

"Listen, we can't pause too long," she went on. "They'll track you here." She tapped at her neck under her ear to indicate my auditory implants.

"They can track these?" I asked. "But this is a Squelch. They shouldn't be able to follow."

"Your trail ends five feet from here," she said, pointing out to the passage. "They'll get to the building, make their way up here and start smashing in the walls if they have to. If you thought Lucretia was bad before..."

She grabbed another book and pocketed a silver grapple.

"What will she do?"

"Whatever she needs to," Kiely said. "She's already got the Commander-in-Chief Justice involved in taking back Portland now. Your best option is to leave the country."

I shook my head. "I have to find my sister. My friends. My parents." My fear rose with each word.

"Look at me," Kiely said, squinting at me. "You can't do everything." I realized that she wasn't just staring at me—she was examining my eyes. "Kel has your sister and some of your friends at a spot not far outside the dome. That's where I'm taking you."

My heart wanted to soar, but stumbled on the word *some.*

"Who?" I asked, praying everyone was safe.

"I don't know." Kiely pulled a device out of her bag, this one shaped like a spoon. She held it up near my face. "This is going to hurt."

I grabbed her by the wrist and stopped her. "What's going to hurt?"

"I'm going to short out your corneal implants. I wish I could do mine, but they were made before the Oxicure™ Patent challenge."

My fingers kept gripping her. I'd had enough pain, and I still wasn't thinking clearly.

"I can't do this if you fight me," she said. "But if you let me, they won't ever be able to shock you again." When I continued to hesitate, Kiely sighed impatiently. "Your sister is waiting."

I released my grip, and she raised the spoon-shaped device up to my left eye. The device emitted a faint high-pitched whine, stopped, and suddenly there was a flash and a blinding pain. My head dropped into my hands.

"Do you know if Saretha is okay?" I gasped in a broken voice, trying to blink away the pain.

"I believe so," she said. "Let's finish this." I raised my head. I felt like she expected me to be tougher, more like her. The pain hit my right eye, but I was more prepared for it this time.

"They broke the DRM," Kiely said proudly, putting the device away. "Thanks to you. So they could heal her. That's a big deal. They used the book you took from Rog's collection."

She put a hand on my shoulder for a moment and smiled, then turned away. I blinked several times, trying to see straight, and was surprised to find everything looked clearer.

Kiely ran a hand over a stack of her own books. "It wasn't *the* book, but it was as useful as anything I've ever found."

"Is that what you've been looking for?" I asked, scanning

her titles. I couldn't believe how much more easily I could read the spines now. "*The* book?"

"*The* book is a myth," she said.

"Then what are all these?" I asked.

"These are how I figured out it's a myth," Kiely replied, looking at them sadly. "Rog played both of us on that one." When I didn't respond, she added, "We should move. Are you ready? Can you see okay?"

"Yeah," I said, surprised. "Is it...weird that I can see better now?"

Kiely nodded wryly. "Your guardian probably adjusted the focus to be just slightly off so she could sell you a prescription upgrade later on."

"Damn Mrs. Harris," I muttered. That sounded about right.

Kiely turned to open the exit and paused. "I don't know what we're facing out there. If something goes wrong, you get to the roof and head east. Don't worry about me."

I looked down at myself. I was still wearing Lucretia's service-gray outfit with its white sleeves. One of my shoes was in her office where I'd thrown it. I took off the other, figuring it was more important to be balanced than to have one foot covered. I didn't know if I was ready for this. I still felt shaky, and I had so many questions. "How will I know where to go?"

She put a hand on the lever that sealed and unsealed the room. "Your friends are to the east, but I can't explain more than that. If you lose me, you'll be on your own."

Then I'm not going to lose you, I thought.

Kiely pulled up on the lever and the square shifted. She put a finger to her lips, moved the square aside and pulled herself out.

THE BLIND ORDER: $32.97

Four dropters were perched outside, hovering just beyond the grate we had entered. They whirred to attention as we neared and spread themselves out. The street below fell silent as the Ad screens clicked off. All four began to beep in alarm.

Kiely fretted at this only for a minute. She tapped at her Pad, and the dropters wobbled before plummeting to the ground. She held up three fingers, then two, then one and kicked the grate open. She shot out a line and zipped away to a building across the street, her body streamlined as an arrow. I scrambled after her, only to find her gone when I reached the roof. I scanned the skyline and only barely caught sight of her as she vanished over a higher building farther up the street. I struggled to keep up. She had to know I wasn't at full strength—my imprisonment had taken its toll. But maybe this was as slowly as she could go without risking being caught. Maybe I was about to lose everything.

The word "Halt!" echoed through the air. I chanced a look back. Police cars and Lawyers' sedans peppered the street. Faces scanned for us and locked on me.

Suddenly a car mounted the curb and smashed into the side of a building, and another went out of control and grazed it. People all over the street froze. I wondered if this was some trick Kiely had up her sleeve, but then I saw her falter up ahead, her grace suddenly gone as she hit the next roof hard and rolled, squeezing her palms into her eyes.

"Dammit, she's blinded me," she called out. "Go on! Get out!" she ordered, trying to wave me off without knowing where I was.

From the chaos below us, it seemed Kiely wasn't the only one blinded. I landed next to her. People staggered in the streets below—even Affluents. There were accidents all down the street.

"She's done it to the whole city."

Kiely shook her head in disgust. "She'll stop at nothing now. You need to leave me here and escape."

If I left her, Kiely would be done for and I'd have no way to find my friends, or my family. The police were still on the move. For some reason, they hadn't been blinded.

Kiely suddenly reeled forward. I heard moans rise up from all around the city. The hairs on the back of my neck stood up. I knew what Lucretia was doing to their eyes with those malicious patterns. I wondered if Victoria was being spared this torture, or if freeing me was the last straw for her mother.

I grabbed Kiely's hands and put them together, aiming the grapple for her.

"I'm getting you out of here," I said. I held her tightly and squeezed the trigger. The two of us shot upward. She had no way to know when to slow the line as we were reeled toward an angled hatch on the roof of the dome. We hit hard and were almost knocked loose. I had to scramble to reach a handhold as Kiely writhed in anguish.

"We're almost there," I told her.

Heart racing, I undid the hatch's magnetic lock and it

swung open into the sun. I made sure Kiely had a grip on the handhold before I hauled myself up through the opening, then turned to help Kiely up. I grasped her hands with mine and pulled with all my might to get her through, then kicked the hatch shut.

Kiely fell back onto the angled surface of the dome, breathing hard, her clothes drenched with sweat. She held her palms to her eyes, clearly still in agony. Apparently the WiFi extended up here. I looked around wildly, trying to find a way to help her. The DC dome was so vast, its surface seemed almost flat. Unlike our honeycomb, this was one smoothly printed shape, peppered with occasional hatches and antennae.

Antennae. I raced for the nearest one and gave it a yank, snapping it in half. I darted to another, and then to a third. When I turned back, I saw Kiely roll over onto her knees. Had it worked?

"FiDo," she confirmed with a half cheer, looking at me with sore, red eyes. Before they were taken from me, my parents had lived for the moments when the WiFi would go down. Everyone called them FiDos, apparently even in DC, though this one would only be in the small area where I'd knocked out the antennae.

Kiely got to her feet and shook off the pain, drawing herself up to her full height. She pulled something from her bag that looked for all the world like an expandable skateboard. Young Affluents would sometimes breeze through the Onzième on these, weaving through the poor kids for fun.

Kiely caught hers under one foot to hold it in place, then beckoned me to stand on the back of it. She meant to ride the board down the angle of the dome. This might have been thrilling, except from where I stood, it looked like we'd be riding off the edge into oblivion.

Something hit the hatch near us, and Kiely kicked off. I didn't have time to do anything but hold on for dear life, hoping she had a plan for the way the dome sloped away.

"There's a WiFi patch ahead," she shouted as we began to move faster, "but it's meant for the city, not out here—I should be able to see again before we hit the edge."

My stomach dropped. What if she didn't? She kicked again and again, needlessly adding to the speed the angle already provided. I peeked back, my short hair fluttering in the wind. The hatch had rolled out of sight, obscuring anyone who might be following us.

Far ahead, past the edge of the dome, I saw greenery and a scattering of buildings. The trees here were alive, and one of the buildings was an actual stone ruin from some part of American® history too exclusive for someone from the Onzième to know about. Vines climbed it, and some stones had fallen away. Beyond were more gutted, split and derelict buildings like the ones I'd seen before Lucretia captured me.

My heart fluttered—at the speed, the drop and with worry about my friends. Kel had my sister, but I knew nothing about the others or who was even there.

The steep drop-off was coming up fast.

"Can you see?" I cried.

"One sec," she grunted.

I kept expecting her to slow, but she let the momentum build.

"Now?" I asked, panic whirling inside me.

"I got it. Hang on tight!" she said, which wasn't a *yes*, but I did what she asked.

We went flying over the edge, airborne. Kiely quickly clamped her shins around the board, leaving my feet dangling. She shot out a line. It hit and stuck to the high wall of the ruin. Suddenly we were swinging, from one line to a second, and then we came to a stop. It all happened in just a few seconds, but felt like so much longer. I'd done some dangerous things as a Placer, but that was all nothing compared to this.

Kiely alighted on a wall and carefully separated us, rubbing her eyes. She motioned for me to be careful—the fall on either side was twenty feet. I stood as still as possible while balancing and counterbalancing myself, the way bodies do at terrifying heights. I got my own grapple ready, just in case I slipped. She saw this, nodded approval and then pointed to a van that was partially concealed behind a listing building overgrown with greenery. That was where we were headed.

She shot another line out, straight into the weeds creeping up the side, and I followed her. The van bore a picture of a thin woman's torso, squeezed to absurd proportions. The OiO™ logo was emblazoned across the middle. My stomach seized. Had it come from up north, from the town where we'd been caught? I looked at the windows, but they were the same sort of black glass that Rog's Meiboch™ had.

"Are they inside?" I asked, dropping down to the side of the van. Kiely didn't answer. Behind me, she had made her way up a braced wall where a WiFi node had been installed on a pole. She carefully extracted the silvery NanoLion™ battery pack, then used some tool to cut it free without causing an explosion.

I opened the van door. The cab was empty. My shoulders sagged as Kiely dropped down next to me. My brain took a second to focus and shake off my disappointment that no one had come to greet me. But that was foolish—they would have been in danger this close to the dome.

"Where are we going?" I asked as we climbed in.

"Twenty minutes west," Kiely said, closing her door. "To a temporary camp we're building in a WiFi blind."

"We?"

"Kel and I," she said.

"And Saretha?"

"Yes. Saretha and your friends."

I took a moment to breathe. Maybe she meant all of them. I hoped she did—I was afraid to ask.

I gathered my courage. "Who's there, other than Saretha and Kel?"

She took too long to answer for me to feel reassured. "I don't know exactly. We've only communicated in short bursts because they're staying on the move and out of the WiFi."

"But everyone is okay?"

"Everyone I saw."

We pulled away through the living trees. I wanted to press her more—maybe make her describe them.

"So, why'd you do it?" she asked before I had a chance. "Why'd you go silent?"

I hated to disillusion her, but I felt like I owed her the truth. She'd saved me, after all. So I explained it all as best I could while we rode, and hoped she wouldn't be too disappointed.

PHOTOCLOUD™: $33.99

"Impressive," Kiely said when she'd heard it all. It was not the reaction I'd expected.

"None of it was intentional," I explained. Surely she realized I hadn't done much?

"You say that, but it was still brave, and you survived things that would break most people. And you didn't have to go after Rog, or the WiFi or any of it. You *chose* to do those things."

"It didn't feel that way."

"Courage never does. You've forced them to fight for Portland. I've given them something to deal with in DC. The last Central Data node is in Delphi™," she said, her eyes flashing. "If we take that out, we might really shut them down."

"Won't that cause chaos?" I asked.

"There'll be chaos, all right. But once the network comes down, we'll be able to get the food printers working without the WiFi, thanks to you."

For a second, that idea seemed lovely to me. With the WiFi out, and the book of PrintLocks™ codes, people could freely tell each other how to print food. But my excitement was brief. Portland had been a mess with the WiFi down. Being able to talk didn't mean people would communicate.

"Everyone is so spread out, through the different domes," I

said. "It will take forever to get the information out to them all." A sick, hot feeling went over me. This would be terrible, no matter how successful we were.

"Don't think for a minute that this solution isn't for the greater good just because it's painful," Kiely said. Her eyes were fierce. "If we don't put an end to it, kid, there will be worse suffering for generations to come."

I couldn't wrap my head around how to manage it. I'd heard threats about suffering for generations from the Rogs enough times to know she was right.

"Let me ask you something," she said. "Do you know anything about your family history, past your parents being Indentured?"

I shook my head.

"It isn't accidental," she said. "They keep rewriting history. I've tried to collect what pieces I can—that's why I kept stealing books, even after I figured out there wasn't going to be any *one* book that somehow solved everything. But they can't change the actual past. Remember that. Your family history is part of that. When people can speak freely, they pass on stories with words." She paused, then smiled and added, "Kel felt so strongly about it, she had this idea that if we knocked out the WiFi while we were Placing, we might be able to help."

"You Placed with Kel?"

"For six years," she said with a note of longing. "Did your family never take advantage of those FiDos?"

I hadn't considered before that it was Kel who'd made it possible for our parents to speak with us freely. To learn that Kiely had been part of that, too, made my head spin. Those FiDos had allowed my parents to kiss and hug us without paying, even if those occasions were rare.

Grateful tears welled up in my eyes. "My mom told me she had some family pictures from a long time ago, but by the time we were toddlers, she had to make hard choices about what she could afford to keep in the PhotoCloud™. She and my dad chose pictures of us. Pictures of when we were little, babies—toddlers. She chose those over pictures of her own mother."

My voice started to give way. Silence was easier than this.

"Then it stopped mattering. We couldn't afford any subscription fees for PhotoCloud™. My parents could scarcely afford to say the company's name. Every month they sent a notice of the tiny thumbnails of the pictures they would permanently delete if we didn't pay. But we *couldn't* pay. My parents were gone by then. Saretha, Sam and I would gather around and peer close at those little thumbnails of our family as they winked away, punishing us for our debts."

I brushed at my eyes to clear them. Even when I was little, it had felt like pieces of us were being ripped away.

"Our guardian," I said between gritted teeth, "Mrs. Harris. She told us we didn't deserve what we couldn't afford. She said even *looking* at those tiny pictures was immoral."

I flashed to the moment when I had saved Mrs. Harris from the mob and wondered if I should have let things go another way. Then I remembered Sera had long ago called us thieves for looking at those thumbnails, too. When we'd argued, Sera had yelled back, *I never had any pictures to get deleted!* I'd thought she was lying, that she didn't deserve to have pictures. I had been so angry about what we'd lost I couldn't see how much worse things had been for her. Now I just felt sick and ashamed for the way I'd treated her.

Kiely kept silent, watching the road, giving me space. After a while, she said, "I've been kicking myself for not thinking of finding a book with the PrintLocks™ codes. I thought I could hack them. I poked through the systems. Who knew they would actually *print* them!"

I had to laugh at that.

"But now I have a plan for how to coordinate," Kiely went on. "With a place like Portland, where the city is free, even if only for a while, I can recruit help. We can arm them—not with weapons, but with the PrintLocks™ codes to crack the DRM. We'll fan them out across America®. If we can get that center in Delphi™ down, the WiFi and everything will go with it. And we won't have to worry about people starving."

She made it sound so easy. My head hurt as I thought about who she could recruit. "You'll only be able to get kids like us to do that," I said.

"I didn't say it was fair," Kiely answered.

A moan escaped me. "And what about the Indentureds? What will happen to them when the WiFi goes out? How will they eat?"

"The farms will be fine. They grow food. The others... Hopefully we'll be able to reach them in time. If there was a way to do it without disabling the whole system, I'd do it, but I don't see how."

My mind tried to work through this, searching for another solution. My body slumped, dispirited. It all seemed so insurmountable.

"All I want is to bring my family back together," I said more sharply than I intended. "That's all I ever wanted."

"It isn't up to you to solve everything," Kiely said gently. "It isn't up to you to solve the problems of the world. You're sixteen, and, trust me, you've more than earned the right to take your family and go."

"Where?" I asked. "I have a friend who feels our best bet is Téjico, but..."

Kiely's intense face broke into a small grin. "I did a little digging into your family history when Kel went to bail you out of jail," she said, nodding her head toward her bag. "Look inside. There should be a black book with the number twenty-four on it." She waited for me to retrieve it. "Flip to the page labeled Jiménez."

ANCESTRY®: $34.99

Kiely had written about my family in ink. The idea of it was both exciting and frightening. The name Jiménez was large and heavily inked, like she'd written the word over and over again many times. I couldn't help but think of Norflo and how happy he would be to see this.

I found the dense tiny handwritten words difficult to read as the van jostled along a road that was barely a road anymore. Still, what I saw sent a shiver through me. I'd never seen words written down on paper before. It was forbidden to us.

There were a bunch of names written on the pages, all connected with little lines. I was descended from these people—*all* these people. They spread like branches or roots, to me and from me. A few generations back, Carlos and Eleanor Hernandez, my great-great-grandparents, had come from Mexico to live here back when Téjico was still called Mexico. What had they expected to find? The Jiménez side of my family had apparently lived in America® for hundreds of years before their name was shortened to Jime by something Kiely called the "One People's Act." I wanted to shake Kiely's book for more answers, but all I could do was stare and try to understand everything she'd written.

Toward the bottom of the page, Kiely had written a note that sent chills down my spine.

JIMĒNEZ

Speth Jime

LAST DAY BRANDING PROFILE NOTES JIME IS NOT HISTORICAL FAMILY NAME

Roberth Jime + Mayra Teg

Lexi Mosa + Austin Jime

JIMES IN PORTLAND DOME

Alvador Teg + Samantha Swaine

NAME SHORTENED TO JIME BY ONE PEOPLE'S ACT

AMERICAN CONFEDERACY FOR CULTURAL UNIFICATION?

Evi Dez + Orlando Jime

JIME PRICED @ $1.99
JIMÉNEZ PRICED @ $3799.00

Carlos + Eleanor Hernandez

CAME TO USA FROM MEXICO

Roberto Jiménez + Catherine Starr

Jiménez family in U.S. dates back to at least 1860 according to Rog historical Archive.

Flora Ortiz + Arthur Jiménez

Flora was tagged in historical ISP data for an illegal download. "Unapologetic" Data held by Butchers + Rog. Why?

The algorithims appear manipulated to ensure early Indenture date for both sisters before independent families can be created.

"'The algorithms appear manipulated to ensure early Indenture date for both sisters before independent families can be created.'" I read aloud. "What does that mean?"

"They like your genes," Kiely said grimly. "They wanted to take you all into Indenture before you could have children. It's likely the reason they kept your parents together when they were assigned. They probably thought you all would make nice workers for generations to come."

I stared at her in horror. Many kids didn't know what became of their parents once they were taken. They weren't allowed any contact. We were restricted to a few nervous, awkward, aching calls each year. Many of my friends—Penepoli, Mandett, Nancee, Sera—were only allowed to talk to one parent. The other parent was simply gone. But when your parents couldn't really afford to say anything, how much did it matter? What could any of our parents afford to say? I'd never realized that we were lucky our parents had gone together—I'd just thought it was unlucky they had been taken in the first place.

My head kept shaking in disbelief. Kiely pulled us down a wooded dirt road and began to slow the van.

"I lived most of my life never really thinking any of this was odd or wrong," I whispered. "How could I have been so stupid?"

"Not stupid," Kiely said. "Ignorant and unprepared. That's by design. They didn't want anyone to know what they were doing."

She stopped the van and looked around. There were a few plastic shelters out in the dark, each shaped like half an egg and printed roughly around a tree. One was only half-constructed, with a small, drone-like printer circling and building the shelter up slowly in the dark. Kiely frowned after a moment.

"What's wrong?" I asked.

"This is the blind where we were supposed to meet," she said, rubbing a hand through her short blond hair. "Site's been abandoned."

"Why?" I asked, panic creeping into my voice. The little printer kept moving.

"It's okay," she reassured me, putting a calming hand out. "Could be lots of reasons. If they'd been caught, they wouldn't have left the hacked printer going."

I squinted out into the shadowy forest, hoping to spot Saretha or one of my friends. Despite what Kiely had said, the abandoned printer didn't make me feel any better.

"There's a second site not far from here," she added, putting the van in Reverse and backing down the dirt road. "Don't panic. We'll find them. There's just no WiFi to communicate. We mapped out a plan."

Kiely reached into her bag and pulled out a Pad. She tapped the screen to update something, then handed it to me.

There was a line of WiFi blinds dotting the map from OiO™ down toward the outskirts of DC. Some were green, some were red. Beyond, all the way into the Archipelago of Disney™, more dots spread out, like an infection. A corruption of the system.

"How did you get this map?" I asked, centering in on Carolina.

"I stole it, obviously," she said. She turned us around and started to speed up.

My heart started to pound. The words *Crab Creek* appeared between the Agropollination™ domes. Small red dots spattered the area around it.

"Crab Creek!" I cried. "That's where my parents are!"

"I know," she said, smiling. "Saretha told us."

"Can we get them out?" I asked. If anyone would know how, it was Kiely. "Can we free my parents?"

She took a deep breath. "I don't know much about how those farms are guarded." She paused and looked at me. "There are overseers, and the Cuffs keep them tethered to the area. The chaos you and I've created... Well, it can't hurt."

"You didn't answer my question. Is it possible? Is there a way to break my parents out of there?" I stared at the spot and burned its location into my brain.

"I know you have to try. You're lucky they're both in the same location."

I thought on this a moment. She wasn't going to give me a *yes.* Kiely wouldn't make an empty promise.

"Why do you think they kept my parents together?" I asked.

Kiely looked at me sidewise. "I imagine in the hopes they would—" she paused, and the next word stuck in her throat "—breed."

I felt sick to my stomach at first, then felt a small surge of relief. "Well, that certainly didn't work out the way they planned."

"That's fortunate," Kiely said, turning the wheel toward another densely wooded path. "The companies take direct ownership of any children born to parents in Indenture."

I recoiled in horror. *"What?"*

"It's *slavery,*" she explained. "They are born into slavery. You probably don't know that word. They priced it too high for anyone to speak. When the government wants to destroy freedom and limit thought, they control speech. They don't want you to understand the concept. If they could, they'd have erased it from the Word$ Market™ entirely, but that isn't allowed. Slaves are people whose lives, freedoms and fortune are under the absolute power of others."

"But that's everyone," I cried.

"No. The Law is clear on how it works." She recited: *"Neither slavery nor involuntary servitude, except as a punishment for crime whereof the party shall have been duly convicted, shall exist within the United States™, or any place subject to their jurisdiction."*

"Except a ton of people are in involuntary servitude."

We came into a clearing. "Like your parents, most have been 'duly convicted' of a debt crime," Kiely reminded me.

"Duly," I muttered.

Kiely slowed the van. The lights washed across another plastic printed structure. This one stood alone, but it wasn't abandoned. Saretha was sitting there, her back to it. When she spotted our van, she rose, unsteady on her freshly healed legs, and began to run toward us.

My heart broke. Seeing Saretha stand made me want to cry with joy, but seeing how unsteady she was filled me with tears of a different kind. Before Kiely had the van at a full stop, I pulled at my handle and jumped out of the van, tossing Kiely's book and Pad back inside.

"Speth!" Saretha cried. I ran to her and pulled her into a fierce embrace. She squeezed me back, shaking, more desperate than even the hugs our mother had stolen during FiDos. I felt her heart beating through her chest and my own matching it, fast and hard. I didn't care what happened next. I would never leave her again.

The van's engine cut away, and I pulled back so I could look at her.

"I'm sorry!" I sobbed. "I'm so sorry I left without you."

"I'll give you a minute," Kiely said in a low voice, wandering away from us and the structure.

"Are you okay?" I asked, looking down at Saretha's legs.

She shrugged and hiked up her skirt to show me. I felt myself take a sharp breath. Her legs were bruised and blotchy, puckered at the shin where the worst break had been. She fingered that indentation. "It still hurts," she said.

I pulled her back into my arms. "I'm sorry," I said again, aching for her. I waited and hoped for her to say it was okay, but the words didn't come.

This time, she broke off the hug. Her eyes were clearer than the last time I'd seen her. The pain had overwhelmed her then, and before that, for a long time, Zockroft™ had dulled her. But she wasn't back to what I thought of as normal. Her eyes looked different—not misty, but farther away. When she spoke her next words, I understood why.

"I want to forgive you," she said.

"You..." I couldn't find a word to say after that. It felt like she'd kicked me in the stomach.

"I wish there was a BoneKnitter® for our hearts," Saretha said, touching her legs again. She looked so sad. It was the kind of sappy comment Sam would have made fun of, and I felt his absence deeply in the space now between us. I wondered if she did, too.

"If I'd spoken," I choked out, thinking of that day on the bridge, "they still wouldn't have... They might not have—"

"We'll never know," Saretha said. Unsaid was, *You could have tried.*

I felt dizzy from the ache in my heart. Blinking back tears, I stared beyond her at the hastily printed structure. Two printers zipped back and forth, building it up, thickening the walls. They hadn't been here that long. Mira's head poked out through the door, curious, then slipped back inside. One piece of dread fell away. Mira was okay. She was safe, but a pang of jealousy hit me. Sam was still gone.

"I need you to believe it wasn't my fault," I begged Saretha. "Please?"

Saretha's forehead wrinkled. The last time she'd looked at me with any real pride had been on my Last Day. She had been so excited for me. She put a hand to my chin and lifted my head just a little to look at my scar.

"What happened that night?" she asked. She hadn't bothered to back then—the night I was attacked—because she knew she'd be met with silence. That silence sat between us like a wedge.

"I had to keep quiet," I told her. "I couldn't let some random lunatic make me speak. I was attacked in Section 14. This drunk Affluent..." I swallowed. "He knew I wouldn't scream. He wanted to do...things to me. If Henri hadn't broken from the Placers to help me..." I looked at the door where Mira had been, desperate to know whether he and the others were safe.

"Henri rescued me and got the Placers to take me in," I said. "I had found a way to help the family—to keep us out of servitude. I wanted to tell you so badly."

Saretha's face softened a little. She took my hand and squeezed. I squeezed back, wanting this to be forgiveness, but I could feel it was less.

"I did everything I could," I said to her. "I tried to find every way I could to keep us together. I wanted you and Sam to know I was a Placer, I really did."

"Sam would have really liked that," she said. It wasn't meant to be cruel, but the reminder hurt. Sam would have been thrilled to know I'd made it onto a crew. But he'd died before he could truly feel happy.

"If I'd spoken, Keene would have taken us all," I tried to explain, but the words came out sounding weak, like they didn't have enough substance.

"Not if you'd read just your speech," Saretha said. She tried to make the comment sound light, but for her, it wasn't. "I could have pulled it up for you. Arkansas Holt said you could read it anytime."

"Maybe," I admitted. "But there was more to it than that. They'd stolen your image long before my Last Day. I...I wanted to do something about it."

"I know," she said. Her eyes flashed with a momentary thrill. "I was Carol Amanda Harving the whole time."

That wasn't exactly how it worked, but it was easier for me to agree. I looked at the light coming from the shelter. Someone paced inside.

"Did you meet them?" I asked her. "My Placers?"

Saretha swallowed hard and reached out to hug me again. "I'm sorry, Speth," she whispered.

She had something awful to tell me. I knew it from her voice. My body started trembling. I wanted to push her away—to run from the news she was about to deliver—but I held on more tightly. We hadn't even been able to mourn Sam properly. I wasn't ready for more appalling news.

Saretha spoke as gently as she could. "Your friend Henri—he didn't make it."

HENRI: $35.99

Inside the shelter, Margot was sitting on the ground with her back to the wall, staring out with empty eyes. She barely seemed to notice us. Mira sat by her side, watching as I entered. Norflo stood, shaking his head, and wrapped me in a bear hug. I squeezed back as best I could, my strength feeling all but gone.

Saretha couldn't mean Henri was dead. There had to be some other explanation.

"What happened?" I asked in a broken voice. For a moment, no one answered, and I let myself feel a brief surge of foolish hope. "Did Lucretia's people take him?" That would be awful, but we could go back to DC and free him.

"No," Margot said darkly. Her face twisted with pain, and she snarled, "They just left him there."

"But why?" I cried. I'd heard the shot. I'd seen Henri fall. I saw the blood. "Why? He was supposed to be safe!"

Margot choked back a sob. Mira clung to her more closely.

"But he was owned," I protested. "That should have protected him from being killed."

"For Lucretia Rog, it meant *she* couldn't own him," Norflo said darkly.

I slumped against the far wall by the door. Saretha sat carefully beside me. "Surely she could have bought him," I said, desperate to believe we could still rescue him. "She has the money. Why would she kill him?"

Outside the door, the DC dome loomed beyond the clearing and the trees, low across the sky. It looked so massive and wide, despite being miles away from where we were. I couldn't entirely comprehend the size of it. Why couldn't Henri be somewhere inside?

"He was owned by his father," Margot said, shaking her head. "The Rogs knew Henri's father would never sell his son. That was the point of owning him. That is what Henri always said when he defended him. His father had bought Henri and Henri's mother to protect them."

She didn't sound like she believed his motives. I didn't blame her.

"Kel checked," Margot continued. "So we could be sure. Lucretia paid out a huge settlement to Henri's father—five times the earnings of a Placer's full career, plus pain and suffering damages because he says he loved Henri."

"No," I whispered. "No. No. No." My mouth kept saying it, like an incantation against what I knew. The awful, empty pit of a feeling that I'd shoved away after Sam's murder opened up before me. Henri and Sam were both innocent, with such shining, good hearts. Why did the Rogs need to destroy everything that was good in this world?

"Did you see him?" I asked, wishing what I'd remembered wasn't real—that it was sleep gas or one of Lucretia Rog's tricks.

Margot shook her head. "We ran through the woods," she said, keeping her tone as even as she could manage, still staring out the door with glassy eyes. "We lost Lucretia's men in the trees."

"I thought there were bears," Mira said, shivering.

Margot stroked her hair absently. "I told her those men—they are worse than bears."

Kel entered the shelter, eyeing Margot and me. Sera was not with her. Where was she?

Outside, the van started up again. The lights flashed as it moved off.

"Worked our way back toward OiO™," Norflo said solemnly. "Only place we knew. Took days. We sneaked in. They were focused on keeping Indentureds in, not us out. But the Indentureds knew the Silent Girl had passed through. Was a small uprising behind us, started by those women in the street. They had the factory locked down. Margot took down an overseer. Used his Cuff to get a message to Kel."

"I did not think she would receive it," Margot said, her voice weaker than I'd ever heard it.

"But she did," Norflo said. "Only took a few minutes 'fore Kel had a new message scrolling in Margot's eyes."

Margot dropped her head into her hands and let out a sob. "It took days for Kel to reach us there."

"Thought we could still save Henri," Norflo whispered.

A tear formed at the edge of Kel's eye, and she quickly pushed it away. "I'd been using the WiFi incursion in Portland to monitor when I could," she said. Her voice was gentle, almost funereal. "But it wasn't enough."

Was this what a funeral was like? I had never been to one. You don't get a funeral in the Onzième—not with debt scores like ours. All you get to do is pay for disposal of the body and say what few words about the dead you can afford.

"Shut down OiO™ for two days," Norflo told me. "I took down the power. It was an uprising. Full-on. Shut the tunnel. Held 'em back 'til Kel arrived."

"Word has begun to spread," Kel said. "People know about Portland."

"How could you hold back Lucretia's people?" I asked. It didn't seem possible.

"Weren't hers," Norflo said. "Once they took *you*, the Rogs had what they wanted."

Margot's head dropped down even lower. They hadn't wanted Henri.

"'Twas OiO™ security," Norflo said.

"I knocked one out," Mira said proudly. Margot patted her hand without looking.

"What about Sera?" I asked.

Margot hesitated for a moment before answering. "Taken," she said, harshly wiping at her eyes. "With you."

"But I never saw her," I protested, which proved nothing. Why would they take her and not Henri? But I knew. She could be Indentured.

"Lucretia Rog has her in DC," Kel confirmed. "Kiely dug up the transfer of ownership. She bought the girl down to her DNA."

"But not Henri?" I begged.

Margot shook her head.

The blood drained from my face and my heart started hammering. "We have to get her out," I said, feeling panicked. I knew what Lucretia would do to her—what she might be doing at this very moment. Sera wasn't perfect, but no one deserved this.

"Kiely barely got *you* out," Kel said, avoiding my eyes. She looked to the door, like she expected Kiely any moment.

"Sera is on her own," Margot added without pity.

Sera is always on her own, I thought sadly. I felt tears stinging my eyes, remembering the years of loneliness she'd endured.

"Sera is lost," Kel confirmed softly. "You have to accept it."

Saretha rubbed my back with her hand to comfort me. I couldn't catch my breath. Nothing made sense. I shook my head against it all.

"If it was Henri, we'd go back," I said coldly.

"But she is *not* Henri," Margot retorted angrily.

Mira's eyes widened at her sister's tone, and I felt as if I'd been punched in the heart. "You…" I stopped myself. What was there for me to say? That Henri mattered to us more than Sera? Our world assigned a value to everything and everyone. Did that sick truth have to condemn Sera to a life of torment?

My head was too jumbled to make sense of it. Were we as bad as the Rogs, who saw us as little more than debts for them to move from dome to field to work until we were dead? We were all supposed to know the Affluents mattered most and the Indentureds not at all. Did we need to create a pecking order in between?

I forced myself to stand. Saretha's hand slid from my back. I took the few steps to the door and rushed out into the night. The DC dome loomed over the horizon like an empty eye. I'd wanted nothing more than to be together with everyone, but for a moment, I just needed to be alone.

REGRET: $36.99

Outside, in the night, the DC dome glowed, half-obscured by trees, but too large and luminous to ignore. The sky above it glowed, lighting up the clouds and air. Off to one side, a crescent shape caught my eye. It was the moon, smaller and so much more detailed than I'd expected it to be. I couldn't think how to describe it, except that it seemed intensely real and separate from our world. I envied that.

I paced out farther into the grass. Each time my mind drifted to Henri or Sam, a sob would well up and I'd have to press it down. I didn't want the others to hear, but Saretha soon stepped outside, limping across the distance to join me.

"The moon looks like your scar," I said.

Her hand went right to her shoulder. Without that scar, we might never have known Carol Amanda Harving was a fake.

"Sort of," she said.

We stood quietly for a moment. I struggled to keep myself together. Henri and Sam were dead. Sera was doomed to a life of torment under Lucretia Rog.

"You're not going silent again, are you?" Saretha asked, half joking. It reminded me of something Sera would say, and suddenly, I could no longer contain the tears. I collapsed to the ground, sobbing, and started hammering at my knees in frustration. What had I done?

"Oh, Speth," Saretha said, her voice trembling.

"You're right," I cried, breaking apart. "If I had just read my speech, we all could have had a few more good years. Then..."

When I thought of *then*—of what would have come next—my insides ignited with fury. Our futures would have been bleak no matter how obedient I might have been. The Rogs had built a maze with no exit for people like us.

"Beecher couldn't find a way out," I said, my lip trembling.

"It was awful," she whispered. She was the one who'd screamed when he threw himself off that bridge. I'd kept my mouth shut. Mrs. Harris had been proud, not knowing what use I would put my silence to.

I stared into the distance. The moon cast its light through the haze over DC.

"Inside that dome," I said, "Sera's toiling away, punished hour by hour. Or maybe Lucretia Rog is just torturing her for fun."

"You never liked Sera Croate," Saretha said with care.

"That doesn't mean..." I broke off with a sob. I couldn't face thinking about what plans Lucretia might have for her. She might spare Victoria her wrath because Victoria was her daughter, but Sera wouldn't be so lucky. "Sera has no family. She has no one." My heart lit with a need to do something. I began to pace.

Kel had moved outside the shelter and was quietly attending to one of the printers nearby. When I called her name, she turned and walked over to us.

"Can't we send Sera a message?" I asked.

Kel held the small printer in her hand. It whirred and struggled, like it wanted to get back to work.

"There's no WiFi out here," she explained, holding the printing drone out for me to see. "These are hacked."

"And we're going to Crab Creek!" Saretha exclaimed. "To find our parents, remember? Not to save Sera in DC!"

My breathing hitched. "If we make it to Crab Creek, and *if* we find our parents and manage to free them, what will we tell Sera's mother? She's there, too."

Saretha looked taken aback.

Kel let the printing drone go. It flittered off to find the rim of the shelter, where it began printing again. "If I can get a message to Sera, I will," she said. "But I doubt it will be possible. Lucretia Rog is going to shut everything out now, no matter what Patents or Laws she has to break. She knows by now Kiely hacked in and contacted her daughter. She blinded a whole city just to stop your escape."

"What do we do?" I pleaded.

"Leave," Kel said. "Find your parents. Go with Norflo and Margot to Téjico. I know you feel awful for Sera, but there are millions of people worse off."

Kiely had said much the same thing—I couldn't do everything, no matter how much I wanted to help.

"Look, I don't know what you'll find at Crab Creek," Kel continued. "But they're not going to just let you walk in and set your parents free. I wish I could tell you what you're facing, but communications are shut down."

Two lights shone in the distance. Kiely was back. The van turned, silhouetted against the long low form of the DC dome, and then turned again, blinding us with its light.

Kiely stepped out, and the lights from the van dimmed. It wasn't the same van from before—it was larger and decorated with fruits and vegetables, all held in the claws of an enormous stylized crab. My heart started to race. In the faint light of the printer, I could just barely read the words below the image.

Crab Creek Farms—Exclusive, Garden-Fresh Produce.

"This, at least, should get you inside," Kel said as Kiely reached us. Her face was bright and exuberant, and for a second I thought she was going to sweep Kel up into a bear hug. Then her head tilted, like she'd heard something.

"Are our parents..." Saretha started.

Kiely held up a finger. She stepped over to the shelter door and waved everyone out, then moved to the printer, her eyes searching the night. Without looking, she managed to catch the printing drone midprint. It struggled for a moment before she shut it down, leaving a messy ribbon of plastic squiggled in the air. The area fell dark, save for the glow of the DC dome.

"Grab a stick," she whispered to us all, her shadow reaching down to grab one off the ground. Something was out there.

I heard Mira whimper, "Bears?" Margot shook her head and shushed her. I put my hands to the ground and, after a moment's searching, wrapped my fingers around a thick, weighty branch.

"Dropters," Kiely whispered.

I heard a faint hum, then spotted the tiny blue light of a NanoLion™ battery bobbing a few yards off. It was easier to see if I looked away and used my peripheral vision. There were more behind it. A breeze blew across the clearing, and the dropter motors pitched up and down, compensating for the wind while holding steady.

Suddenly, there was one right near me. The dropter whipped by my ear, followed by a hard crack. The blue light went spinning off and sparked to the ground. Kiely had batted it away.

"Four more," she said, putting her back to me. "Don't let them escape."

The remaining dropters spread themselves out, silhouetted against the DC dome. Behind us, something swished as Mira took a practice swing. When I turned to look, one was moving straight at my face. I hauled back, swung and missed. Saretha stood frozen as it passed her. It tilted and started to move off. I bounded after it, raised the stick over my head and brought it down fast. The hard crack of the dropter's plastic casing told me I'd gotten it. It plummeted into the grass, and I stepped on it for good measure. Its engines whined in protest, then ceased with a hard *snap* as it shattered under my foot.

Behind me, Margot swung and knocked one sideways, right into Kiely's path. Kiely hammered it hard enough that the battery hissed and sputtered blue-white flame in the dirt, then erupted, filling the clearing with crisp white light.

"Two," Kiely counted off.

"How did they find us?" I gasped.

"I should have been more careful," she growled.

The two remaining dropters abruptly turned and flew off, calculating the danger. I caught one with a lucky smack. Kiely swore as the other one sped out of reach, but Kel reached back, plucked the fist-sized printer from its spot and hurled it out into the night.

It arced perfectly into the retreating dropter, knocking it to the ground. Norflo hustled after it and pounced before it could recover.

"You are incredible," Kiely said to Kel. Kel beamed at the compliment, hiding her smile behind an embarrassed hand.

"They transmitting?" Norflo asked, cupping the last one as it sputtered in his hands.

"No," Kiely said, taking the small dropter from Norflo and looking it over. "They're out here looking for what caused the WiFi to go down. When they find it, they head back in and report."

"*We* are what caused it," Mira said, coming closer. She reached a finger toward the dropter.

"You should not touch it," Margot warned. "If it was connected, it might *zap* you." She stomped her foot, which made Mira jump. Margot's face sparkled for one brief moment with playfulness, but then I could see her remember Henri was gone. The air seemed to darken around her.

"Just be careful," she said, businesslike once more. Margot dropped her stick. Mira picked it up, trading hers out, then moved closer to her sister.

"We're going to have to move," Kiely said, gesturing toward the white-hot glowing battery fire. "When they don't return, someone will come looking, and this mess is a beacon."

KEL'S ADVICE: $37.98

"I want you to leave this behind," Kel said to me. She meant more than the camp, and more than the Dome of DC, where Sera had been abandoned. I sat in the van's driver's seat. The faint smell of fruit hung in the air, remnants of whatever delicacies the van had delivered before Kiely stole it.

"You did your part," Kel went on. "More than any fifteen-year-old should have to."

"I'm not fifteen anymore," I said. I didn't know exactly how long we'd been on the road, or how long Lucretia Rog kept me, but I was sure my birthday had passed by now.

"I'm going to return to Portland, to help your friends there and fend off Lucretia as long as we can. We'll help the people you inspired. You don't need to feel bad about leaving this behind. What's ahead of you will be hard enough."

"She's right," Saretha said, settling herself in the passenger seat. The others were gathered around Kiely by the shelter, absorbing some kind of instruction or wisdom from her.

"I don't even know what's happening in Portland," I said. "How can they—"

"I have good people in place. Placers I know and trust. Your friends Mandett and Nancee are dedicated to rescuing others the way you rescued Nancee. What you choose to do now is all that matters."

Nancee. I hadn't thought of her once since we'd left Portland. "She never would have been taken if she hadn't copied me," I said hoarsely.

"Did you make her do that? Did you tell her to go silent?"

"No, of course not, but..." I paused, searching for the right words to say. "What if Portland needs me?" I asked.

"What if every place needs you?" Kel answered.

Saretha was shaking her head. "I don't ever want to go back," she said, pressing her hands down on her legs. "And *I* still have followers there." Kiely and I both turned to look at her in astonishment. Was she really still thinking about *followers*? Can you even have followers without a Cuff? I didn't ask aloud—it would only hurt her feelings.

Can you have followers after the world has been destroyed?

Kel pulled out a Pad. "I wish I'd had time to plan with you and get you a Pad and a map before you had to flee," she said. "Though, I will admit, I would never have sent you to Crab Creek. I don't know what you're facing there." Her expression turned fierce. "You have to promise me you will abandon this plan if it looks too dangerous."

I wouldn't make that promise. She knew it.

"Your parents might not even be there. Lucretia Rog could have—"

"No," I said. "She'd have played that card when she had me." I didn't know if I would have been able to withstand watching her torture my parents.

Kel sighed and tapped a few commands into the Pad. A map of our area popped up, outlining the route to Crab Creek. Kel handed it to me with a serious look.

"Security will be heavy at Crab Creek, even if they *haven't* clued in to the fact that your parents are there. Use the van as camouflage. Be patient. Figure out exactly where your parents are being kept, and how, before you do anything. Then come up with a plan. Use your Placer skills. Quiet. Careful. If the alarm is raised, it's all over."

A weight settled in my chest. Sera's mother was there, too. Hundreds of people were trapped. Was I supposed to leave them all behind?

Kel saw the thoughts behind my eyes. "You have enough people to look after," she said, looking at the group around Kiely. "You can't save everyone down there."

"This is an awful pep talk," I told her.

Kel flashed a bright smile, but it was also a little sad, like she was sorry that we wouldn't have time to talk now that I was speaking. "You have to get away," she said.

"To Téjico?" I asked, feeling dread about a place I knew so little about. I had to push what I'd seen in movies aside. Had they wanted us to fear it? They had fed us so many lies. Why would this be any different?

I wanted to ask more, but there wasn't time. Dropters and worse would be crisscrossing the area soon, looking for the ones we'd downed.

"Find your parents and go," Kel insisted. "Let yourself be happy."

"That's ridiculous," I laughed. I didn't know how. I could hear Sam's voice in me as I kneaded at my brow with my fingers. I was leaving too much behind. Sera, Nancee, Penepoli and Mandett—would I ever see them again?

"What if our parents want to go back to Portland?" I asked, knowing that was a terrible choice, but feeling the pull of it all the same. Our whole life had been there. Was it foolish to feel even a moment's homesickness for the small plastic room that I'd hated my whole life?

"They won't," Kel said, shaking her head. "If you can be a family again, let that be your victory."

"Every choice feels wrong," I said. "Sera—"

"It would be worse for you all to be caught," Kel cut in. "That's all that waits in DC."

The group behind her broke up and started heading for the van. Kiely scanned the area, watching for any sign of dropters. Kel took a step up and wrapped her arms around me. I hugged her back, something I hadn't been able to do before. I wondered what it would have been like if we'd had more time. I'd never had the chance to let her know the real me.

THE BREAKING GOODBYE: $38.97

Kiely said there was no time for goodbyes, but they happened, anyway. As we left, even she and Kel took a minute with each other. Kel seemed like a different person in that moment. She and Kiely clasped hands, looking into each other's eyes. Kel seemed younger, and Kiely less severe. It was only a second or two before they both climbed into the OiO™ van and headed off into the night. I hoped, someday, I would see them again.

I peeked back as the last curve of DC's dome vanished behind us.

The fruit van we were in was open from the cab to the back. There was plenty of room, but it wasn't very comfortable. Margot and Mira sat silently on one side of the floor, with Norflo across from them.

The van seemed cavernous without Henri and Sera. "Do you want to sing?" I asked Mira. I needed a distraction.

"Why?" Mira asked, her voice very small.

I shrugged. The muscles in my back were taut and aching, and we'd barely started our journey. I turned the shrug into a shoulder roll to loosen them.

"Norflo," I said, suddenly remembering. "Kiely showed me a history of my family. You were right about Jiménez."

His bright enthusiasm had dimmed while I'd been held

prisoner. Who could blame him? Still, he looked up and gave me a pleasant smile in the rearview mirror.

Saretha exhaled loudly and shook her head. "Our parents never said anything about it."

"Lots don't. Mine spent a lotta time back in the FiDos talking names and history."

"But yours is spelled wrong," Saretha said.

Norflo laughed. "How can you *hear* how I spell it?"

"Your brother told me," Saretha said, leaning back in her seat and adjusting her legs with a little groan.

Norflo sighed. "True. Couldn't afford Juarez—they spiked the price on Latin names long back. Like, crazy expenses. But Juarze counts."

"I can't hear the difference," I offered.

"War Rez," Saretha said loudly. "Not *Warz*."

Why was she being so difficult about this?

"Anyways," Norflo said, "my dad and his dad let us know all the names got changed. Said to 'member them. Jime from Jiménez. Gark from Garcia. Gonz from Gonzales, Tide™ from Fernández."

Saretha clicked her tongue. "How do you get Tide™ from Fernández?"

"Corporate sponsorship," Norflo said. "Didn't name me Norflo after the nasal spray 'cause they wanted to. Offset the cost of holding that Juarez surname."

"Except you didn't," Saretha needled at him. "You had to change it to Juarze."

"Me? Nah," Norflo said. "'Twas long 'fore me. Juarze still counts, tho. Still pricey, too."

"Your brother Wuane acted like this was *so* important. So what if the names got too expensive?" Saretha said like she was bored. "You change it to what you can afford. What's the big deal?"

"That's Harris talking," Norflo said.

"They do it to break us apart," I answered. "They don't want us to know anything outside of what we owe. They hold back our words so we can't connect to each other or our past—" a chill ran down my spine, thinking of Beecher's lost hope "—or our future."

"I don't even know what that means," Saretha complained.

"I do," Margot said. In the mirror, I saw that she was no longer looking down, but staring off into space.

Mira grabbed her arm and shook it. "What?" she whispered. "What?" Margot wasn't going to answer. She was thinking of Henri, but she put her arm around her sister and pulled her in tight.

Saretha scoffed. I didn't want to be angry with her. We hadn't been able to talk for so long, but the things she was saying made my jaw tighten. "Saretha, can't you see what it did to us?"

Saretha's face crinkled. We bumped up onto a new road that Kel had marked for us on the Pad. A red line threaded across a green landscape on the screen.

"The thing that split our family apart was you going silent," Saretha snapped.

The lack of compassion in her voice troubled me. Her mood had darkened since we'd left the clearing, and I wondered if the drive was making her pain worse.

"No, Saretha," I said, keeping my emotions in check. "They took our parents long before that."

"But..." she started.

"Think of what they did to make Beecher so desperate. Think how they destroyed him."

"He was funny," Norflo said. "'Fore his Last Day gutted him."

"Henri was funny," Margot said. Mira nodded.

I felt a lump in my throat. "I still can't believe he's gone," I said.

Margot's eyes met mine in the rearview mirror. There was a hard look on her face. I knew it was the sort of thing I should ignore—that was polite, and she was hurting. But I'd stayed silent about so many things.

"Are you still mad for what I did to get Henri's device?" I asked. She didn't answer.

I glanced back at her over my shoulder. "I'm so sorry," I said. "I apologized to him back in Keene. It was an awful thing I did. It wasn't fair to trick him like I did—that's what the Rogs do."

"What upset me most was not that you tricked Henri into thinking you liked him," Margot admitted. "It upset me more that he liked you back." I started to protest, but she raised her voice. "He was in awe of you," she said. "Even before you ever met."

"He was in awe of what the Silent Girl had done," I replied. "But he was in love with *you*."

Margot was quiet for a moment. A tear slid down her cheek. "Knowing that only makes losing him harder."

Mira hugged her around the middle and squeezed. I opened my mouth to apologize again, but Margot suddenly snapped to attention. She raced to the van's rear window, steadying herself against the uneven bumping on the ancient, pitted roads.

"There is something back there," she said.

I checked my side mirrors, my rearview, even quickly turned my head, but I couldn't see anything. Norflo hurried to Margot's side, which meant I couldn't see out the back at all.

"What is it?" I yelled.

"One of those small dropters," she called back.

I tried again to see it. Nothing. It was too small for me to see from where I sat. This wasn't good. "Just one?"

"I think so," Margot said, her head whipping from side to side as she tracked its progress.

My instinct was to panic and floor it, but I doubted the fruit van could outrun a dropter. I forced myself to stay calm. If we'd hit a WiFi bubble, it might be broadcasting a live feed. While I could hope we weren't visible inside the van, it was safer to assume the worst.

I took the next turn, spiraling off an exit calmly.

"What are you doing?" Saretha asked, watching us depart from the path on the Pad's screen.

"Throwing them off the trail," I said. I held firm. I didn't speed up. The van was silent around me.

"On the count of three, I want you to open the back doors," I said after a mile or so. "Everyone hold on. I'm going to slam on the brakes."

"What?" Saretha asked.

"Do it!" Margot yelled. She understood. Norflo gripped the wall.

"One," I called out.

"Margot?" Mira asked.

"Two."

"Hold on to Saretha's seat," Margot said with a flick of her hand.

"Three!"

Margot slammed her door open. The van suddenly filled with a rush of air. Norflo fumbled and got his door open, too. The pavement rushed by, and I finally spotted the dropter as it hovered and bobbed, matching our speed.

I jammed on the brakes. Margot yanked her door shut and held on, but Norflo went flying, smashing into my seat.

The dropter whizzed to the front of the van, turned on me with a big glassy lens and zipped away. Margot slammed Norflo's door shut just in time to stop its escape. The dropter's motors whined. Mira leaped up to grab it, clapping her hands together.

"First try!" she said, catching it.

"No!" Margot called out.

A thin, electric crack sounded, and Mira screamed. Her arms flew apart. The dropter hit the roof, its motors flaring, buzzing around like a trapped, angry hornet. Margot burst into a karate kick, her foot connecting with the small machine. The dropter smashed into the other wall and fell. Margot stomped on it, then rushed back to Mira.

"Are you okay?" she asked, her voice shaking.

Mira sniffed. Her upturned palms were bright red.

"This is nothing," Margot assured her at once, though she was visibly upset. "See what we have in the kit for burns," she said with forced calm to Norflo. Norflo instantly obeyed, rifling through Margot's Placer bag.

Saretha looked on, her mouth hanging open. She pressed on my arm, like I hadn't seen any of it. Like I wasn't paying attention. Like I didn't need to drive.

"We should assume that whoever sent the dropter has seen

us," I said, looking back. I turned the van around. "I doubt they were fooled by my exit, but we can hope."

"We can hope," Margot replied mechanically.

Norflo found a sealed package of Banded® Advanced Bialoe™ cream and quickly handed it to Margot. She tore it open and squeezed it into Mira's hands and had her rub them together. Relief showed instantly on Mira's face.

"Nextime," Norflo said, rubbing his head where he had banged it, "hope your tactic isn't *sudden brakes*."

I sorely wanted to tap the brakes right then, just to be funny. Norflo would have laughed, but this wasn't a time to be mischievous. We had to get back on the path to Crab Creek. Maybe then I could make a joke, or take a rest or let my mind wander from the list of what I had to do. Once we arrived, my parents could figure out what came next.

But until then, it was up to me. I pressed a little harder on the gas and forced myself to believe that soon, things would be better.

CRAB CREEK: $39.99

Our route took us on a new road. The van hummed quietly when we hit the vast black pavement. Sponsorship signs lit up to let us know we were in Agropollination™ territory. This was different than what we had encountered before. This outdoor space wasn't abandoned—it was owned.

"Should I be proud of Carol Amanda Harving?" Saretha asked. I guess it made sense to have something to talk about.

"What do you mean?" I asked. I tried to make my voice sound curious, but somehow my agitation must have gotten through because I could feel Saretha bristle.

"I *mean*, since she wasn't real—since she was actually me, it's like *I've* been in a lot of movies."

Norflo nodded like this made sense to him. "Sure," he said.

"But you were not the actress," Mira said.

Saretha started to list the films. "*Phat Dash. Truly, Lovely, Danger. Name of the Sparrow. Girl ReBranded.* What was the one where she gets sued because she's sick?"

"Autumn's Trial?" I asked, a little disgusted. "That was her first movie. It wasn't a big role. She dies in the first twenty minutes and you're supposed to be glad because the movie makes it seem like it was her fault for not having the money for the cure."

"No. It *was* her fault," Saretha said. "She ignored the Terms of Service."

Sera and my sister probably would have gotten along well back in Portland.

"She had cancer," I said.

"They show her using the food printer wrong. She tampered with the inks. That's why she got the cancer."

"Propaganda," Norflo commented.

"Her character still didn't deserve to die," I insisted.

"She got an award for that," Saretha continued. "That should be *my* award."

"You should message them," I offered.

"Don't be a brat," Saretha snapped.

"But who acted it?" Mira asked.

"No one," Margot explained.

"Wonder who sponsored that flick?" Norflo muttered.

"Mandolin..." Saretha stopped, realizing Norflo was being sarcastic.

Outside, the scrub grass was gone, replaced with lush greens. A new dome loomed as we came over the rise of a hill. This dome was small compared to the others I had seen, just large enough for a dozen buildings a few stories tall. Another of these smaller domes was a little farther off, and opposite both were fields.

"I hated her a lot, you know," Saretha said after a moment.

"I did, too," I said in a rush. "It felt so wrong that she got everything and you were supposed to be nothing. When I found her apartment, before I knew she was a fake, I seriously thought about hurting her."

This made Saretha smile.

Long rows of green plants extended into the distance, water

spraying out in geyser fans between them. I didn't know what kind of crop I was looking at. It was odd and bulbous. We didn't get a lot of produce in the Onzième, and I'd never seen whatever this was.

"And then it turns out she's me," Saretha said, her tone growing darker. She'd once pinned her dreams on meeting Carol Amanda Harving, only to be betrayed by her idol, locked away, then betrayed again when the actress turned out to be a digital shadow.

"She was never you," I said. "She *looked* like you. You're more than that."

Saretha lolled her head over at me—a sign of real irritation.

"Speth. I'm *your* big sister. It isn't the other way around. I've been giving you advice since you were little."

My jaw tightened. I'd been doing everything I could to take care of our family from the moment Saretha was locked in our apartment. But she wanted the role of big sister. If that made me bristle, maybe I had to suffer a bit to make her happy.

Soon we began passing rows and rows of trees. These were easy to identify by the peaches hanging off them, unripe and green as they were. Thinly netted mesh fences bracketed them for protection or, from the look of it, to keep them warm. Farther on were more greens, viny ones with thick bunched yellow flowers.

"Just because I had to desist didn't mean I stopped being in charge," Saretha went on.

Instead of arguing with her, I thought it would be easier to just thank her, but the words caught in my throat. In among the vines, there were men and a few women, bent low to the ground, brushes in hand, dabbing at an apparatus attached to their Cuffs. I slowed. The Indentureds ignored us.

At the field's rim, a few guards in tan jumpsuits turned—men of odd and troubling proportions, with that same heavy brow and dim, thuggish look as Lucretia's bodyguards and the brothers who had murdered Sam. Each clutched a black metal gun slung around their shoulders. They seemed agitated and suspicious, but made no move to intercept us. The van was doing its job.

I scanned the vastness of the fields and felt the insurmountable task we were facing close in on me, even as the space seemed to sprawl out to infinity.

"How will we find them?" I asked Saretha. We weren't even in Crab Creek yet. The farm was still miles away on the map, an hour's worth of travel.

Saretha gasped. Her face was horrified. The outlook was bleak, but her gasp seemed somehow out of place and melodramatic until I spotted what she'd seen.

Two children were looking up at a guard, showing him something in a roughly printed basket. He nudged one of them back with his gun. The younger one started to cry, then smothered her tears so as not to attract any more ire.

There were *children* working in those fields. Kids as young as Sam was and younger. One woman had a baby on her back, sleeping, brown-skinned in the relentless sun. A boy of about ten ran a hand across his brow, and one of the guards yelled at him for the pause. A child-sized Cuff was on his arm.

"How's this possible?" Norflo whispered, his eyes wide. "Kids aren't supposed to be here. You got to be at least fifteen 'fore you face Indenture."

Norflo's face reddened with anger as Mira and Margot moved to look out the windows. His head shook, refusing to believe it.

"We could have been with them all along," Saretha said.

At first, I couldn't quite take in what she meant. I couldn't really understand anything for a moment. "Who?" I asked.

"Mom and Dad," Saretha said. "We could have come and worked with them, like these families."

My insides filled with ice. Did she really believe *that* was a solution? How could that really be what she wanted?

"Saretha, do you realize what this means?" I asked. "This isn't about paying off some family debt. This is about them making families—*our* family—slaves."

"Slaves?" Saretha said.

Margot held Mira close, as if someone might snatch her and put her to work in the field. Worried that her fear might not be unfounded, I drove us faster. I checked the mirrors in case someone was behind us, but I saw no one other than the Indentureds. The land around us was lush and green—beautiful, really, save for the people forced to work it, suffering, dead-eyed and broken.

"It's worse than being Indentured," I said. I explained what Kiely had told me as we began passing untended fields. Water sprayed up in high jets, misting back to the soil. The sky was a clear, deep blue, made deeper by whatever the black glass of the van did to filter it. A low, dark cloud smudged the horizon, like an ominous warning.

The road became straight and flat. The foreboding clouds hung low and strange, billowing in thick swells, like they were spewing forth from something just over the horizon. I was new to the sights of the outdoors, so it took me a while to realize I wasn't looking at clouds.

"I think that's smoke," I said. I felt everyone shift to look.

"Is that a volcano?" Mira asked.

"No," Margot said, moving Mira gently back as if it might be. "The road is blocked ahead."

A security van was parked sideways, purposely blocking the way. Several more lined each side. Guards were gathered around it in the same tan overseer jumpsuits we'd seen earlier. Some were out in the field, but I couldn't see any Indentureds.

"We should find a way around," Margot said.

"There isn't any," I said, removing the Pad from its perch and handing it back to Norflo, since he was closest. He and Margot leaned in, scrolled and swiped, looking for an alternate route. Mira jumped to try and see.

"We'd lose too much progress," Norflo said. "We're almost there."

The source of the smoke came into view. It billowed from a long, low barracks, like those we'd seen in OiO™. A large crab listed from the roof, its claws emptied of fruit.

My ribs seemed to tighten around my heart. We'd arrived at the edge of Crab Creek, and it was on fire.

A DRAWN ARROW: $40.97

Kel's reminder to proceed with care rang in my head, but I don't think she'd expected Crab Creek to be in flames. We'd expected a fight, but it had happened before we arrived.

"Is it time to abandon this idea?" Margot asked, her voice flat, her eyes scanning around for other routes.

"Abandon? This is *it*," I said, worry and despair churning up through me. "All I wanted was to find my parents. This is where they're supposed to be."

Margot's face told me she thought it was too late.

"Maybe we can fake our way through?" Saretha suggested, terror in her voice.

"The only thing protecting us is the black glass," I said. "If they see inside…it's over."

"Floor it," Norflo suggested.

"Speth," Saretha said my name like I needed to *listen* to her. She wanted me to slow, to come up with a plan. She wanted me to trust that *she* knew best, but I couldn't.

I squeezed the wheel. We drew close enough that I could see the men were facing away. There were more men in jumpsuits out in the fields, sweeping the area, like they were looking for something. They weren't blocking the road into Crab Creek—they were blocking the way out.

"Slow down!" Saretha cried.

I ignored her and kept up my speed, looking for a way around that wouldn't involve mowing any of those men down. To the right, I found my opening and pulled on the wheel. A blast of wind hit the guards, knocking the hat off one of them. He raced to pick it up, receding into the background. None of the others raised their weapons. None tried to give chase. A few watched us, scratching their heads in confusion. But whoever they thought we were, we weren't worth their time, or pursuing us wasn't one of their orders.

Ahead, a small dome was burned out, leaving a mound of melted plastic behind in a ring around skeletonic shapes of whatever had been inside. Smoke wisped up in thin sheets. Beyond, a larger dome burned steadily along its perimeter. The plastic casing flared and noxious black smoke rose, carried and thinned by the wind into the distance, where it spread in a neat, ugly line. It appeared to have been burning for days.

"No one's putting it out," Norflo noted.

He was right. The landscape was empty of inhabitants. The larger dome seemed to be at the tail end of a massive fire. Nearby, long molten bands of plastic sludge smoldered—the remains, it seemed, of more barracks.

"Saretha..." I paused, trying to find the right words to say. Her gaze was frozen out the window, likely thinking the same thing I was. Fear rose up in me. This was where our parents lived.

"Everyone has fled," Margot said mechanically, taking Mira by the hand and sitting down as the van raced past the fire. "There is nothing here for you."

"Maybe they 'scaped?" Norflo suggested.

"How do you know?" I asked unsteadily, desperately hoping they were right.

"The workers are not in the fields, but the guards seek them," Margot said, a little more life in her voice. "The company would not set fire to its own property. It would not kill its workers. They are worth money. The road is blocked to prohibit escape. They did not care about us coming in, but they *will* care about us trying to leave. We are, again, trapped."

"We aren't theirs," Saretha said. "What do they care?"

"Stole this van," Norflo said. "That's one thing. Has a big crab on the side. They're gonna want it back. Also, 'spect they'll want to know who is inside eventually."

I scanned the landscape for clues or ideas. My mind kept coming up blank. What was the point of all this if I couldn't put my family back together?

"I am sorry, Speth," Margot said, like she understood the depths of my disappointment.

"Who's that?" Norflo pointed. In a field among more vines with yellow flowers was a solitary figure, brush in hand, dabbing at his arm and then into the petals. There were no guards, just him. He brushed a flower, then the next, took a step and repeated the process.

I slowed the van, curious.

"Speth, what are you doing?" Saretha asked me.

"I'm going to ask some questions," I said, pulling the van into the field and bringing it to a stop.

The man had to have noticed us, but he didn't acknowledge us as Margot, Norflo and I exited the van and approached. He kept at his task, robotically moving from one flower to the next. He looked like he'd led a difficult life, or was very old—perhaps both. His skin had the same leathered look as my parents', but it was darker and much more wrinkled. His hair was a mix of bleached blond and white, with a large tuft missing over his right ear. As we came closer, he watched us with a side-eye, but kept on brushing.

I didn't bother with an introduction. "What happened?" I asked.

He painted a few more dabs, then wiped his brow. The air was warm, and the fire burning nearby added to the heat.

"He can't afford to answer you," Norflo whispered in my ear. He and Margot stood on either side of me. Saretha and Mira watched from the van.

"Is that true?" I asked. "You can't afford to speak?"

He stopped. He held out his Cuff the way people do when they want you to pay for their speaks. In return, I showed him my blank forearm. He didn't look. He kept his eyes on his chore.

I took a nervous look around. We wouldn't go unnoticed for long.

"We can remove your Cuff," I said. Margot had a little blue teardrop device out. Kel must have given her a new one because Henri's was lost—with him. Sorrow washed through me.

The man shied away, putting his body between us and his Cuff. His Cuff was different than I was used to seeing—it was larger and held a long container full of pollen.

He bent down and wiped a hand in the dirt. It seemed like a meaningful gesture, but I couldn't work out what it meant. He made sure to hold his Cuff out, away from his body. He kept his head up, looking at the flowers, but scratched at the soil.

"Might have lost his mind," Norflo whispered.

"No," I whispered back.

The man went back to painting flowers. At his feet was an arrow. He'd *drawn* an arrow in the dirt. He'd used his finger and made the mark, and beneath it, he'd written a letter *T*. This was more frightening to me than any words he could have spoken. Even children weren't allowed to do this—though they occasionally would, often when they were too young to understand. They were badly punished for it. When Sam was five, he was beaten for it. As Mrs. Harris lashed him with a belt, she coldly explained that writing words, symbols or marks like this simply wasn't allowed. The Rights Holders had money to collect.

Despite the fear they'd instilled in us, I'd known for a long time that such a thing was possible. You didn't technically need paper or a pen to write. But in the Onzième—in the entire dome of Portland—there was no place for it. The plastics they used to print buildings weren't always great, but you couldn't easily scratch a message into them. Sam had only managed because he'd made shapes out of crumbs from a stale UltraGrain Harvest™ Bar.

It took a minute longer for my brain to realize what the old man was communicating. He casually brushed the arrow and the *T* away with a foot as he moved down the row to the next tangle of vines. He'd been careful not to look at his message, or its erasure, so his ocular implants wouldn't pick up on what he'd done. The arrow clearly meant something, but what? I followed the line of it, but all I saw was a break in a line of trees at the edge of the field. I needed more.

"What does the *T* mean?" I pleaded. He turned and stared blankly into the distance. He made no sound and no gesture. He glanced for a moment at his brush and then away. I looked down at it, too. It rested in his shaking hand, casually, not in any way you could describe as significant, but it was pointing right at my heart.

"I'm looking for my parents," I told him. No answer, of course. "Do you know them? The Jimes?"

A little smile appeared. He knew them. He flipped the brush around, so it pointed to him, but then stepped out of the way so it was pointing at precisely the same angle as the arrow he had drawn. This was no accident.

"Did they escape? Did they go that way?"

He nodded so slightly I would have missed it if I hadn't been watching so carefully.

That made no sense. If my parents had escaped, they would head to Portland. They'd do exactly what we had done, but in reverse. They would try to rescue us. They would come for Saretha and me. *Wouldn't they?*

"8391." A voice spoke urgently through his Cuff. Margot and I jumped, but the man seemed unsurprised. *"Have Indentureds returned to your location?"*

A pause.

"We will pay for your response," the voice added.

He licked his lips and twitched a smile.

"Haven't seem 'em in two weeks," he said. "Not since that OiO™ revolt where everyone *escaped*."

He lingered on the word *escaped*, like he loved the taste of it in his mouth.

His Cuff buzzed with the cost and its transfer. Then an InstaSuit™ popped up for his "overarticulated response." Five hundred dollars. He laughed to himself.

"8391, please limit response to necessary communication," the voice reprimanded. *"Are you alone?"*

"Who?" he asked.

"Are you alone?" the voice repeated irritably.

The man paused, thinking. I realized he was stalling. He hadn't looked at us purposely, so they wouldn't see us on his feed. His Cuff, though, must have registered talk in the area. He was stalling so we could get away.

"Alone," he said, looking contemplative. "No one's helped me since everyone ran."

"We are proceeding to your location. Do not move!"

Margot tugged at my arm, and the three of us broke into a run for the van. They were going to figure out we were here, if they hadn't already. I climbed inside and started the engine.

"What did you find out?" Saretha asked.

I put the van in gear, seeing a route between two rows of differing crops. It was in the same direction as the man's arrow. "We're heading that way," I said, pointing.

"To what?" Norflo asked.

I thought of the *T* and the only thing it could mean.

"Téjico," I said.

MEXICANS: $41.99

I pulled us into the field, following a long set of tracks on the ground and a trail of crushed, unripened fruit. I couldn't tell how many vehicles had driven through, but it was definitely more than a few. In some spots there were footprints, like the ruts had been examined, or maybe there was a struggle. I didn't know how to read them, only that sometimes on crime shows they could see things in the tracks people left behind. I was left with the distinct impression the Indentureds had been pursued.

"If our parents escaped, do you think they went home?" Saretha asked. I had to think for a moment to realize that she meant Portland.

"Nah, man pointed to *Téjico*." Norflo said the name as if that other country would magically provide answers to everything. I understood how he felt, and I wanted to share that feeling, but my heart was uneasy. If my parents *were* in Téjico, how would we ever find them?

We had to trust that the old man's arrow would lead us toward something better. My parents had come this way, I felt sure. I prayed we could pick up their trail.

"I don't understand," Saretha said. "Why aren't they looking for *us*? Why wouldn't they go home?" Her voice was pleading. She felt like we'd been abandoned and left behind.

Margot gave her an uncharacteristic bit of comfort by putting a hand on Saretha's back. I didn't have an answer for her, so I just said, "We can't be disappointed until we know what happened. We don't know that they had a choice."

Margot sighed, like I'd made her sadder.

Dirt and caked mud scattered out across the pavement where they had escaped. I turned the van to follow, no doubt leaving our own trail of dirt behind. The soil thinned as I followed the path. Soon it became little more than an occasional dirt clod. Then nothing.

"Maybe they knew?" Norflo said. "Maybe they felt the same pull?"

Margot silently fumed for a time before finally bursting out, "Téjico is not *pulling* us." I could feel angry heat radiating from her. I knew she was devastated by the loss of Henri, but something else was stewing inside her. Part of me wanted to remind her I'd lost Henri, too, *and* my brother. I'd expected my parents to be at Crab Creek, only to find them missing. How did she think that felt? But I couldn't think of a way to say those things that didn't feel petty and awful.

"Following the direction of that old man's arrow is our only real choice," I said.

"Yes," Margot said. "That is my point. Téjico is not *drawing* us toward it. We simply have no options."

"Téjico's an option," Norflo insisted.

"Is there somewhere else we could go?" Mira asked, her voice a little afraid.

"You're gonna like Téjico," Norflo assured her.

"Do not tell her that," Margot warned. The whole van was thick with tension now.

"I'm just trying to help," he said.

"What is our real name, Norflo?" Margot demanded. "What Spanish name do you get out of Chem?"

"I don't," Norflo said, taken aback.

"What do we even know about Téjico?" Margot went on.

"It's not here," he said. "Sometimes they call it Mexico."

"That is not much to stake our futures on and certainly no reason to tell my sister she will like it."

"What do *you* want to do?" I asked her, my patience reaching an end.

She didn't answer at once. I kept my eyes on the road. America® seemed to simply crumble away as we traveled. There were no more domes or even abandoned towns. The road was flat and cracked as we crossed from Carolina into Kennessee. Then the bleached grass and dirt of Kennessee gave way to sand that streaked the pavement from trucks that had passed this way. I found myself squinting as a strip of luminous white cloud extended to the horizon under a glowing morning sun.

Margot moved to the front of the van and stood behind me. After a good long while, she leaned in and whispered into my ear. "I do not know what to do," she said. "I fear there is no good place for us in this world."

She didn't want Mira to hear the hopelessness in her voice. I wanted to pull over and reassure her, but I had to keep driving, and I couldn't find the right words to say. The ones that would matter most to her.

We passed the old metal skin of an abandoned truck, rusted

and half-buried, sideways in the sand. Then another farther out, and a third, right at the side of the road.

"The domes were built for two reasons," Margot went on. We passed the scattered remains of homes, stores and bill-boards, but they had all eroded to little more than wooden bones and rusted metal beams. "To keep out the weather… and people from places like Mexico."

Something about this idea made me sick. The Mexicans were my ancestors—she knew that. Saretha and Norflo and I *all* had a connection to Téjico, even if Mira and Margot didn't.

I suddenly understood why she'd asked about the name Chem. "Margot," I said, matching the low tone of her voice. My sister leaned in so she could hear me, too. I probably should have thought more about what I was about to say, but the words forming in my head felt right, and if I could de-cide one day to be silent and stick to *that* choice, I could fol-low through on this one.

I let my voice get louder. "You will always have a place with us," I swore to her. "If you want it. No matter what."

BOLLARDS BETWEEN: $42.98

Far in the distance behind us, something else was on the road. I didn't intend to let it get close enough to learn if it was someone with ill intent.

On our left, a searing, glimmering mass appeared beyond the dirt and sand. The brightness of it was overwhelming. Saretha blocked the light with her hands and scrunched up her face. Margot sank down lower in the van and told Mira not to look.

An awful thought gripped me. What if some terrible accident had happened? Wasn't there a NanoLion™ factory near here? What if thousands or millions of those batteries detonated, chain reaction–style, like the explosion I'd caused back in Portland—but ten thousand times worse? What if it was the result of sabotage, inspired by me?

Then I caught a glint of blue. "S'the ocean," Norflo said with wonder, holding up the Pad so everyone could see the map of it.

A strange, nervous excitement ballooned in my chest. The sun's light sparkled against the distant water. "Look!" I cried to Saretha. From so far away, the ocean was a flat, brilliant expanse that didn't even look like water.

"Should we take a detour?" Saretha asked, squinting at it.

"No," Margot insisted.

"Probably shouldn't delay," Norflo said.

Saretha pouted. The water was too far away for us to really appreciate.

"But it's the ocean," I consoled her. "We're finally seeing the ocean, like we always talked about."

She gazed at the shimmering horizon, trying her best to appreciate it. "I don't know if this counts," she whispered. I wasn't sure, either. I'd always imagined being at the water's edge when I'd let myself dream about it.

At the end of the road before us, a dome rose up, shining above the horizon at first like it was floating, then dropping into a shining pool of water. The road appeared flooded. I wanted to slow down, but the car behind us kept coming, and I had no idea if it was chasing us or just following the same route by coincidence. Either way, there was no choice but to plunge on. At least we'd get to see the water up close.

But the closer we got, the more the water seemed to recede, like it was being siphoned away for our arrival—or, more aptly, like a special effect that didn't quite get the physics of water correct. But this was no digital trick. My ocular implants had been deactivated by Kiely. All of ours were. Whatever I was seeing was real, or, at the very least, a trick of some other kind. As we got near, the shimmering haze evaporated, like it had never been there at all.

On either side of the dome, as far as the eye could see, a massive concrete wall rose three stories high, stretching into the distance. In front of the wall sat a smaller chain-link fence, peppered with years of debris blown from across the landscape. A few pieces of trash rolled over the ground, buffeted by heavy winds. Both barriers snaked toward the water on our left and a distant rise of hills on our right.

The dome itself had a face of smooth plastic in three equal stripes of green, white and red. A gold star was perfectly centered within it. The bottom was a band of dull gray metal, inset with four massive metal doors, all shut tight. A series of thick steel posts jutted up from the ground, bollards arranged in a semicircle to further block our entry. I slowed the van and stopped a few feet from the first of these. This was the border we had to cross. Téjico was right before us, just out of reach.

"What now?" I asked.

Saretha pulled open her door. "Maybe there is a bell or something," she said.

"A bell?" Margot asked.

"Honk the horn!" Mira suggested.

"Please do not," Margot said.

"I got it!" Norflo said enthusiastically. He rushed out between the metal bollards and toward the shuttered doors. He was scarcely a few feet past the posts before something small careened to a halt in front of his face—a dropter. Norflo shirked away, then righted himself and began speaking to it.

I lowered the windows to try and hear what he said, but I caught just a few stray words under the wind. *Téjico, freedom, border.* The response from the dropter was, unfortunately, clear enough.

"Thank you for calling on the Independent Republic of Téjico. Admission to the IRT requires proper identification, as well as a visa in compliance with the Laws of both the IRT and the United States of America® East and West. These may be obtained in most major cities and domes."

Two other dropters appeared on either side of the van, their jewellike lenses focusing first on Saretha and then on Mira.

Norflo said something else, his arms outstretched. The response was broadcast through all three dropters.

"Due to the high administrative costs of vocal interaction demanded by the Rights Holders of the United States™, the Independent Republic of Téjico requests no further communication at this time."

The dropters zipped off. Norflo turned back to us, deflated and stunned. I shared his disbelief. Were they really going to just turn us away? Norflo didn't even bother returning to the van. He just leaned against a barricade pole and slumped in defeat.

"What now?" I asked. I dropped my head to the steering wheel. I was sick of this van. I was sick of this journey. I just wanted to be home—or, more accurately, I wanted to find one.

"We wait," Margot said, her face determined in a way I hadn't seen in a long while.

"For what?" Saretha asked.

"Until they allow us to enter or we bake to death in the sun," Margot said fiercely. "Let our bodies weigh on their consciences."

"I don't want to bake in the sun," Mira said.

"You do not," Margot affirmed—or corrected.

"You should take the van, Margot," I said, eyeing the rearview mirror. Whoever had been behind us was getting closer. They would arrive in minutes.

"And do what with it?" she asked, sounding a bit more like herself. "Drive back to Portland? It is too late for any of that. We have all agreed Téjico is our only option."

I looked at the colors of the small border dome blazing in the sun. I wondered if the star was made of real gold. Gold was very expensive, but only because the Patent to print it was priced so high. Was that true on the other side of that wall, too?

"How did our parents get through?" I wondered aloud.

"Maybe they went somewhere else," Saretha said. "Maybe they went north, to Portland, to look for us."

The truck behind us was quite near now, and I was suddenly struck by an idea. I pulled us to the side so we could be prepared for whoever was following.

"Norflo!" I yelled, calling him back to the van.

"What are we going to do?" Saretha asked as Norflo ran doggedly toward us.

"Fight," I said firmly, but before the word had even fully left my mouth, I saw the truck behind us was from Mandolin Inks™, not Lucretia's people. It pulled up and rumbled to a stop, bringing a hot, oily smell with it. Despite my half second's hope it would turn out to be a driverless vehicle, there was a man behind the wheel, staring intently ahead.

"He's not even looking at us," Saretha said.

The Mandolin Inks™ driver lowered his window and one of the three dropters approached him. Another hovered in front of the truck's front license plate, and the third seemed to sniff in a low circle around the bottom of the vehicle. The driver didn't speak. The dropters didn't ask any questions. The whole interaction took only a minute before the metal bollards retracted into the ground.

Ahead of the Mandolin Inks™ truck, one of the four enormous metal doors growled open and the driver headed straight toward it. I didn't wait to think about it because we might not get another chance. I knew it was probably illegal—or at least not what the people on the other side of that door wanted—but I put our van in gear and jammed on the gas to follow the truck inside.

BORDER CONTROL: $43.98

We were forced out of the van at gunpoint by uniformed guards, and made to stand in a line against the far right wall. The Mandolin Inks™ driver was sent to the left side and never once looked over at what we had done.

"No digas ni una sola palabra," the leader said in a low, intimidating voice. Behind us, the huge door closed, sealing the dome off from the sandy landscape.

The man wore a green, white and red badge that read Advik Ramírez—IRT Border Control, with a small yellow star beneath it. His skin was sun weathered and dark, though he seemed much healthier than my parents or the man we'd seen in the field. There was a pistol on his hip, but no Cuff that I could see.

"What?" I asked.

"¿Qué?" Norflo translated for me, a huge smile on his face. Despite the gravity of our circumstances, he was plainly thrilled to have made it onto Téjican soil.

Advik closed his eyes, as if that might give him more patience. Two other guards continued to point their guns at us while the rest swarmed our van and poked around inside.

"No apuntes les armas a los niños," Advik chastised. The guards lowered their guns.

One of them looked at me and said, "La Muda."

Advik nodded, then examined everyone else. His shoulders drooped when he got to Mira. His face scrunched up when he saw Saretha.

"¿Es usted Carol Amanda Harving?"

Saretha couldn't suppress a proud grin. His expression was one of confusion.

"¿Quiénes son ustedes?" he asked slowly, and when it became clear we couldn't understand him, he translated. "Who are all y'all?"

Norflo stepped up, barely able to contain himself. "Norflo Juarze," he said.

"Juarze?" Advik asked. "Not Juarez?"

Norflo shrugged and put out his hand. "Either way, I'm glad to meet you. ¡Me da mucho gusto conocerlos!"

"You're not afraid it'll costcha?" Advik laughed, shaking Norflo's hand. This normally would have cost $3.99 per second.

"We only know un poco español," Norflo said, embarrassed, struggling to get the Spanish part out.

Several of the border guards watched me as their cohorts searched our van. One of the guards in the van called out in surprise. "It's empty."

"There's no fruit in your fruit van?" Advik asked.

"We are fleeing an oppressive regime," Margot said. "We did not stop for fruit." Margot's sense of humor was mostly absent these days, but her cold sarcasm remained.

"I am Mira." Mira put her hand out, too.

Advik knelt. "Hello, Mira." He took her hand and shook it delicately, as if she was precious.

"Is that really free?" Mira asked.

"Absolutamente," Advik said.

"And talking?"

"Also free," Advik said, and then a little more sadly, "until you go back."

"I'm Speth," I said. "Jiménez. And we're not going back."

Advik's eyes widened. "La Muda," he said in wonder. "The Silent Girl. But…you're not silent?"

"Not anymore," I said.

Advik tapped at his thigh and looked from me to Saretha. "What happened? Why are you talking? Why is the leader of the Silents traveling with Carol Amanda Harving?" He waved over the other agents, who were eagerly listening to our conversation.

"I'm not the leader of the Silents, and she's not Carol Amanda Harving," I said. Saretha let out a breath like I'd spoiled her secret. Advik scrutinized us, unsure if he believed me.

"I've seen all her movies," he said, as if he might convince me that I was the one who was wrong.

"There is no Carol Amanda Harving," I explained. This confused him. "She's made-up," I clarified. "A fiction."

"A simulacrum." Norflo grinned, pointing to Saretha.

Saretha straightened her clothes. "They stole my image, if you want to know."

"Mmm." Advik did not seem to believe her.

"Look, we're just trying to find our parents," I said.

"In Téjico?" His brow knit with confusion. "How'd y'all get separated?"

"How did we get separated?" I asked, a little thrown by such a strange question. "My parents were taken from us when we were little. You know they do that, right? They split up families. They Indenture thousands of people in America®."

I began to worry they weren't here.

Advik's eyes darted over to the Mandolin Inks™ truck, which was just pulling away. "That information's proprietary, no?" he asked, shaking his head while tracking the truck out the door.

"I'm sure it is," I said. A frustrated breath escaped me. "How can you not know our parents are taken to work as slaves, and yet you know who Carol Amanda Harving is?" My voice rose with every word.

"They export movies, not information," Margot reminded us.

Advik's voice got low and very serious. "I know they make people work as Indentureds. We hear things. We see things. We've..." He looked around at the other guards. Was he wondering if he could trust them? "A lot of folks have turned up recently," he continued, "but I can't say if we let them in, because we can't be caught breaking any international Laws. ¿Comprende?"

"No," I said coldly.

He swallowed and spoke even more quietly, looking around as if he was worried someone would hear. "You don't have any idea what the Americans® did to us here, do you?" When we all looked at him blankly, a resolved expression crossed his face, and he added, "Follow me, I'll show ya."

NO ONE FLIES: $44.97

Advik took us into an office. There wasn't really room for all of us, but we jammed ourselves inside, anyway. A screen ran a loop of news silently on one wall. There was a story from Dallas. Another from Guanajuato. There were images of roiling water and stormy weather in a place where people were shuttering beautifully printed homes. There was a stunning gold building and a ribbon being cut.

Advik sat and pulled his hat back on his head, like he was overwhelmed. "Help yourself to water," he said, gesturing to a tall, clear tube of crystal clear water with a levered spigot below. I could tell he was stalling.

"What flavor?" Mira asked.

"It's just water," Advik said with a laugh. "Agua." He leaned forward, plucked a paper cup from a stack and held it out to her. Mira turned to Margot.

"But what flavor?" she whispered to Margot, as though Advik wasn't able to understand. She took the cup from Advik's hand and looked for a logo on it. It was blank, which felt weird.

Advik returned his attention to the rest of us. His amusement faded. "Y'all know some of this used to be part of the United States™, right?" he asked, waving a hand around as if he meant just the room.

We all hesitated, but I was the first to say, "Geography is proprietary. So is most of the history they fail to teach us."

He typed something on a membrane keyboard and pulled up a map like the one we'd seen in the truck back in Sylvania™, but these borders were different. There was no Téjico. There was the United States™, spread out from sea to sea, with Canada above it and Mexico below.

"You don't know any about of this, do you?" he asked. I got the distinct impression he had been through this before.

"We know a little," Margot said.

"Ever heard of the North American no-fly zone?" he asked. He tapped a button, and the map changed. The coastlines eroded a little, and a huge circle encompassed the whole map with a label: No-Fly Zone.

"Like the little insect?" Mira asked, buzzing for emphasis.

"No," Advik said slowly. "It's for planes. Do y'all know what planes are?"

Mira took a sip of her water and made a face. Margot shifted. None of us knew, but *she* did. "They were little more than flying bombs people once used to travel around the world," she said.

"Not exactly," Advik replied. "A few planes were used that way—a few out of literally millions. A couple of attacks—*terrible* attacks—changed everything."

He showed us an image of a huge gleaming bus with wide metal wings like a bird's, frozen midglide. It flew low over an undomed skyline, like the biggest dropter I'd ever seen.

"The US reckoned it was safer to ground all air travel to protect everyone. Anything larger than a goose caught flying over North America is blasted out of the sky now."

There were limits on dropter size—they couldn't be large

enough to carry a man. I'd never questioned why. I'd always assumed it was because of Patent fights—or maybe I'd never really thought about it at all.

"The middle states in particular were against that shutdown, but that wasn't what made us leave. That happened when they mandated we must *pay* to speak. *That* you know all about. But Texans—¡Dios mío! We couldn't put up with that. We revolted, and seceded from the US."

"Texans?" I asked. "Is that the same as Téjicans?"

"Not exactly," he said. The map reappeared, and suddenly Téjico expanded, taking over a state called Texas and a few others around it. Canada expanded, too, but downward, so that the eastern and western states of the US were separated. The Texas name changed to Téjico as it merged with Mexico below. "Texas far preferred to be part of a free Mexico than a United States™ that charged even for the word *freedom*."

"But I don't understand," I said. "How would the US go along with this? Why did *our* states agree?"

"They didn't exactly agree," Advik hedged.

"That is what caused the Civil War," Margot said. She seemed confident, but it turned out she wasn't right.

"No, the Civil War was different. Much older. There wasn't a war this time—only punishment," he said grimly.

"What punishment?" Norflo asked.

Advik typed a little more and pulled up a gorgeous landscape image dotted by thousands of fat brown-and-black animals.

"They didn't call it punishment. Maybe a consequence? They said they were protecting intellectual property Law. MonSantos™ claimed the genetic pattern of the cow. Y'all know what a cow is?"

We all did. Affluents could get BeefMilk™—you'd sometimes see Ads for it in wealthy neighborhoods. It was a rare delicacy we were told came from cows. I realized the animals in the image must be cows, though they didn't resemble the grinning, long-lashed cartoon versions I'd seen once in an Ad.

"Our farmers had to pay a million-dollar fee for *each* cow inside our nation's borders, or turn their cattle over to MonSantos™."

He brought up another picture showing even more cows. The sheer number of them was mind-boggling. I thought they were rare.

I leaned over to Margot. "Did you know about this?"

She shook her head, looking a little stunned.

"Obviously they couldn't pay," Advik continued. "There were a hundred million cows, spread out on cattle ranches across thousands of miles. If we were inclined to turn them over, it wouldn't have been physically possible to move that many cows—though a few ranchers put together a massive protest and tried to drive a hundred thousand cattle through here, just to show 'em."

"So what did they do?"

"MonSantos™ let them die. All of them."

"Why?" Mira asked sadly.

"How?" was the question I asked. How could they make the cows die?

"That company had been altering the genetic code of cows for years to increase yields of milk and meat. Most farmers liked it and paid a subscription fee to have these better cows. Even the ones who didn't eventually ended up with the Patented genes in their cows, so they had to pay, too. But that meant *all* the cattle were dependent on a specially modified grain stock. Without that specific grain, the cows couldn't eat;

they couldn't digest anything else. Most didn't survive more than a month. You can't imagine what came next."

"You said they died," Margot pointed out.

Advik nodded. He held his fingers over the keyboard for a moment, but decided against showing us the next part. "That much death is a catastrophe. There were more carcasses than could be managed. It caused massive outbreaks of disease. We didn't just lose a vital source of food; tens of thousands of people died from necrotic bovine infections. Infections which MonSantos™, by the way, owns the cures to. They raised the prices on the cures and made sure very few infected people survived."

"Awful," Norflo murmured.

"But it was all *legal*," Advik said, his voice hitting a high, troubled pitch. "That was very important to them. It had to be exactly legal according to the Terms of Service between our nations. They won't ever go to war, but they still have the ability to wipe out our corn, chickens and pigs that same way. They could kill us all." He turned toward the screen, avoiding our eyes. "I'm sorry."

"Sorry?" I asked. "For what?"

He looked sadly at the device in his hand. "For turning you in."

BETRAYED: $45.99

"Your Commander-in-Chief Justice issued a lawful extradition demand for you, Miss Jiménez, long before you arrived," Advik said regretfully.

"Then just take me," I said. I wasn't going to put the others in danger any longer.

"No, Speth!" Saretha cried out.

"The order is clear," Advik said, looking uncomfortable. "We have to turn over everyone and everything found with you."

I looked Advik over. Margot, Norflo and I could probably overpower him and get his gun. I wasn't afraid to try, either, but once we got out the door, where could we go? The guards were still out there, and armed.

"I don't have any choice," Advik said.

Norflo shook his head in disappointment.

"You should be so very proud," Margot said, holding on to her sister. Mira gave a little head nod to punctuate.

"I haven't even done anything," I protested, still trying to think of a plan.

Advik tapped a few times and posted the order on the screen.

"The list of crimes is extensive," he said.

"It's mostly lies," I replied.

"I don't doubt you, but I have no way to adjudicate," he said.

The Legalese grated at me. "Can't you help us? Isn't there some way..."

Advik was shaking his head before I finished. "If *they* were breaking the Law—if there were some way we could prove *that*, we might stand a chance to fight them, but we can't. We have no grounds." Advik's face darkened. He stood, signaling that we were done here. He gestured to the door. "You have to go."

"We'll end up tortured and worked to death!" I screamed at him. "They've promised not only to take me, but generations to come. Think about that. Think about what it *means*!"

He winced. "We can't harbor La Muda. I..." He ducked his head down low and whispered, eyes on the door. "Three weeks ago, we let through a few dozen refugees from the Archipelago of Disney™," he admitted. "A few days later, nearly a hundred more turned up from a factory dome that had turned to riots. Do you know why?" I shook my head. "They were following *your* lead."

"I never told anyone to riot."

"But they have taken inspiration from you. A mass of people from a farm in Carolina even *named* you when they came through. There aren't many places they—"

"What farm?" I interrupted. These had to be the Indentureds who escaped from Crab Creek. Had my parents made it?

"I don't know what farm," Advik said, as if he didn't see the significance. "Please don't make this difficult."

I watched the pistol on his hip in case he went for it, or in case I changed my mind and did it myself. Then the door to his office opened. There were more guards, in military black this time, and a man in a suit—a Lawyer, from the look of him, but he had a tag that marked him as a Téjican government official.

"Our parents escaped from a farm," I said desperately. "In Carolina."

Advik regarded me with pity. "I'm so sorry. I shouldn't have told you anything."

The official in the suit gave Advik an admonishing look. "We must ask everyone to stop talking."

"If we get caught, we'll have to turn them *all* out," Advik whispered. "All the refugees will have to go back, not just you and your friends. This is awful, but it is the Law."

As the official took my arm, something clicked in my brain. "What about Carol Amanda Harving?" I asked.

"It is too dangerous to keep her as well. She is too famous." His eyes drifted toward Mira and softened. "I might be able to keep the little girl—maybe we can do something for her."

Mira looked horrified and clung to her sister. The official didn't seem hopeful, even about this.

"You don't understand." I shook him off. "I'm talking about *Carol Amanda Harving*."

"What about her?" the official asked. His eyes darted to Saretha.

"You said she isn't even real," Advik said.

"We said she was *stolen*," I explained. This was a fight I had never finished, and suddenly, the injustice of it was boiling back up inside me. "They copied what Saretha looks like, made a digital re-creation, then filed a lawsuit against my sister in the name of that re-creation. They sued *her* for looking like the digital image *they* stole!"

Saretha pushed herself forward between the guards.

"They murdered our brother to cover it up," Saretha said.

I blinked. Had she finally stopped blaming me for what had happened?

"None of it was legal," I went on, desperate to make them see. There was a way forward, and it was all bound up in Carol Amanda Harving's stupid movies.

"Ma'am," the official said, unconvinced. He nodded for his men to take me.

"None of it was legal," I repeated, like I was driving a nail into a coffin.

Advik backed away, bumping into his desk. "I'm sorry," he said, brushing at his face. "Real sorry about your brother. But we aren't able to get involved in that. That happened inside your borders, not across ours."

"There must be something you can do!" I pleaded, but he wasn't getting it.

"He just told you, we can only do something if *they* break the Law across *our* border," the official said. "We're going to have to report the words you've spoken to your Rights Holders. US Law requires it."

The new guards in black had Norflo and Margot and were pulling them out the door. Another went straight for Saretha, then paused, as if trying to figure out whether she really was Carol Amanda Harving.

"Let her go!" Mira said, aiming a sharp kick at the guard who had her sister.

Words had failed me before, but I couldn't let them fail me this time. "They sold my sister's stolen image across your border."

"Stolen?" Advik asked, brow furrowed.

Two guards came up on either side of me and took my hands. Saretha tried to stop them, but they pulled us apart.

"My sister's image. They used her likeness *without* her consent," I said as they clamped my wrists into cold metal handcuffs behind my back. "Or my parents' permission. They broke the Law."

Saretha let them cuff her and spoke with surprising calm.

"'International Copyright Law, Section 17A, prohibits the use of a person's likeness without legal consent,'" she quoted. When she saw my astonishment, she explained, "I read that damn DESIST letter a hundred times."

Advik went a little pale. The official held up a hand.

"You sound like a Lawyer," Mira said to Saretha. "Except you said the *D* swear."

"They knowingly sent illegal material here?" Advik whispered. He pressed his palms to his forehead.

"Yes," I said, excitement mounting in me. They were getting it.

The official faced me. "You can prove this?" he asked.

"Yes," I said, nodding my head at Saretha. "She is all the proof you need."

NONE SHOULD SUFFER: $46.97

Saretha beamed beside me as we were escorted deeper into Téjico. They were letting us in. For now. The same guard who had manhandled us now kept telling Saretha how important she was. She was incontrovertible proof the US had engaged in illegal activity across the international border with Téjico. He kept pulling up Carol Amanda Harving's movies on his personal device and marveling at the resemblance.

"They didn't get your eyes right," he said.

The funny thing was that I'd seen *their* country in movies and shows before, with low adobe buildings and dirty slums that made the Onzième look like paradise. They didn't get that right, either. The reality of Téjico was very different. Each building we passed had been carefully and beautifully printed in terra-cotta and sand, with ornate designs accented in gold. I felt like we were driving through a utopia.

"How can you afford all this?" Saretha asked. "It looks like everyone here is an Affluent."

"Printing doesn't cost anything," the official, named Arturo, explained kindly. He had big brown eyes with long lashes, and he spoke in a soothing, deeply earnest voice.

"For you, señorita," he continued, "they make printing an expense, and that is both needless and very sad. No person need ever feel hunger. No building need ever be ugly. We have the technology and the aspiration to provide everyone with what they require, at the very least."

I'd wondered for a long time what the world would have been like if everything wasn't tied to demanding profit from every little idea. Now I had a chance to see. People walked along the sidewalks in gorgeous, perfectly fitted clothes. They had lovely hair and shoes and could walk in peace without Ads chasing them, telling them they were too fat or thin or ugly. The few screens I did see were decorative or informational.

"We have a saying," Arturo went on. "*Ninguno debe sufrir necesidad o querer, todos tienen que sufrir sueños.* It means *None should suffer need or want, all must suffer dreams.*"

"Why does anyone have to suffer?" Saretha asked.

"There is always an ache when you long for something better," I said, looking around, wishing we'd grown up in a better place.

"I like that," Norflo said.

Arturo went on, "We strive to let everyone live beyond need and want, so our work can be on dreams." He cleared his throat, suddenly looking serious. "Whereas those like your Commander-in-Chief Justice work to keep most toiling under need, leaving them unfulfilled. Our biggest impediments are what your nation has done to us and the constant threat of what they will do. Our hands are tied in many needless ways."

"I thought everywhere was like America®," I said, half choking on the words. I suddenly felt ashamed to have lived my whole life in a small dome, never really knowing about anything beyond it.

"When you build walls between nations and people, you make every life smaller," Arturo said.

"But..." Norflo trailed off, a shadow of doubt crossing his face. He so clearly wanted everything to be perfect here. "You *are* a wall. We just saw it." He jerked his thumb back toward where we'd come from. "Téjico and Canada make a barrier 'tween East and West."

Arturo nodded. "We do," he said, though without pride. "An ugly necessity—our greatest bargaining chip is separating East from West."

As we traveled, we tried to fill Arturo in on as many facts as we could remember. There was so much to say about what the Rogs had done that it all came pouring out of me. Thinking about how they'd so completely inverted the truth made my blood boil.

"They are so used to manipulating facts they forgot—they can *never* produce Carol Amanda Harving," I said feverishly. "That is their greatest flaw!"

When I stopped to take a breath, Arturo asked me to slow down.

"You are in a state of anxiety," he said calmly, like he was practiced at reassuring people. "You should rest, and tomorrow we can go over everything more carefully, with a team to support you."

"Okay," I said, letting out a deep breath. "I just feel so desperate to get it all out."

"I understand," Arturo said, looking at Saretha. "We have proof now that they cannot refute."

Saretha smiled at him, grateful that she'd found a role to fill.

"We have been looking for something like this for a very long time," he said. "I share your impatience, but we must be thoughtful and plan well. The Rog family is formidable, and the consequences of a misstep would be terrible."

"S'ben a very upsetting trip," Norflo commented.

"Of course," Arturo said. "That is why I suggest a pause."

"And our parents?" I asked.

"If they are here, we will find them."

"They have to be here," I said quietly, trying to ignore the fact that they hadn't come looking for us. They took off without any reason to think we would be able to follow them. Though I hadn't voiced it like Saretha, I couldn't understand why.

"We have sent for someone to take a DNA sample so we can match it against our refugee database," Arturo told us.

"Can't you just look up our family name?" Saretha asked.

"We do not take names. Names can be tied back to their owners in America®," he explained. "If your government requests extradition, we can legally claim we do not have a Speth Jime or La Muda. Anyone who made it inside the border has been counseled to change their name."

"I'm dropping Norflo," Norflo said. "Changing my name to Javier. Javier Juarez."

"No more Juarze?" Margot commented, but she said it with a smile. Norflo grinned back.

Did I want to change *my* name? I'd hated the name Speth my whole life, but changing it now felt like hiding, or being silenced—or, worse, erased.

Saretha frowned. "I've always liked *my* name," she said.

"You will need to keep it, anyway," Arturo said to Saretha. "We will need to legally establish your identity."

"But then can't the Rogs claim they own her?" I asked. "What happens if they try to take her back?"

Arturo took a moment's pause before answering. "They can't while this case is pending. If we win, they will not be able to make such a claim. You will be safe here."

"And if we lose?" I asked, dreading the answer.

"Then I am sorry to say, we would be obligated to turn you over to the Rogs."

"Both of us?" I cried.

Arturo shook his head. "More than just you and your group, I'm afraid. A loss in international court will have terrible consequences for you, for the refugees and likely for all of Téjico."

A dreadful, bitter anxiety roiled through me. "The Rogs don't play fair," I said.

"We know," Arturo answered.

"Should we not do this?" I asked, ashamed for wanting to flee. Kel had told me to go and be happy. "Couldn't we just find our parents and go far, far away from the Rogs?" I didn't know what lay beyond Téjico, but maybe there were more and better things.

"I wish this were possible," Arturo said. "It is not up to me. But I also hope you will make this last sacrifice. I know you have been down a very hard road, and this is a lot to risk. For all of us."

I swallowed hard. "Swear to me it's worth it. Swear we have a real chance."

"I swear," Arturo said with conviction. He truly believed it, but I couldn't. He didn't know the Rogs like I did.

I didn't want to rest. I wanted everything settled now, but we were put up in a hotel, anyway. Margot and Mira were given one room, Norflo another. Saretha and I were placed in a third.

We each had a bed of our own, something Saretha and I had never experienced. They were huge and soft—a million times more comfortable than the pullout couch we'd shared in our Ad-subsidized apartment.

Saretha flopped down on the bed near the window, spreading out her arms and sinking into the mattress. The other bed, I guessed, was mine.

"We're going to see Mom and Dad," Saretha said, her eyes closed. "We're going to be together, finally."

I sat down on my bed. I hoped she was right. I tried to feel relieved and joyful, but I couldn't. Worry still nagged at me. We had irrefutable proof that Saretha had been copied, but when had the Rogs ever let truth defeat them?

And there was another worry, simmering under everything.

"Saretha," I said, as gently as I could, "Mom and Dad still don't know about Sam."

She didn't answer at first. I wanted to look at her, to get some sense of what she was thinking, but I couldn't bring myself to do it. My vision blurred—it was so unfair that Sam was gone. I closed my eyes to hold back the tears.

"I'll tell them," she said at last. The warmth was gone from her voice.

"But..." I started to say that perhaps I should, but I didn't want to finish. Did she still believe it was my fault? Did I?

Her bed squeaked. "I'm older," she said. I could tell she was standing now. "It's my responsibility." I let my eyes stay closed, even though I'd suffered Lucretia Rog's cruel blindness and had wanted so badly to gulp in the world when my sight was restored.

"Do you still blame me?" I asked her, the words catching in my throat.

Her answer took too long. "No," Saretha said at last. The bed sank beside me as she sat. "No," she said again, with more conviction this time. "Those men killed him."

I opened my eyes. She was sitting with her hands in her lap, staring off at the wall. Even the simple hotel we were in looked like a palace.

"But, Speth," she said hesitantly, beside me, but not touching. "I can't not wish it had been different. I can't not wish you had spoken, and that it had saved him—that the Rogs might have forgiven us. He said he would let me be Carol Amanda Harving. Did you know that?"

"I suspected."

"What if that was our life?" she asked, brushing away her tears. "What if you and Sam and Mom and Dad and I all got to live somewhere special? We could say whatever we liked. It would have been wonderful."

"That was never going to happen."

"I know," she said in a hoarse whisper. "But I can't not want it."

"That's why Rog offered it," I answered, sitting up. I worried about how present her fantasy was. "Saretha, even Lucretia Rog's own daughter is so miserable in this world she went silent."

"I don't know what that has to do with wanting our family to be..." She couldn't finish the sentence. Instead, she sobbed, knowing our family would never be whole.

"No one can be happy in the world they've made," I said. "Not even them."

A long pause followed, and Saretha's face reddened with shame. In a humiliated whisper, she said, "Before you went silent, I was."

WHAT YOU COULD BE LIKE®: $47.99

I slept for a few hours, though it was still the middle of the day. Saretha was gone when I woke. She needed some time and space to herself, and I understood that. I hadn't been alone in a long time, unless you counted the sightless, deaf hours I'd spent locked away by Lucretia Rog.

We'd been given a lovely room with two beds, plush blankets, a chair and pictures of rolling sands on the walls. It was larger and nicer than the room we had grown up in. There was a wide window, covered by two layers of curtains, and the screen across the room was dark and silent. There was even a book on a chain by Saretha's bed.

I ran a hand across a wall. I couldn't feel any printing lines, only a fine pebbled texture. It might not have been printed at all.

The bathroom had a glass mirror instead of the screens that videoed you back to yourself at home. You could never quite trust those. They constantly popped up Ads about your flaws, and often altered your appearance to *What You Could be Like®*.

I hadn't really studied myself closely since the night before my Last Day. I wasn't the same person anymore. The girl in the mirror looked tired. She stared at me with a mixture of guilt and fire. Her gaze was a little detached. I brushed back her hair. The pixie cut wasn't very pixie-like anymore. If I'd seen this girl on the street, I'd have avoided her. She'd have worried me. She worried me *now.* She was hollowed out. She was angry. And she had a zit on her chin, which made me laugh at my own melodrama. For just a moment, I saw the connection between Sam and me, and my laugh died away.

The bumps on my neck beneath each ear filled me with anxiety. I wanted to claw out Rog's auditory implants. They couldn't hurt me now, but they reminded me of how far she'd been willing to go, and I wondered if they left me vulnerable in some way. I prodded them with disgust. Sera, I knew, must have been treated the same, but she was still subject to Lucretia's cruel whims. For the moment, I was free. Maybe if we won the case, we could find a way to free Sera, too.

I didn't want to think about Sera anymore, but I felt I owed it to her. I needed to remember her and Henri and Sam and everyone I might never see again.

The room was so quiet and my thoughts so loud I had to leave. I went into the hall and crossed to Margot and Mira's room. The door was partway open.

"Are you okay?" I asked as I pushed inside to find Margot sitting alone on her bed. She shrugged and put the Pad Kel had given us facedown.

"Where's Mira?"

"Taking a bath," Margot said, her voice a little strangled. I heard the gentle sound of water from behind the bathroom door and quiet singing. I'd never had a bath—we'd had no tub in Portland, only a shower—but I imagined it was nice.

I sat next to Margot. She wouldn't show me her face.

"Can I see something?" I asked, trying to respect that she wouldn't want to talk about what was bothering her. She was barely able to nod.

I reached over and picked up the Pad beside her. I wondered if it would have access to the Téjican WiFi. But when I turned it over, a frozen picture of Henri was grinning at me from the top of his file. Beneath the photo, his status was listed as *Deceased*.

"You can clear it," she said, wiping her face.

I didn't want to. I understood. Looking at Henri's broad, grinning face was agony, but neither of us should forget. His appeal score had been zeroed out because he was dead, but his employment status was still hidden.

"Please," she added, seeing my hesitation. I cleared the screen. Henri winked away along with his status. I wished I could remove the tag, that it would change what had happened. But these tags weren't magic. The definition of *deceased* was still *dead*. It didn't actually matter what the database said, or if the definition changed.

I stared at the Pad now, my mind a blank. I tapped at the news icon, but it just came back with a red flash and a *No Connection* message.

"There has been nothing about us on their news," Margot said, turning on the wall screen for me—maybe to distract me. A Téjican newscaster spoke seriously to the camera in Spanish. "Do you really think your Carol Amanda Harving information will let them do something?"

"They've been caught red-handed. We have proof," I said, sounding more optimistic than I felt.

"They will have proof, too," Margot said.

"Of what? Their own crimes?"

"Of whatever they want," Margot said. "The Téjicans seem to believe they will have a fair trial, but I don't believe it. Not with the Rogs involved. We should see if we can reach Kel."

"Kel?" I asked. "Why?"

"We will need all the help we can get," Margot said, her eyes rimming red. "And, however the trial plays out, I plan to take them to account for Henri."

"How..."

A knock came on the door, and Norflo's head popped in, grinning in a way that didn't match our mood.

"Gotta sec?" he asked, holding on to the doorframe to show he wouldn't cross inside without permission.

"Sure," Margot said, taking another wipe at her eyes and changing her face from sad to stony.

"DNA guy's here," Norflo said, beaming at us. "Found two matches for me!"

"Who?" I asked, as Norflo urged the DNA man into the room with his small kit. Arturo came in after him.

"We don't keep a database of names," the DNA man said, shooting a look at Arturo. "Someone should have told you."

"I did mention it," Arturo said. "But I can go over it again."

"We get it," I told him. "So you don't have any idea *who* the DNA matches are?" I asked Norflo.

"Gotta be my brothers," Norflo said. "Unless it's the 'rents. That would be amazing. I can't wait to see."

How could he be so happy about it? Didn't that mean his parents or his brothers had taken off and left him behind? Norflo didn't seem to care. Maybe they'd all agreed to be okay with whoever made it to Téjico, but we hadn't. Our family hadn't had a plan like that.

I hadn't said a word to Saretha about being disappointed our parents hadn't looked for us, but that feeling was replaced by a worse one. I didn't *know* that my mom and dad were in Téjico. We'd followed the trail of refugees from the fields, but that didn't mean my parents were with them. I'd been fretting about the idea that they hadn't looked for us, but it would be worse if they had. What if they headed to Portland alone? What if they never made it anywhere?

"We're only looking for close matches," the DNA man said. "And we can provide you a health and heritage profile if you wish."

"I came up Mexican, Ecuadorian and Argentine," Norflo said proudly.

"Argentine," I said, repeating the word I'd read on an illicit slip of paper long ago.

"Means something," Norflo said with a smile. I wasn't quite ready to change his name to Javier in my head just yet. Arturo clapped him on the back.

The DNA man held up a pair of small appliances the size of a spoon handle. They were wrapped in clear plastic packages, labeled DNA Sampler. He handed one to Margot and one to me, as if we would know how to use them. Margot turned hers over in her hand.

"You place it in your mouth and gently brush the tip against your cheek until it chimes," the DNA man said.

I peeled mine out of the package. Margot handed hers back. "I do not feel there is any point for me," she said. "I do not have any heritage you are looking for."

"Unless you object, I'd still like to put you on file," the DNA man said.

"After all, what if someone comes looking for you?" Arturo asked.

"That is not a concern," Margot replied. The DNA man regarded her with sympathy and took the sampler back with a nod that showed he understood.

It took just a few seconds for my tester to chime. The DNA man held out his hand, and I passed it to him.

"What does it say?" I asked.

"I need to send the data out," he said as he dipped my tester into a small slot in his kit and held it there. "It will take a few minutes."

"What are you guys doing?" Mira asked, her body wrapped in a towel, but still somehow dripping all over the floor.

"Put on your clothes, please," Margot said.

"My clothes smell," Mira answered. "What are you doing?" she repeated.

"A science test with spit," Margot said. "You will not want to do it. Go get dressed."

Mira ran over to Margot, awkwardly holding up her towel. "I want to try it!"

"No," Margot said.

"What if I get dressed first?" Mira asked. Arturo looked away to keep from laughing.

Margot seemed to struggle with this for a moment and then relented.

"Fine, she and I will do the test as well."

DEOXYRIBONUCLEIC ACID: $48.98

"Are you part Chinese?" the DNA man asked Margot.

"One eighth," Margot said. "On my father's side. Why would you ask? The test should show you in a moment."

"I can't do this job and not be curious about such things," the DNA man said, removing her tester from the kit. "Her, too?" he asked, looking at Mira, who was now dressed and itching in her dirty clothes.

"She has a different father," Margot said in a low, reluctant voice.

"What difference does it make?" I asked, wondering if that had anything to do with why they didn't seem to care about going back to Portland.

"For this test? None," the DNA man said.

"But you should know, we are supposed to give priority to people with certain heritages," Arturo added.

"Priority?" I asked. This sounded deeply troubling. I was tired of the idea that some people were more important than others. "Priority for what?"

"Housing. Printers. Jobs," Arturo said. "America® has a history of mistreating Latino, African and Asian people, to name a few. The Téjican government has taken some steps toward reparations."

"I do not have Latino heritage," Margot said flatly.

Arturo and the DNA man exchanged a look. "Perhaps not, but Chinese ancestry is considered a subset of Asian," Arturo said.

"Is subset bad?" Mira asked.

"No," Arturo replied with a smile.

"It means part of a greater whole," Margot said.

"Am I Chinese, too?" Mira asked.

"Probably not," Margot said.

Mira looked disappointed. Norflo widened his eyes at me. Neither of us had known this was going to be so complicated.

"Are we having a party?" Saretha's voice made my head turn. She entered the room with a little swish, swinging a bag beside her. She was wearing a new bright yellow dress. It was stunning. She seemed refreshed and happy again.

"Where did you get that?" I asked.

"Arturo showed me where to have it printed," she said, sending him a grateful smile. "They thought I was Carol Amanda Harving!" she added with a laugh.

The DNA man cocked an eyebrow. "Can we get her sample now?" he asked. Arturo passed a sample kit to her.

Saretha put down her bag. "I had them print clothes for all of us," she said, then looked at Norflo. "Well, for the girls. Sorry, Norflo."

"Meh," Norflo said, sniffing at his shirt.

Arturo told Saretha what to do with the test. "If your parents are here," he said, "that will be excellent for our case. DNA proof of your lineage."

"It would be nice for us, too," I said, feeling a little sour. "Getting to be together. You know, as a family."

Arturo looked like I had slapped him. "Of course. My apologies, señorita."

"Would that mean our parents would have to testify?" I asked.

"I am afraid so," he said. "A great deal is at stake."

I shared a look with Saretha. She paused in opening her package. Did she understand what this meant? If we lost the Carol Amanda Harving case, we would *all* be sent back.

"You don't have to take the test," Arturo said to her.

The kit's screen made a sound. "Ah," the DNA man said. "The results for you three are in," he said, meaning Margot, Mira and me.

"It shouldn't matter," I said, suddenly wishing everything wasn't so complicated. "I just want our family to be together."

"The little girl is one-eighth Guatemalan," the DNA man said.

"Is that Latino?" Mira asked.

"Latina," Arturo corrected. "Or Latinx, if you prefer."

Norflo cocked his head, looking at me. I shrugged. The word was new to me, too.

"No familial match," the DNA man said to Margot. "Neither you, nor your sister, have parents or siblings here." Margot showed no concern. Did she know, somehow, that her parents were safe in Portland? "You are Chinese, French and English," the DNA man went on.

"No surprises," Margot said with a yawn.

"For you," the DNA man said, looking at me, "I have good news. You have both Mexican and Colombian DNA, *and* we have found a familial match."

"My parents?" I asked hopefully. Saretha moved closer to the screen.

"It seems likely," Arturo said, looking at the kit's screen, too.

"We have located three close relatives in a refugee camp set up just south of here," the DNA man explained, pointing at a small map.

"Three?" Saretha asked, looking as confused as I felt.

There should only have been two possible matches. "Could the third be an aunt or an uncle? A grandparent?" I asked. I'd never met any, but I would have loved to. The hope of it, like so many other hopes I'd had, was very brief.

"No. These are first-degree relatives," the DNA man said. "Parents, full siblings or children. Neither of you has had a child?"

"No!" Saretha cried, holding her stomach.

"Who could be the third?" I asked, utterly baffled.

DNA man shrugged and read from the screen. "Two males and one female, in a refugee camp twenty miles south."

Saretha's eyes widened. "Speth!" she said excitedly. Pins and needles ran down my back. "It has to be Sam!"

An odd feeling formed in the pit of my stomach. I closed my eyes, and Margot grabbed my arm to steady me. I sat back on the bed. I knew for certain that it couldn't be true. "That's impossible," I said, holding back a sob. "We saw him dropped off the bridge."

"We didn't see him hit," Saretha countered. "We never *looked*." Her face filled with anticipation.

How could he have survived? I began to wonder, then shook the question off. I refused to get my hopes up. Not about this. Both Rogs had tried to fool me into believing he was alive. I couldn't believe again.

"Could this be a mistake?" I asked. "Are these tests ever wrong?"

The DNA man forcefully shook his head. “Almost never.”

“That isn’t the same as *no*,” I said, my voice shaking. It was wrong to make Saretha hope this way.

“It is unlikely,” Arturo said. He could see the turmoil between us and put a hand on each of our shoulders. “This is easily settled. After we meet with the Lawyers tomorrow, we will bring you to your family,” he said. “And you can all be reunited.”

VS. BUTCHERS & ROG: $49.98

The next day, Arturo took us to a government building. There, seated around an enormous table, we recounted all the details we could remember about how Saretha's identity had been taken. Lawyers and government officials listened intently as I gave them my whole history, telling them about being picked up by Kel and her Placers, and how I'd discovered the fraud the day I went to Carol Amanda Harving's address and discovered no one was home.

They seemed to think this case was going to change everything for them. Their enthusiasm and hope was inspiring. Saretha shone in her bright yellow dress, believing every hope they offered. Her smile returned to full wattage, like when she had been happy and thought being Branded was an honor, and paying for words was a privilege.

"We would like to establish a timeline," Arturo said. He was careful to mediate and proceed slowly with us. I half wondered if he was afraid we might run.

"Our records indicate Saretha would have been just over fifteen when Carol Amanda Harving's first movie came out," he noted. "Would she have been in contact with any member of the Rog family before then?"

"The Rogs were the ones who sued us into debt in the first

place," I explained. "That's why my parents ended up Indentured. But they do that to everyone."

"We don't know how you, specifically, came to the attention of the Rogs. Were you in contact with the general public?" one of the Lawyers asked Saretha.

"After my Last Day, I worked for Mrs. Nince, at the Nince Boutique," she said. There was still a bit of a sales lilt in her voice. "I used to model clothes for the customers."

I wondered if she could see that what she remembered as happiness was really only her hope that things would someday be better. Hope was what restored her now. I was beginning to feel some optimism, too. The case looked good, to hear the Téjican Lawyers tell it, and when we were done, we were finally going to see our parents.

And discover the identity of the third person who matched our DNA.

"This Mrs. Nince—" Arturo started.

"Mrs. Nince was a horrible woman," I said quickly. "I wouldn't be surprised if she illegally scanned Saretha while she was changing and sold off the data."

"At fifteen?" Arturo's face scrunched up in disgust. Saretha looked horrified. The idea made me sick as well.

"There are literally billions of infractions," one of the Lawyers said, pointing to a dense legal text on a large screen. "Each frame of each movie they exported is potentially subject to a $10,000 fine. And that is just here in Téjico. There are other nations as well. France, in particular, is eager to join the suit, and China, Canada, Romania, Turkey and Vietnam are all looking into participating. It is a strong coalition, and we would be beating the Rogs at their own game."

They had even found a few examples of where they had

simply used scans of Saretha, right down to her crescent-shaped scar.

"We have contacted the US government," another Téjican Lawyer said. "They acknowledge there may be 'some' cause for a trial." She rolled her eyes at the word *some*. "Our only setback—and I don't see a way around this—is that the case will need to be tried where the crime was committed. Especially with an alleged murder involved."

"Portland," I breathed. I closed my eyes and tried to think of something else. In an hour or two, I would be able to hug my mother for the first time in years. I would be able smell my father's hair, though I realized with an ache that I'd been small enough to ride on his back, my chin nestled in his hair, the last time we were together.

"I can't go back," I said, my body chilled by fear.

"Without you, and your family, there is no case at all," Arturo explained.

A thin Téjican official was looking over the odds. "Based on our interpretation of the Law, and our computer prediction, we have a 94 percent chance of winning. But only with all of you. They would have to come up with something extraordinary to defeat us in court."

This all sounded convincing, but as the official finished speaking, a voice crackled to life, intruding into my thoughts through the implants just below my ear.

"Speth..." the voice said, though I could barely hear it. My stomach did a slow roll. I shook my head, hoping it would just go away. I'd been afraid this would happen—that Lucretia Rog would somehow be able to reach me through the implants. She must have obtained access to the Téjican WiFi. I put my hands

on my neck and pressed at the bumps, vowing to get them removed somehow.

"Something extraordinary?" Saretha asked, sounding fearful. We both knew the Rogs were more than capable of coming up with something astounding and terrible.

Before any of us could even speculate what that could be, I held up a hand. "Stop," I said, my joy and optimism draining. "She's found me."

Everyone looked at me like I'd lost my mind.

"Speth?" the voice said again. The static that came with it made my eyes twitch. I just wanted to get through this. I wanted to see my parents again. *"The Rogs are setting a trap,"* the voice said.

That startled me. It wasn't Lucretia.

"What is it?" Arturo asked.

"You can't win against them in court," the voice said, like it was doubt personified, sitting on my shoulder. *"Especially not up here."* I didn't want to listen. I'd fought enough. There had to be some way to win.

"Someone..." I pointed to my neck where it met my ear. "Someone is contacting me."

"Speth, it's Kel," the voice said. My insides unclenched a little, but I still hesitated. It sounded like Kel, but what if Lucretia Rog had a filter for that? What if she was impersonating Kel to win my trust?

"Someone has breached the WiFi," one of the officials confirmed, looking at a Pad. "At address X0562.1.1." He pointed to me.

"Shut it down!" Arturo shouted.

I held up a hand. "Wait." I didn't want a voice in my head, but if it *was* Kel, I needed to hear what she had to say. The room fell utterly silent. Saretha leaned in, putting her ear close to mine.

"You can't beat them with the Law," the voice in my head continued. *"They will rewrite the Law."*

"Who is that?" Saretha murmured, leaning in to hear.

I pushed her back, away from my neck. "Kel, what was the last thing you told me to do?" I asked the air in front of me.

"Let yourself be happy."

My whole body sagged. It wasn't Lucretia. But her words were bittersweet—how could I be happy? I had just wanted to see my family, but the specter of Sam's death cast a shadow on that coming reunion. I wanted to be safe, but I was being asked to return to the most dangerous place I could go. I never wanted to think about the Rogs again, but I had no choice.

"It's Kel," I explained to the room, pointing to the terrible spot beneath my ears. "She says we can't win this case." *If that's true, at least I won't have to return to Portland,* I thought.

"They'd have to produce Carol Amanda Harving herself to beat us," the lead Lawyer laughed. He clearly found the idea preposterous. A scattering of chuckles followed, but I didn't laugh with them.

Arturo tried to reassure me. "Even the Rogs can't create a living human being to suit their needs."

The blood drained from my face as I realized what the Rogs would do next. They had no other choice.

"If they need to create a living, breathing Carol Amanda Harving to win, that's exactly what they'll do," I said.

"How?" Arturo asked, struggling to take my concern seriously.

"Plastic surgery and genetic reengineering," Kel said in my ear. I repeated the information to the officials.

"This is what they're like," I added. The smirks fell away, gradually replaced by looks of horror.

Kel made a sickly gasp in my ear. People started talking around me, but I shushed them. I needed to listen. Kel's voice crackled through the static in my ears again.

"Speth," she said, as tentatively as I'd ever heard her. *"I need you to remember your training. We have to stay calm."*

We? When had she ever included herself in such a suggestion? Her voice was agitated. She was struggling.

"For their Carol Amanda Harving, it looks like they are going to alter the genes inside Sera Croate."

COMMANDER-IN-CHIEF JUSTICE: $50.99

Discussion and argument broke out around the table. I could barely focus on their voices. I couldn't stop thinking about when our family Lawyer, Arkansas Holt, had suggested we maul Saretha's face so she didn't look like Carol Amanda Harving—and he'd actually been looking out for us. What the Rogs would do to Sera was similar, but more diabolical.

I begged them to help her, but what could the Téjican government do? They had no power to extradite Sera, or even to request her records. Even if they did, they would have found nothing. Kel said they all had been erased. Sera Croate no longer existed, and Carol Amanda Harving was suddenly listed as Indentured to Silas Rog.

The lead Lawyer insisted the case was still strong. "I do not see how they can get away with such a ruse. The Commander-in-Chief Justice himself will be the Judge. Surely that will count for something."

"He's in their pocket!" I screamed. "They have his picture on their walls, like he's family!"

"No one even knows who he is," Kel reminded me.

"But the Commander-in-Chief Justice will *have* to abide by the Law—he is hardwired into it, is he not?"

"You don't understand," I said. "Those Judges are hardwired through their visors so they can *control* the Law, not so it can control *them*!"

"No," the lead Lawyer contradicted me. "We must presume good faith adjudication of the Law, or we will have no Law between nations at all."

There were nods all around the table. How could they be so naive?

"Not having Laws would be better than the Laws they've created," I protested.

"You're describing lawlessness," Saretha said. Wasn't she anxious about all this? She seemed far too calm.

"She is describing anarchy," one of the Lawyers corrected, looking affronted.

"Without Law, there would be only chaos," Arturo said.

"Is slavery preferable to chaos?" I asked.

That gave them pause.

"The Laws just need to change," Saretha said, as if it was that easy.

"And who will change them?" I asked, standing up. My legs felt cramped and itchy.

"Something more radical is needed," Kel said in my ear.

"Enough," I said. "I'm done discussing this. I want to see my parents." I turned and pushed through the doors, out into the late-afternoon light. Without Arturo's help, I had no way to actually get to them, but if I couldn't see them, then at least I could have a moment alone.

Then I remembered Kel was in my head. I couldn't be alone.

"You okay?" she asked.

A new fear gripped me. "Kel," I said, "if you can connect to me, what's to stop Lucretia from doing the same?"

"She's not going to do that, Speth. If she connected to you, it would be an easily traceable international crime—this one on the Téjican side of the border. She can't give them that kind of evidence to work with. Even the Rogs wouldn't be able to defend that."

"Aren't you breaking the same Law?"

"Yes. If they want to prosecute me, they can."

Arturo came outside looking for me. Clearly, I would have no peace.

"We will try to expedite the proceedings," he said, trying to soothe me.

"What good will that do?" He no longer made me feel calm.

"The faster we go to trial, the less time they will have to alter your friend."

"Kel, what exactly are they going to do to her?" I asked.

"They have genetic material from you, Saretha and Sam," Kel said. *"They are going to splice it into her DNA."*

The idea was so sickening that all I could do was scream. It ripped from me, like it had in my dreams, but it didn't ease the pain. Across the street, in the filigreed light of a protective glass awning, a few people stopped and stared.

"Why alter her genes?" I cried. "It isn't enough to change her face?"

"They will do both," Kel said. *"If they isolate the right genes, they can use them to alter her appearance through rapid chromosomal generation and get a better match."*

"Why Sera? Why not Victoria?" I asked, though I didn't actually wish this on the girl who helped me escape. "Why not *anyone* else?"

I glared back at the people gawking and they awkwardly moved on, mixing in with the others who passed by, unconcerned with me.

"Victoria isn't an option," Kel said quietly. *"The process will be agonizing, and they'll need compliance from whoever they change. I suspect they have offered Sera a movie star's lifestyle in exchange for putting her old life behind her."*

That wouldn't be a hard choice for Sera to make. Silas Rog had offered it to my sister, and I knew she had been tempted.

"If they would really dare to genetically alter your friend," Arturo offered, "it will take time—weeks or months. If we move fast, they won't have an opportunity."

"They will move faster, at the expense of her health, but he is right. The sooner you can get the trial set up, the better."

"The trial they will win," I said, my voice hollow. "You said so yourself, Kel."

Arturo moved to respond, but then thought better of intruding. He could only hear my half of the conversation.

"They're pouring resources into stopping you," Kel replied. *"They're afraid of you. That is a remarkable accomplishment. They're massing troops in every tunnel and on every road in the nation to prevent you from making it to the courthouse. And they're retaking Portland in case you make it that far, so they can trap you there."*

"So we'll be dead before the trial even begins?" I exclaimed. "How is that useful?"

Arturo looked worried.

"If you can find safe passage to the courthouse, they will be forced to have the trial. The Commander-in-Chief Justice will have to preside and rewrite the Laws from there."

"This all sounds terrible," I said. "Even if we make it, we'll still lose."

A family walked by, a dog on a leash. They all seemed quite happy, but the dog was restricted and straining by the neck to get at a colorful bed of flowers she desperately wanted to smell. I understood how she felt.

"I know," Kel admitted. *"It isn't fair, what I'm asking of you. You don't deserve this. I truly do want you to be happy. But if you make it to Portland, it will put all eyes on you and give us a real chance to strike at Delphi™. We could take down the last Central Data node."*

The dog jumped and the owner let out the leash. Arturo stared at me intently, waiting. "And what happens to us then?" I asked.

"If we succeed, the entire system will be destroyed. They won't be able to beat you at trial because they won't be able to have a trial. There will be no more Laws, Ads or WiFi. They will have no more power than you. We'll all have a fresh start."

I honestly didn't know if what she was describing would be better. "I know we cracked the DRM, but people… Some people aren't going to make it."

"Just because a solution is painful doesn't mean it isn't right," Kel said.

"But it *isn't* right!" I exclaimed. "People will starve. People will *die*."

Arturo put a hand on my shoulder, but I shook him off. I didn't want his comfort.

"Let me rephrase that. Just because a solution is painful doesn't mean it isn't for the greater good."

That was almost exactly how Kiely had phrased it back in DC. I swallowed hard. "What if you fail?"

"Fail at what?" Arturo asked, alarmed.

"You can't tell the Téjicans what I'm suggesting," Kel warned. *"It would only put them in danger, and they'll cut me off from you.*

The aftermath of what I'm suggesting will be a difficult time for everyone."

"What if you fail?" I asked again.

"There is a small chance you could still win the trial," Kel said, but she didn't sound hopeful. She'd already been clear about the prospects. *"But you need to know that even if you win—even if they admit they faked Carol Amanda Harving, and they pay the Téjicans and let your family go—they will never let* you *go. The only way we're getting you out is if Kiely and I can take down that data center in Delphi™."*

I turned to Arturo. "I don't really have a choice in whether or not I go, do I?" I asked.

"We can't force you to be part of the trial," he said, looking at the ground. "But I am sorry to say that if you don't participate, we would be required to turn you over to the American® authorities. There is no choice for us in this."

Kel was silent for a minute. Then she whispered, *"If you want to escape, I will help you. You don't have to agree. I know this isn't fair. I can get you far, far away."*

Of course I had to agree. Where would I go? How could she help me? She couldn't help us all. I knew that, and so did she. I thought of all the times I'd seen people forced to tap AGREE on a screen. The choice wasn't a choice at all.

In this case, there were too many people who needed my help. I thought of this whole Téjican nation that I'd barely seen. I thought of Mandett and Penepoli fighting in Portland right now. I'd rescued Nancee from her owner to set her free, not so Rog and people like him could take her again. Those women in OiO™ who had blocked the way to save us deserved a chance to see the Rogs and their Laws brought low. In my mind, chaos had to be better than slavery, but I couldn't let Arturo know that.

Finally, I thought of Sera, whom I'd known for so long, but hadn't really seen clearly. Her life had been like mine, but with even fewer choices and comforts. I was supposed to bring her to Crab Creek to find her mother—her only family in the world—and I had failed her. I could do almost nothing for her from here, but if I went to Portland, there was a slim chance I could help her.

"If we won the case," I asked Kel through the static-filled air, "would they let Sera go? Could *she* be free?"

Kel took a while to answer. *"If they're claiming she's Carol Amanda Harving, and she confesses otherwise, then yes."*

I didn't know what state of mind I'd find Sera in. She wouldn't know or understand any of this. Her prospects were likely as grim as my own.

"I have to go," Kel said suddenly. I heard a faint zipping sound, static, then silence.

Arturo gazed off into the distance, uncomfortable in the role he'd been given. "Can I go see my family now?" I asked him. I didn't elaborate, but I wanted to do more than just see them. I wanted to do something I hadn't really been able to do since I was nine years old: ask for my parents' advice, and say a proper goodbye.

SPIDER JUPITER: $51.98

The day had waned by the time we reached the outskirts of the refugee camp. The sun had sunk out of sight and left behind a cobalt sky caught between twilight and night. Music played on live instruments far off, from somewhere I couldn't see. People walked in the warm glow of both streetlights and colored lamps strung down the lane under a vaulted latticework canopy. They called this town Glimmer, and I could see why.

All of this was under another dome. Instead of geometric hexes, the roof was crisscrossed by curved, printed scaffolds and thin shapes of translucent glass that Arturo called Art Nouveau. This dome's biggest difference from the ones back home was that there was no wall around its circumference. In Téjico, the domes were open to the outside. Breezes blew through. They provided cover from the sun and rain, but allowed the people to come and go as freely as air.

"The camp is inside the dome?" Saretha asked.

"The camp *is* the dome," Arturo said. "We began work when the first refugees arrived weeks ago."

Norflo looked around in wonder. It was hard to believe they'd built this so quickly. Margot and Mira had stayed behind, but now I wished they had come, if only to see it.

"You built all this in weeks?" I asked, awestruck.

"And so beautifully?" Saretha added.

"Many people came to help," Arturo said. "And the printers can be very efficient, especially with the right hands working them. Some are still at work, you can see."

He pointed with a long finger up to the tops of the buildings. Some were finished, but many were still being printed on their upper floors, printers zigzagging elegant structures.

"But they look so fancy," Saretha said. "It looks like it was designed long ago."

"It is just as easy to print a beautiful shape as a blank wall," Arturo replied. "Why make them ugly?"

A tall, lanky man about my father's age was bent over one of the printers, tinkering with it four floors up, harnessed astride the wall and deep in concentration.

"See that man?" Arturo asked. "He was one of the first to arrive. Very clever. A genius, really. This is what you lose when you don't let people explore their gifts. In your country, he was nothing. His abilities were utterly shackled to the DRM you all suffered. Here, he can make these printers do almost anything. Half of the beauty here was created by his hand."

Arturo put his fingers in his mouth and let out a loud whistle. The thin man above us looked around and then down. He waved, then bent his head like he couldn't believe his eyes. He seemed to recognize us, but I had no idea who he was.

In a heartbeat, he'd grabbed the rope that was holding him safe and begun to rappel down the side of the building.

"What's he doing?" Saretha asked.

"I suspect he wants to meet Carol Amanda Harving," Arturo said. "Or the Silent Girl."

But he didn't. He hit the ground, bending his long legs at

the impact and unclipping himself as he stood. He came striding toward me on his long legs, his eyes shining as he called my name. “Speth!”

Something about his gait was familiar to me. I had no clue who he was, but Saretha recognized him when he got close.

“Mr. Stokes?” she said, stunned.

“Beecher’s dad?” I asked her. I saw the resemblance now. He was taken into Collection years before Beecher and I grew close. I might have seen him before then, around the Onzième, but I wouldn’t have committed him to memory. Beecher, of course, had no pictures of him. He and his grandmother weren’t allowed any contact at all once he was taken away for circumventing a food printer’s programming.

I didn’t know how to feel about seeing him in Téjico, but when he held his arms out, I felt like I owed him a hug. I was there the day his son died. Did he know that Beecher had killed himself on my fifteenth birthday? Mr. Stokes didn’t ask about Beecher. He must have been told, or seen the news. How else would he know me now?

“Speth,” he said again, breaking the hug. “I knew you’d make it down here! I’d say call me Randall, but I had to change my name.” He held out his hand. “Spider Jupiter.”

His whole manner was light and jovial, but his eyes were dark and sad—not so different from the haunted look I’d seen in my own reflection.

“Were you at Crab Creek?” I asked, shaking his rough, calloused hand.

He shook his head. “Agropollination™ 3,” he said. “Fixing equipment. Managing walnut trees. They triple-Cuffed me!”

He held out both arms and a leg, though all the Cuffs were gone now. He seemed manic, almost a little unhinged.

"I had not realized you knew each other," Arturo said. He peeked down at his handheld device and stepped back patiently. I knew he wasn't expecting a delay, but it would have been rude to cut this moment short.

"How did you escape?" I asked.

"Oh, that," he said. He rubbed at one arm and then the other. "When you knocked out Portland, you rippled a power spike throughout the system. Rest of the domes had to split the extra power. Saw the surge, so I hacked our dome's hydroponics battery system to store the excess energy until it overloaded. Blew out the dome's grid. Turned it dark."

"But how could you see any of what was going on? How did you know about Portland?"

"The fools gave me three Cuffs!" Randall said again, holding out the same three limbs. "They locked me down three ways, but it also gave me three windows and systems. You can't *connect* me to the WiFi and *keep* me from the WiFi." He started laughing, and Saretha laughed with him politely.

Mr. Stokes put a finger on my neck where the implant was and frowned, his laugh fading. "What did they do to you?"

"Lucretia Rog, our dome's lovely representative, put an audio implant in there," I replied with a grimace. Guilt crept across my shoulders as I remembered how Lucretia had offered to free Beecher's grandmother. I had no idea what had happened to her.

"Do you know if your mother—"

He shook his head, cutting me off. "I hope she's headed here. The farm they had her on revolted during the second power spike. Was that you, too?"

I didn't understand the question.

"Did you take out that second data center in DC?" he

asked, a little louder, maybe wondering if the implants interfered with my hearing.

"No," I said. "That wasn't me."

"Good," he said with relief. "Glad more folks had the chance to escape, but I was worried maybe you were trying to take out *all* the data centers."

A terrible feeling grew inside me. That was exactly what Kel was hoping to do.

"Why? Would that be bad?" I asked.

"It would be if one were seeking to destroy the system that charges for words, for example."

An icy sensation rolled through my gut. "Why? Wouldn't blowing it up knock out the whole thing? Wouldn't that just...end all of it?"

Arturo shook his head. "Destroying the entire system would be disastrous."

"Won't take down the system," Mr. Stokes said. "How foolhardy do you think they are? They have backups. Lots of backups."

I could feel all my hope draining away. If knocking out Delphi™ wasn't useful, the only thing left was the hopeless trial.

"I thought the three data centers *were* the backups," I said, in the desperate hope that this was true. It was my only real chance.

"You should not be concerned about this," Arturo counseled. "Such a plan would be a catastrophe. The refugees alone would be more than we could withstand."

Anger flared in me. "The refugees? Is that what you're worried about?"

"In part. There is only so much we can do."

I understood he was afraid, but I don't think he fully understood the oppression people lived under.

"The three Central Data nodes are more like redundant systems," Mr. Stokes explained. "It'd be better to have a few dozen, but they kept suing each other for rights, like they always do. They're lucky they even managed to build those three."

"Then what are the backups?" I asked.

Mr. Stokes grinned. "Guess," he said, looking from me to Arturo.

"I don't want to guess," I said. This wasn't fun for me. If what he said was correct, I was doomed. An old resentment bloomed in me at his son, for tossing his life away for no reason. He could have fought, but he didn't.

I would fight on my way down, at least. And I would try to save as many lives as I could.

"We should be on our way," Arturo said. I agreed with him on this. I was so close to my parents now, and I wanted to see them more than anything. I didn't want to play guessing games.

"If you just think about it a minute, it makes perfect sense," Mr. Stokes teased.

"We really have to go," I said.

"We do have a time constraint," Arturo offered gently, putting one hand on my shoulder and holding the other out to Mr. Stokes. "They haven't yet seen their parents."

"Oh!" Mr. Stokes said, understanding the situation, but looking a little sad. I could imagine why. His family had been completely and irrevocably destroyed. He shook Arturo's hand, grinned and tapped the side of his head, indicating that we should think about what he'd said.

"It was nice to see you," Saretha said, like we'd all just had an enjoyable chat.

"Thank you," Arturo said with a crisp nod, and then he moved us away.

THE FAMILY REUNION: $52.97

Arturo followed an instruction on his handheld device that led us into a courtyard. The music grew louder as we approached. There were about a dozen people in the center of the printed cobblestones, accompanied by lots of trumpets, a few guitars, two giant basses and a full set of drums. Around the musicians, people were dancing—freely, openly dancing. Some were teaching the moves, and I guessed they were Téjicans. The rest must have been the refugees.

I scanned the crowd for my parents. I saw too many people my age and younger, with both delight and sorrow in their eyes. I saw more with blank faces, like they weren't really there. Many of these latter ones sat out the dance, though a few stood amid it, completely still.

Arturo had crossed the courtyard to a man who must have been in charge. They spoke for a moment, and then Arturo returned to us.

"He will not say if they are here," he said.

"Why?" I asked.

"Understandably, he does not think it wise to admit the parents of the Silent Girl are among these refugees, for their protection, and probably for yours."

Saretha elbowed me and pointed. She'd spotted our parents on the far edge of the crowd. I ached to see Sam with them, even though I knew the third DNA match had to be a mistake. I saw no anticipation on their faces, only a mild relief as they watched the dancers. I grabbed Saretha's hand. I didn't know what she was going to do. I didn't even know what *I* was going to do.

Suddenly, she was running, pulling me along. I couldn't think. Could this actually be real, after all this time? We hadn't reached them yet, and I was already crying. I wanted to believe Sam was here, too. That it was possible. That this was the end of our journey. That this was home.

"Mom," I said. My voice wasn't strong enough against the music. "Mom! Dad!" I yelled. I suddenly felt like I was five years old, running toward them. For a moment, all the burdens on me fell away, and I was just desperate to feel their affection.

My father turned first, his face stunned. I threw an arm around him, grabbing for my mother at the same time. Before I knew it, the four of us were held together by some irresistible force, like gravity. My parents and Saretha and me, finally together. Seconds ticked away with no Cuff clocking us for our affection. I wished we could stay like this forever.

"Oh, my girls," my mother cried.

"Speth!" my dad said. Only he and my mom could say my name nicely, like it was actually worth something. Even Saretha couldn't do that. Only Sam had ever come close.

Sam.

The longer our hug lasted, the more hope I could hold on to. For as long as it lasted, I wouldn't have to answer their questions or explain. I could hope somehow, Saretha had been right: that Sam was *here*, dancing to the glorious music.

I couldn't think of any explanation for it, but I hoped all the same. I could almost see him, freed from the dome, loving the bright, joyful sounds around us. I peeked out into the dancing crowd, celebrating their freedom. I scanned for kids who were his age. I searched for the ones who were dancing. Sam would be dancing.

My mother finally broke away and looked at us questioningly. "Where's Sam?" she asked as gently as she could. She held Saretha out by the arms, as if Sam might be hiding there in the space between, but also like she knew a dark answer awaited.

Saretha swallowed hard. She seemed to hope for one more second that my mom would look around and say, "He was just here." My dad's eyes were already teary from our reunion. He looked like he was certain Sam would turn up. Like he didn't really believe anything bad could have happened to the smallest of us—like he was too tired to really let the truth dawn on him, especially without words.

Then Saretha's lip began to quiver. She pulled my mother in and held her too tight. She was supposed to tell them, but a horrible, gasping sound erupted instead. It was worse than her screams when Sam had been dropped. She had needed to pull herself together then. Now my parents were here, and her emotions came pouring out. She couldn't say the words, so I had to.

"Rog's people killed him," I said, holding back the same painful grief. If she fell apart, I couldn't. They had to know. I heard the darkness in my voice and remembered my face from the mirror, imagining what it must be like for them to see me so changed.

"But why?" my father asked, as if there could be no explanation.

"I..." My voice quavered. How could I explain that they'd killed him to make me speak? How could I say those words?

"Shhh..." he said before I could continue. He wasn't really looking for an answer. He was expressing his distress. We could explain the details later, when reality had sunk in.

My father pulled me into a sorrowful hug. I watched the revelers go on, unaware of us in our grief. The contrast was excruciating, but they couldn't know how our mood had shifted. We looked just exactly as we had a moment ago in our joyful reunion. So many of them seemed happy, but I suddenly understood the ones who stood there, bewildered, unable to celebrate. One of them, frozen in place, was staring right at me. A cold shock prickled down my back. He looked like Sam. How could he look like Sam?

He was much too young to be Sam. I could see that right away. This was what Sam had looked like at five. He had Sam's eyes—or at least the same shape. They were dark, so dark they seemed nearly black in the gleaming light. And he was so gaunt—there was none of Sam's cherublike sweetness about him.

The boy walked toward us, his head cocked in confusion. He pointed at me with a jabbing finger and reached out for my parents. My father broke off our hug and picked him up carefully.

"You can talk," he said, wiping a smudge of dirt off the boy's cheek. My heart felt like it had stopped. "You can say anything you like now."

Saretha looked the way I felt. She was gaping at the boy. Who was he? "Mom?" she managed to ask.

Our mother's face contorted with distress, her eyes shifting from the boy to us. Something wasn't right.

"Mom," Saretha repeated, tugging at our mother's sleeve, looking like she'd seen a ghost. "Who is that?"

"This is your brother," my mother said, sucking in air through her teeth. "His name is Santos359™."

SANTOS359™: $53.99

I stumbled back in shock, flashing to what Kiely had told me about how the corporations owned any children born from Indenture. Born into slavery.

Saretha trembled, yet somehow managed to smile at the small boy. She tried to coax him toward her, but he clung to our father. I forced myself to smile, too, despite feeling weak and sick. Up close, he looked even more like Sam, but with the life drained from him. I examined his fingers, browned by the sun and yellowed with pollen.

"Was he working in the fields?" I asked. My voice came out horrified and accusatory. But how else could I say it? *Was he a slave?*

"Once he could do it, they didn't offer a choice," my dad explained, putting a hand on the boy's head, as if that might protect him now.

"It's just brushing pollen," Saretha said. She painted at the air with a small pretend brush.

My mother blinked at her, shocked, then sad. Some part of Saretha was always going to try to ignore the horrors of the world. I couldn't do the same. I could hear Santos359™ breathing through his mouth—short, careful little breaths. He hadn't said a word.

My brother. A boy I hadn't known existed until now.

Something snapped in me. "Why didn't you tell us!" I cried. I would have pounded on my father if he hadn't been holding that child.

"We couldn't tell you," he said, lifting Santos359™ a little higher. My brother looked slight and underfed. He watched us with mild interest, but didn't seem to understand what was going on. My father tried to keep the tone of his voice calm, but bitterness played at the edges. "Our Terms of Service prohibited it. We were forbidden to speak about him, or he would have been taken away. Remember, we are—were—barely allowed to speak at all. Their terms specifically said that we were never to refer to him as *our* son, or part of *our* family. They were very clear that he wasn't *ours*."

"Not yours?" I asked through the contracting lump in my throat.

"He's owned by MonSantos™," my mother said, anger visible in her cheeks. "They say he is *theirs*." She spit the last word with the venom of a pit viper.

My father's face darkened as he recited the Legalese: *"You acknowledge and agree that any and all designs, works, creations, construction, or formation created while in service to Agropollination™ shall belong to and shall be the sole and exclusive property of Agropollination™ Inc.; its parent company, MonSantos™; and any subsidiaries thereof."*

He finished the recitation with a kiss on Santos359™'s forehead, like a blessing that might protect him.

"But we're his family," Saretha said, as if the Lawyers for MonSantos™ might be swayed by compassion.

"His very existence is proprietary information," my dad replied. He turned to the kids dancing in a tight pack near the trumpets. "They own *all* these kids. They laid claim to their likenesses and the sounds of their voices. They Patented their DNA."

Saretha moved toward Santos359™, crying both in joy and horror. Her arms went out to take him from our father, but he shied away again, curling his head down into our father's neck. I stood, frozen, an icy horror prickling across my skin.

"I'm your sister, Santos," Saretha cooed to him.

"359," my mother corrected. "He is Santos359™. That one is Santos362™," she said, pointing to a boy the same age in the crowd, then another who looked slightly older. "That one is Santos248™. They didn't even allow us to name our own children."

"You should change it," I said, my thoughts jumbled and fighting to get out. "That isn't his name. How could you let them do it?" I cried.

Tears formed in my mother's eyes. My words were unfair. I knew she had no choice.

"If we didn't do exactly as they asked, they would have taken him away," she said, and then she weighed her next words carefully, unsure if I was ready to hear them. "They would have changed him—altered his genes and made him into a brute they could control. They would have made him into little more than an animal to command."

I thought of Uthondo and Bertrand and shivered. "They call them Modifieds," I whispered.

I told myself he was safe now. But only for now. The trial loomed—a trial we would lose. All of us would be sent away to do things far worse than pollinating. My parents were supposed to come with us, to give us a chance, but how could I ask them now?

A hand caressed my shoulder, all knuckle and bone.

"You're so tall," my mother said. I turned, and my heart broke a little as we stood eye to eye. We hadn't been face-to-face in seven years—of course I was taller now. I grabbed her and held on, and she did the same to me.

They'd taken my mother from me and made me think that it was normal. My body heated with anger. I tried not to let the fury be the only thing that lived in this moment, but an awful sound came out of me—a low, terrible groan like the one I'd made the day Sam died.

"I love you," my mother said. "I love you so much." Her eyes were streaming tears, and so were mine. I'd never doubted that love, not once. They could keep us all apart, but they couldn't take that away from us. A distant pang twinged at my arm where my Cuff had been. I wanted some peace, but my thoughts were churning too fast. There were so many things I couldn't express.

The music went on, unconcerned with us. The drummer drummed faster, the bass notes thudding in my gut.

"I don't think he likes me," Saretha said, failing to coax a smile from Santos359™.

"He needs time," my father said, his voice trembling. His neck was reddening. "We couldn't afford to raise him the way..." His words choked off in anger and frustration. "That's going to change now. Now that we're together."

My heart sank. I wanted everything to be over—for this to be happily-ever-after. All of us did. But that couldn't be.

"Has anyone told you about Portland?" I asked, turning away, unable to look at them.

"That you took out Rog's WiFi?" my mother asked, pride

and emotion swelling in her voice. "Yes. They shut down all our access to the news after that."

"We have to go back," I said, shaking my head.

"No, honey, you can't go back. It's too dangerous," my father said. He turned me around to look at him, so I would know he was serious. He didn't realize the plan was meant for all of us.

"We have to," Saretha said. "They need me to sue the Rogs."

"For what?" my mother burst out. They didn't know about Carol Amanda Harving.

I pulled myself together. We couldn't all fall apart. I understood now why our parents hadn't looked for us. They'd made the right choice, fleeing here. If we won this case for Téjico, it would mean all these people—the escaped Indentureds, and whoever had followed—could live safely.

But not me. Not me and, I realized with horror, not Santos359™. MonSantos™ would claim him. Maybe my parents, too, or maybe they would be able to return with Saretha. I could sacrifice myself for this, but I couldn't sacrifice this little boy.

"You need to change his name," I said, refusing to let my emotions take control.

My parents glanced at each other, then back at me.

"You need to change *all* of your names, right now," I insisted in an intense whisper.

"They have to go to Portland, Speth," Saretha insisted. "We need them for the case."

"No," I said firmly. My father's head cocked to one side, as if he wondered when I'd taken charge. "You and I will be enough. They need to take care of him," I said, looking down at Santos359™'s hollow eyes.

Saretha looked at me like I'd gone off the deep end. "Speth, they *need* to be witnesses. We need them to prove I'm their daughter. Otherwise the Rogs will win for sure."

"What are you talking about?" my mother asked.

I kept my eyes on Santos359™. I'd never know if I'd failed Sam back on that bridge, but I knew I couldn't fail this boy.

"You can't be our parents," I said, forcing myself to keep it together. "Rog will win no matter what we do. He'll take anyone who shows up on American® soil."

"Then *you* can't go!" my father said.

"*We* have to," I said, turning to Saretha. "But he can't."

I pointed to our new brother. He had a tentative hand out now, reaching for Saretha's long hair, more like a baby than a small child. They'd already changed him. He didn't have the joy a child should. He was stunted. We had probably been stunted, too—probably still were. We'd all grown up in a place where our parents could barely talk, though he got the worst of it by far. I would not let them change him more. "He *has* to stay," I said resolutely.

Saretha's shoulders slumped. I knew she wanted to argue, maybe to prove she was still the big sister, but she knew I was right. She drew herself up again. "Mom and Dad have to stay, too," she said to me, like I still needed to be convinced. She turned to them. "You have to take care of Santos."

I nodded to support her. My eyes scanned the crowd, seeing the adults who were trying to make the best of their new life, and the ones who couldn't. On the far side of the courtyard, I saw Arturo, smiling and talking to a pair of men who were printing desserts and slicing some kind of food from a rotating spit. I waved for him to come over, already agonizing over how all-too-brief our reunion had been.

"But what about you?" my mother asked, worry masked by sorrow in her eyes. She wanted answers, but instead I gave her the sign of the zippered lips. She looked at my father and Santos359™. She opened her mouth to speak, but then understood. She made the sign back to me and grabbed me for one last hug.

"Please come back to us," she said.

"I'll try," I said, knowing there was nothing to be done. My father reached out his free arm and embraced me, too.

Arturo walked over with a broad smile, no doubt thinking we'd had a happy, if emotional, reunion, but his smile fell as he got closer and sensed our mood.

"Is everything okay?" he asked.

I shook my head. "They don't know where our parents are." Arturo stared at me in disbelief. Tears came to my eyes, and I let them come. I had plenty to feel sad about. "They say they didn't make it out."

My mother shook her head, looking at the ground.

"Forgive me," Arturo said, glancing at my mother and father. "I was certain they *were* your parents," he whispered to me. He definitely suspected something—of course he did. My mother and I looked too much alike. I hadn't realized that was part of what I had seen in the mirror, but we both had the same eyes—maybe because we'd suffered the same sadness of being ripped apart.

"Family friends," Saretha said unsteadily.

"Oh," Arturo replied, looking downcast. "It is very unusual for the genetic test to be wrong." He had to know this was a ruse, but he bit his lip.

"The test can't always be correct," I said.

He paused for a moment longer, then said, "Perhaps that is why it returned three results." I looked at him gratefully, knowing that he didn't really believe this. "You will have to do this alone."

"Not alone," I said.

"We'll be together," Saretha said to him. This brought me some comfort. My parents, too, I thought. There was no reason to dash their hopes that we would be together again soon.

I wiped my eyes and put aside my heartache. I looked around, partly for show, but also to take in everything and remind myself how much was at stake. I wanted to remember what I was fighting for. So many lives had been ripped apart. Only Saretha and I had a chance to keep it from happening again in the future.

My parents melted reluctantly into the crowd, arms wrapped protectively around Santos359™. I watched them walk away, hoping they would be happy.

There was just one last task for us to do here. Somewhere in this mass of people, I remembered, was Sera's mother. I needed to tell her what had happened to her daughter. I owed Sera that, at least. The idea weighed me down, but then I spotted Mrs. Croate. A jolt of hope ran through me as I realized that I was able to recognize her because she looked so much like her daughter.

If Mrs. Croate agreed to come to Portland, we wouldn't need our parents with us to win the case. We would be able to prove without a doubt that Sera wasn't Carol Amanda Harving—because Mrs. Croate shared her daughter's DNA.

THE ROUTE REVEALED: $54.97

Like my parents, Mrs. Croate had woken before sunrise each day, drunk three cups of Metlatonic™ and was transported to whatever field they ordered her to pollinate. Once there, she'd mindlessly brushed pollen where she'd been instructed. She was warned to work faster if she worked too slow. She was warned to keep her pace when she worked at the speed the company expected. If she worked faster, she said, they'd expected her to match that speed from then on.

"Was a thin line to walk. They weren't gentle about it," she'd said without any real feeling. "Theyn't much reason to forgive mistakes."

We had told her about what the Rogs had in store for Sera, and she agreed to help before we could fully ask. The Lawyers and officials quickly forgot about our parents once they realized how much more useful Mrs. Croate would be as both witness and evidence. Now she sat with Saretha and me in a car, journeying on a route Arturo insisted would provide a secret way into Portland.

Mrs. Croate stared out into space for a good long while, then said, "I'll be glad to see Sera." She had a low, raspy voice from years of misery and disuse. "Nice to be able to talk," she added. "Even if I sound like a sickly toad."

I soaked up everything she told us about what life had been like in Crab Creek. Even if it was miserable information, it gave me a glimpse into what my parents had endured, and made me feel closer to them. It made me sad, though, that I was able to talk to her when Sera couldn't. It wasn't fair. Once again, Sera was being robbed of something I was given.

"Worked us year-round 'th whatever they could find," Mrs. Croate said. "Wasn't just pol-nation. Spoke no more than a few words allotted each day. Could save them up, if it didn't interfere with my work. Parents like yours saved theirs best they could to call a few times a year. Wouldn't let me talk to Sera. Her guardian said I wasn't a good prospect, whatever that meant. Too prone to muttering, I know that. And I was alone. Your 'rents had chother...and 359," she added, reflecting on her loneliness. "That's a hard worry. Boy had to work once he could walk. Can't turn a kid out right in those circumstances. Your dad says that boy can speak, but I've never heard it."

I wished it were my parents I was sitting with on this journey instead of her. I felt a little guilty about that, but I doubted anyone could blame me. I had to pretend they hadn't been found. I had to make peace with the fact that I probably wouldn't see them again. We hadn't had enough time together. But Mrs. Croate was the next closest thing, and she didn't mind talking. Nothing seemed to upset her—or make her happy.

"I turned all that off long ago," she said.

"Sera will be glad to see you," I said, trying to make her feel better.

"I doubt that," she replied with a shrug. "If them Rogs offered her a life as a star, I 'spect she'll be might put out I'm there to ruin it."

I hoped Mrs. Croate's presence would be enough to make Sera admit who she really was, but her shrug was not inspiring. The better hope was in her DNA, but none of us knew exactly how the change to Sera's DNA would affect the tests—or Sera herself.

The car was moving fast. We had to hurry. The Rogs had "magnanimously" agreed to begin the trial as soon as we could arrive in Portland, which was likely meant to flush us out. They had assembled an army to delay us—or kill us, if it could be made to look accidental. The Téjicans had been required to apply for a travel visa and supply details about our planned journey to Portland.

To evade the trap the Rogs had planned for us, Arturo and his people had submitted a fake route that used the main roads, from dome to dome, all the way up to Portland. It was as obvious a path as we could have taken. A caravan of unmanned trucks would travel in our place as a decoy. Arturo fully expected they would meet with a terrible accident somewhere on the road.

He had different plans for us, but so far, he had refused to reveal them.

Norflo, Margot and Mira were trailing in a car behind us, but they wouldn't be coming to Portland, no matter what route we took. They were only coming to see us off. Norflo had offered to join our team, even though he'd found two of his brothers and it was painfully obvious he was exactly where he'd always wanted to be. I couldn't bear the thought of him suffering or dying because he wanted to help—and there was really nothing he could do. Margot hadn't offered, but I didn't blame her. Only Mrs. Croate, Saretha and I were heading back—and Beecher's father, Randall Stokes.

Just before we'd left Glimmer, he'd dashed up to us and asked if he could come. Arturo had told him it wasn't possible.

"Am I not a free man?" Mr. Stokes had asked.

"It isn't that simple," Arturo had replied.

"Maybe I have some skills to help?" he'd said, eyes flashing at me.

"You did say he was a genius," I'd pointed out to Arturo. "What if he can help us in some way we haven't thought of?"

I wanted to know where the backups were. If the system couldn't be destroyed by taking out the last center in Delphi™, maybe there was some other way. I hadn't explained this part to Arturo, but he saw the overall wisdom and relented.

Randall wouldn't say anything about Central Data with others around. He recognized Arturo and the Téjican authorities were fearful of what would happen if the system was destroyed. I hadn't revealed Kel's plan to them, but they must have had an inkling. Kel may have been worried they suspected, too. I hadn't heard from her since before we'd gone to see my parents.

The Rogs had set everything up so the destruction of Central Data would mean misery for America®'s neighbors. But I couldn't shake the idea that whatever Téjico would suffer was nothing compared to the suffering of the millions of Indentured people in domes across America®. I couldn't share this opinion with them, but fortunately, if there was one thing I knew I could do well, it was to keep silent.

"You want to tell us your secret plan?" Mrs. Croate asked, shaking me from my thoughts. My back prickled, fearing she'd somehow divined what I was thinking. But she wasn't talking to me; she was talking to Arturo. "How you gonna get us there?"

Arturo leaned in close with a sparkle in his eyes. "It's proprietary," he said, grinning.

"Is it a plane?" Saretha asked.

"No, they'd blast a plane out of the sky," Arturo answered. "It isn't quite as fast as a plane, but we'll arrive in a little more than two days. The Rogs are counting on six."

He was gleeful about this.

"The Rogs are counting on us not making it at all," I said.

"No. They are hoping to stop us, but preparing for everything."

"Everything? Even the way we're getting there?" Saretha asked.

"I don't think so," Arturo replied. "I don't think anyone will have thought of this."

Randall was shaking his head. "It's a ship," he said, like it should have been obvious to everyone.

"A what?" I asked.

"A ship," he said more slowly. "A boat?" He cupped his hands together, palms up, and showed them to us, like that would help. Arturo gave him a look, like he'd spoiled some secret.

"I don't know what those words mean," I said.

"That shows you something." Randall began nodding, half satisfied, half angry. "Don't need a word to know its meaning. They can price it out so you can't afford to see it, but the idea still exists. They can pretend the Word$ Market™ holds the meaning of words, but it isn't so. You'd figure out what a boat is, given half a chance, even if you didn't call it such."

He touched his temple with a long, rough finger. "It's like a car, only it floats across the water."

I was having trouble picturing this. There were only a few small ponds in the Dome of Portland. I'd seen them and their rippled surfaces. I'd felt the top of the water, though I wasn't supposed to. Water did not seem strong enough to hold anything more substantial than a Wheatlock Puff™.

"How do you know what a boat is if no one else knows?" I asked Mr. Stokes.

"Well, I came about it the hard way," he said. "Invented it. I mean, it already existed, but not knowing it did, I realized it could be made—got in trouble with Agropollination™ for that one."

"And we'll all fit?" I asked, doing my best to make the cupped-hand shape.

"Boats are small. Ships are big," Arturo said. "The ship we are taking is very impressive."

"Why would they hide the idea of a ship from us?" I asked.

"The idea is proprietary," Arturo said, getting the sparkle back in his eye. "*Our* property. There's a consortium of nations that bought the Patent to the idea of conveying people and goods over or through water. It was mostly done to keep the Americans® away, since most nations find the idea of such a Patent absurd. But the Americans® had already done away with planes in their space, so it wasn't unprecedented. No one wanted them crossing the ocean to sue us. France led the effort and offered the use of their historical art and architecture, as well as the mouche."

"The what?" I asked.

Mrs. Croate pointed to her cheek. "A fake little mole. Your

mother wore one for a while. When that was popular in the Onzième."

I stared at Sera's mother, speechless. I'd never really thought about the fact that they'd grown up in the Onzième together.

"Would you like to see the route we will take?" Arturo offered. He showed us a long line that curved along the blue water and squiggled through the Archipelago of Disney™, up the coast past Delphi™ and directly to the Dome of Portland.

"Saretha," I said, elbowing her as I realized what this meant. "We're going to *really* see the ocean at last."

CERULEAN: $55.99

The ship was more massive than my brain could handle. This was no Wheatlock Puff™ floating on a puddle. It was bigger than the refugee dome, and it bowed out in intimidating but supple lines. It was so enormous that, from inside its massive hangar, the ocean was entirely blotted out. All we saw was metal, glass and sleek lines reaching up ten stories. A small army was waiting for us on board.

Margot, Mira and Norflo hurried over to say their good-byes before we walked up a thing Arturo had ominously called a gangplank. Mrs. Croate made her way up and onto the ship without us. She had no one to see her off, which made me sad.

"Must feel weird going home," Norflo said.

"Portland isn't home," I answered.

Saretha nodded from behind him.

"Must feel even weirder, then," he chuckled, but we all knew it wasn't funny.

"I wish no one had to go anywhere," Mira said.

"We'll be back soon," Saretha said. She gave Mira her warmest smile and Mira jumped into another hug. I smiled, too. No one else needed to know this was more than likely a one-way trip for me. I hoped I could at least protect the people we left behind.

Norflo gave Saretha a careful hug, and me a far less cautious one.

"You end them, Jiménez," he said.

"Okay, *Javier*." I knew Norflo was a terrible name, maybe as bad as mine. He deserved better than to be associated with a cheap nasal spray. Still, I imagined it would always be difficult for me to think of him as Javier instead of Norflo.

"Jiménez," he repeated.

"Jua-*rez*!" I said back to him, glad he could take back his family name.

"You will be careful, Speth," Margot said, half asking, half telling me, fretting in a way she normally reserved for her sister. Mira wrapped her thin arms around me and squeezed so hard she nearly took me down.

"I will."

Margot glanced over at Norflo and Saretha with a look that said, *Could we have a moment?* They both retreated back a ways. Mira continued to hold on to me at the waist.

"I do not blame you," Margot said, her eyes welling up. "I know you might blame yourself, but what happened to Henri was not your fault. What happened to your brother..." She took me by the shoulders. I wasn't expecting this. Mira let go of me, sensing the seriousness in the air. "That was not your fault, either."

I felt tears stinging my own eyes. "Thank you," I choked out, overwhelmed not just by her compassion, but by her knowing so well what I needed.

"You do not always know this. I can see it," she said.

I smiled, but with a pang of sadness. Margot and I had been

battered by so many events that we couldn't help forming a deep friendship, but we'd rarely had time to talk or reflect. We'd never really had a moment to enjoy it.

"I wish we had the time to know each other in a world without chaos and danger," I said, speaking the sort of thing I normally kept to myself.

"*Chaos and Danger* sounds like a Carol Amanda Harving film," she said, wiping her eyes. I had to laugh. Her comment told me she understood we would probably never have that time.

"When will you be back?" Mira asked, tugging at me, maybe sensing what was to come.

"Soon," I lied. "I just need to stop some bad people."

"The ones who hurt Henri?" she asked, her expression shading with a darkness a nine-year old shouldn't feel.

"Yes," I said, resolute.

Margot bit her lip. "I wish I could go. But you understand why I cannot."

I looked at Mira. "Of course."

She couldn't put Mira in danger again, and I didn't blame her. I could also sense that something was wrong in the way Mira had been treated back in Portland, and that Margot had been powerless to fix it.

"I could take a message to your parents," I offered.

"You cannot." Margot shook her head. She teased Mira's hair and then playfully covered the girl's ears as she whispered, "They fled the very first day."

I was thunderstruck. I wanted to ask why she hadn't told me, but I knew. Margot was too proud.

"I could have gone with them," she said with a great, shaky breath, "but only me. That is the offer my father made."

She removed her hands from Mira's ears, reached out and hugged me.

"Oh, Margot," I said.

"What?" Mira asked, putting her hands on her own ears. "Did you do that on purpose?"

"Yes, my monkey," Margot said and then looked at me. "Goodbyes are hard."

Arturo led us up to the top deck, grinning at the ingenuity of what Téjico had achieved. Margot, Mira and Norflo waved at us from below.

"Here, I can *show* you the difference between a boat and a ship. This," Arturo said, gesturing to the whole huge thing, "is a *ship*." He then brought us to the side and showed us a much smaller craft attached to the ship's side on armatures. They were shaped not unlike long cupped hands, but sleeker, with the word *LifeCruiser*® emblazoned on the side. "These are boats."

"Why is there a restricted mark after the word *LifeCruiser*?" I asked, unsettled. "I thought you didn't do things like that."

"We still have Laws," Arturo answered. "LifeCruiser® is a brand. We have brands. It is only fair and right that the company's name be reasonably restricted to use only by that company. They make a good product. The LifeCruiser® boats are very durable and fast."

"I didn't even notice," Saretha said to me.

I wasn't sure what to make of it, but I moved on. The military personnel saluted as we passed, which made Saretha duck her head to conceal her smile. I knew she liked the attention.

"I will not make you agree to a Terms of Service like you might in *your* country," Arturo said. I think he was stinging a little at my implied criticism. “But you should note the location of these boats. In the event of a catastrophe, these lifeboats are designed to take everyone to safety.”

“That doesn’t sound good,” I said.

“Don’t worry. They are merely a precaution.”

Behind us, the gangway lifted and retracted into the ship. My stomach lurched and spun a little as we began moving, slowly and backward, in a way that made it seem like the world was moving away. I took Saretha’s hand and pulled her over to the rail to see the water.

“We made it,” I said.

The ship made an unhurried turn, like it was slowly presenting the horizon to us. Margot, Mira and Norflo continued watching us from the shore, receding until I couldn’t see them anymore.

The waves of the ocean grew, the shapes changing from gentle cups that intersected each other to clearer, deeper ridges and valleys that shifted and undulated through the cerulean sea.

Saretha let go of my hand and grabbed onto the rail, giggling and nervous. “It feels so…”

I didn’t have a word for it, either, but the ground beneath our feet no longer felt entirely solid. The ship carried us out of the bay and farther into the ocean. The waves grew in height and breadth, and the unsolid feeling beneath us became more pronounced as the ship sluggishly tilted one way, slowed, then gradually tilted back the other.

“Keep your eyes on the horizon,” Arturo said, putting one hand on my back and one on Saretha’s. “It will help if you feel at all sick. The motion of the ship on the water can make some people feel ill.”

"Will it be like this for the whole two days?" I asked, taking a deep breath and steadying myself. A fresh, salty mist sprayed my face.

"On the water, the ocean decides," Arturo said. He sounded like he'd been on a boat before. The ship cut through the water and stabilized some, churning up a great white bubbling foam behind us. "If we are lucky, this will be the worst of it."

"Is this what you pictured?" I asked my sister.

She shook her head. "I thought the waves would be more like big ripples." She undulated a hand.

"But on TV, they look more like this," I pointed out.

"Why would you trust anything they show?" she asked. "You know it's all digital and fake."

"Good point," I said, though she couldn't possibly have thought about it this way growing up.

"I'm glad we've finally gotten to see it for ourselves," she sighed.

We stayed there, side by side, staring at the water for a long time. It felt good being with Saretha and knowing my friends were safe, far behind us.

SECRETS OF DATA: $56.97

Arturo continued to hope the trial itself could lead to change. "I have waited my whole life for this," he said. "Many of us have."

The legal team on the boat gathered and collected evidence, getting updated information somehow as we moved out to deep waters.

"How do you get WiFi out here?" I asked.

"We have satellites," Arturo explained, pointing up at the night sky from a high deck on the ship. The stars shone in multitudes. I wasn't quite prepared for it. There were so many more than we'd seen outside the domes on the road. They sparkled and swayed with the motion of the ship. "They stay above us, in orbit."

Saretha crinkled her nose at this. She didn't understand. Neither did I.

"Think of them as small WiFi centers, floating around the Earth," Arturo explained.

"Like balloons?" I asked, still unable to picture what he meant.

"Sort of," Arturo answered. "This way, a signal can exist anywhere."

I shuddered at the thought. "Scary."

"Why?" Arturo asked.

"We worked hard to destroy the WiFi in Portland," I said. "The WiFi invaded every part of our lives."

"The WiFi isn't the problem," Arturo explained. "It is like blaming the air for a storm."

"If the shoe fits," Saretha said.

"But air lets you breathe. It lets you communicate with sound," Arturo said.

"Will Kel be able to contact me here?" I asked. I had not heard from her in a long time, and I was beginning to worry. I needed to let her know that her plan to destroy the Central Data node in Delphi™ wasn't going to work.

"I don't know what her methods are," Arturo said, shifting uncomfortably. "But if she could reach you in Téjico, I think she should be able to reach you through our system at sea."

It was growing cold out on the deck. I had my arms crossed tight. Saretha shivered beside me with a long, chattering sigh. One good thing about living in a dome was that the temperature was always steady.

Arturo pulled a blanket from a bin that seemed to serve no other purpose than to provide blankets. He spread it so that it covered Saretha and me over our shoulders. The last time someone had done something like this for us was the first week after our parents were taken away. I had asked Mrs. Harris to tuck us in.

"There should really be a charge for this," she'd said, throwing the blanket on top of us without much care. From then on, Saretha and I took care of each other—and Sam.

"You can *see* the satellites in the night sky, if you look very carefully," Arturo said, looking up. "A satellite will catch the light of the sun and move slowly across the sky, like a drifting star."

"Why doesn't the American® government blow them out of the sky?"

"Technically they aren't *in* the sky, they are *above* it, outside the designated limit of the Rights Holders. Plus, I think this is another example of the Patent Wars holding America® back. I think they have lost the ability to reach so high."

The stars flicked steady in the sky. None drifted.

"I don't see it," I said.

"You have to be patient," Arturo explained.

I laid myself flat on a second blanket to look up.

"Fun!" Saretha said, lying down beside me. We'd never had the chance to sleep outside. Sam had wanted to sleep on our apartment roof, but we all feared it might keep Placers away.

"Do you think Mrs. Croate might want to join us?" Saretha asked.

"I suspect she's comfortable where she is," I answered. She had a nice room and a warm bed and a weak hope of saving her daughter. I don't know that she wanted anything else just now.

Arturo excused himself, but returned a short while later with two guards.

"To keep you safe," he said before he wished us good-night. The two large Téjican officers stared off into the distance, the way Lucretia's brutes sometimes would, although these men had softer, unaltered faces. I wondered what Arturo thought they were protecting us from.

I was so mesmerized by the glittering beauty above us that I was startled when the moon rose over the edge of one of the raised lifeboats. I watched it, still not understanding. Could I unlock its secrets if I stared long enough? It was three-quarters full, like the opposite of a crescent. The shape changed a little each night. I didn't understand why, but I took comfort in knowing it would go on shining, changing from crescent to full, regardless of what we did down here.

Eventually I slept. The moon drifted from my thoughts into my dreams. It was a luminous dome in the sky that held the final backup of Central Data. It was full at first, then a crescent, which spread into a ring for Saretha to wear instead of a Cuff.

"It will turn my words to moonlight," she explained. "It's beautiful."

Her words scrolled across the sky as she was charged for each one.

Saretha Jime—word (IT'S): $100,000,000.
Saretha Jime—word (BEAUTIFUL): $1,000,000,000.

My heart was struck with terror. We could never afford what she'd said. The dome had to be destroyed before we were all taken into Collection.

I awoke with a start. Saretha slept beside me. The boat listed to one side and then, very slowly, to the other. The moon rocked gently above, solid in a bluing sky, with a handful of stars and few streaks of cloud.

The guards still kept watch, maybe for things that came from the sea. Leaning on a rail above me, Randall Stokes looked toward the lightening half of the sky and then down at me. He motioned for me to come up.

"Sunrise should be spectacular," he said when I'd found my way up to him. He pointed to where a pink band of light had appeared on the horizon. He had a Pad in his hand, and on the screen was the outline of the coast and a dot crawling north, representing our ship.

"I need to know about the backups for the system," I said, dropping my voice to a very small whisper. I didn't know if the guards could hear us, or if they would even know what to do with the information if they did. "Is what you said before true?"

"Of course," he said.

"I need to know if it can all be destroyed."

"Your friends don't want it destroyed," he whispered, nodding down at the Téjican guards and, presumably, Arturo and his team.

"It will make life harder for them," I said with a sigh. "But—"

"It made life impossible for my son," he said sadly. Then he shook that sadness off. "If you blew up that last center, the backups would take over," he told me in a hushed voice.

The line of pink in the sky had turned orange, and the waves sparkled in the warm light. It made his face look brighter, but it also revealed finely broken capillaries around his nose and under his eyes. Mr. Stokes peered down at the Pad. Our progress was so slow, you couldn't really even see the ship move.

"They said you were a Placer. Ever use one of these?" he asked, holding the Pad out to me.

"Yes," I confirmed, trying to be patient. "But I asked about the backups."

"You can figure it out," he said, shaking the Pad in front of me.

"Why are you making this a puzzle?" I asked, my voice rising.

"Puzzles are good for the mind. They occupy your brain when you need it. I sure did need it, all those years. And it's good for you. It's good to think things through."

"Thinking things through might not be my strongest suit," I admitted. I'd made a lot of decisions I felt terrible about.

"No one gave you the tools," Mr. Stokes said. "That's why it's important to learn."

Orange and yellow flared on the horizon. The water seemed to churn with fire as the sun rose from the sea, its light a thousand times more intense and crisp than the videos they showed on screens.

"The backups would have to work off-line," he said, offering a hint.

"Like the Pads?" I asked, and then it hit me. "The Pads?" I exclaimed, much too loudly. I lowered my voice. "You're telling me the backup is the fucking Pads?"

"I didn't tell you anything," Mr. Stokes said with a mischievous smile that reminded me of his late son. "You figured it out on your own."

THE EXPLORER'S HEART: $57.97

Beecher Stokes had been impish before his Last Day came. He was curious and funny and clever with words. But once he had to pay to speak, his life drained away. I never understood why I let him kiss me after that, when I hadn't before. I don't think I ever truly wanted to be more than friends, but he seemed so hopeless that I wanted him to have something to hold on to. It was twisted—I knew that now. Until that day on the ship, talking to his father, I hadn't really understood how important that hope had been for him. He didn't know I'd go silent, but he knew we would probably never be able to afford to speak to each other again. He made my last day of freedom his last day in the world.

Now his father stood in front of me with the same sort of impish glee, like a part of Beecher still survived in his dad, even though I knew it should have been the other way around.

"Everyone knows they're special," he went on about the Pads. "Work off-line. That off-line storage is awful handy."

"But they're everywhere," I said. "Placers. Overseers. Even real estate agents have them."

"But not anyone in the Onzième. Right? And they *have* to be everywhere. They update in staggered intervals, once every fifteen minutes. Discovered that about two years into my Indenture. Damn overseers aren't nearly careful enough. And they're lazy. So lazy, they had me do my work and theirs, too.

"If the Pads don't find Central Data, they look for other Pads instead. You blow up that last major node in Delphi™, and all the Pads will go into fail-safe mode. They'll become a distributed backup network, communicating with each other like a swarm. There'll be tens of thousands of them. Like a hydra."

"A what?"

"Doesn't matter. Point is, blowing up that data center would be worse than leaving it be."

"Wait, that doesn't make any sense," I said, trying to keep up. "How can everything in Central Data be stored on a Pad? The information couldn't possibly fit. If it did, why wouldn't they just make the Pads the Central Data system in the first place?"

"Each Pad doesn't store all of it. Central Data stores *all* data. Movies, 3-D scans, history, news, every piece of surveillance footage ever gathered from an Ad screen—you get the picture. But the Pads don't. They each store a bit, which is clever, because the whole thing doesn't end up in any one person's hands.

"They all store an index of which Pads store what. And, most important, they *all* store the important stuff. They all carry the lists of debts and debtors. Lists of property and owners. The prices of all the words. All the nation's Laws. For all their apparent verbosity, these bits of data require very little storage space. Even the entire Word$ Market™, with its definitions for every word, hardly amounts to any kind of data. It's easily stored."

"That's all saved on here?" I asked, tapping the Pad.

"This? No. This Pad is Téjican. It isn't part of the backups. Set up very differently. Nicer screen, too," he said, admiring it.

"So if all those Pads store the data, there's no way to destroy it," I said, confirming my worst fears.

"Anything that can be made can be unmade. There's *some* way to destroy it." He dropped his voice down even lower. "I wouldn't have come on this trip if I didn't think so."

"But how?" I asked.

"That's what I'm trying to figure out."

"You don't have a plan?"

"You didn't have a plan when you went silent. So I've heard."

"Are you trying to needle me, or encourage me?" I asked.

He laughed. "Can I do both?"

I thought for a moment. "Maybe we could make all the NanoLion™ batteries in the Pads explode at the same time."

"Again with the exploding! That won't work," he said. "They care about those Pads too much to use NanoLion™. There must be something we can do with that last center—besides explode it."

"But that's the plan," I whispered. "My Placer friends want me to buy time for them with this trial so they can destroy the center at Delphi™."

"You know what?" His face suddenly lit up, his sagging posture straightening. "You can do something less dramatic. You could destroy all their records, sort of like what you did with the batteries, but without exploding anything."

"How?" I asked.

He had a gleam in his eye now. "The Pads store what Central Data tells them. When things change, they have to erase a few old things to make room for more. I might be able to instruct the system to wipe out everything instead."

My heart started pounding again. Could this work after all? If we could shut down the system, I might be able to go back with Saretha. I might just survive.

"It'd cause the same chaos, though," Mr. Stokes went on. "There'd be no Laws. No communication. No nothing. Everything would have to start over." The gleam faded as he realized what this would mean. "Printers wouldn't work. People would starve. People in need of medical care… Even with a cracked DRM, you'd have no way to get word out."

"People could talk," I said, wanting this to work. "They could travel and explain. We had a plan for this." Kiely had even made me feel a little hopeful about it.

Mr. Stokes seemed to do some calculations in his mind. "There's a lot to that. I understand why our friends down there don't want it to happen. Some folks aren't going to make it. Could get really bad."

"It's *already* really bad," I said. "Bad enough that…" I didn't want to speak about the Jumpers. That was too cruel. "Did you worry about how bad it would get when you escaped?"

He smiled at this, the sun shining in his eyes. "I see your point."

"Do you think we could manage it? Could you explain to my friends how to do it?"

Mr. Stokes put a hand on the back of his neck. "That would be hard. It'd be better if I could do it myself."

"Could you do it with that?" I pointed to his Pad.

He shook his head. "Central Data can rewrite Pads, not the other way around. If it worked both ways, I'd have taken the system down long ago! I'd have to be inside, with your friends."

"Inside the Central Data node at Delphi™?" I asked, a bit too loudly. The two guards below us looked up. "I don't even know if my friends can get in," I continued in a whisper. "I don't know what their plan is. I haven't heard from Kel in days."

I scrutinized the map again. The Dome of Delphi™ was maybe ten hours away, and everything was falling apart. "Could you do it alone?" I asked quietly.

"I know how to break into printers, not buildings. I'm no Placer. I'd need your friends' help as much as they'd need mine. Plus, how am I supposed to get to Delphi™? We can't exactly ask Arturo to make a quick stop."

"No," I said. "We can't. But I have another idea." I looked up to where the lifeboats hung and gave him the same kind of grin he'd given me. "I'll bet you can puzzle it out."

THE DOME OF DELPHI™: $58.96

We passed the Dome of Delphi™ at midday. It was nearly as large as the Dome of DC. We saw it looming over the horizon well before we saw the coast it hugged. I didn't know if Kel was inside yet. She still hadn't contacted me, and time was running out. I couldn't let Mr. Stokes leave without a place to rendezvous, though he had grown so eager, I was concerned he might bolt off on his own, anyway.

"I really love the idea of these boats," he said to Arturo, which made me uneasy. I didn't want Arturo to guess at our plans. "I suppose because I feel as if I invented the idea—even if it had been invented before I'd ever been born."

Arturo looked at him with interest. "I've wondered how they taught you the history of the world if they could not even mention boats on the water."

"They didn't teach us any history like that," Saretha said. "Was there something we missed?"

I didn't understand how she could ask that. Of course we'd missed something. We'd missed nearly everything.

"Much of human history consists of men sailing," Arturo explained. "Exploring, conquering lands they found, sending their plunder back to their ancestral homes—and, sadly, bringing back slaves to work those lands."

"We knew none of this," I said, feeling bitter at the idea that slaves had been part of history for so long—even if they called it something else. "I didn't even know what the word *slave* meant until I escaped."

"Maybe I don't want to lay claim to this boat idea," Randall said, then shifted subjects. "How fast do these lifeboats go? How far?"

"I should have known," Arturo responded, making my heart seize for a moment, fearing he'd caught on to our plan. I breathed a bit easier when he said, "You have an explorer's heart. With all your curiosity, I should have seen it before. Alas, these lifeboats wouldn't suit exploring. They are meant for emergencies, to get passengers quickly to shore. Bad weather can come on suddenly."

Randall nodded. "Which is the fastest?" he asked. I shot him a look that begged him to stop.

"They are all exactly the same," Arturo answered, amused.

"Sir," one of the officers called from the deck door. Arturo turned. "You should come to the bridge. We've got news from America®."

We all raced to follow him down into a wide room near the level of the sea. Every once in a while, a wave would swell high enough to roll over the thick window and show the murkiness beneath the surface.

On-screen, a news report sputtered, showing the Portland dome. Silas Rog was talking, but the sound was broken up too much for us to catch anything but a few scattered words. His face was blocked again, his bodyguards were behind him and he was free.

"What happened?" Saretha asked before I could.

"They have reclaimed Portland and declared a state of emergency."

My body went icy, thinking of my friends there. What would become of them now?

The scene changed to show smoking wreckage in a tunnel somewhere between domes. Crane Mathers was on the scene. Though his voice was obscured by static, the words *Téjican Attack* labeled the image.

"That is our decoy," Arturo said. "They will have discovered the trucks were empty by now."

"They meant for that to be us," Saretha said, stunned.

"I don't know why this horrifies me so much," I commented, laughing nervously. "We knew this is what they were going to do."

"It horrifies you because it is horrible," Randall said, his eyes glued to the scene.

"I wish I could get in touch with Kiely or Kel," I said. "They could tell us what is going on. Are you sure they can reach us at sea?" I asked Arturo.

The communications officer looked at him with discomfort.

"They can." He swallowed, shifting his weight from one leg to the other.

"What is it?" Saretha asked, looking worried. There was something he wasn't telling us.

His cheeks darkened. "They can reach you, but we have been blocking any incoming signals broadcast to X0562.1.1," he said. "For your protection."

"What?" I yelled. "But you knew I needed to talk to them! They're on the inside. Do you have any idea who Kel and Kiely are? They can help us."

"Or harm us," Arturo said. "We have reason to be concerned.

You discussed blowing up the last data center. You know that would be a disaster."

"Yes," I said, realizing I needed to be careful now. "They *are* planning to blow up that last data center at Delphi™. I need to tell them to *stop*."

Arturo looked stunned. Randall threw his hands in the air.

"Unblock her signal," Arturo said quietly. The communications officer obeyed.

I waited. The screen sputtered an Ad for a new Carol Amanda Harving movie. When had Rog found the time to put that together?

"Now what?" Saretha asked.

"Now we wait," I said, then added, looking Arturo in the eye, "If they don't assume I'm dead or unreachable."

"You must understand our predicament."

"I think I understand your predicament better than you understand mine," I retorted.

The communications officer cleared his throat. "Someone has pinged X0562.1.1 every fifteen minutes for the last twenty-four hours. They haven't given up."

"I need some air," Randall said, launching his lanky body into the wall as he rushed off, like someone who felt unwell. I doubted he was sick, but I wasn't going to stop him.

"How long until the next ping?" I asked.

"Seven minutes," the officer answered.

"You swear you are going to talk them out of blowing up that center?" Arturo asked me.

"I promise."

He digested this for a moment. He gazed at the waves rolling by the low window.

"If I make this signal, you will cut off the transmission,"

Arturo said to the communications officer, making a slicing motion across his neck. "You understand," he said to me.

"I do," I answered with a glare. In the Onzième, that gesture meant *You're dead*, and usually preceded a fight. It cost $1.99, cheap enough that even kids without resources could intimidate each other. I was going to explain this to him, but before I could, an alarm suddenly blared. Arturo and all of his men tensed. One of the officers took off, tearing up the stairs, in the same direction Randall had fled.

"What's that?" I asked, hoping I didn't sound like a person who already knew.

"The alarm for the lifeboat," Arturo growled. He seemed to consider running up top, but then thought better of it. "Can we stop him?" he asked the nearest guard.

The guard was ready for action, but he looked helpless. "At top speed, we could follow, but we wouldn't catch him until he hit shore. The lifeboats are all the same."

"Which is fastest," Arturo muttered, repeating the question Randall had asked. He must have felt like a fool.

"I'm going to find them," Mr. Stokes said in my ear. His voice echoed into the room. I didn't understand how he was accessing my implants, but he was clever, and they had repeated the frequency in front of him at least once.

"You're monitoring what comes through these?" I demanded, pointing at my neck. "You're *broadcasting* it?" The communications officer dropped his head in shame. Arturo's cheeks flushed.

"I gave him orders."

"They can't destroy Delphi™," Mr. Stokes added. *"It would be a terrible mistake."*

A boat engine roared in my head under his voice.

"Should we go after him?" one of the officers asked.

"What is the point?" Arturo asked, then turned to me. "Did you know he was going to do this?"

"Yes," I admitted.

His frustration was immense. "We are supposed to be working together! I need to be able to trust you," he said.

"I'm supposed to trust you when you monitor private communications in my head? Do you have any idea how much I hate these things Lucretia Rog put in me? It isn't bad enough that I have to worry that at any moment she might pop into my head, but also that you could listen to *any* conversation I have."

"We would not do that."

"No?"

Arturo stiffened, his pride wounded. "I give you my word."

"Then you have to trust me as well."

"Of course," he said, but his face, and the faces of the officers around the room, looked skeptical. I needed them to understand that the final data center at Delphi™ would not be blown up, but they could not know our plan was still to destroy the entire system, just in a different way. The chaos they wanted to avoid—the hordes of refugees—would be exactly what they feared. I had to prepare myself to walk a very fine line, to give Kel the information she needed and keep silent about what I must not say. I knew words had power, but silence had power, too. I needed to find a way to use them both in just the right combination.

WORDS & SILENCE: $59.97

Kel's voice sounded in my head, right on time. *"Speth?"*

I took a deep breath and hoped the sentence I had planned would do what I needed. "Kel, you can't blow up the center in Delphi™. The consequences will be disastrous."

Arturo breathed a sigh of relief, but I didn't know if it was enough. I still felt hot and obvious. A drop of sweat trickled down my back.

"We're in Delphi™ now," Kel said in a low, frustrated growl. She wasn't alone, and it must have taken considerable effort to travel, again, from Portland.

"They have backups. Destroying the center at Delphi™ won't do what we want."

"She is right," Mr. Stokes called out over the engines of his boat. It felt especially strange to have two people talking in my head. *"It won't work like you think."*

"Who is that?" Kel asked.

"Spider Jupiter," he said quickly, before I could call him Mr. Stokes. The name felt ridiculous to me, but maybe it was safer for him not to give out his name.

In my time working with her as a Placer, Kel had learned to read my face. Now I had to hope she could read my voice.

"Spider Jupiter may be able to help," I said.

"Help with what?" Kel asked. *"If we aren't destroying the data center, what are we going to do?"*

This wasn't a question I could answer. Not like I wanted.

"Find Spider Jupiter," I said. If I could get him to her, Mr. Stokes could explain.

Kel paused. She was considering. She knew something was up. *"Who else is listening in?"*

There was an uncomfortable shifting in the room.

"I'm here," Saretha said, and then, because no one else would take it on, she added, "And there are lots of Téjican officials and Lawyers here to help us with the trial."

"Hello," Arturo said.

Saretha still had faith that the Lawyers could work everything out for us, despite their uneasy caution.

Kel paused again. *Come on, Kel,* I thought. *You can figure this out.* In the window, a wave swelled up and blocked the view of the horizon. The gray-green water darkened the room for a moment, and a school of silvery fish flashed past.

"What is your plan?" Kel asked.

"We've found a way to Portland," I said. "We have a trial everyone thinks we can win."

"Everyone?" Kel asked. She knew I didn't think so.

"Yes," I lied.

"And everyone *is okay with the consequences?"* She also knew that, even if we won the trial, I would be left behind.

"Yes," I said.

Again she paused. I thought I heard Kiely in the background.

"Do you want us to meet you there?" Kel asked.

"No," I said, perhaps too quickly. "I don't even know what we'll find when we get there. Do you know?"

"The Rogs restored WiFi to the city. They have a temporary system up and are building a new, stronger core."

My heart sank. "What about my friends?" I asked.

"We got a lot of kids out," she said. *"We had to scramble for places to stash them. Speth, if we can't find a way take the system down, I don't know how long we can hide them. The Rogs are especially keen on tracking down anyone from the Onzième now."*

Arturo exchanged a look with the communications officer. I could see they were considering shutting off my connection.

"Even if we could take the system down, it would be chaos," I said with my jaw tight. "Could we get them to Téjico?"

I looked at Arturo and hoped he would think it was better to have a trickle of refugees than a flood. He nodded, but it was obvious we were only going to pretend to trust each other. Maybe if everything else failed, a few kids from the Onzième could survive.

"Now? I don't think so," a different voice said. It was Kiely. I was glad to know she was there, but her appraisal did not encourage me.

"Maybe Nancee and Penepoli. Kiely has them pretty far south," Kel said.

"I don't know if they would go," Kiely chimed in, her voice ringing with approval.

"Why not?" I asked.

"They're on a mission, Speth. I know you'd be proud," Kel said. She didn't want to say more.

"What about Mandett?" I asked.

"Mandett was taken in Portland," Kel said quietly. *"A lot of people were rounded up in Portland."*

My fists clenched. It wasn't fair. No one was safe. I'd understood that, but it was different to have it proved. The only hope for any of us was to wipe out the database, Pads and all, and soon. But how could I let her know that? She still needed the distraction of the trial to get into the data center—maybe even more so now.

I looked at the communications officer, knowing that as long as I was on the ship, I wouldn't be able to talk to Kel without being monitored. If I took off, like Mr. Stokes, that would jeopardize the trial. My next chance to talk would be when we arrived in Portland.

"I've landed," Mr. Stokes called out.

"How long until we reach our destination?" I asked.

"Six hours," Arturo said.

"Kel, I need you to do what I ask."

Her response was instant. *"What are you asking?"* There was no doubt in her voice.

"Find Spider Jupiter," I said.

"39.9179, 75.1472," Mr. Stokes called out, then repeated the numbers again.

"Coordinates near Delphi™," the communications officer confirmed.

"And then?" Kel asked.

"I'll tell you when we arrive. But, Kel?"

"Yes?"

"Please remember: just because a solution is painful, doesn't mean it isn't for the greater good."

The water splashed by, covering the window in a spray that streaked with our speed and then washed away at the next wave. Kel quietly said, *"Understood."* A faint click followed, and the ambient noise behind her vanished.

"What does that mean?" Arturo asked, with equal parts curiosity and suspicion.

I examined the window again. Another wave washed by.

"It means she knows that however this turns out, I'm not likely to make it," I said honestly.

"That's not true!" Saretha said.

"Think about it. If we win the trial, you'll be able to go back to Mom and Dad and Santos359™. The Téjicans will be in a position to negotiate a way to keep their food sources safe. But me?" I shook my head. "They'll never let me go."

"We will negotiate for your freedom as well, of course!" Arturo said. "We have already planned this."

"I know," I said. "But you won't succeed. They'll give you what you want, but they will demand that I not be part of the bargain. And you won't sacrifice everything for me."

Arturo opened his mouth to say otherwise, but we all knew anything he said to reassure me would be a lie.

Saretha's eyes were wet with tears. "Why didn't you tell me?" she cried. "I can't lose anyone else. I *can't*."

"You need to understand." I took a step back to address everyone in the room. "You *all* need to understand, that what I'm doing is for the greater good, even if it seems like a terrible thing."

Saretha looked devastated. I wanted to tell her that there was still hope, but if Kel had failed to understand me, at least she would be prepared for the worst.

TWO OF US™: $60.99

The rest of my journey was spent with Saretha, crying and occasionally laughing as we reminisced on the deck of the ship. The coast crawled along in the distance to our west, marking the passage of what little time I had left. A knot sat in my stomach, a tiny bit of hope surrounded by a mound of worry. What chance did I really have to change things now? I had come so close, only to find I wasn't nearly as close as I had dreamed.

Arturo brought us some food. He called it a quesadilla. I'd never seen anything like it.

I sniffed it. It smelled warm and delicious. "Was it printed?" I asked. It was flat, but also a little uneven.

"Printed? No. This was made by hand."

My stomach might have been in knots, but I was also starving. I took a bite. The flavor was amazing, cheesy and earthy at the same time. There was an undertone like CornLock™, but without the chemical edge. There was also a slight tang, something red I couldn't identify.

"These have actual tomatoes," Saretha said. I had devoured half of mine by then.

"Thank you," I said, my mouth full, and Arturo left us alone.

My stomach craved more, like I couldn't eat fast enough.

Saretha laughed at my greed. The moment between us was so normal, like how things had once been. Before she turned fifteen and had to pay to talk, we could be silly like this without a thought.

"I wish we had more time," I said wistfully. "I wish we could be close again."

"We *are* close," Saretha answered.

I didn't want to disagree, but we had grown apart. We'd been split and separated by my silence and by circumstance—and by how we had changed from who we had once been. Even before everything fell apart, things had begun to change between us. There had been no time to say I'd felt misled by her leading up to my Last Day. She'd told me my Cuff was beautiful. She wanted me to be excited for my Branding. It wasn't her fault—Mrs. Harris had taught her to do this—but I felt let down. I knew she felt the same way about me. I knew she believed that if I had just broken and said one word that day on the bridge, those brothers might have spared Sam.

"Can you forgive me?" I asked suddenly.

"Forgive you?" Saretha asked in total surprise. "For what?"

"For Sam," I burst out.

"Oh, Speth."

"I'm sorry," I said, my voice shaking. It should have cost me $10. It should have been a legal admission of guilt. But it was more than both those things. It was more than an apology for Sam or for drawing Silas Rog's eye onto us. It was also an apology for the state of things and that they couldn't be different. I struggled to find a way to explain that to her.

"It wasn't your fault," Saretha said, and then, with more conviction, "It wasn't. I'm sorry I made you feel like it was."

We pulled together for a sisterly hug. It was just her and me now—she knew that. And I loved her with all my heart. If we made it through the trial, and what might be the end of the world, maybe we could talk about everything then. But that was a slim hope, and it would have to wait.

It was a comfort to be with her. Like something I'd lost had been found again. I was just so sorry that the world had to be like this. I wished I had spoken the word sooner, for a hundred different reasons. Whatever definition the Word$ Market™ had for *sorry*, it could never capture everything I felt. Whatever it cost me to say, the Word$ Market™ couldn't calculate its worth.

If Kel succeeded, if she'd understood me and could make it inside, and she and Kiely and Mr. Stokes could hack into the system, the definitions and Laws would be gone tomorrow, their values erased. The Rights Holders would have nothing to hold.

If we destroyed everything, if we erased it all, it would be so satisfying to watch everything horrible vanish, leaving the Rogs and their kind with nothing. But so much would be taken with it. I felt horrible about that. *Sorry* wasn't enough. Its meaning was too thin.

As the ship crested a swell in the water and dropped, leaving my stomach behind, a new thought hit me. What if erasing it all wasn't our only option? What if something else was possible? There wouldn't be much time to work it out, but a new hope bloomed in me that I might have found another way.

LUCRETIA'S REVENGE: $61.98

As Portland came into sight, a new and tenuous hope flickered inside me. I wished I could contact Kel, but there was nothing I could do but wait. I'd never seen Portland's dome from the outside. None of us had. We'd all gone out through the tunnel and saw nothing of it, not even Mrs. Croate, who vividly remembered the day they'd taken her away. I'd wondered about what it looked like from out here, mostly hoping to see the ocean someday. But I'd never dreamed that I'd see it from the waves, gently undulating on an enormous floating ship that had been Patented out of the public mind.

The dome wasn't so different from what I'd imagined. The concave hexagons I'd grown up with as my sky were convex out here, forming the bubble over the city. Between them, an iridescent sheen of solar paint gathered power for the city. The ocean lapped and crashed right up against the dome's eastern edge.

I had been taught there was no way in or out from the eastern side. It was all water, we were told. But a tunnel crept up out of the coastline and curved its way into the dome. I knew the city well enough to know that it would line up with the city's massive courthouse. That was our way in. The sight filled me with apprehension, but there was no turning back now.

The ship slowed and stopped farther out than I would have expected.

"You'll need to go belowdecks, to the bridge," Arturo instructed.

"Why?" I asked.

"They have mined the water. We need to clear the way."

"Mined?" Saretha asked.

"Explosives, under the waves," he said as he ushered us toward the door inside. "They must have known we'd detect them. A show, so we'll understand that we're not safe."

A host of dropters rose up from the Téjican ship, buzzed forward and plunged into the water. A moment later, the first explosion came.

An immense, foaming bubble broke the surface of the water. A massive column of water burst up in a geyser of spray. As we hurried to the bridge, a deep, rumbling *pop* rocked the ship. Another exploded behind it, then two more, each with massive gushing detonations and thundering sounds that reverberated the sides of the Téjican vessel. A cacophony of sound and showering vapor rose between us and the dome. It looked and sounded like the world was ending.

Then the noise subsided. The last few scattered explosions died, and a fine mist fell reluctantly over the roiling surface of the waves.

A few of the dropters resurfaced from the water, but most of them had been sacrificed in order to detonate the mines. Those that emerged turned to face Portland, proceeding in front of the boat, like a shield as we moved toward the dome.

"You're here early," a voice said in my head.

It wasn't Kel. I felt at my neck, seized with panic. It was Lucretia Rog.

"This is inconvenient," Lucretia continued. Seeing the terrified expression on my face, the communications officer hit a button, and Lucretia's voice was broadcast through the room. *"Miss Harving is scarcely ready to greet you. She is still so upset with your sister for trading on her looks. I don't know if she will be ready for the trial for a few more days."*

Everyone on the ship's bridge heard her. I don't know if they all understood what she was doing, but Arturo did. His face turned ugly for the first time since I'd met him, like he'd eaten something spoiled and sour.

"Your Commander-in-Chief Justice promised the trial could begin as soon as we arrived," I said.

"Did he?" she countered. *"Well, if Father said so."*

I didn't fully understand at first, even though her words were clear. Ahead of us, several sections of the tunnel motored open, leaving a wide expanse of road exposed to the air, eighty feet or so above the ocean, right at the level of the high deck. Was that how we were meant to enter?

I tried to cover my neck so she couldn't hear me, but I realized too late that the effort was futile as the word *Father* formed in my throat.

"Oh, of course," Lucretia said in her exaggerated mimic of innocence. *"I forgot that the family lineage of the Commander-in-Chief Justice is proprietary information. I should have had you agree to a nondisclosure. I didn't mean for you to know that our father writes and administers the Laws of these United States™."*

"You are bound by international Law!" Arturo said, shouting a little nearer my face than I would have liked.

"Is this not a private conversation?" Lucretia said in mock sur-

prise. *"I didn't agree to have the likeness of my voice reproduced. I'll have to add that to the wealth of suits we'll be prosecuting."*

"You're not prosecuting," I said. "You're defending stealing my sister's likeness and selling it across the border."

"Yes, I saw that," Lucretia said. *"One of many cases the Commander-in-Chief Justice, my father, will adjudicate today."*

"Inter… International Law—" Arturo sputtered.

"Yes, yes, yes. Naturally we will abide by all international standards as agreed to by our countries, including statute C117-A, which requires the Laws of the nation of trial to be adhered to. For example, you need to immediately extradite any and all criminals, including Speth Jime and that mimic sister of hers."

Arturo appeared ready to argue, but I made the sign of the zippered lips.

"You will all, of course, be required to remit payment for all the words you speak, as you are now within US jurisdiction."

There was something in the tunnel. I couldn't make it out at first. It looked like little more than a line of dots.

"We don't have access to your Word$ Market™," Arturo said. "How can we—"

"Don't worry," Lucretia said gleefully. *"Access is coming."*

Whatever was in the tunnel was moving fast, like a black snake slithering through the air. It wasn't until it got closer that I recognized it as a chain of tiny dropters leaving from the dome's tunnel and whirring toward us over the water.

"What is that?" Saretha asked.

"It is our WiFi, made manifest," Lucretia boasted, her voice gleeful. *"A WiFi cloud. An actual cloud, made from thousands of tiny drones, each acting as an amplifier for the signal."*

The communications officer's mouth hung open.

One of the Téjican Lawyers went gray. "It shouldn't be possible," he whispered. "They have disputed this Patent both domestically and internationally—"

"It has been fought over in Patent courts for years," Lucretia interrupted, *"but Father has declared a state of emergency. The representatives of the United States of America® East and the United States of America® West have agreed it is more important to unite at this time than to keep bickering over a small Patent. They have also been compensated handsomely for their cooperation."*

The swarm descended over the ship, resolving from a blackish, billowing fog to thousands of tiny gray drones, no bigger than flies, spaced inches apart. The ship was moved to within a few hundred feet of the tunnel, its base battered by waves. The fog of drones swelled and swayed, forming a bubble around the ship as it moved.

I made a slicing motion across my neck at the communications officer. He pointed to himself, like he wasn't sure I meant him. Or maybe it intimidated him because it had two meanings for him, too. I pointed at the implants and made the gesture again. He looked to Arturo, who nodded. The officer cut the signal.

"Can you do that when we get inside?" I asked. "Keep her out of my head?"

"If you're within half a kilometer," the communications officer answered.

"Could you do it so Kel can still reach me?"

His eyes flickered over his screen. "I think so. I could block any signal coming from within the Portland dome, and allow others in. I'll have to connect via the satellite. It might not be perfect."

"We shouldn't leave the signal out too long," Arturo warned.

"Let her stew a minute," I said. "We'll tell her the signal dropped."

After a moment, I gave the communications officer the thumbs-up. He reinstated the connection.

"You dropped out, Lucretia," I said. Her name felt disgusting in my mouth.

"Did I?" she asked.

"I demand we begin the trial at once," Arturo said. "That is what you have agreed to."

"I demand that you turn the Silent Girl and her sister over to the court at once," Lucretia shot back, her sickly sweet voice dropping to a menacing growl.

"There is no one here by that name," I said.

The Lawyer who had turned ashen looked up at me, impressed.

"Speth Jime," Lucretia insisted with a disgusted sigh. *"And her sister, Saretha. We demand the Jime sisters at once. They are our legal property."*

"We have no one here by those names, either," I said. Saretha stared at me in shock. "We are the Jiménez sisters."

Norflo wasn't there to beam at me, but Arturo was. He was so proud, it rendered him momentarily speechless.

"Perjury is a serious offense," Lucretia warned.

"Perjury only takes place in a courtroom," the ashen Lawyer said, regaining a bit of his color.

"I'm sitting *in a courtroom,"* Lucretia hissed.

"But we are not," I said. "You can't prove you *own* us without proving we are who you claim we are. To do that, you will need to see us in the courtroom and, for avoidance of doubt—" I grinned a little at myself for throwing in some Legalese "—you will need to match our DNA."

My words were met with silence, which I took as a very good thing. After a moment, a long platform extended from the tunnel onto the deck of the ship. It rose and fell with the slow swells. The cloud of drones inched away to clear more space.

"I will send a driver for you," Lucretia said, returning to her falsely polite tones.

"No need," Arturo said, snapping his fingers. Something roared below us, and a massive car appeared on the deck, skidding into place. "We have our own."

OBSEQUIOUS APPLAUSE: $62.98

The courthouse was as imposing inside as it was from the outside. My stomach twisted with nerves. The massive stone bricks and pillars were not just a facade; they made up the interior of the main courtroom. The drone cloud snaked its way inside ahead of us, powering the WiFi and silencing the waiting crowd.

Only the Affluents had kept their Cuffs on, and they glared at Mrs. Croate, Saretha and me as we passed. Everyone else in the crowd must have removed theirs in the days following the WiFi's fall. Sadly, they all still had implants in their eyes, ready to shock them if they spoke, shrugged or screamed. All of them were silent and rounded up into one corner of the room, probably to watch Lucretia make an example of me. My skin began to crawl.

A row of open Cuffs was lined up for us on a table at the front of the courtroom. We would all be required to wear them to give testimony. That was the Law. Once the trial began, they would go into Lie Detector™ mode and notify the court if we knowingly failed to answer truthfully. We would also be fined double the cost of our words.

Mrs. Croate began to massage her left forearm, where she'd worn a Cuff for years. You could see where her arm was smaller and misshapen—something Mrs. Harris claimed would never happen, though we'd all suspected it could. I scanned the room for Mrs. Harris, but didn't see her. I wondered which side she would choose now.

We could, and would, refuse corneal implants. The very thought of them made me nauseated. The originals were still in my eyes but dead. We would have no ocular shocks to worry about, at least, but that didn't help the majority of the crowd. The silence of so many people was unnerving in contrast to what I had seen and heard in Téjico, or even to the spray and churn of the sea. My heart longed for music and the ocean. What it got was the thin sound of a thousand drones and shuffling people making the maximum amount of noise legally allowed.

News dropters pushed through the cloud of drones, leaving eddies behind as their lenses found Saretha. She walked up the center aisle with hard, proud steps and me at her side. Her limp was almost gone.

I felt surrounded and unsafe. There were Modifieds everywhere. I had a dozen Lawyers with me, but I knew what little difference they would make in a fight.

Silas Rog entered right after us. The last time I'd seen him, he had been hauled away by the police. It was no surprise he was free now, though I didn't know the circumstances of his release. Either he'd been bailed out or, more likely, the charges against him dropped—or removed.

I saw no police now, which I took as a bad sign. They didn't want the Law here. I also remembered Rog had tried to murder me and failed, but only because without the WiFi, his gun wouldn't fire. There was WiFi now. I wouldn't be so lucky this time if he tried again.

Silas Rog moved heavily to his seat, radiating anger. Just behind him was Lucretia, though I didn't recognize her at first. Her face was not what I had seen in DC; she could no longer make me see her illusions. Her real face suited her much better. It was made of cruel angles, beady eyes and a thin, miserable mouth. She wore an elegant yet intimidating legal gown that appeared custom-printed, probably just for this trial, and likely more flattering to everyone who still had working ocular overlays.

Grippe and Finster flanked her, and Andromeda trailed behind. Victoria was nowhere to be seen. I would have expected her to bring Victoria, so her daughter would finally get to see me speak.

I looked around to see who else was here.

I recognized Bhardina Frezt and Itzel Gonz. Mandett was beside her, looking stone-faced. Nearby, I was devastated to see Sam's friend Nep. He'd grown since I'd last seen him, but he was still a child, his round face nervous and terrified. There were scores of others from the Onzième—I almost couldn't look. Even if we won this case, it would do nothing for them. Sera and Saretha and Mrs. Croate could go home. Those who'd made it to Téjico would be safe. But I realized I wasn't the only one who would suffer during the aftermath. The fate of everyone they'd corralled into the side gallery would be terrible. I was sure the Rogs had gathered them there to intimidate me.

Saretha's face was too calm for her to have pieced this together. I'd come to it too slowly myself. I needed Kel to contact me, but we were already here, and so far, I'd heard nothing. I worried that the communications officer hadn't been able to keep her access to me open—or, worse, was blocking her.

We had a team of Lawyers three deep, tapping away at screens and trying to compile more evidence even now. They had DNA Samplers at the ready. A quick test of Sera posing as Carol Amanda Harving would link her to her mother. Some of the Lawyers thought that could be grounds to demand an early judgment, and they had the fees ready to make the request. Mrs. Croate sat quietly by, scarcely daring to move, her eyes on the Cuff meant for her arm.

"Even their Commander-in-Chief Justice has to accept DNA evidence, doesn't he?" Arturo whispered, leaning over to me and gripping my hand. I shrugged.

"What do you think will become of them?" I asked, gesturing to where Bhardina, Itzel, Nep and Mandett stood in the crowd. He didn't have time to answer. The silence of the court was rippled suddenly by music. It was loud and bombastic—an announcement by horns. They lacked the crisp sound of real horns, and the joy of the players I'd heard in Téjico. They were used instead to intimidate and bash us with harsh sound as the Commander-in-Chief Justice arrived. He walked slowly out of the shadows from a door beyond the Judge's bench, pushing through a line of nine monstrously proportioned men who looked just like Uthondo and Bertrand.

"All rise!" a court official barked. The Judge mounted the stair, his expression blank behind his glowing judicial visor. He took his place and looked up, expressionless.

"The honorable Commander-in-Chief Justice of our United States Supreme Court®," the court official called out, his voice echoing through the stone chamber.

For most in the room, and for anyone watching on screens,

the Judge's face, like Silas Rog's, would be blurred away, but I could see him. I knew who he was. He was elderly, but I couldn't tell just how old. The very wealthy had ways to extend their lives. His white hair was trimmed to perfection, just like Silas Rog's. Unlike Silas, his demeanor was calm and precise. Once he sat, he didn't move. The nine brothers lined up behind, towering over him.

I'd never seen a Judge in person before, but in movies and on shows, they were always neutral and impartial—heroically so, right down to their emotionless expressions. Without being able to see the Commander-in-Chief Justice's eyes, it was hard to know what he might be thinking or feeling. His mouth and face looked characteristically detached, but also pitiless and unyielding.

The nine brothers stared ahead with watery eyes. On the end, I was certain, was Uthondo, who stared at me with an expression I could not unravel, because his face had been bred to menace and scowl.

Saretha's posture changed. Her eyes scanned the room, like she was looking for ways to escape.

"You okay?" I whispered.

"Mmm," Mrs. Croate answered instead.

"Before these proceedings begin," the Commander-in-Chief Justice announced, "I must say a few words."

His voice, amplified by some unseen microphone, echoed through the room. I steeled myself. We knew they would never let the trial proceed without trickery. I waited for an update from Kel, but heard no sound from the implants beneath my ear.

"While I am within my legal right to recuse myself from this judgment, I have decided not to avail myself of that right.

As *the* Commander-in-Chief Justice of the Supreme Court®, I have the latitude to preside over any case with objectivity and impartiality. Regardless of the facts of this case, I will discharge my duties impartially and without bias."

I assumed everything he said meant the opposite, and would be bad for us in the end. But even with that terrible knowledge, I could feel something worse was coming. My heart thudded against my ribs, waiting for it.

"For avoidance of doubt, and in compliance with International Code Section 5B, I hereby disclose that my legal name is Silas Weston Rog, father to Silas Charles Rog and Lucretia Hale Rog."

His impartial, neutral expression twitched to a half smirk as he banged his gavel and told the court to come to order. He was met with stunned silence from all sides until, after a moment of confusion, the Affluents began their applause.

$1.99 per second.

THE PERSISTENCE OF MOONLIGHT: $63.97

"And now," the Commander-in-Chief Justice said in a booming voice, "a word from our sponsors."

A large screen over the elder Rog's head popped to life. Moon Mints™ appeared, sparkling in a cascade over a full, golden moon.

The line of news dropters reconfigured their swarm to ensure everyone had a good view. Nothing in America® was so important that it couldn't be interrupted by Advertising.

I'd seen the real moon now. The one on-screen paled in comparison. Whatever the moon was, they didn't own it. They could force people to live in the shade of domes, but they could not stop the moon from casting its light.

I was acutely aware of who wasn't in the room with us. Sam, Henri and Sera. There was a hole in my heart that I realized was never going to be filled. But for Sera, at least, there was still hope. Beside me, Mrs. Croate watched the Ad as the Keene name on-screen faded to black.

"You will call the first witness," Justice Rog said to the Lawyers.

A bailiff picked up a Cuff from the table and held it out, waiting.

I felt at my neck. Still not a sound. I told myself it was possible Kel was still breaking into Delphi™. She needed time. I was the distraction. That was my job.

"Will there be no opening statement?" I asked.

"You will call the first witness," the Commander-in-Chief Justice Rog repeated.

My Lawyers took a moment to readjust. Arturo caught my eye and gave me a thumbs-up. What about this did he think was going well?

"We would like to call Miss Carol Amanda Harving to the stand," Arturo said in a rush. I wished I could tell him to slow down. We needed to give Kel as much time as possible.

Lucretia Rog stood. She adjusted her black legal gown. "If it pleases the court," she said, sneering at me and the Téjican Lawyers, "we feel it is only appropriate that Miss Harving be called to the stand as the *last* witness. This befits someone of her high stature and top billing."

"Objection," one of my Lawyers said. "Statute 117A-451A clearly states that the prosecution chooses the order of witnesses."

Silas Rog the younger stood and addressed his father. "Your Honor, Statute 117A-451A should be amended to allow an exception in the case for persons of high public profile, Influence and Affluence, like Miss Harving. Anything else would be an insult."

Several of my Lawyers chortled at this and were met with the sound of the gavel. Finster and Grippe glanced at each other and smirked. The Commander-in-Chief Justice paused for a moment, and then, with a finger on his visor, said, "Statute 117A-451A has been so amended. Said witness will be last as befits a person of high public profile, Influence and Affluence."

My Lawyers were stunned, but I wasn't. They leaned over and whispered to each other. Arturo looked crestfallen. Saretha was shaking her head. Who did they think they were dealing with? As the Affluents in the court applauded, I finally understood how Silas Rog had wielded such power all these years. Of course he never lost a case. If the Law worked against him, he had his daddy rewrite it.

One of my Lawyers stood up. "Your Honor, permission to approach the bench."

"Denied."

"Speth," Kel said through my ear receiver. I could scarcely contain the relief I felt at hearing her voice. *"Security pulled off as your case started,"* she explained. *"We're in."* Her voice was breathless and eager. This was just what we'd wanted.

"This is highly irregular," the Lawyer said. "You cannot simply rewrite the Law in the middle of a court case."

"Federal Statute 19D of the Patriots Act® allows the Commander-in-Chief Justice to amend, rewrite or expunge any and all Laws pursuant to the safety and economic welfare of the citizens of the United States of America® and its assigns," Justice Rog recited.

"That is not in accordance with international Law."

"Correct," he confirmed without emotion.

"This isn't right," Arturo muttered. He'd finally realized what I'd known from the beginning. The trial was a sham. It was impossible for us to win. I saw his posture change as the truth sank in.

"Speth, we're going to need a little time."

"I'll do what I can," I said. "But before you do anything, wait for my instructions."

Arturo thought I was talking to him, and that was my intent. I didn't want the Rogs to spot that I was communicating through the implants Lucretia had provided.

"I don't know if we can," Kel whispered.

I peeked over at Silas and Lucretia Rog. Lucretia was smirking. I tried to anticipate what their next move would be. The Rogs had the court tied down—we couldn't win here. Would defeating us be enough?

No. They would want more. The forces moving off at Delphi™ weren't a misstep. It was an intentional move.

"They *want* you to destroy the system," I whispered, but in the quiet court, my words were heard.

The Commander-in-Chief Justice banged his gavel. "I will have silence in the courtroom."

Lucretia turned and scrutinized me, her eyes narrowed in suspicion.

"Why?" Kiely called out from somewhere near Kel, but I couldn't answer without drawing more attention to myself.

"You will call your next witness," Justice Rog said, his tone filled with warning this time.

"We haven't called our first," Arturo muttered. My Lawyers were still reeling, trying to figure out how they could function if the Laws were simply written out from under them.

"Call *me* to the stand," I said quickly.

"I should go," Saretha argued.

"No," I said, grabbing her arm. I needed an opportunity to speak. "Please, I have an idea."

Saretha didn't understand, but she relented. I stood.

"We call Speth Jiménez to the stand," one of my Lawyers offered, still a little off balance.

"Please place your arm in the court-provided Cuff," a bailiff ordered. Behind him, two of the watery-eyed Modifieds glared at me. They were all over the place. One by the main exit with a shaved head had wide, deep creases around his mouth that reminded me a little of Henri. I wondered if that was intentional. He appeared less brutal than the others, but that might have been my imagination—or part of a typical Rog trick. I wouldn't put it past Lucretia to choose someone who looked like Henri—or even alter them—to rattle me as much as possible.

As I walked past her to the stand, she muttered something into her hand, then waited for my response. She got nothing. She didn't know she was being blocked from being in my head. I was glad even for this small victory.

The bailiff held a Cuff open for me. Lucretia wore a sick grin. I never wanted to wear one of these again, and she knew it. I hesitated, then put my arm forward. The bailiff snapped the Cuff around as quick as he could. It clicked, sealed and hissed. This one was the heaviest I'd worn yet. An AGREE button popped up, accompanied by Terms of Service that permitted the Cuff to analyze my answers and levy perjury fines if I lied. I tapped it, and an Ad for Arkansas Holt appeared. I swiped it away, but I had to admire his ability to keep afloat.

"Do you swear to tell the truth, the whole truth, and pay for all words representing that truth?" the bailiff asked.

"I do," I said.

Speth Jime—phrase, nonmarital (I do): $13.99

"Have a seat," the bailiff commanded. I obeyed, putting myself within arm's reach of the Commander-in-Chief Justice and a few of the Modifieds similar to Uthondo and Bertrand.

Lucretia stood up and said, "Please state your name for the record." She looked much too pleased with herself.

"Speth Jiménez."

Lucretia faked a patient smile and turned to her father. "If it pleases the court, this girl's legal surname is Jime. I have the records."

She flipped them from her Cuff. The Commander-in-Chief Justice nodded.

"It is legally registered so. The witness will give her legal and rightful name," he instructed.

"The Cuff has detected no lie. I have given you my rightful name," I said. "Speth Jiménez."

"Aka the Silent Girl," Lucretia said, her voice full of effort. "Why, you have so many aliases, I don't know how anyone could be expected to keep track." She turned to the Commander-in-Chief Justice and held up her Pad, showing the list. I wondered if her father saw her, or her digitally enhanced self.

"You will comply with my lawful order," Justice Rog demanded.

"I have complied." I held up my Cuff and pointed out the Lie Detector™ mode. The Cuff buzzed, showing my words and a $3 fee for pointing.

"The witness is mistaken," he said after a moment of reflection. "You will comply and give your legal name."

"Kel," I said.

Lucretia narrowed her eyes.

"Speth?" Kel asked. *"Can you talk?"*

"Perhaps the Lie Detector™ doesn't work on someone so practiced at trickery," Lurcretia offered.

"If I said my name was Kel, that would be a lie, even if you legally assigned it to me," I said to the Judge.

"No, my dear," Lucretia said, her voice dripping with disdain. "That is what you fail to understand. I can assign you any name I please. You are legally obligated to accept it."

"You could assign anything to me," I said, choosing my words very carefully now.

"Assign anything?" Kel asked. *"Me?"*

"You—" I said, adding a thoughtful pause "—could assign *everything* to me."

"What?" Lucretia asked suspiciously.

"Everything?" Kel asked, her voice unsteady.

The Commander-in-Chief Justice banged his gavel. "Your outbursts will not be tolerated."

"I move to strike her comments from the record," Silas Rog burst out.

"They are so stricken," his father replied.

I was suddenly delighted. They'd given me the perfect opening. "Don't erase everything," I said slowly, so Kel would understand. "Assign it all to me."

"Oh..." Kel's voice trailed away, then she yelled in excitement. *"Kiely! Spider!"*

Silas Rog erupted to his feet. "She is obviously incompetent."

The Commander-in-Chief Justice banged his gavel again. "This is your last warning, Miss Jime. Each infraction will be fined according to Courtroom Statute 39-1, and you will be charged the maximum amount of $10,000 per violation."

"Why not make it a billion dollars?" I asked.

"Statute 39-1 dictates fines between $1,500 and $10,000. That is the Law."

"You can rewrite it to be anything you want, though, right?

Why waste time with small amounts? Why not make each word a trillion dollars?"

"Is she asking what I think she's asking?" Kiely yelled to Kel with glee.

Lucretia narrowed her eyes at me and whispered, "I'm going to call your bluff."

Lucretia didn't understand what I was doing. Neither did my Lawyers or Saretha or anyone else in the gallery. But I didn't care—all that mattered was that Kel, Kiely and Mr. Stokes understood.

"Your Honor, if the 'witness' wishes to be fined a trillion dollars for each infraction, perhaps it would please the court to oblige her," Lucretia said with a sinister smile.

The Commander-in-Chief Justice mashed his lips uncomfortably with his fingers.

Kel breathed deep. *"I hope this works,"* she said in my ear.

I was ready to fail. There was nothing else I could do now. I had to hope, and enjoy what freedom I had left.

"The amount suggested is fiscally and administratively imprudent and therefore rejected," Justice Rog said finally. "However, the fine in Courtroom Statute 39-1 is hereby raised to $800,552.99 for each immaterial, extraneous or irrelevant word you speak while being questioned."

I didn't know how he arrived at that number, but it was probably some absurdly specific calculation of the fiscal and administrative maximum.

Lucretia nodded in satisfaction. "Now, please state your name for the record," she said, turning back to me.

"Tattoo, polecat, flipper, beef," I answered. My Cuff bleated wildly with warnings for the cost of each irrelevant word. Kel laughed in my head.

"Enough!" Silas Rog Junior barked from his seat. "She is making a mockery of this court. She is in contempt!"

"Is that an objection, Attorney Rog?" the Commander-in-Chief Justice asked.

"Yes, sir," Silas muttered, sounding like a sullen teenager.

"Objection sustained. The witness will not be allowed to testify if there is another outburst. Is that understood?"

Saretha sent me a pleading glance. My Lawyers conferred with each other, trying to think of good rational questions they could ask so they could get good, rational answers in return. Did they still believe they could win a case like that with the Rogs around?

"Do I need to agree that my name is Jime?" I asked the Commander-in-Chief Justice.

"It is legally required," he said.

"Spider says we can do it," Kel whispered in my ear. *"But it's a lot more work."*

"Luscious, effervescent, surreptitious, cruft," I said, letting my tongue linger on the sound of each syllable. My Cuff shuddered at the expense, like it feared for me.

"Remove her from the stand," Justice Rog said. Behind me, one of the nine brothers stirred. It was Uthondo. He held out his hand, rather than grabbing me, and I took it. He escorted me to my seat and then thumped back to his spot. The one next to him—Bertrand, I realized—looked at him askance. Andromeda watched them both with care.

"Please tell me there is a reason for what just happened up there," Saretha begged me. Arturo leaned closer to hear my answer.

"There is," I said.

"We'll put your sister up next," one of the Lawyers said.

"Then we have testimony from—"

"No," I said. "We're not calling any more witnesses. Make them bring out Carol Amanda Harving."

"I hope that gives me enough time," Mr. Stokes grunted, as if whatever hacking he was doing required physical effort.

"But, Speth!" Saretha whispered urgently. "I need to explain! And we have other witnesses. Mrs. Nince is here! She can testify about giving me the scar."

So someone had found her, the old prune. She was in among all the other clapping Affluents and surely couldn't be trusted to do anything but turn on us when the moment came. They must have all thought this was the way to safety for them.

"Mrs. Nince would never admit to injuring you in a court of Law. She'd be liable," I said.

Saretha knew this was true.

"I don't want to leave Sera to them any longer," I added. "If we call the last witness now, hopefully she'll be spared some suffering. Who knows what they're doing to her back in whatever room they've got her in."

Saretha and Arturo didn't like it. None of the Lawyers did, either. But all that mattered to me was getting Sera in the room. If my plan worked, I wanted to see her face when everything changed.

ANOTHER CAROL AMANDA HARVING: $64.98

Sera walked up the aisle with as much movie star attitude as she could muster. The dropters went a little crazy at the sight of her. She took hard steps in her heels, swaying her hips, her head held high. Her hair—I couldn't tell whether it was a wig, extensions or genetically enhanced—was full, dark and wavy, just like Saretha's. Her eyes were an icy blue—nothing like Saretha's, or her own, but the exact shade of blue of Carol Amanda Harving's eyes on-screen. The shape of her face had changed, too; it was a little fuller. The skin was a little raw, as if it had been scrubbed.

She didn't look entirely like herself, but she didn't look like Carol Amanda Harving, either.

"I don't know who she's supposed to be," Saretha said dismissively.

"Miss Harving," Lucretia said, like she was awed. Silas Junior grinned behind her. The faces in the courtroom were transfixed, and not nearly as skeptical as Saretha's and mine. Even Mandett looked impressed out in the crowd. Then I realized that we weren't seeing the same thing as everyone else. They were being fed a perfect digital re-creation over the reality of Sera. Saretha, the Téjican delegation and I were immune without corneal overlays. It made me wonder why they'd bothered to change her physical appearance at all, but then I remembered how cruel Lucretia Rog was.

"I'm sorry," I whispered to her as she passed.

Her glee crumpled. "What?" she asked. Then her eyes darted to her mother and widened in shock.

"Sera?" Mrs. Croate said hesitantly. Sera shook herself and glared at her mother like she was a scuff on the floor.

"I'm sorry we left you to suffer under her," I said with a nod toward Lucretia.

"Charming, but a distraction," Lucretia said, taking Sera's hand and pulling her away. "Please enter the witness box."

"You aren't sorry," Sera sneered, unable to let it go.

"I am," I said. "I've felt awful about it every day. I kept trying to think of a way to free you. You never deserved this."

"Sera!" Mrs. Croate called to her daughter as Sera moved toward the witness stand.

Sera shirked away from her mother's voice. Her eyes reddened.

The Commander-in-Chief Justice banged his gavel again. "Order!" he commanded.

"We're going to need a little more time," Kel whispered in my ear.

"Miss Harving," Lucretia said, taking her by the arm, but getting nowhere. She nodded for help from the brothers, and Bertrand stepped out of the line.

"*She's* taking care of me," Sera said to her mother, her icy blue eyes looking unreal up close.

"Please sit," Lucretia Rog asked.

Sera's anger boiled away, and her phony grin returned. She tottered into the box and settled down, assuming a proud posture and folding her hands obediently in her lap.

"Do you swear to tell the truth, the whole truth, and pay for all words representing that truth?" the bailiff asked.

"The Rogs will be paying for my words," Sera said haughtily, "but yes."

"We need more time," Kel whispered in my ear.

"Please state your name for the court," Lucretia said, smirking, looking out toward the gallery like she had us.

"Stall!" Kel whispered in my ear.

"Objection," I shouted.

Lucretia's face pinched with annoyance. Her father turned to me, his gaze an eyeless, glowing line. The Lawyers from Téjico fell in around me. The objection wasn't mine to make.

"On what grounds?" Lucretia laughed.

I stood. "The Law requires words be used with intent to convey their proper meaning," I said, bracing myself. I didn't speak Legalese, but felt the need to mimic its sound. "Does this not include names?"

"Names are a special class that are not assigned meaning," the Commander-in-Chief Justice said.

"With all due respect, Your Honor, names *do* have meaning."

Gasps rippled through the court. I had just disagreed with a Judge in his courtroom—and not just any Judge. The Supreme Commander-in-Chief Justice himself. Lucretia shook her head, like I was being foolish.

Justice Rog turned his head toward me. "It is not the responsibility of this court to educate you on points of Law. Unless you have a legal point to make, please be seated."

"I would argue that all words *are* names," I insisted. "They are sounds assigned to ideas, things and actions. If you are angry, the word is *not* the feeling itself. It *conveys* the feeling."

"We know what words are," Lucretia Rog said coldly. "We own more of them than anyone in this nation."

I went on, ignoring her, instead fixing my attention on Sera, "Rights Holders are not allowed to void, change or reassign meanings. For example, if I say *I'm sorry*, we all understand it is both an apology and a legal admission of guilt. If I did not see that someone had grown up in even worse circumstances than I had, or if I failed to help them when they needed me, I can speak *'I'm sorry'* and convey how terrible I feel. I can let them know how I wanted to help. I can explain how hard it was to understand what they were going through. *If* I can afford the $10 fee."

Sera squinted at me, unsure what I was doing. The Commander-in-Chief Justice banged his gavel, but I went on.

"But if I can't say it, because the cost is too high, then we are forced to live in separate worlds. We are divided, even from the people closest to us. We cannot share our experiences. We cannot hold on to our culture. We go unheard."

"But..." Sera trailed off, holding out her hands, unsure what she wanted to say.

Silas Rog shouted, "Objection! This is a mockery of the court!"

"Sustained," the Commander-in-Chief Justice boomed. "You will cease speaking."

"It leaves us all alone," I continued, raising my voice and keeping my eyes on Sera.

"Two minutes," Kel whispered in my ear. *"The WiFi will need to go down first. We won't be able to communicate until everything reboots."*

"Remove her from my courtroom!" Justice Rog called out, his visor glowing more intensely. The two brothers on either end—Uthondo and whoever was on the far side—moved to take me. Saretha clutched my arm as the Téjican delegation closed ranks around us.

"You don't have to do that," I told them.

"We pledged to protect you," Arturo said firmly.

"You have one card to play while the WiFi is down," Kel said. *"Nancee and Penepoli have Victoria Rog."*

I shooed the Lawyers away and met Sera's eyes again. She stared back at me, trembling.

"Victoria has one request," Kel said, as her connection crackled out. *"That her mother not be harmed…"*

There was the faintest thud, and then, from outside the courtroom, a distant ticking. Along the dropter chain, starting at the door and moving inside, the drones fell one by one, wobbling, pitching and careening to the ground. The little ones scattered to the floor like sand and the news dropters fell like dominoes. The screen behind the Commander-in-Chief Justice's head went dark, and so did his visor. The WiFi was down.

He immediately put his hands out, searching. Emotion finally registered on his face.

"Desist!" the younger Silas screamed at me.

"No," I said, clucking my tongue at him. It was such a simple word. "*You* aren't supposed to be speaking with the WiFi down."

"Enough!" Lucretia cried out to her bodyguards. "No one's watching now. End her!"

The bodyguards all blinked in confusion and wiped at their eyes. With the WiFi down, the low-level shocks that usually kept them obedient must have abated. A few, like Uthondo, took tentative steps toward me. Andromeda, wild-eyed, raced for the door. She wasn't alone. It was chaos as Affluents and Silents both tried to work out what was about to happen.

Lucretia's face turned a violent shade of red as she and Silas decided to take matters into their own hands.

"Without your bodyguards, do you really think you can take me hand to hand?" I asked. That gave Lucretia pause, but not her brother. "The only thing protecting you now is..."

I was about to speak Victoria's name, but before the words could leave my mouth, the WiFi returned.

RESTRICTED®: $1,000,000,000

"Desist!" the Commander-in-Chief Justice shouted, terrified, patting at his visor like he was worried it was gone. The dropters woke from the floor and hovered unsteadily.

"Uthondo!" Lucretia commanded, tapping frantically at her Cuff. Uthondo stepped closer to her, enraged.

"It's all yours now," Kel said.

"I've taken control of the database," I warned.

"What database?" Silas Rog demanded.

"The only one left," I said.

Uthondo paused. His eyes shot to me.

"Lies!" Silas Rog spat.

"Try me," I taunted, wondering how much loyalty and devotion money and cruelty could buy as Uthondo tried to shake the Rogs from his head.

The Commander-in-Chief Justice began speaking. "Whereas Speth Jime, the party of the first part, has shown blatant and unrepentant contempt for this courtroom and its authority—"

"I do have a lot of contempt," I said, a sense of giddiness bubbling up under my fear.

"Be careful out there," Kel said.

"—and whereas the party of the first part has refused to comply with a lawful order to speak her legal name, and whereas the party of the first part has practiced Law without deference to her legal counsel—"

"Sorry, guys," I said to my Téjican legal team as they began to pack up and work out an escape.

"What is happening?" Arturo asked.

"—I sentence the party of the first part, Speth Jime, aka Speth Jiménez—"

"You're not even on trial!" Arturo said, outraged.

"They don't care," I said.

"—to death," the Commander-in-Chief Justice roared.

"Objection!" one of my Lawyers called out. "That is not legal procedure! You—"

"I will amend the legal procedure," the elder Rog shot back.

"I think you'll find that you can't," I said quietly.

The Commander-in-Chief Justice's brow furrowed under his visor.

"And even if you could sentence me to death, how would you determine the sentence has been carried out?" I asked.

Uthondo stood worryingly near, unsure what he should do. His brother followed his lead, waiting.

"Death is just an assigned value according to the Law," I explained. "Like my name. Every word has a meaning, an owner and a price. With a simple tap, I can wipe them all out."

"If she erases the database, words won't have any meaning," one of the Affluents in the crowd cried out.

"No one will be able to understand anything!" Silas protested.

I held up my arm and the Cuff they'd given me.

"If the word *death* ceases to mean anything, will it bring my brother back?" I growled.

"Erase that database, and you'll destroy the entire economy," the younger Silas bellowed.

"Do you think that worries me?" I asked.

Lucretia put a hand on her brother's arm to calm him. "Do it," she said. "Erase the entire system and see." She rubbed a thumb over the Pad in her hand. If we wiped everything out, I'd be willing to bet it would give her control. She'd allowed the other data centers to be destroyed.

Silas Rog Junior gripped his Cuff with his right hand and searched for a clear line to me.

"We've shut out the Patent for projectiles," I warned. "I know how much you'd love to shoot me, here, in front of the whole world."

"I would have expected you to blow everything up, like a terrorist," Lucretia sneered. "But this is no different in the end. Erasing everything is just the long way around to the same thing. Chaos and death are exactly what you want. *That* is what the world will see." She cocked an eyebrow at me, and it was clear she didn't share the fear that hung in the room. She wanted the last center destroyed, one way or the other.

"I *could* erase it all," I said to tempt her. I hovered my finger over the Cuff. No one dared step near me now. "Or..."

"Or what?" Lucretia asked, her calm chipping a little.

"I could just assign all the words to me."

Kel had helpfully shunted a list of options to my Cuff, leaving the choices in my hands. With a simple tap, I became the only Rights Holder in America®. It felt powerful and good and a little scary.

"Kiely has my back," Kel said. *"Spider's hard at work. We're still inside if you need anything else."*

"She can't do any of this, Silas," Lucretia reassured her

brother. "Meaning is protected by the Second Act of Connotation, and Verbal Code 371 prohibits transfers exceeding—"

"Verbal Code 371 has been revised to require you to shut up," I said.

This wasn't one of the options, but Kel laughed in my ear and said, *"Got it."*

"The Second Act of Connotation had been repealed," I confirmed, feeling Cocky™.

"You cannot rewrite the Law to suit your purposes!" the Commander-in-Chief Justice snarled.

"Why not?" I asked cheerfully. "You do! It's all you've ever done!"

"I am the elected leader of these United States of America®!"

"Elected?" I snorted. "By who?"

"I won 100 percent of the eligible vote."

"And who decides who is eligible?"

"Father, don't answer her!" Lucretia called out.

I persisted. "How *many* people in the United States™ are eligible to vote?"

The Commander-in-Chief Justice fell silent.

"The answer is sixteen, by the way," Kel whispered in my ear. *"I'm looking at the rolls now."*

"Every word you speak makes me money now. Do you know how rich I'll be? What if I took the price of every word and—"

"And made them free?" Lucretia finished my sentence for me with a scowl. "Typical liberal fantasy. You don't understand anything about how the world—"

"Don't interrupt me," I snapped. "I'm not going to make words free. No, I have a different idea."

The Silents and my friends in the gallery now looked

shocked. I tapped and put the Word$ Market™ up on the large screen behind the Commander-in-Chief Justice's seat, where everyone could see. Words and their values crisscrossed on the florid green background.

"She's bluffing," Silas Rog protested.

Lucretia's eyes went wild when she realized, too late, what I was about to do.

I tapped my Cuff again, and each word's value skyrocketed into the billions.

A hush fell over the room. A single word from anyone now would mean more debt than anyone had ever known.

"I'm the only person in the country who can speak now," I said, pacing to the front of the courtroom. All eyes were on me. No one could believe it. Saretha looked hurt that she couldn't speak, too. Sera glared from her place on the stand. All three Rogs were rendered mute.

"That makes all of you Silents," I announced with a laugh.

NULL

I could have kept the nation silent like this indefinitely, with everything in my control. But what kind of monster would that make me?

A few actual Silents who were in the room appeared thrilled. Was this what they had wanted all this time? Did they even know anymore? I would have to disappoint them, but first I let the silence sit a minute. I had a point to make.

Silas and Lucretia stewed furiously. Their father sat paralyzed, which wasn't so different from his usual stony, eyeless expression. I wanted them to know, just for a minute, what it felt like for most of us, to know the fear of speaking more than you could afford.

"This is the endgame," I said. "What every Affluent dreams of—getting as rich as possible. I own *everything* now—every single word, gesture and Copyrighted move."

I did a quick little salsa move, like I'd seen in the courtyard in Téjico, and felt Sam's mischievousness in my heart.

"Idiot!" Silas Rog called out, throwing a few billion dollars away in his anger.

"Oh," I said innocently. "You don't like it? Jealous you didn't think of it yourself? Angry you laid the groundwork and I got here first?"

He glared at his Cuff. He was rich enough to survive another transgression or two, but greedy enough not to dare.

"I own," I said, shaking my head and showing them my Cuff. "Go ahead and look. I'll waive the fees. I've put my name on everything. Your homes, your cars and your Indentureds." I paused, glaring at the Rogs. "Or should I say your *slaves*?"

Some of the Affluents looked taken aback as I continued, "Think of how imbalanced that is—one person owning *everything*. But the Law says it's all legal. If I can figure out how to manipulate the Laws, whatever I decide will be legal. It doesn't matter what anyone else actually wants or needs. That is *all* we care about—how things are defined by Laws, regardless of what is logical, fair or right."

My voiced echoed through the courthouse, bouncing from stone to stone.

"Is it really so different when it's a few dozen people that own *almost* everything? Or a few hundred? When millions have so little, and most own less than nothing, can you count on the wealthy to be generous when their pitiless greed is what brought them their wealth and power in the first place?

"Did you know you can own *children*?" I asked, looking around at the crowd. "They didn't teach us that in school. I was taught you can only be taken into Collection *after* you finish school. But they don't tell you about what happens to the kids born to parents who are already Indentured. They're owned from birth, with no more rights than a Trademarked logo. They take them and put them out to work in the fields almost as soon as they can stand."

I paused to let that sink in. Even some of the Affluents seemed troubled by the idea.

"Now I own them, too." It was a sick thought. "I own *every* Indentured logged in the system."

I took a breath. I had to use this moment to make something right.

"That includes you, Sera," I said.

Sera's brow creased. She hadn't understood my attempt to apologize earlier. She was raw, still, with hatred.

I pointed at Lucretia. "*She* doesn't own you anymore," I explained. Sera opened her mouth before I could stop her.

"But *you* do?" she snapped. She shouldn't have spoken. Each word cost her billions of dollars. It was a laughable amount, or it would have been if her Cuff hadn't started buzzing wildly. A high-pitched whine sounded. She looked down at it, alarmed.

"It's warm," she said, her eyes blazing with fear. People began to shuffle back, away from her. A warm Cuff was a prelude to a total meltdown of the NanoLion™ battery inside. "What do you want from me?" she screamed, not understanding this wasn't what I was trying to do. I wasn't trying to punish her. I hadn't made myself clear.

"Kel, wipe out every debt."

Cheers rose from the Onzième crowd at this. The whine of Sera's Cuff stuttered and then dropped away. Lucretia's nostrils flared.

"What do you want?" Sera begged me.

"Charge her speaks to me," I said quickly. Billions were charged to me and then forgiven, because I was the only Rights Holder in America®.

"I want your forgiveness," I said, relieved her Cuff had stopped buzzing.

Sera looked like she'd swallowed a lemon. "Why?" she asked. Everyone else was frozen and held hostage to the silence, save for the two of us. I would have preferred to work this out in private, but I had no choice now.

"Because we were kept apart by a cruel system that left us to raise ourselves and wouldn't let us speak."

Sera sniffed, "You act like you didn't have fifteen years of talking. You could have apologized anytime you wanted before that. You could have said it after, too. It's only $10. You're the one who went silent. You didn't have to do that."

"I didn't," I admitted. "We had words, but we didn't have any guidance on how to use them."

"What the hell does that mean?"

"They took our parents, Sera. They took our families away. I'm not just talking about the system of words, but everything that made us scrap over every little morsel. We were pitted against each other from the start for everything—how much Wheatlock™ we could print, or how much space we could have. We even had to compete for Mrs. Harris's time. They kept us working against each other so we would never work *with* each other."

"So I'm supposed to be your friend now?" she asked, a little bewildered. Sera wasn't the type to get all sappy.

"No," I said. "There is a difference between friend and family. I want you to be my sister."

Sera's eyes streamed with misery and her mouth opened in shock. She gestured across the courtroom. "But you have Saretha!" she sobbed.

"Family is more than just blood," I insisted, stepping closer. "I can have more than one sister."

Just like I could have more than one brother. Sadness washed over me as I thought of Sam and Santos359™.

Sera stood there, uneasy in her skin, looking almost like a

Jiménez now because of what they'd done to her. I walked over and put my arms around her. They had charged us for this. They had made that seem normal.

Lucretia Rog watched us, disgust written across her face. Silas Junior kept looking at his Cuff, waiting for his status to change. I broke away from Sera.

"Speaking of blood," I said, turning around and addressing the nine brothers held in place by my billion-dollar threat. "If I release the words and make them free, I'd like you not to spill any," I requested.

They all sent me the same watery-eyed glare that said, *Don't count on it*—except Uthondo, who glared a little less.

"In a moment, you are going to be free. Your eyes will no longer ache with that low-grade shock they've used to control you. You'll be able to decide for yourselves what to do with the incredible strength MonSantos™ gave you."

At the head of the room, the Commander-in-Chief Justice folded his hands—a public domain gesture I was surprised to see. He was patient. He was ready. He seemed much too sure of what was about to happen. Whatever he had up his sleeve, I only had one more move to make.

I turned and again faced the courtroom.

"According to Silas Rog, words have meaning only because they are assigned meaning in a database. His father, the dishonorable Commander-in-Chief Justice, ruled, legally, that *without* the Word$ Market™, words have no meaning. They claim that if the database is wiped, none of us will be able to speak or understand anything. If I say the word *zebra*, it will mean nothing to you."

I raised a finger, ready to blank the assigned values, meanings and ownership of each word. Everything else I'd leave intact. There would still be WiFi. The printers would still work. The Patents were all mine now. People wouldn't starve. They wouldn't die for lack of medical treatment. We would still be able to communicate with each other. I held my Cuff high and waited, bringing my finger a millimeter away for dramatic effect.

"But if the meaning and value of every word is wiped out, and you can *still* picture a horse with stripes when I say *zebra*, it will prove, beyond a shadow of a doubt that the system is—" I turned slowly so the whole assembled crowd could hear "—absurd, ridiculous, farcical, broken, illegitimate and, frankly, utterly dishonest."

While I spoke, I pressed AGREE to wipe the Word$ Database.

Of course my brain still worked. No one realized, at first, that I had done anything at all. Our brains were not tied into the system like they'd always told us.

Silas Rog looked down at his Cuff. "Take her!" he shouted the moment he realized he could speak again.

The nine freed Modifieds just stared at him, wiping at their eyes. I could only imagine how good they felt now, after a lifetime of constant, threatening pain. They looked to me with grateful, pain-free eyes—all except Uthondo. He had already pushed past me, heading straight for Lucretia Rog. His brothers followed him, and Silas and Lucretia tried to back away, their fury morphing into panic. The crowd behind them tightened, and Saretha and Sera both moved to either side of me.

"Do you know what you've done?" Lucretia screamed as she pointed to her father.

On the high bench, the Commander-in-Chief Justice sat, hands still folded, eyes still blank behind his judicial visor. He didn't move, like he was waiting to pass judgment.

"What is he planning?" Saretha asked. Sera took a step closer to me, her shoulder pressing against mine.

"Creepy," Sera said, pulling at a strand of her long dark hair nervously.

Lucretia kicked out at the giant men advancing on her, but it was no use. "You fools! You've rendered words meaningless to him!" she screamed.

"What is she talking about?" Sera asked.

I stepped up to the bench and waved a hand in front of the elder Rog. He reacted, moving back, unfolding his hands like a spooked animal. He stood, as carelessly and awkwardly as a toddler, and then began to move off. His status as the leader of our nation still seemed to intimidate some of those around him, but there was no malice left in him now.

"He was directly linked to the system," I said, sickened and sad that he'd been rendered mindless. "For him, the meanings of words *were* tied to the database. His thoughts have been reduced to feelings. His mind can't call up any meaning."

"It will be like that for all the Judges, I'm afraid," Kel said.

Uthondo took hold of Lucretia.

"Don't hurt her," I said.

I couldn't tell who looked more stunned, Lucretia Rog or Uthondo, who was seconds away from taking his revenge for a lifetime of pain. The mob was pressing in, and Lucretia took advantage of his distraction to twist out of Uthondo's grip. She flung her Pad across the room, to the Modified by the door. "Go!" she shouted.

He snatched it from the air gracefully and seemed fairly pleased with himself for the catch. He quickly stuffed it into his bag and took off with the speed and style of a Placer. I didn't know how she'd brainwashed him—maybe he didn't understand what was happening. I didn't have control of the situation anymore.

"Don't hurt *her*?" Silas Rog roared. "What about me?" As if I owed him anything. Victoria wanted me to protect her mother, but she'd made no such plea for her uncle.

Silas Rog was swallowed up by the crowd. I wouldn't have any further part in his fate. He sputtered vicious Legalese as he went down. I'd worked hard to save a lot of people—I would not try to save him. Lucretia was enough.

Uthondo was clearly struggling to resist every violent urge he felt toward Lucretia. "Hand her over to them," I told him, indicating the Téjicans with me. Uthondo looked crestfallen, but he obeyed, which made the whole thing feel sicker to me. I didn't want his obedience, but I saw no other way to fulfill my promise to Victoria.

I glanced back at the gallery and saw Mandett and Itzel cheering for me, which roused those around them. The Affluents remaining didn't know which way to turn. Everyone was looking to me.

"I never meant to be a leader," I said loudly to the crowd. "I just wanted to be free. I want all of us to be free. Now it's up to you—*all* of you. We *all* need to talk, not just me—and we need to listen. They kept us apart by controlling what we could say and what we could know. They took nearly everything: our parents, our sisters and brothers, our friends. They didn't want us to know each other, or ourselves. They didn't want us to *have* selves. They didn't want us to know where we come from. But they failed."

I took a deep breath. "Every little act of rebellion, and every little thought you held close in your mind, preserved something. Now we need to preserve more. We need to be known. The good and the bad, from our history down to what makes us our best selves, needs to be remembered. We need to share all of it. What we say can't be restricted."

A cheer went up. Mandett whooped from the crowd, his face glowing. I knew what they expected me to do next, but I wasn't going to do it. I couldn't. I didn't want to be a leader.

I had to stop. Sam would have been proud of me, and that made it so hard to know that he didn't live to see this moment.

But he would have understood what I had to do next.

It was time for me to leave. It was time to go home.

EPILOGUE

Santos359™ looked at me as I knelt beside him on the flagstones. A warm wind blew through the small, open-sided dome over us. I wanted to hug him, but worried he would bolt off. Would he feel different from Sam, or the same? Both ideas tugged at my heart. Sera knelt beside me, her arm pressing against mine, shaking.

"He won't bite," I promised. She wasn't afraid of that—she was still unsure of her place with us.

A light flashed in our brother's eyes. He barked and gnashed his teeth, then fell backward into giggles. I'd been making progress with him. I dreamed that one day we would speak to each other, but for now, he only listened—a silent boy.

I giggled right back at him and gave him a playful bark of my own. This was something Sam would have done when he was little. Maybe this boy had the same mischievous heart. I hoped so. I didn't want him to replace my Sam, but he helped me remember everything I'd loved about my lost brother. I could love him for himself, too. That didn't seem like a terrible bargain.

He stopped and examined his forearm to check it was still free of his Cuff.

"No more Cuff," I said. I showed him my arm. Sera

showed him hers. My father had warned me MonSantos™ had swapped out his Cuff each year on this date—their sick birthday present to him as he grew.

My father watched from the edge of the courtyard, hanging decorations for Santos359™'s birthday celebration. It would be his first. My mother was half-hidden with Mrs. Croate behind leaves and vines in the garden. I wouldn't have thought they would want to do such work after so many years enslaved on a farm, but the two of them found the garden soothing. It helped to know *they* would reap the rewards—in this case, tomatoes, peppers and squash. I could smell them in the air, ripe for the picking, ready for the party. Mrs. Croate and my mother didn't talk much as they harvested, but they could, and that seemed enough for them.

Saretha hurried out of the building that had been printed for us. It was Mr. Stokes's design: a Spider Jupiter original. He'd made a space for each of us here, deep in Téjico, near other refugees. The house was wildly ornate and maybe a little too much, I thought, but I'd rather have too much space made than see it cruelly printed away. Mira, Margot, my parents, Mrs. Croate, Sera, Saretha, Santos359™ and I each had a bedroom, plus there was space for guests. We would need that space today.

My father wanted Mr. Stokes to join us, but Spider Jupiter had been gone for weeks. As he'd hoped, his mother had escaped with a group of Indentureds after the data center in DC went down, but no one knew where they had gone. He intended to find them.

Saretha made her way over to us. We all knelt before our brother like he was a little king. This was his day, after all.

"Is it dumb that I'm just a *little* bit sad he won't have a Last Day?" Saretha asked.

"Yes," Sera and I said together. The three of us laughed.

"We could create something new," I said. "We could call today a First Day."

"Día del Primero." Saretha smiled.

"Trademark!" Sera called, mostly joking.

Santos359™ looked at us and took off running. He hid behind a pillar and peeked out, grinning. He needed another name, too, but we'd all agreed it was up to him to change it when he was ready.

"We all need a little time," I said, rising to my feet. Sera followed my lead.

"Or Día del Comienzo," Saretha suggested, warming to the new tradition she was cooking up.

"Norflo's Spanish lessons are paying off," I said to her, peeking up the road to his house. I expected Norflo and his brothers would walk over any minute.

"Javier," Sera corrected, tucking her hair behind one ear.

On the road, a car headed toward us, glinting in the sun. I wanted Kel and Kiely to be inside, but they were too busy. The people needed leaders. Their broadcast of the DRM codes made them very popular and it would be a good while before a real, fair election could be mounted. Until then it appeared Kel and Kiely were in charge.

The car slowed at the edge of the courtyard. Its doors swung open, and for half a second I feared Lawyers would step out.

Instead, it was Victoria Rog.

She crossed the courtyard flagstones and headed directly for us. Behind her, Nancee and Penepoli unloaded presents from the car. It had taken them weeks to make it from DC to us. Despite the hope that things would improve, the transition wasn't simple, and travel was slow.

Santos359™ peeked out, sensing the gifts were for him.

Victoria looked at Sera, her head cocked. "I know you," she said in a quiet voice. She gave Sera a gentle hug. "You were at the house. My mother did this." She put a hand on Sera's face. It would never be the same. But whether it was on the outside or the inside, none of us would ever be the same.

"You saved my sister," Saretha said, putting a grateful hand on Victoria's shoulder. I'd told Saretha the story on our way back to Téjico.

Nancee and Penepoli hurried over now, laden with bags. I had no idea what they'd brought. We wanted for nothing here. We had food and shelter and each other.

I hugged Nancee and Penepoli. I'd missed them. "It's been so long." I meant more than the weeks it had taken them to travel or the months since I'd left Portland's dome. I had missed them since my Last Day set us apart. I hoped no one ever had to have a Last Day again.

"I am sorry," Victoria said with a tight swallow. "A legal admission of guilt I was never permitted to speak." She put a hand to her forehead, like she was pained. Her uncle was dead. Her grandfather, the former Commander-in-Chief Justice, was spirited away by fleeing Lawyers, but there was little hope for him. Like many Affluents, we had heard, they were trying to get to the western United States™, beyond the stretch of Téjico and Canada that cleaved the nation in half.

Lucretia had been taken by the Téjican authorities and granted asylum, so I could keep my promise that no harm would come to her. I didn't know what that would mean for her. I looked at the car, worried she might be inside it.

"Your mother isn't here, is she?" I asked.

Victoria shook her head.

"She's up on a solar farm," Penepoli whispered, her eyes darting north toward the mountains.

"Earning her keep," Nancee added.

Victoria's face went red.

"She's not Indentured, is she?" I asked, a little alarmed, even if it would be a suitable punishment.

"She has a job," Victoria said. "To her, it is the same."

From the front door, Mira came blazing out of the house and rousted Santos359™ from his hiding place. He ran from her and circled us, with Mira right behind, teasing she would catch him. Margot hung back in the doorway and watched.

"You could stay here," I said to Victoria.

"That's kind," Victoria said, her eyes dropping to the ground. "But I can't."

"Don't be ashamed of caring about your family," I said. "Your mother—"

"It isn't my mother," Victoria whispered quickly. "I'm going back to find Andromeda."

Santos359™ widened his circle and zipped behind my mother and Mrs. Croate, then across the courtyard by my father. All the while, Mira was close behind. I felt like they were corralling us—trying to keep us together. I looked at Norflo's house up the road. He and his brothers were emerging, party hats on their heads. If there was one thing I was glad to keep from the Onzième, it was the Juarez brothers as neighbors.

I looked at Nancee and Penepoli. "You could all stay here. If you want." I wanted good people around me. I wanted to be surrounded by people I could trust—by people I loved.

My two oldest friends shook their heads.

"We're going back, too," Nancee said, jerking a thumb toward the north.

"Not tonight," I said, trying to hold back a lonely feeling in my throat.

"No. After we visit," Penepoli said, mussing my hair.

I nodded, but I had to ask, "Why?"

"You said you never wanted to lead a revolution," Nancee explained, "but you led one, anyway. Now that it's started, we want to see it through."

Penepoli gave a bright-eyed nod. A warm wind blew up around us all.

I had to digest Nancee's words a moment. I'd hoped the revolution I'd started had finished, but it hadn't. There remained generations of work to be done—just not by me. I had done enough, both bad and good. I had what I wanted, and needed, and maybe even what I dreamed. I had my family here—less than I should have, but more than I'd ever hoped for.

★★★★★

ACKNOWLEDGMENTS

In the time between writing *All Rights Reserved* and this sequel, a lot has changed in the United States. I want to acknowledge how much closer we appear to have moved toward the world I have written. But, scary as it is, I also find hope in knowing, dear reader, that people like you still want to fight against such a troubling future. So, first and foremost, I want to thank you. Seriously. Thank you for reading this book.

I want to thank my publisher, Harlequin TEEN, who gave me the license and liberty to write a second Word$ book. They gave Speth a chance to finally, truly speak, which she desperately needed. Lauren Smulski, Shara Alexander, Laura Gianino, Siena Koncsol, Evan Brown, Linette Kim and a host of others have done so many things to get this book and its predecessor out in the world and into your hands.

I need to thank Oscar Kochansky for meeting with me to give me notes, even though it meant forgoing bread; Johnny Frank Dunn, for his insightful commentary; and the Fayerweather Street School, for providing access to these brilliant minds and others.

Thanks also to Catalina Bertani and Annette Gaudino, who both offered counsel in several very important ways. Lia Novotny and Jennifer Dorsen, who provided invaluable feedback, and, of course, Lee Gjertsen Malone, whose help was, as always, immeasurable.

I must also thank the talented Frankie Corzo for giving voice to Speth in both Word$ audiobooks.

Finally, I must thank my wife, who makes all things possible, and my daughter, who makes everything worthwhile.